ALSO BY ARI BARAN

The Penalty Box Series

Game Misconduct
Delay of Game
Home Ice Advantage
Goaltender Interference

Goaltender Interference contains descriptions of depression, under-negotiated kink, drug and alcohol use, and homophobia.

GOALTENDER
INTERFERENCE

ARI BARAN

HARLEQUIN

HARLEQUIN®

Recycling programs for this product may not exist in your area.

ISBN-13: 978-1-335-00442-0

Goaltender Interference

First published in 2025. This edition published in 2026.

For questions and comments about the quality of this book, please contact us at CustomerService@Harlequin.com.

Harlequin Enterprises ULC
22 Adelaide St. West, 41st Floor
Toronto, Ontario M5H 4E3, Canada
Harlequin.com

HarperCollins Publishers
Macken House, 39/40 Mayor Street Upper,
Dublin 1, D01 C9W8, Ireland
www.HarperCollins.com

Printed in U.S.A.
1 2 3 4 5 6 7 8 9 10 HDC 29 28 27 2

GOALTENDER
INTERFERENCE

I.
SUMMER

CHAPTER ONE

July

Sometimes it felt like Aiden Campbell had closed his eyes at twenty-six and woke up thirty-six. One day he'd been a kid with a kid's body and energy and recovery time. And then the next, he had to be even more religious than he used to about stretching and yoga, or his body tied itself up in knots and ached when he lowered himself into bed.

Sometimes it did that anyway.

Normally, at this point in the offseason, Aiden would be headed to the gym, the same way he had done for countless mornings over the course of almost two decades. Or he'd be driving to Tarrytown to get some work in on the ice. Even in the summer, there was never much of a break.

Today, Aiden had nowhere to go, nowhere to be, nothing to do.

It was the first day of the offseason after the New York Liberty had been eliminated from the playoffs, but he couldn't even accurately call it the offseason anymore.

With the season over, Aiden was officially retired.

The decision hadn't really been deliberate. He'd been

getting hurt a little more often these last few years, a groin pull here, a tear or a sprained ankle and a knee surgery there, the kinds of betrayals his body never used to make. When he'd have to wake up for morning skate, instead of feeling the thrum of excitement in his veins, he just felt tired.

Gabe Walker, his backup, took over the bulk of the starts.

When the last year of his contract came up and talks should have started, he'd put off reaching out to his agent for long enough that it started to get uncomfortable. He'd put it off until Caroline, because she was used to him, called and asked, "So do you want to make a decision, or is this your way of telling me you've done it already?"

Aiden thought about it. The pause went on longer than it should have. Finally he said, "Caroline, I think I'm done."

He didn't have many regrets. He'd brought two Cups back to New York. His home was decorated with individual awards. He'd been the backbone of the team for years. He was a lock for the Hall of Fame, first ballot or otherwise.

He'd known, in the very back of his mind, that it would be a good idea to make plans for the rest of his life. Consider the direction he wanted to take. Figure out where he was going from here. It had been too much. Instead, Aiden had boxed the thought up and put it away. The same way he boxed up every thought that he didn't want to consider, the things that were out of his control, the messy, unpleasant aspects of life he couldn't ignore. It was easier not to look at them.

He'd focused on the things he *could* control, which

in this case turned out to be shepherding a team full of playoff virgins through the postseason. That had taken a lot of time and mental energy, and it had worked.

But now the playoffs were over.

It wasn't working anymore.

Aiden went downstairs to make himself breakfast in his white and shining kitchen. He had eaten basically the same thing every day for fifteen years, but he still took care in preparing it. The Routine was important, even if most of the Routine had been ripped away from him along with hockey itself.

Aiden took the toast out of the toaster.

Mom had been asking when he was coming home, but he didn't know when he wanted to do it. *If* he wanted to do it. He'd stopped going back to Winnipeg in the offseason about five years ago, after his last long-term boyfriend had broken up with him. That had been when his parents really started pressing him about whether he was happy, whether he was going to meet anyone, if he thought maybe one day he'd like a family of his own.

Instead of answering, he'd quietly shelved his plans to buy an offseason residence in Manitoba and went all in on New York.

Aiden spread cashew butter on the toast and poured himself a cup of coffee.

Today was the first day of the rest of his life.

These days, Aiden's phone notifications were full of missed calls, voice mail and passive-aggressive text messages from his family.

A voice mail from his mother: *Give me a call, beta, I'm worried about you.* Even the childhood endearment, in his mother's comfortingly warm, brisk voice, didn't make him feel any better. A text message from his sister: You're really not coming home? That was more aggressive than passive-aggressive; Aiden hadn't been answering his sister's calls for a reason. He didn't know *how* to answer. So he didn't.

Hannah meant well, but she worried, the same way his parents worried. Aiden didn't have an explanation or anything to say about what his future held. He didn't want to spend his time reassuring the family that he would be okay. He would probably be okay, but he didn't know how, and he didn't know when.

Mostly he just wanted to be alone.

Aiden locked the door to his empty house and went for a walk.

New York City in the summer always felt bittersweet. This time of year, his mind wandered to the past. Running used to help, but the older he got, the harder it was to deal with the brutal heat and humidity. By the time he had gone a few miles, his shirt stuck sweaty to his back and he wished he'd remembered a water bottle.

He ended up in Central Park, sitting by one of the fountains and watching children splash and play in the water even though they weren't supposed to. A twenty-something kid recognized him and came up for an autograph; Aiden sighed and signed the snapback shoved into his hands. He politely but firmly shut down the attempt at starting a real conversation and started walking again.

He hadn't been to the MoMA in years; he had no reason to go. Today, Aiden spent a few hours walking around the exhibits, looking at the art in complete silence, avoiding meeting anyone's eyes. No one bothered him.

He stood for a long time in the contemporary gallery, looking at the wall with Cy Twombly's *Leda and the Swan*, and wondered how the hell he ended up *here*.

The days went by.

Aiden's phone rang while he made himself lunch. He didn't pick up.

He checked the voice mail a few hours later: *Your jersey is ready, please come and get it anytime during regular business hours.* After every season he'd played, he framed the jersey, from mini mite to the Harriers, his juniors team; Worlds and Olympic and All-Star jerseys, his minor league gear and every single variant of the Liberty's jerseys from the first year he'd played through his penultimate season, when they'd had a new third alternate.

The one he was avoiding picking up was the last game-worn jersey he'd ever put on his body, framed and ready to hang, the capstone to his collection. Aiden knew it was stupid. Leaving the jersey at the store didn't change the fact that his career was over. But he still wasn't ready to pick it up yet, and he didn't know when he would be.

Aiden woke up.

He went to the gym.

He came home.

He sat on his couch and stared at the ceiling.

He ignored phone calls from his mom, texts from the team, phone calls from Hannah.

He remembered to eat mostly because paying careful attention to his meals, macros and intake had been ingrained in the Routine for years.

He sat on his roof deck and stared at the skyline.

He intended to fall asleep at a reasonable hour.

He did not.

Aiden woke up.

The Routine had used to help him feel grounded and at ease. But now, at a certain point, he realized he was more bored than he had ever been in his entire life. Before, he always had something to work toward, but now it didn't matter how many times he went through his yoga routine in the morning, how long he spent in the gym after. No matter what he did, it felt like running in a hamster wheel.

A few of the guys from the team texted him regularly, the ones who stayed in New York City over the summer permanently and the ones who just hadn't left yet. Even then, Aiden was painfully aware that he was five or ten or in some cases fifteen years older than them, and he couldn't bring himself to accept any of the offers to hang.

Eventually he stopped responding at all.

For the last few years, there hadn't really been anyone steady in his life. When he had first—when it had happened, at first he had slept around for a while. For a long time after that, he'd dated, serially monogamous relationships that would always fizzle out around a year, when the other guy realized Aiden couldn't give him what he wanted. That even though Aiden could commit to a relationship, that no matter how good the sex was, sex and companionship was all it was ever going to be. Aiden was never going to be emotionally available the way any of them wanted.

And it wasn't like he *never* hooked up, but at a certain point it was almost more effort than it was worth for an ultimately unsatisfying reward. None of those men understood what he wanted—and he'd learned, a long time ago, that with the wrong person, even asking for it could be disastrous. You couldn't just say to a guy you barely knew *hey, I'm in kind of a mood today, you should hit me so my brain will shut the fuck up,* and expect anything like what you were looking for. Anything like what he'd—

So in the end, sex was just that. Sex and nothing more.

The worst part was that he didn't even know why dating felt so empty. It wasn't even like he really wanted romance. It was just that sometimes, he thought he'd kill to be able to talk to someone the way he used to talk to—

Well.

What it came down to was: there were no answers he could give himself about how to fix this. At a certain point you woke up, realized you were almost middle-aged by normal standards and already ancient by hockey standards, and that you had spent the first half of your life failing to set yourself up for the second.

Aiden went running.

It was a hot day. It felt good to sweat and suffer. For a time, he could stop thinking, exist only in the pounding of his feet on the pavement, the gasp of breath in his lungs and ears, the city streaking by.

He stopped to stretch out his legs and rest his knee. Someone said, from behind him, "Soooooouuuup!"

Aiden sighed, turned and smiled. He posed for a picture.

Aiden went running.

The thing was. He couldn't outrun the past.

The doorbell rang.

Aiden checked his phone and sighed. There was Gabe, on his stoop, arms folded over his chest, tapping his foot impatiently. Against his better judgment, Aiden slipped on a pair of shorts and went downstairs to answer it. He had the feeling that if he didn't, Gabe would still be there hours later. He was stubborn that way.

When Aiden opened the door, Gabe's face visibly brightened. "Soupy! You're alive!"

"Still breathing, anyway. What are you doing here, Gabe?"

"Well..." Gabe trailed off and chewed on his lower lip. "I was worried about you. You haven't really been answering anyone in the group chat."

"It's because I'm not on the team anymore."

"Well, yeah, *technically*, but you're still there in *spirit*."

Aiden had never felt as old as he did in that moment. "Thanks, Gabe, I appreciate it. I'm fine, though, you don't have to worry."

Gabe was already pushing past him, and Aiden didn't fight back. He allowed himself to be gently bodied aside. Sighing, he followed the kid into his own home and closed the door behind them. It was difficult to say no to Gabriel Walker, mostly because he always refused to accept no for an answer. Because he never *had* anyone have to tell him no.

Over his last season, Aiden had been for Gabe what Aiden's own mentor, Derek Ward, had been for him almost two decades ago. Before Aiden's retirement, he and Gabe had a good tandem going. No hard feelings on Aiden's part when Gabe took over the crease. The experience of mentoring another goalie had been challenging but rewarding, especially as he started to see the tangible results; watch Gabe grow in confidence and ease in front of the net.

Gabe didn't remind Aiden of himself at that age in anything except his level of play. Talented, driven, competitive, twenty-two years old, his whole future ahead of him. Gabe was all of those things. He was handsome, with his huge brown eyes and the kind of mouth and eyelashes that some people paid good money to obtain. Gabe was cheerful, goofy, a little arrogant, and one of the first openly gay prospects taken in the first round of the entry draft. He *was* the first openly gay prospect to play a major league game.

There were a few conversations they'd had early on that Aiden obviously hadn't been able to with Ward. Mostly about being gay and a minority in a sport that was very straight and very white. Aiden's mother had immigrated to Manitoba from Gujarat, and Gabe was a Black kid from Scarborough, but they had more in common than anyone probably would've guessed considering the disparity of their backgrounds.

Gabe had a chip on his shoulder the size of Nunavut when he'd come up, ready to fight anyone who looked at him wrong, even if they were a teammate. It had been on Aiden to tell him that wasn't necessary *here* because the team was already used to it. And that neither Aiden nor Isaac Pearson, the Libs' captain and official You Can Play Ambassador, would tolerate any shitty behavior from the team, on the ice or off it.

Gabe had stared at him for a very long time and said, "*You?* Really?"

Aiden hadn't really known how to answer that.

Aiden envied Gabe, the certainty and confidence he had at such a young age. Even though everyone on the team knew Aiden was queer *now*, he hadn't ever come out to the general public. He couldn't see himself doing it, either. It still felt uncomfortable, having eyes on him for things that weren't related to hockey. Even when he didn't play hockey anymore. But Gabe had never seemed to give a shit who looked at him, or why.

Gabe, frowning at Aiden, stood in his space. "But I'm serious, Soupy, I'm really worried about you, you know?"

"You don't have to be. I'm enjoying retirement."

"Doesn't look like it from where I'm sitting."

Aiden just looked at him, level and expressionless.

"Come *onnn*, Soupy," Gabe said, cajoling. "Come out with me tonight? You can let yourself have fun for at least one day, and then you can go back to hibernating by yourself in here, or wearing your hair shirt, or whatever it is you're doing, okay? I just think it'll be good for you to get out of the house."

Gabe's hand rested on Aiden's arm, and he looked up at Aiden with big, pleading brown eyes. Aiden had to shake his head to clear his vision, assaulted, suddenly, with a memory he hadn't thought about for years. It was such a strong image that he almost felt like he had to sit down.

"Soup?" Gabe did sound really worried now. "Are you okay?"

"I'm fine," Aiden said. His voice sounded hoarse, rusty with emotion or disuse. "I'm fine. You want to go out? Fine. I'm yours for the night."

Gabe smiled and pressed his fingers against Aiden's arm again. "Good. You won't regret it."

Aiden regretted it immediately.

They ended up at a dive bar not far from Aiden's house, and Gabe kept ordering shots, which Aiden felt obliged to drink, and which he felt obliged to either match or pay for, because Gabe was on the last year of his ELC and Aiden was a multimillionaire.

Gabe set yet another round in front of him. "There you go, Soupy."

"Another one?" Aiden asked, rubbing his eyes. He drank anyway. Gabe watched him do it. "Aren't you training? Don't you have to go to the gym tomorrow? Aren't you going to regret this?"

"Well, yeah," Gabe said, flashing his dimples. "But I don't really get hangovers, at least probably not like you do, because you're ol—you're, you know, retired. So it'll be fine, probably. Anyway, I can suffer a little tomorrow to cheer up my favorite goalie tonight."

"I thought *you* were your favorite goalie."

"You're my other favorite goalie." Gabe patted Aiden's hand reassuringly. "And besides… I wouldn't be half the goalie I am without you. Like. You know." He looked away, suddenly shy in a way that was very out of character. "I owe you a lot, okay? So I really don't wanna see you so sad all of the time."

"I'm not *sad*."

"Oh, right, Soupy, you were just hiding in your house for weeks and weeks not talking to any of us for no reason. Just some casual hermiting."

"It wasn't *weeks*. Gabe…come on, have mercy on an old man."

"Nah, no mercy," Gabe said, beaming, and then, "You are *not* drunk enough right now, and I told you we're going to have a good time—hey, lemme grab the bartender—"

Aiden loved Gabe, but he was *so* young. He wondered, vaguely, whether any of his teammates had felt the same way talking to Aiden back in the day as he felt talking to Gabe now. That choking combination of fond protectiveness, absolute confusion, amusement and vague horror at the entropy of the universe in relation to himself.

Gabe, clueless, chattered on about anything and everything. "And then I told Richie that I'm going to work on my lateral movement, but I have a lot more explosiveness than they thought, they're underestimating me, so…"

Aiden was drunk, but not drunk enough. He could feel himself fidgeting, the uncontrollable way his body moved sometimes, when he was overwhelmed and couldn't handle it. Aiden's leg jiggled, bouncing; the table on its uneven leg shook even worse. He didn't want to be a dick, so he bit down his exhaustion and nodded and offered encouraging remarks at the appropriate times. Gabe bloomed under the attention, smiling and intent, kept touching Aiden's arm to punctuate his points.

"Excuse me, Gabe," he said, lurching to his feet. "I'm going to go get us a pitcher of water."

"Oh—um, okay."

Aiden took a deep breath as he wove his way through the crowd, fishing for his wallet so he could settle the tab, too. He leaned against the bar, waiting to catch the bartender's attention. And then he looked up and the universe punched him in the face.

"Oh," Aiden said, before he could stop himself.

Matthew Safaryan, the captain of the Montreal Royal, stood at the bar, apparently just as shocked to see Aiden. They hadn't been this close off of the ice in over a decade. Seeing him, here in New York City, out of hockey pads and close enough to touch, almost took Aiden's knees out.

Matt was still a few inches shorter than Aiden, but he'd filled out since his early twenties, broad and solid and muscular. His sharp, owlish features had aged well: laugh lines at the corners of his eyes and his mouth, flecks of gray in his black hair. A scar still cut through one of his eyebrows.

It had been an errant skate blade; Aiden remembered watching the replay after the game and wincing as they tried to stop the bleeding before he vanished down the tunnel for stitches, then wincing again when Matt had gone back on the ice for the next period. Winced a third time seeing the blood still smeared on his forehead behind the cage.

The patchy beard Matt used to have was fully grown in now. His dark brown eyes fixed on Aiden's face, but Aiden couldn't read the expression in them anymore. Matt wasn't wearing his wedding ring. Somehow, he was even more attractive than he had been when they were kids, all of the raw material he had weathered by time.

Aiden should say something. He *had* to say something. His throat felt like he'd swallowed a bowl full of glass shards.

Gabe stumbled up behind him and threw his arm over Aiden's shoulders in a way that Aiden was really going to have to talk to him about later. When his heart wasn't pounding so loudly.

"Safaryan?" Gabe said. "What are *you* doing here?"

"Not really your business, Walker." Matt's voice even sounded the same, calm and level, and he looked from Aiden to Gabe and back with something like disdain.

"Matt, what—?" Miles Safaryan, Matt's little brother, appeared from the crowd behind Matt's shoulder. His eyes narrowed when he saw Aiden. "Oh. Campbell. Jesus Christ, of course. Okay. Okay. This is—I can handle this. All right. Campbell. *You* need to leave."

"Uh, excuse me," Gabe cut in, "this is totally unnecessary, okay?"

"Oh, cute. You got a kid fighting your battles now?" Miles' lip curled in a sneer. "Seriously, Campbell, fuck off and get the hell away from my brother."

"I'm not—I wasn't—" Aiden tried to work his way through a silent mantra, a breathing exercise, *anything*, but all he had was the yawning grief in his chest. "We'll go. I was just settling the tab."

"*Soup*—"

"I'm settling the tab, Gabe. Night's over, buddy."

The barest hint of a flinch flickered over Matt's face. He hadn't spoken since that first time.

Aiden looked away. Pulled a hundred-dollar bill out of his wallet, handed it to the bartender. "No change, please." He turned and walked quickly through the crowd, his shoulders hunched and his head down, like that alone could make the rest of this, somehow, go away.

Outside, he tried to get air into his lungs. It was a summer night, thick and humid, so the actual air didn't do anything to help. He tried anyway. Distantly, he could hear Gabe.

"Soupy? Are you okay? What the *fuck* was that?"

Aiden didn't answer, just kept walking west down the street, ocean roaring in his ears.

"Hey!" Gabe said, grabbing his arm. "Soupy, please,

you're kind of scaring me, man. What's happening? What's wrong?"

Aiden didn't know what his face looked like when he shook Gabe off, but he wasn't far gone enough not to feel bad when Gabe flinched.

"Gabe, I'm sorry, I..." Aiden groped for something to say, anything to explain. "I'm sorry. I have to go home. I can't. I can't do this."

"Soupy..." Gabe looked up at him, eyes wide, face flushed. He reached out to touch Aiden again. His hands were warm and soft. "Soupy, just tell me you're okay."

Aiden shook his head. Carefully disentangled his arm. He walked home, leaving Gabe behind.

Aiden walked into the empty living room of his empty house. He needed to scream. A curse, a cry, *fuck*, anything, rose up in his throat, but he choked it back. There wasn't anyone to hear him; a display like that wouldn't help anything.

He tried to get himself under control. He poured a glass of water from the pitcher in the fridge. He drank the water. He rested his head against the cold metal of the freezer. It was past midnight and he was drunk; yoga and meditation were both probably out of the question. He could drink more, or he could just go upstairs and try to sleep. But that seemed like a stretch goal.

Aiden had been fairly responsible since his retirement, but this was an emergency. He tried not to feel too guilty for pouring himself a generous glass of whiskey. He drank the whiskey. He didn't feel better. He didn't even feel more drunk.

The doorbell rang and Aiden ignored it. The doorbell rang again and again and again and again, and Aiden set the glass down on his counter, turned to go to the door and fling it open and tell Gabe that he needed to *mind his own fucking business.*

"Gabe, you need to go *home*—"

Matt was standing on Aiden's front stoop.

Matt was fucking standing on Aiden's front stoop, handsome and furious and lost. He looked at Aiden like he was drowning, like he wanted to be anywhere but here, like he hated that he was. He said, roughly, "Let me in."

Aiden instinctively took a step back as Matt stepped over the threshold and shut the door behind him. "How did—how did you—?"

"I just asked Duncs."

Aiden's former teammate. Matt's juniors buddy. A lump rose in Aiden's throat the size of Mount Everest. Aiden couldn't say anything, or move.

It didn't matter. Matt moved for him. In two steps he closed the space between them and took Aiden's face in both of his hands. Aiden had a brief moment of eye contact, staring directly at Matt: his pupils dilated and expression wild, entirely unlike him. He pressed his mouth against Aiden's. It felt exactly the way Aiden remembered, the way he'd tortured himself remembering, warm and demanding and a little mean. Aiden opened instinctively, a muscle memory. But then he really *was* responding, tongue learning the new line of Matt's teeth, the gap where one of them was missing. Rediscovering the way he tasted. Like whiskey, like salt.

Matt made a strangled noise, or maybe it was Aiden.

Aiden's hands flew up to grab his wrists. At first, he wanted to push Matt away, but he couldn't do it. Instead he ran his hands down Matt's shoulders, his sides, half wondering at the now-unfamiliar lines of his body, half unable to believe he was here, real and solid under Aiden's touch. Matt's tongue, slick against Aiden's. Matt's hands, thumb stroking Aiden's cheek, tracing the line of Aiden's beard, his jaw, tangling into his hair. When he wrapped his fingers there and tugged, Aiden made an awful whimper, and finally pulled back to gasp for air.

"Matt, Matt—*what*—"

"Please," Matt said, and his eyes were huge and so, so dark, "can we—not talk right now?"

This was a terrible decision.

It was the worst decision he'd ever made.

Aiden didn't need to tell himself that.

He allowed Matt to push him backward and crowd him against the door, still kissing him furiously, desperately, like he'd die if they stopped. He allowed Matt to worm his hand under Aiden's shirt, splay his fingers against Aiden's abs, tracing the line of each ridge of muscle, a muffled noise of frustration when he realized that Aiden had the same definition he'd always had. He allowed Matt to trail from his mouth down the line of his jaw to his neck, eyes closing when Matt's teeth dug into the particularly sensitive spot right below his ear.

Aiden felt like he had completely lost his mind, like this was some kind of fever dream. His hands were all over Matt, his hair, his biceps, his face, his ass, fingers digging into the muscle of it. No rhyme or reason to where he touched. Couldn't decide what he wanted to touch first, wanted to touch all of him at once, wanted to cut him open and crawl inside.

Matt was still sucking a mark onto Aiden's neck, hard enough that he gasped. Matt pushed up against him, hard enough that the friction made him squirm. Matt's hands tugged Aiden's pants down, and Aiden wanted to say *no, stop, this is a terrible idea* and Aiden wanted to say *I missed you, I missed this, please, please,* please.

He realized, belatedly, that he *was* saying, "Please, please, please—" whenever Matt allowed him to breathe. Begging over and over again for something he couldn't even bring himself to describe. Not now, not from Matt, not after all of this time.

But Matt gave it to him anyway, his calloused hand too hot, almost feverish against Aiden's skin. Aiden managed to get his hand down Matt's pants, too; Matt hissed when Aiden rolled his thumb around the head of his dick and through the moisture beaded there.

Matt was so close there was barely any space for their hands to move, grinding up against Aiden's body, their knuckles bumping, clothes pushed down and disarrayed. Matt wrapped his hand around both of them, and Aiden's entire body flinched at the sensation as Matt's hand sped up.

They had stopped kissing, didn't have the coordination for it, just panting into each other's mouths. The air was humid between them, lips barely brushing, and Aiden clutched Matt's arms like that alone could somehow keep him on his feet. His entire body felt like it had been hit by lightning, an electric current running between all of the places his skin touched Matt's. He was so keyed up, so sensitive, that he couldn't possibly hold out long. Matt's hand was merciless, on the edge of too much.

Aiden shivered and came, wet against his shirt, sticky between them. His knees buckled with the force of it, but Matt kept going, shoving him back against the door so he couldn't move, so he had to keep standing. And then it *was* too much, oversensitive and rough, and Aiden's gasps sounded very loud in the quiet house.

He didn't say *stop.*

He didn't want to stop.

He didn't want—

Matt buried his face in the crook of Aiden's neck when he came, and Aiden could almost feel the thud of his heart trapped between them.

They didn't stay that way long. Matt pulled away and swallowed hard, looked down at the mess of his shirt and Aiden's clothes, at Aiden's softening dick hanging sadly out in the open. He pulled his pants up and tried to adjust his shirt while Aiden stared, dumb and unable to move, even to try to preserve his dignity.

Their eyes met and Matt's face softened almost imperceptibly before setting in the mask again.

He said, "Let me go."

Aiden moved to the side, and let him.

For several long moments after he left Aiden's house, Matt stood on the front stoop, swaying on his feet.

He was *fucked up*, and even though he was still kind of drunk, his current state was only about a quarter alcohol. The rest of it was just Aiden Campbell, the same way Aiden had always fucked him up. He put his hand out to grab the doorframe and tried to process what he had just done.

Matt had been the captain of the Montreal Royal, an Original Six team and the oldest and most storied franchise in the league, for years now. It was a position that required steadiness and responsibility and always doing the right thing and being conscious of your public image. It was a commitment as much as it was a job. He'd voluntarily taken the honor and weight of that onto his shoulders.

The captain of the Montreal Royal didn't get drunk in New York on a family vacation and fuck his ex against a door. Except, apparently, when he did.

It had been more than a decade since things fell apart. Matt had thought he was over it. He had done the work to get over it. It was very clear in that moment, shivering in the dark and still unable to get his feet to walk down the stairs of Aiden Campbell's front stoop, that he wasn't over it at all.

His head was still spinning and he knew his hair was sticking up at all kinds of insane angles, his face was red and his mouth swollen, and his shirt was a fucking *mess*. There was no way that he was going to be able to make it back to the house the family had rented without Miles asking all kinds of uncomfortable questions.

He'd probably already figured it out; after Aiden and Walker had left the bar, Matt made it a little under fifteen minutes before saying, "I have to go."

The look Miles had given him said it all.

The stupid, self-destructive part of him, the part that had reached out to Duncs in the first place, said: *Ring the bell. He's still in there. Go talk to him. Actually* talk *to him.*

The part of him that had any kind of self-preservation whatsoever said: *run.*

He made himself consciously put one foot and then the other down those stairs. Forced himself to walk away from Aiden's beautiful, soulless brownstone. Forced himself to walk away from beautiful, soulless Aiden.

It shouldn't have been possible that a brief encounter in a crowded bar could have messed him up this badly, thrown him out of the carefully controlled routines of his existence like that.

It wasn't like he had *never* seen Aiden over the years. Their teams played each other at least three times a season; they both appeared in the All-Star Game every few years. They'd been on the same Olympic team once and won a gold medal together. He'd survived all of those things. None of that was the same as looking up and feeling the immediate gut punch of seeing Aiden's face, really *seeing* him, for the first time in over a decade.

Aiden hadn't even looked the same. His light brown skin had a grayish pallor. His hair had gotten long and shaggy and he had a scruffy beard that did nothing to hide the lines at the corners of his mouth and eyes. His wide brown eyes looked haunted. There were dark circles under them like he'd been punched repeatedly, and his expressive mouth, which Matt mostly remembered smiling and laughing and teasing, turned down at the corner in a frown. The whole effect was a little like a medieval painting of a saint being martyred. He'd looked so worn down that despite everything Matt had felt the immediate urge to fold him up in his arms before he realized how fucking stupid that thought was.

Aiden's body had felt the same, though. He'd panted for it the same eager way he always had. The noise he'd made when Matt took what he wanted from him had been the same. The faint, dark brown freckles on his nose were the same. Matt wondered whether the freckles on his shoulders were, too.

God, what the fuck had he been thinking? He *hadn't* been thinking. Not with his head, anyway.

He walked briskly down the street back toward the house. When his parents had said they wanted to visit

New York, he'd protested, but hadn't fully been able to explain why. It was a huge city, and he hadn't even known where Aiden lived anymore. As far as his parents knew, he had moved on when he married Emily. If anything, they were still worried about him *after* Emily, two years post-divorce, and that was why they'd dragged him down here. Part of him had dreaded going. And part of him had hoped that even in a city of eight and a half million people, there was a chance—a chance.

Still. The universe's mysterious conspiracies weren't a good excuse for stupid decisions.

He tried to open the door quietly, but his hands were still shaking as he fumbled with the key.

Aiden Campbell.

Aiden *fucking* Campbell, after ten years and change.

There was a time when Matt, young and stupid, had really fucking thought things were going to last forever. When he'd bought a ring and everything and he'd had all kinds of big, expansive plans about coming out, about telling the Montreal media to go fuck themselves if they had a problem with him, when—

It hadn't mattered. None of it had mattered. Heart in his throat and all of the stupid fucking hope in his chest, he'd asked, *would you marry me?* and Aiden had looked back at him with those big, sad eyes and said that they wanted different things, and he couldn't be what Matt needed him to be, and he was sorry.

I'm sorry, Matty, Aiden kept saying, and *I just want to do what's best for you.*

His stomach lurched, remembering. Even now he could recall with exact clarity the sick, sharp nausea he had felt in that moment, like he'd been thrown physically back into it. The despair when he'd insisted, *I know what's best for me, and that's you.*

By the time Matt stumbled into the living room, Miles was still up, watching TV. He'd clearly been waiting, and he looked sharply at Matt's disheveled state. "Jesus fucking Christ, Matt, where the hell were you?"

"I have to. I gotta, bathroom—"

On his knees on the cold tile, he leaned over the toilet and puked until there wasn't anything left. Until his stomach heaved and twisted and acid soured his tongue, nothing to give but trying to expel it anyway. He didn't feel any better afterward because the problem wasn't the alcohol. As much as he wanted to, it had become really fucking clear he couldn't purge Aiden from his system.

Matt stripped off his come- and sweat-stained shirt and shivered, sweat beading cold on his back under the blast of the air conditioner. He counted to fifteen. He stood up, swaying. Ducked his head under the running water from the faucet, drank and spat it out in the sink.

"What the fuck *happened*?" Miles demanded, when Matt came out of the bathroom. "Matt, I was fucking worried about you."

"I—I had to take a walk," Matt mumbled. He couldn't look Miles in the eye. "I had to clear my head."

"Don't fucking tell me you—"

"I didn't. I didn't. I just—I just had to clear my head. I was more fucked up than I thought I was."

"Because Jesus, Matt, we were all with you through that and I—he's not *worth it.* That piece of shit isn't worth one more second of your time or effort or emotion."

"I know. I know, Miles."

Miles stared at him again, a combination of worry and pity and fury, and Matt had to look away so he wouldn't throw up again. "I'm just… Matt, you know how much we all love you, right? He's *not worth it*."

"I have to go pass out. I—I'll talk to you in the morning."

Alone in a bed that wasn't his, Matt lay on his back, stared at the ceiling with his hands folded over his chest. He wondered what the fuck, exactly, he thought he was doing.

I wonder if he's thinking about me.

It took him a long time to fall asleep.

Aiden didn't sleep much that night.

He watched the sunrise on his roof deck, because eventually he'd just given up.

Pears texted him around five in the morning: Gabe said you had a rough night, everything cool?

Aiden typed you're not my captain anymore and deleted it. He said, Everything's fine.

Copacetic, bro. But he said Safaryan was there, so I was just thinking, maybe not.

I left right after we ran into them. We didn't talk.

OK, Soup. Yo, just because you're not technically on the roster anymore doesn't mean you're not a Lib. Got it?

Thanks, Pears.

I can send you a playlist.

No, thanks.

Pears sent him the playlist anyway. It was called *some classic songs to get over your ex to because it's been maaaaaaybe a lil too long*. The first song was Juice Wrld's "Life's a Mess."

Thanks, Isaac.

Anytime, he said, with a sunglasses emoji.

Aiden went to the gym. He came home. He sat in his house. He did not bother putting on pants. He did not look at the front door. He got up. He picked up a book on the history of goaltending he'd been meaning to read, but only made it about two pages in before he put it down. His eyes wouldn't focus. He spent an hour folding laundry. He did meal prep for the next few days. He played the guitar, but he couldn't remember any of the songs he was playing.

He did not touch the tender bruise on his neck. He looked at himself in the mirror, the lines on his face, the dark circles under his eyes. He sat down on the couch and flipped through various cable channels he wasn't interested in watching. Finally, he just stopped and sat, and put his head down in his hands.

Aiden woke to find that the sun already down, the doorbell ringing. He stretched out the knot in his shoulders and neck and unlocked his phone. He had about thirty texts from Gabe he didn't read. He opened the door camera app.

Matt, again, pacing on the stoop like a caged animal.

Aiden took a deep breath. He thought: *maybe I won't answer.*

He went down the stairs.

Matt's shoulders were hunched forward, tense and

miserable, by the time Aiden opened the door. It was raining, not hard but steady, and Matt's hair and jacket looked damp.

"What are you doing here?"

"I don't know. I don't *know*."

"Why are you in New York?"

"My parents wanted to take a family vacation." His laugh was low and bitter. "We're here for another week. My parents and my brother; his wife and kids. And me."

"Why—"

"It's not a small city, I didn't think there was any chance of, of running into you."

"I—Jesus, Matt. It's been—"

"A decade. More." They stared at each other for a long time before Matt said, again, "Let me in."

Aiden took a step back, and Matt closed the door behind him. He slipped the wet jacket off and dropped it on Aiden's floor.

"The kid. Walker. He's…?"

"My replacement."

"You're not—"

"Jesus fucking Christ, Matt, he's twenty-two. He was my rookie. *No*, I'm not."

"I'm sorry, I just—the way he looked at you, the way he touched you—"

"It's been a decade. You got *married*. Even if I did, it's none of your business."

"I know," Matt said. His voice was very small and very rough. "I *know*."

Matt's hand on his shoulder, in a way that used to feel warm, steadying. Aiden couldn't bring himself to say anything.

"Tell me to go."

"Matt—"

"If you want me to go, tell me to go."

Matt's mouth set in the same determined way it used to look when they played each other, right after they'd broken up, like he was ready to crash the crease and fight Aiden at a moment's provocation, like all he needed was a signal.

They'd done it, once, right after Matt got married, beat the shit out of each other before the linesman could get in between them, kept fighting even then. Matt, focused only on Aiden and flailing, had blacked the linesman's eye. They'd both gotten game misconducts. It was the only real fight Aiden ever had. After that, Matt barely even looked at him unless he was shooting on the net, and Aiden thought, every single game, about slashing his leg with his stick, giving him a shove, getting some kind of reaction, any reaction.

He never did.

Now Matt's eyes fixed intently on Aiden's face, the same look that used to make him shiver, like Matt could see right through him, like Matt knew everything about him and still desperately wanted to know more. Aiden licked his lips, trying to think of what the hell to say, but all he could do was lean forward and crush his mouth against Matt's.

"Tell me to go," Matt mumbled into the kiss.

You know I can't, Aiden wanted to say, but instead, he walked Matt backward to the couch. It wasn't a very comfortable couch, made more for aesthetics than with the expectation that anyone would sit on it, but it was wide enough.

He pushed Matt down to a sitting position. Slid down to straddle his lap. It was surreal how much time had passed but how his body still remembered so clearly doing this hundreds of times before, remembered exactly how it felt to press up against the hard length of Matt's body.

"Aiden—"

"This is so *goddamn* stupid."

"Mm," Matt agreed, because Aiden was kissing him again, because his hands were sliding under Aiden's shirt, tugging it up.

"You shouldn't be here. This is such a bad idea."

Matt's thumb caught against Aiden's nipple, lightly, then a sharp press of his nail. He swallowed Aiden's gasp with his mouth. Did it again. "Tell me to go."

"I hate you," Aiden said instead.

It didn't sound convincing. He didn't even mean it, not anymore, he was just so tired. It had been so long since he thought about this. It had been so long since he put it to rest. And now his entire body was on fire with the way Matt touched him, the way he touched Matt.

Matt, surging up against him eagerly, grinding his hips into Aiden's. Matt's hands, teasing and searching for the sensitive spots he still knew on Aiden's body, laughing when he found them, and Aiden swore and twisted against him.

"I know," Matt said.

Aiden mouthed at his jaw. Bit his earlobe, sucked it briefly and dug his teeth in again.

Matt groaned. "*Fuck.* God—I hated you, for so long, for so—"

"Matt, can we just—can you just—without—"

Matt stopped moving, his hands very still on Aiden's collarbone, his neck. Then his thumb brushed a line along Aiden's shoulder. His voice was scoured raw. "Whatever you want, baby."

Aiden's dick jerked, leaking, and Matt swore. Maybe Aiden should have been embarrassed, that he was still so easy for Matt's endearments, Matt's hands, but he was too busy exploring Matt's body. The same boy he'd always known; the man he didn't know at all. He was still just as responsive under Aiden's hands, still just as eager, although Aiden's fingers caught on old scars he'd never seen before, tracing the lines of them at Matt's shoulder and his hip and his knee.

Impatiently, he tugged Matt's shirt up and over his head, but he didn't have much time to admire the view before Matt pushed Aiden off his lap and down onto the couch. They wrestled, flailing arms and limbs, the same way they always had. The only difference was that Matt felt heavier on top of him, pinning him down.

Maybe that was just Aiden, getting old and tired.

Aiden pushed experimentally at the hands circling his wrists, but there wasn't a lot of give, and he wasn't trying to turn this into a real struggle. Matt stared down at him with a wild, half-panicked expression, like if he looked away, Aiden would disappear. Aiden couldn't tell him, in enough words, how he could never do that.

"Can I suck you off?" Aiden asked instead, a faint feeling of satisfaction when Matt swallowed hard. "You should do it like this. Hold my arms down, fuck my face, come *on*."

"Jesus Christ, Aiden, you haven't changed at all."

Matt pulled away to struggle out of his pants and boxer briefs, and then he was moving up Aiden's body, dick nudging at Aiden's lips, his hands pinning Aiden's arms down again.

Aiden looked up, ran his tongue over the head of his cock. Too light, too teasing.

Matt said, "*Fuck* this," and pushed forward.

Aiden stopped fucking around and swallowed him down. It wasn't exactly a comfortable position—his wrists hurt, his shoulder ached, Matt was rough enough that Aiden choked a little—but he closed his eyes and breathed through his nose and relaxed into the discomfort, the familiarity of it.

"God," Matt was saying, above him, "god, *god*—"

It had been a while since Aiden had done this, either with a boyfriend or a casual hookup, but the weight of Matt in his mouth, the way he felt at the back of Aiden's throat, the way Aiden's eyes watered when Matt's body thrust forward, the broken sounds Matt made, the bruising weight of Matt's hands on his wrists...he fucking loved it. He moved his tongue when he could, relaxed his throat when he couldn't, and just *took it*, because he didn't have any other choice.

Because he'd already made his choice.

Matt fell forward with his weight on his hands when he came, gasping. Aiden gagged again, not quite able to swallow everything at that angle. Did his best anyway. His whole body buzzed, the kind of endorphin high he hadn't felt in longer than he wanted to think about.

Matt pulled out, shifted so his weight was back on Aiden's hips, and before Aiden could wipe away the mess with his aching arms, Matt was kissing him, lips trailing down the side of Aiden's mouth, his warm tongue cleaning up what he'd left behind.

Aiden closed his eyes so he didn't have to look at Matt after that.

"What do you want? Hand or mouth?"

"Your mouth." Aiden's voice sounded wrecked, hoarse and scratchy. "It—it's not going to be long now."

"I forgot just how fucked up you get from sucking cock," Matt said, too soft, yanking Aiden's underwear down and looking at the painful situation he had going, the wet spot on the fabric and the sticky streaks on his skin, how absolutely desperate he was, hips hitching up in search of *anything*. Matt's thumb traced the cut below Aiden's abs, a touch so gentle that Aiden thrashed under him, like that could somehow get him more. "How could I forget—*Jesus*, Aiden—"

Aiden shoved his head down so he'd stop *talking*, and Matt snorted but didn't fight him. Matt's mouth on him felt like being thrown backward in time, like dying, like the best thing Aiden had ever felt. He struggled up onto his elbows so he could watch Matt doing it, because he was ruthless, cheeks hollowed out, looking up with something almost like defiance. He couldn't tell for sure, but it was probably only a minute or two before his body seized up and his brain shorted out.

When he opened his eyes again, Matt was crouched over him, looking down with the same cocky little smile he used to get sometimes, if Aiden had especially embarrassed himself. "Still easy," he murmured.

Aiden, panting, tried to get his stuttering brain back online. It didn't quite connect.

"Aiden—"

Aiden, still trapped underneath the full weight of him, pushed at his chest. "You should go."

"You don't—"

"You should *go*."

Matt moved away from him and stood. Aiden tried not to be too obvious about staring as Matt leaned forward to grab his underwear and pants, turning away as he struggled into them and went to search for his shirt.

Aiden watched him do it in silence. He shrugged his jacket on. His face looked the same way it did when he first showed up on Aiden's doorstep, lost and furious and so fucking sad.

"Aiden?"

"Don't. I'm *telling* you to go."

Matt's shoulders slumped, but he opened the door, and left without another word.

Aiden took a while to get up from the couch. He wasn't really sure what was going on in his head. It felt like screaming static, a whiteout without any thoughts or feelings.

Eventually, he stood up and put his boxers back on. His phone rang. Gabe. He shouldn't answer, but the last thing he wanted right now was for the kid to turn up on his doorstep again. When he could think again, when he could—function—he had to talk to Gabe about boundaries, apologize for any wrong ideas he might have inadvertently given him.

"Hello?" His voice sounded just as bad as it had right after Matt finished.

"Soup? I just—you haven't been answering my texts, and I was really worried about you after the other night."

"I'm fine. Gabe, you need to, you just need to give me some space, okay?"

"You don't sound okay, Soupy, and you're, uh, really important to me, so—"

"Gabe, *please*. You need to back off."

There was a long silence on the other end of the line. "Okay," he said, finally, very hurt and extremely young, and Aiden felt like the biggest asshole in the world.

"I just have to figure some things out. Then we'll talk, okay?"

"Okay."

Aiden went upstairs and took a long, cold, shower.

He was going to get his life together, and he was going to make better choices about it.

He was going to be better.

There was just a single problem.

Matt hadn't been sure what to expect when he came to New York with his family. He was familiar with the city; there were obvious reasons he'd visited the most of anyone in his family. He had figured it would be a long, boring trip.

It was just…he loved Miles and Jess. He loved being an uncle to their two small children, Ellie and Theo. He loved his parents. What he didn't love was the way everyone treated him with kid gloves, the way they danced around the fact that he was thirty-five and divorced and alone. That was the thing about families, especially happy families: they felt that if you didn't have that too, you were somehow less than, and they were determined to fix it.

Or in Matt's case, fix *him*.

It was tough in close quarters like this, when he couldn't evade the questions about whether he was seeing anyone, if he'd talked to Emily recently, if he wanted the phone number of one of Miles' teammates' sisters. Always a woman, like they didn't know he was interested in men, too. He had never lied to his parents, but they had never been exactly *comfortable* with it, even if they'd accepted Aiden up until the disastrous end of things. And after that, it had been like they'd hoped he'd come to his senses and settle down, provide the horde of grandchildren they'd always dreamed of. They'd been overjoyed when he had met Emily. It had been tough over the years, even the years that he hadn't really thought about Aiden very often.

But now it was impossible to think of anything else.

He hadn't intended to go back to Aiden again. He told himself that he absolutely couldn't go back to Aiden again. But it was like his whole body oriented itself magnetically toward that house, knowing that Aiden was there, knowing that Matt would be able to touch him again.

Matt had been sober—actually sober—for a few years after their first breakup, and he'd briefly attended meetings. He wasn't sober anymore, once he'd gotten his shit together, but the first place his brain went was: this felt exactly like a relapse. It wasn't alcohol, or Xanax, but… He was going off the rails, and it didn't even matter when he had Aiden again, panting underneath him, wrists tense under Matt's hands, eyes watering when he tried to choke Matt down.

It was ironic, that he'd spent time in player assistance after Aiden had dumped him and after he'd made the disastrous decision to propose to a girl he'd known for all of three months. Outpatient rehab and intensive therapy. The guilt and shame of knowing how badly he'd spiraled after all of it. How hard he'd worked to pull himself out of it. It had taken years of work, and he was *better now*. He drank moderately when he was out with the boys. He didn't use any other substances. He had his shit together. And yet.

He had been sober from this stupid, destructive relationship for over a decade, watching Aiden from afar, and now… He knew better, he absolutely fucking knew better, and he was still making these stupid fucking decisions. It didn't feel like making a decision so much as falling off of a cliff, the inevitability of going back there knowing that Aiden would open the door for him again.

It was easier when they were out and about doing the touristy things, but even that reminded him of Aiden now, of the summers they'd tried to sneak around under the radar in New York and Montreal and trips outside of the continent. He had a hard time getting through the MoMA because in every gallery they went to he had the most vivid fucking memories. The first summer he'd visited Aiden in New York and the two of them had gone through the whole museum, making out in the elevators after the doors closed and springing apart again when they'd opened, mocking the art they'd been too immature to actually understand.

That was the shit that really got him. Because even though he had Aiden for the week, physically at least, that wasn't what he actually missed the most, what had screwed him the fuck up when Aiden had ended things.

He was the captain of the Montreal Royal. Hockey was a religion in Montreal the way it wasn't anywhere else. He could hook up with almost anyone he wanted, if he'd been so inclined. That wasn't the problem.

The problem was that even though sex with Aiden felt like setting himself on fire, what Matt had really missed were the phone conversations on the road, the stupid inside jokes they'd built up over the years, the way he could make such a serious, tightly wound goalie smile and laugh in a way no one else could, the way Aiden had taken such good care of Matt when he got mono one offseason or was recovering from a concussion.

He'd missed Aiden's stupid dorky smile and the almost comically bad sock tans he got in the summer. He'd missed Aiden's single-minded obsessions with hockey, but also with comic books and music. He'd missed how fucking *weird* Aiden could be, sometimes, the way he never reacted the way Matt thought he would, no matter how many years he'd spent trying to crack the code.

He'd just missed *Aiden*, the whole complicated package of him.

"Uncle Matt?" Ellie asked as they passed through the room with *Leda and the Swan*.

"Yeah, Ellie?"

"Are you okay? You look like you're gonna be sick."

Matt hesitated. He was a little hungover, but that wasn't the problem and that wasn't what he'd wanted to explain to his five-year-old niece, anyway. "I haven't been feeling so great this week," he admitted.

"I'm sorry." Her eyes were very wide. "Do you wanna sit down?"

"Sure."

The two of them sat on one of the gallery benches and stared at the wall in silence. At the far end of the gallery, next to their parents, Miles carried Theo on his shoulders as they looked at one of the larger pieces near the door.

Matt sat in silence with Ellie and absentmindedly rubbed his neck. It was still a little sore; Aiden had left a dark, mouth-shaped hickey there last night. It was fucking stupid to have let him but like the rest of this insane, fever dream of a week, Matt had done all of the stupid things against his better judgment.

"You just seem really sad," Ellie said.

Matt looked down at his hands. The problem with

Ellie was that she was too fucking smart for her age, the kind of little girl who always had a notebook and prowled around the yard of her home, keeping tabs on the neighbors because she wanted to be a spy or a private detective when she grew up. He thought about telling her, *I'm not sad*, but he never liked to lie to the kids. They could see right through him half of the time no matter what he did.

"I'm okay," he lied, anyway.

She looked sideways at him and frowned, like she was trying to figure out what was going on with him. Matt hoped to fucking god that she couldn't. She frowned. "All right. If you're sure."

Matt absolutely wasn't sure.

He somehow made it through the rest of the day, but his mind wasn't in it. His parents could tell something was up—he was distracted and irritable and not very good at hiding it—but they didn't press.

And when they were all about to leave for dinner, Matt took a deep breath. "You guys go on without me. I'm gonna meet a juniors buddy in Brooklyn."

Miles looked sharply at him, suspicious, but he had enough sibling loyalty not to rat Matt out in front of their parents. He bit his tongue, even though it clearly pained him to do it.

And Matt, knowing better, hating himself, on fire with anticipation, made his way to the subway, knowing Aiden was waiting for him.

CHAPTER TWO

July

The problem was that Matt kept showing up at Aiden's door and Aiden kept letting him in. The problem was that Aiden knew he shouldn't be doing it, that it was going to backfire horribly, that years of work were going up in smoke every time Matt touched him.

The problem was that as much as Aiden knew these things, logically, Matt kept showing up at the door and Aiden kept letting him in. For all of his logic and all of his knowing, he couldn't say *no.*

They never made their way up to the bed, and it was mostly just blowjobs and handjobs and a lot of heated making out and grappling on the couch, but Aiden kept doing it.

They never talked about it.

They didn't need to talk about it. The sex was good. It had always been good with Matt, because there was something about him that Aiden's body just responded to instinctively. Matt had been his first. His first *everything*, from the initial angry kiss onward, the only one who'd been able to tear him away when he'd been too absorbed in hockey to even consider trying to date.

The only person who had proved to him that his lack of interest in girls wasn't solely due to a drive to improve, a focus on the sport that couldn't be shaken. And when Aiden and Matt were kids, before things had fallen apart, he'd thought it was familiarity, the kind of thing that happened when you loved someone, when you knew them and their body so well.

But they weren't in love anymore, they hadn't seen each other for ten years, and that feeling hadn't changed at all. Aiden didn't want to think about it too closely. This wasn't a situation where the breathing exercises and mantras he'd used in his playing years could help. This wasn't floundering in the deep water, this was drowning, this was water in his lungs and not even trying to struggle to the surface.

Every time Matt left, Aiden sat and wondered how he was going to feel when the Safaryans went home to Hamilton after the week was over. When Matt was gone again. Every time Matt left, Aiden mentally crossed another night off of the calendar.

Eventually: Saturday, by Aiden's calculation, the last night. He wasn't really expecting Matt to show up, but when the doorbell rang anyway, Aiden felt such an overwhelming sense of relief that he almost smacked his hand against the side of his head, as if that could shake it away.

This time, Matt didn't move immediately to touch him, just stood there in front of Aiden's door, face twisted like he was in actual, physical pain. "Aiden, can we please—can we talk?"

Aiden wanted to say *oh, you only want to talk when you want to talk, huh?* Aiden wanted to say that there was nothing to talk about, *get out*. He said none of that. He couldn't open his mouth.

"Is it true? That you retired?"

Aiden's mouth went dry. "It's true. How did you know?"

"Duncs told me. I really… I can't believe it."

"You can believe whatever you want. I did."

Matt just looked at him for a long time, studying Aiden's face. "Why?"

It felt like being in the *Twilight Zone*, having a relatively normal conversation with Matt about the end of his life. "What do you mean, *why*? I'm old as fuck, it was the last year of my contract, I kept getting hurt and Gabe's perfectly capable of taking over. It was time."

"I just can't picture you not playing," Matt said slowly. "I can't picture you not wearing that sweater."

"It had to happen eventually." Aiden managed to keep his voice even, somehow. He wanted to laugh: hysterical, furious. He didn't. "So it happened now."

"How are—how are you doing? With that?"

"Are we really doing this? You're just going to drop back into my life like nothing happened to talk about retirement?" Aiden couldn't quite believe that Matt would even care about this, let alone that he'd turned back up here, on the last night, to talk about it. Aiden wasn't his problem anymore.

"*You're* the one who ended things."

"No, we both mess—"

"I didn't mean for any of this—"

Aiden was suddenly desperate for the conversation to be over, desperate to keep Matt from telling him why he was here again or what the hell he expected from Aiden, desperate not to spend this last small stretch of time they had together the same way they'd spent the last six months of their relationship, desperate to turn off his brain.

"Matt, can you just—can you just stop *talking*, fuck—"

Matt's mouth twitched. "That's what you want, huh?"

"Yes."

"That's all you want?"

"*Yes.*"

Matt got down on his knees, there in the entryway, looked up at Aiden with anguished eyes that cut right through him. "Okay, baby. Make me."

When it was over, even though he'd come, Aiden didn't feel any relief. Matt started dressing, face expressionless, not looking Aiden in the eye. Aiden watched him do it from the couch. He wondered whether everyone handled retirement as badly as he was handling it, or whether his competitive nature had to be the best at being the worst, too.

Matt said, "So this is it, I guess."

"Guess so."

"We're going back to Hamilton tomorrow morning."

"I know."

"Okay."

"Okay."

"Aiden—"

"*What*, Matthew?"

"Never mind. Have a—fuck it, fuck *you*, enjoy your retirement."

"Doing great, buddy," Aiden said, walking him to the door, "no regrets."

Matt didn't look back when he went.

* * *

Matt said goodbye to his family at the airport. He was grateful that he and Miles had managed to talk them into flying instead of the eight-hour road trips they'd loved to take when Matt was a kid, like they had to make up in quality time for all of the hockey-related travel, for all of the time the Safaryan boys had spent with billet families instead of at home.

Miles and Jess were flying back to Hamilton to spend even *more* time with their parents before they returned home to New Jersey to prepare for the season. There had been a time when Matt would have gone with them, but he was already relieved he'd planned to spend most of the offseason back in Montreal. He'd had a house in Hamilton too, for a little while, but eventually, when he realized he almost never actually *wanted* to be there, he'd sold it.

It was easier not to deal with his parents' quiet disapproval. It was easier not to be under constant scrutiny, like the way Miles was eyeing him now as they prepared to part ways at the security gate, after Matt had hugged Ellie and Theo goodbye and kissed Jess on the cheek.

"I'm fine," he told his brother, for the umpteenth time.

Miles just shook his head, clearly disbelieving, and even though he was annoyed, Matt felt a surge of warmth in his chest, knowing just how much his brother cared about him. They'd always been close, only fifteen months apart, constantly in an intense friendly competition about anything and everything. Both of them had the scars to show for it.

Matt had stuck by Miles through a rough transition from the minors to the big league, and Miles had helped

Matt pick up the pieces of his shattered life after Aiden left. When things had gotten really bad.

"Really. You don't have to worry about me."

"I always worry about you," Miles grumbled, but gave him a brief, tight hug and a slap on the back before they went their separate ways.

Matt put his earbuds in on the plane and turned on a long white noise track and pretended he didn't hear anyone who tried to get his attention. He had to take some time to pose for photos and sign autographs on his way out of the airport no matter what he did, but thankfully, the cab driver was probably the only person in Montreal who either didn't give a fuck about hockey or had a good sense when someone didn't want to be talked to.

It was a relief to get back to his condo, alone, after that week. He still felt a little like crawling out of his own skin, but he tamped the feeling down by unpacking his shit and making sure all of his plants were watered and rotated. He threw in a load of laundry.

By the time he was finally done, he was exhausted, and home was quiet and empty. Emily had never lived here with him; he'd purchased it after the divorce. It had only ever been Matt here, alone with his thoughts, so this wasn't anything new. He'd been content with that for two years now.

He couldn't be content with it anymore.

Every time he closed his eyes he thought about Aiden, about the way he'd melted into Matt's arms that first night, a surrender as easy as memory. About the way Aiden had looked at him the last night, like he was going to cry but didn't have anything left inside to do it. About the familiar smell of his hair and body, like ten years hadn't passed at all.

Every time he closed his eyes, he thought about what it felt like to touch Aiden again, how much he had missed it. On what a visceral level he'd missed it.

He was still furious. The way Aiden had cut him off when he'd tried to talk, tried to say anything. It flayed deep. It was like being thrown back a decade in time again, when all he'd wanted was for Aiden to understand him. To listen to him. All of it churned around in his chest like a maelstrom, confusing and all-consuming. For the first time in five years at least, he couldn't stop thinking about Aiden when he tried.

He *had* to stop fucking thinking about this. He couldn't afford to be distracted this year, his contract year, maybe his last year with the Royal.

Whatever Aiden Campbell was doing with his life, it wasn't Matt's business anymore. Whether or not Aiden Campbell had decided to fuck him again it *wasn't Matt's business anymore*.

He texted the team group chat: Boys. Who's back in Montreal?

Alex Morin immediately wrote back, We never left, mon capitaine.

That was true at least for the Morin twins and for Xavier Fournier, the Royal's starting goalie, all of whom were from Quebec and spent the offseason in Montreal, even though Fourns was really from Saguenay. He got a few responses from the other guys—some of them had returned early; a few others, like Jamie Ayer, were still training at home before planning to come back later in the offseason. Still, there were enough of the team in Montreal that he felt a little more at ease.

Matt asked, Anyone want to skate tomorrow?

Bit early for that, eh Cap? I'm personally planning

to stay away as long as possible, Amanpreet Singh replied. Manny was one of the veteran wingers, a solid third line checking presence whose solemn face belied a jokester's personality. Between Manny and Saari and Jammer, it was sometimes hard to keep a straight face at practice, and Matt was always grateful to have guys who could keep it light.

It would be good for him to get back on the ice as soon as possible, even if there was always the danger of overtraining. But he needed to *do* something. If he sat alone in his house by himself for all of this time, he was going to continue the summer's streak of stupid fucking decisions. And that was something he absolutely could not afford to do.

Nah, he said. I'll be at Brossard tomorrow bright and early, whoever wants to come.

That's our Safy, Manny said, with a winky face.

He just had to get back to work. All he had to do was get back to work, and then he could stop thinking about sex, about Aiden Campbell, about the quiet solitude of his condo.

He'd done this before and he could do it again.

He just had to go cold turkey.

"Bro," Pears said, "you *gotta* get out of the house."

"Actually, I'm doing great in the house," Aiden replied, rubbing his neck. The bruises Matt left there hadn't faded, and Aiden felt Pears' eyes on them, felt the red rising on the tips of his ears. Like he was sixteen, not thirty-six.

"Hmm," Pears said, and his eyebrows went up. Even in his mid-thirties, he still had the same perpetually semi-stoned expression and fluffy brown hair smashed down under a snapback that he'd had since his rookie year, when Aiden had first met him. Something about Isaac Pearson would always look a little adolescent, no matter how old he was. "Don't really believe that, my dude. So that's an order."

"You're not my captain anymore."

"Ooh, harsh. Well, I still got responsibilities, bud, so you're coming with me. You wanna fight about it?" Pears' hands flew up in a comical mock-boxing pose, and he jabbed at the air in front of Aiden until Aiden grabbed his fist and held on.

"Jesus Christ, Pears, no."

"Then come on out, Soup." Pears gently disentangled his hand. "Just you and me. It'll be super chill, don't worry."

"I don't—"

Pears smiled his impish, shit-stirring smile. "It's not like you got anything else to do, huh?"

"Oh, that's low."

"No, that's Pears," Pears said, and flashed a pair of finger guns at him.

"You're fucking awful," Aiden said, unable to hide the reluctant smile twitching at the corner of his mouth.

"That's why I wear that C, baby. Come on, Soup. I got you."

It turned out that Pears' plans involved driving Aiden up to Storm King State Park, dragging him, in silence, around the emerald green–bordered trails and up the mountain for four hours until both of them were exhausted and sweaty, and then smoking him up while they sat at the summit, legs dangling over the edge and watching hikers in the distance below them. Looking at the blue river curving out ahead among the trees.

Aiden had never been a big weed guy—he was too much of a control freak to really enjoy it. The last time had been so long ago, he'd still been with Matt, incredibly young and lost and fucked up in Amsterdam. He remembered sitting down at a bus stop, his head on Matt's shoulder, his body feeling like it had suddenly tripled in weight, half-convinced that he could fall asleep right then and there.

"Bro," Pears said, as soon as it was clear that both of them were feeling it. Pears kept patting Aiden's knee with gentle hands, over and over again. Normally Aiden would have found it annoying. He focused, instead, on the sensation of fingers on his skin as Pears kept talking: "I'm not gonna tell you I'm worried about you, because I know you hate that, but…you seem like you're kinda in a rut."

Aiden exhaled a small cloud of smoke and passed the joint back to Pears. He felt calmer, a little, although whether that was due to the pot, being out in one of his favorite hiking spots within driving distance of the city or Pears' aggressively Zen vibes, he didn't know. "I'm retired and I don't know what the hell to do with myself, of course I'm in a rut. Like, what are *you* planning to do when you're—you're done?"

Pears rested the joint on the rock. He offered Aiden some trail mix he'd had in his backpack and, when Aiden shook his head, dumped nuts into his own hand. "Finish my degree, start a business."

"I—what?"

"Yeah, man." Pears popped a chili lime cashew into his mouth and chewed contemplatively. "I'm thinking, like, maybe a mobile DJ service." When Aiden looked sideways at him, Pears grinned. "I mean, fuck, man,

I don't know what kind of business yet. But I'm definitely gonna do some kind of a feasibility study to make sure it gets off the ground the right way. We're not the kind of guys who can just sit around, you feel me?"

"Yeah. I'm definitely not."

"You don't really seem like you, hmm…put a lot of thought into it beforehand."

"No."

"Why?"

Aiden thought about not telling him. About not saying anything. But once Pears got on the scent, he didn't give up. "It was just every time I thought about not playing hockey, it felt so wrong that I just—didn't. By the end, hockey was the only thing I had left, anyway, so thinking about losing that, too? It was easier to just not do it. It was like my brain just couldn't get itself to focus on the concept at all. Even when I did retire it wasn't a choice so much as it just…sort of happened."

"You ever thought about therapy, Soup? Like. Regular therapy, not a guy talking to you about goaltending to get you into the game."

"No, there's—there's not anything *wrong* with me, the whole thing I'm known for is steadiness, my mental fortitude—"

"Oh, man, no, it's not just because there's something wrong with you. I mean, there's a lot of shit wrong with you, but therapy's not gonna do one damn thing for that." Pears flashed him a smile. "It's to give you better skills for coping with shit and kicking ass at it. In your case, specifically, not hockey shit. It's pretty dope, you know?"

"Isaac, what the *fuck*?"

"I'm just saying, you gotta like…grow up, accept

responsibility for your own damn self sometime, right? For me it's like—I gotta be the best Pears I can be, right? For the team and for myself. Talking this shit out helps me do that. Anyway, Soup, just saying, you might wanna think about it."

Aiden thought about all of the thoughts he'd boxed up and shoved away over the years, all of the shit roiling in his chest and his head, and trying to tell someone about it. The idea was almost laughable. He thought about all of the mindfulness practice he had done over the decades, about being aware of his body, about focusing only on the moment, letting go of the future and the past. About how he was still doing it.

He looked at Pears. Pears looked back, expectant, hopeful.

Aiden said, "I'll think about it."

"Awesome." Pears watched Aiden from the corner of his eye like he was a skittish animal. "There's one more thing."

"Please don't."

"Sorry, Soup. But I gotta know. That night you went out with Gabe—you didn't just walk away, did you?"

Aiden thought about lying. He thought about *accept responsibility for your own damn self.* "No."

"Ohh, buddy."

"Yeah, uh. It wasn't my best moment. Moments."

"Ohhhh, *buddy*."

Aiden stared out into the long distance. There was a disconnect between his body, relaxed in a way it hadn't been in a long time, and his head, cycling through all of the stupid things he'd done over the past week and all of the complicated feelings he'd had about them. Like he could see them clearly for the first time.

"I know it was a bad idea. A really bad idea. But I couldn't let him go…"

"Soupy, you don't have to explain yourself to me, I'm not trying to make you feel like shit. It's just that I remember what it was like when you guys broke up the first time, and I don't wanna have you going through that again while you've already got so much shit of your own going on, you know? Let's climb one mountain at a time, buddy."

"Yeah, well," Aiden said, and laughed. "It's too late for that now."

Pears' mouth tilted up in one of those lazy, rueful smiles. "Well, just remember, Soupy, whatever's going on, you're not *alone*."

Aiden, strangely, did feel a little better. To get it out there in the universe. To hear that, even if it was ultimately a meaningless platitude, as useless as the mantras he'd used to help himself through his season. "Thanks, Pears. For being you."

Pears smiled again, and said, "I'll send you the playlist."

They sat in silence, for a while, watching the sun go down.

Once Matt got on the ice, he felt a little better. He had been playing it pretty cool overall, being extremely normal about everything that had happened to him in the beginning of July. But he'd also played it cool when Aiden had broken up with him the first time, for a few months at least, and that had ended up as a disaster of epic proportions.

Either way. It was good to get back out to Brossard and push himself to his limit. Although there were a few other guys who were back in the city, only the Quebecers humored him and rolled out. The Morin twins, of course, although Matt liked them best in small doses even after all of these years. And Fourns, who would have lived and slept at the rink if the equipment managers had let him.

Matt warmed up by shooting some pucks on Fourns' empty net, then went into a pretty brutal skate that took him the better part of thirty minutes. While he was doing it, he could see, out of the corner of his eyes, that Fourns had shoveled all of the pucks out of the back of the net, dumping them in a bucket beyond. By the time he had gotten into the crease, finishing his own warm-up and humoring his captain, Matt shot some more pucks in his direction.

Fourns gloved the last one and rose gracefully from the ice where he'd been on his knees. It was funny watching him move. He was a very different player than Aiden had been. Fourns was tall and stocky, with an explosive athleticism, while Aiden had dropped down draft rankings because even though he was tall, he was lanky as hell, and relied more on positioning.

But they had that same easy grace, the same flexibility.

Fourns pulled his helmet off and shook out his hair, then squinted at Matt, who was sweating heavily, his face red. Everything ached. He was in excellent shape, even in the offseason, but that kind of skate took it out of you.

"Cap," Fourns said, "you like to tell me why you're bag skating yourself already in motherfucking *July*?"

"Who's bag skating?" Matt asked, looking away guiltily.

Behind them, the Morins fired a series of rapid pucks on the net, the *bang* of the missed shots hitting the boards too loud in the mostly empty practice rink.

Fourns raised his heavy eyebrows and wrinkled his nose. He looked like a teaching assistant who never had enough coffee, a perpetual five-o'clock shadow on his cheeks no matter how often he shaved. "Cap," he said, disapprovingly.

Fourns hadn't been around for the aftermath of Aiden Campbell. He knew, generally, about Matt's bisexuality and the divorce, but the roster from those years had kept Matt's secrets for him. Even if Fourns *had* known, Matt wasn't ready to talk to anyone about that particular open wound.

"I just want to get back in the swing of the season. Make sure my knee's going to hold up," Matt lied, hoping that Fourns wouldn't call him out on the obvious: pushing it that hard this early was a sure way to aggravate things. Thankfully the knee still felt mostly okay. He'd have to make sure he took extra time stretching and keep up with ibuprofen every morning and maybe see about Toradol shots later on, but for now, it was fine.

"Sure." Fourns wriggled his hand out of his blocker; it looked comically tiny in his baggy sleeve before he raised it to brush the sweaty strands of hair away from his eyes. "But, man, I *will* talk to the trainers if I have to shut you down."

Aiden's hair was longer than Fourns' now, Matt realized with a little jolt. When they'd been younger, Aiden had always kept it mostly short and styled. By the time the playoffs came around, it brushed at the nape of his neck, shaggy enough for Matt to get a hand in there and really pull.

"Cap."

"Sorry," Matt said, shaking his head, like that alone

would clear the cobwebs. "I'm a little distracted today, I guess."

Fourns looked at Matt with his tired brown eyes. A level, searching look. He didn't say *do you want to talk* because he probably knew that Matt would never. That was part of being a captain of the Royal. You bore the weight of that mantle, and you couldn't share it with your team, no matter how much you would have liked to sometimes.

Besides. This wasn't anything like losing games and dealing with media shit. This was something beyond. It was funny: years ago, this was the kind of thing Matt would have turned to Aiden for, knowing Aiden would've had something to say, even if it was completely fucking stupid and off the wall, that would have made him feel better. And that was the problem, of course.

He couldn't talk to *Aiden* about it. Aiden didn't want to talk to him.

Couldn't you? The traitor thought wormed its way into the back of his head. *Couldn't you talk to him?*

No. No: he couldn't talk to him. Aiden hadn't let him. But Aiden had been like that before, sometimes, when he was too overwhelmed by the moment. He'd shut down, but it didn't necessarily mean that he didn't want to… Maybe with a little distance, he wouldn't push Matt away. Who the hell was he kidding? It was entirely wishful thinking. Idiocy.

Matt kept up with the fast pace of the practice that he had set for himself, but the whole time, that poisonous suggestion echoed in his head.

Couldn't you just talk to him?

Time went by.

Aiden wasn't over it, but eventually it felt like an old

bruise, the kind that only hurt if you pressed on it. He kept carefully to the Routine, modified for retirement: yoga and gym, cooking, cleaning his house. He learned how to play a few complicated new songs on his guitar. He didn't drink for seventeen days. He only pressed occasionally, when it was late at night and he was alone in his bed, horny and unable to stop thinking about it.

It was easy to remember when he wanted to remember. The end of it, the unraveling. The more serious things had gotten, the harder it had been to be apart the whole year, to keep it quiet during the summer. Matt wanted more than Aiden could see himself giving, when their careers, their *lives*, were hundreds or thousands of miles away, depending on the time of year.

But if there was one thing Aiden could recall with perfect clarity, at any time, any day, it was the way Matt's face had crumpled after he'd asked Aiden to marry him and Aiden had said no. When Aiden had said, *I don't think this is going to work and it isn't fair to you to keep trying when I can't give you what you want.*

Years ago, he'd forced himself to stop keeping close tabs on Matt's career other than news that wasn't actively avoidable, like when the Royal had won the Cup, or when Matt had gotten a Defensive Forward of the Year award the same year Aiden had won one of his goalie awards and they'd spent a lot of time avoiding each other at the awards presentation. It had hurt too much to do it, a kind of self-flagellation that accomplished nothing.

Since Matt had left New York, Aiden couldn't stop himself from reading articles. Matt had gotten divorced. Matt had gotten hurt. Matt had had surgery to repair his MCL. Matt was back on the ice. Matt was in the last year of his contract, although no one seemed sure whether the Royal would bring their franchise player back in free agency. Matt had expressed a desire to retire in Montreal, but after the nagging injuries wasn't playing at the level he'd used to. There was some speculation he might accept a team-friendly deal—even league minimum—just to finish his career there, but that depended on the front office and the cap space they'd have to work with.

Aiden understood, probably better than anyone, what Matt must be going through. Aiden had never wanted to play anywhere except New York, never wanted to get used to the rhythms of living in a city other than New York, never wanted to love another city the way he loved New York. And in the end, it hadn't saved him. He wondered if Matt felt the same way about Montreal. He wondered if Matt didn't. Whether things could have been different if Aiden had tried harder and been braver. Less stubborn.

He'd tried to stop thinking about the *what-ifs* years ago, because there were so many it drove him a little fucking crazy. It was easier said than done.

He looked at a few listings for therapists, but ultimately, the thought of running through mindfulness exercises, *again*, or telling a complete stranger about all of the things he had spent years ignoring, wasn't particularly appealing. And his sports psychologist was a sports psychologist, he couldn't help with…whatever Aiden was doing right now.

He thought about what Pears had said, about having a plan after hockey, and none of the options he could come up with sounded appealing, either. He couldn't really see himself going back to school in his late thirties.

He couldn't really see the point in any of it. Couldn't really see the point in anything.

Technically, Aiden never had to work again. Caroline had negotiated him several very generous contract extensions, and his financial adviser had made sure he'd invested it wisely. He didn't have to do anything if he didn't want to. But the thought of spending the rest of his life like *this*? Aiden could feel the tightness in his chest whenever the thought came up.

The clock, glowing red in the dark, read two in the morning. He rolled over, tossing and turning. Nights like this, trapped with his own thoughts, the room felt a lot smaller than it was, too hot, like there wasn't enough air.

His phone buzzed.

Hi.

The text wasn't from a number he had saved in his contacts. It didn't matter. He recognized it anyway. You never changed your number?

You never changed yours.

Never got around to it.

Yeah. Well. Me neither. Can we talk? And don't say there's nothing to talk about.

He hesitated for a long time. The thought of talking to Matt, in his house, with nowhere to go and no way to escape if he said something he didn't want to, had been terrifying. Had made him feel like he wanted to peel his skin off. He had control now that he hadn't had before.

Matt wouldn't *see* him, wouldn't see how desperately Aiden *wanted* to talk to him, how desperate he felt in general, whenever Matt was involved. It was probably still a stupid idea. A disaster. Asking for trouble.

We're all going to die one day, Aiden thought, the way he often did when he was trying to calm himself down. *None of this really matters.*

Aiden said, Okay.

It was strange seeing Matt's number pop up on the screen without an accompanying picture. "Hi."

"Hi."

He could feel his heart beating rapidly in his chest, almost too loud in his ears. His free hand, twisted around itself, was damp with sweat. *Nothing really matters,* he told himself, *we're all going to die one day.* It didn't matter if he was *talking* to Matt again. Whatever happened, he'd already made a disaster out of it. It was done.

"I—Jesus, this is fucking weird."

Matt audibly exhaled. "Thanks for not hanging up."

"Yeah, I—it's fine."

"I just wanted to talk to you about what happened in, in New York. Don't cut me off just yet. I'm sorry. I wanted to apologize for the way we left things but for all of it, too. I shouldn't have done it, but I saw you, and I saw how Walker was with you, and it was like everything just came rushing back to me, I couldn't just stand by and watch without trying to talk to you, trying to—"

"We didn't exactly do a lot of talking."

"I was trying, but it's not fucking *easy*, Aiden, especially when you wouldn't let me. But I wanted to fucking, I don't know, apologize. To tell you if you weren't comfortable with anything we did, I'm sorry for pushing.

And to tell you, uh, I've been divorced for two years, in case you didn't know."

He knew *now*, but he hadn't thought about it at the time beyond noting the lack of a wedding ring, which Aiden certainly knew meant nothing. He didn't like realizing that he hadn't thought about it. "In case you didn't notice, I wasn't exactly turning you away."

"I know, but it was—fuck, I can't stop thinking about it. About *you*. It was like no time had gone by at all when I was with you. And now I feel so fucking old."

Aiden exhaled. "I'm sorry I kicked you out. I wish I hadn't, I just, I've been—it's been fucking hell. Trying to adjust to life without hockey, to figure out what the hell I'm doing, it's been…and then to see you like that…"

Matt's breath sounded a little ragged. There was a long silence on the other end of the line. "It's been a weird decade, huh?"

"Yeah. I—how are you?" He almost wanted to laugh: *how are you.* Such a banal fucking question, after all of that time and all of their history.

"I mean, I'm okay. I guess. No complaints about the career. But my knee's been giving me some trouble again, no idea what the fuck I'm going to do about my contract extension…you know. The usual."

Aiden thought about his last season, his weak knee and hip huge pains in the ass no matter how he stretched before games. The inevitable countdown until one or both of them gave out again. "More than you know."

They sat silent for a long time. It was almost 2:30 in the morning now, but Aiden was wide awake. He listened to Matt's quiet breath and remembered all of the other nights of his life he'd done the exact same thing, in New York, in Winnipeg, in hundreds of anonymous hotel rooms while Matt was in Montreal or Hamilton or somewhere across the continent.

It had always felt comforting then. A lifeline. No matter what was happening around him, no matter how chaotic his life had gotten, there was Matt's steady, warm breath, just a phone call away. Now it just felt like a bitter reminder of all of the years he'd lost. And yet, the thought of losing even this connection…

"Are you living in New York in the offseason now?"

"Yeah, I…well. It was easier than going home, after a while."

"I mostly stay in Montreal. Same reason." Matt hesitated. "Aiden…are you okay?"

He'd never really been able to lie to Matt. "No. Not really. Not having anything to do? It's pretty terrifying and kind of lonely, actually."

"You're not seeing anyone?"

"What the fuck, Matt, I wouldn't have let you do that if I'd been seeing anyone."

"Would you have? You didn't ask about my marriage, I just—"

"I should go."

"Yeah. Yeah, you should. It's late."

"Matt…"

"Yeah?"

"Nothing. Good night."

CHAPTER THREE

August

It had been fucking stupid to do it, Matt knew that much. For all of his high-minded talk about going cold turkey he'd just mainlined it instead. After he'd hung up, he couldn't fall asleep. It was like the rush of adrenaline that he felt after a game, one of the really good games where he was on the ice with a one-goal lead and the goalie pulled as the final seconds ticked down, and the other team just couldn't even it up.

Those were the kinds of nights he'd always wished that he and Aiden had lived in the same city because he always had the urge to go home and fuck it out. They'd usually had to settle for phone sex.

And now, just a conversation had thrown him off of the rails. He tried jerking off, but that just made it worse, because all he could think about was Aiden that last night in New York, his hands twisted in Matt's hair and his voice shaking when he told Matt what he wanted. When he *begged* for it.

All of the complicated emotions he'd felt in New York were still bubbling there under the surface, but for all that he knew it was a stupid thing he'd done and an even stupider thing to hope, he couldn't help it. Eventually, he got up to wash his hands and splash cold water on his face, and then just got up. He went up the stairs to the roof of his condo building and watched the sunrise and tried to figure out what to do with the rest of his day.

Jammer was back in town earlier than expected. He'd recently broken up with his poet girlfriend and decided that the best way to get over her was to get onto the ice, a thought process Matt could definitely understand.

Matt went to meet him for breakfast near Jammer's apartment in Old Port. He was well aware he looked like shit. He'd been sleeping badly even before Aiden, but there wasn't anything he could do about it besides melatonin and CBD gummies and hoping for the best. Maybe Aiden would decide to stop talking to him again. Maybe he could just go back to normal and forget any of it had ever happened.

Ha. That was funny.

"Cap," Jammer said breezily when Matt met him outside of the crepe spot.

Jammer looked the same he always did: a giant barrel of a man, dead-eyed, tanned and wearing an absolutely ridiculous outfit. Matt didn't know a whole lot about fashion outside of various brands of athletic wear, and the custom suit shop he had been patronizing since his rookie year. Jammer, on the other hand, liked to experiment. His outfits frequently cost as much as Matt's mortgage and were always a statement.

Jammer hadn't been on the team during the breakup either, had been acquired from the Long Island Railers the following year as a rehabilitation project. He'd flourished in Montreal and helped them win a second

Cup. And he'd only ever known Matt as a steady, reliable two-way presence, on the ice and off.

"Jammer," Matt said, grabbing him in a brief but effusive bro-hug. "Sorry about Diya."

"It's cool," Jammer said. He broke away, shrugging, and held the door for Matt. "I get it; it's hard when you aren't really cut out to be a WAG. Our schedules didn't exactly line up, either. Not with her tours and my travel."

"I know you really liked her, though. So I'm still sorry."

Jammer smiled his charming, crooked smile at the hostess. Once they were seated, he said, "Probably loved her, but who can tell at all with those things?"

"In my experience, when you're in love with someone, you know it."

Jammer's keen eyes fixed on Matt, and he raised one eyebrow. "Sounds like there's a story behind that one."

Matt snorted. They both looked down at their menus. "Well, yes, and no. I guess with my wife, it was pretty clear neither of us had ever been in love. Once it was over and you're mostly relieved, you know."

"It doesn't matter now. I'm very, you know. Accepting. The pain is momentary, but the experience and the memories are forever."

By now, Matt was used to Jammer's little aphorisms. "Well, the memories are certainly forever, anyway," he said dryly, "whether that's a good thing is really up to the individual."

"Oh, no. No, even the painful memories are a learning experience." Jammer was so painfully earnest it was almost too much to handle.

"Jammer, I love you, man, but come on. I haven't even had a cup of coffee yet."

Jammer laughed. "Touché."

Matt ordered a breakfast crepe with eggs and cream cheese and smoked salmon, with a side of potatoes, and Jammer ordered two of them. They ate in silence for a while, which was nice. It was a pleasant spot, huge-windowed and sunny with red brick walls. The tables were a bit too small to comfortably fit two hockey players' legs underneath, but the food and coffee were good enough that Matt was willing to suffer.

"You look like shit, Cap," Jammer said, after they had gotten halfway through.

"It's been…a weird summer."

"Tell me about it. Rhetorically, and in the empathetic sense that I am also having a weird summer."

Matt stared at him. "Jammer, you're one weird fucking guy, you know that?"

"It's part of my charm."

He wasn't wrong, but Matt wasn't about to give him a bigger head than he already had. He poked at his crepe, suddenly not very hungry.

Jammer's shrewd eyes saw right through him. "Seriously, though, Cap. Are you good?"

"I'll be good to start the season. I'm just—have you ever known something's a bad fucking idea and done it anyway?"

"All the time. Most recently, dated a poet," Jammer said, sawing one of his crepes with immense satisfaction. "Pretty good couple of years. Best sex of my life. Pretty sure there's gonna be a poem about me in her next book, though, so that sucks. Would I do it again? Every time."

Matt pushed the crepe across the plate and frowned.

While Jammer ate, he took out his phone and composed a text message.

Aiden woke up later than usual. He worked his way through the morning Routine, with more emphasis on a longer yoga session in the hope that that would help his brain stop screaming at him. The results were inconclusive. When he finished, lying on his back on the mat, he checked his phone.

Matt had texted a picture of the sunrise from the roof deck of what was presumably his condo, and: I couldn't sleep last night.

Aiden stared at it for a long time. He wrote back, while he waited for his coffee to brew. Haven't been sleeping much lately myself.

It was strange, talking to Matt in the same way they'd started talking so many years ago, stilted and awkward, overthinking every interaction. Not exactly the same: Matt had spent most of the first few months pulling Aiden's metaphorical pigtails just to get his attention. This new fragility was different. The worst part was that he *wanted* it. He wanted it as badly as he'd ever wanted anything, Matt sending him pictures the way he'd always done. It wasn't real. It didn't do any good pretending. But *god*, he wanted it.

Matt said, You can just tell me to fuck off if you don't want to do this. I'd understand if you don't.

I don't know WHAT I want. Things have been kind of fucked over here in case you didn't notice.

Oh, I did. For one thing, who the fuck decorated your house?

A startled laugh burst out of his mouth before he even realized it was coming. I hired an interior designer because I didn't want to think about anything.

Looks like they didn't think about anything either. Hope you didn't pay them too much. That couch fucking sucks.

It's pretty terrible, he agreed. Aiden poured himself a cup of coffee and chewed on his lip. Feeling daring, he added, Didn't hear any complaints from you at the time.

Had other things on my mind, I guess.

Aiden burned his tongue and wondered, yet again, what the fuck he was doing. Are you still in the same condo?

No, my ex got it in the divorce.

He stared at the text message and his fingers itched with the desire to ask about it. He remembered the first time he had seen a picture of Matt's wife—it was their wedding photos, in a piece in *The Athletic* about what various Royal players had been up to over the Christmas break. Emily Safaryan had been a very pretty woman, tall and slim and tan, with wavy dark brown hair pulled up in a complicated braid, a distinctive nose, striking light brown eyes that were a similar shade to Aiden's and dark freckles dusting her nose and cheeks and shoulders. She looked radiant in her wedding dress, smiling over her shoulder at Matt, handsome in his gray suit, in the middle of the dance floor.

Aiden had stared at the picture for a very long time, and then he'd gone out and gotten so drunk that he'd woken up from a blackout in the airport in Montreal. No luggage. No plans. Nothing except a hundred missed calls and three hundred text messages, from the coach, his team, his family, all increasingly panicked and furious. He hadn't tried to see Matt, or even talk to him: he'd turned right around and bought a ticket back home. It had taken him a really long time to clean up *that* mess. He still flinched, inwardly, thinking about it.

Sorry.

It's fine. My new place isn't bad. A fresh start wasn't the worst thing.

Matt sent Aiden a brief video, panning around the kitchen in what was presumably his new condo. It was modestly sized, pleasant and modern with industrial touches: exposed pipes and concrete countertops and green plants in every available window space. Toward the end of the video, Aiden caught a glimpse of Matt's plate, with a half-eaten breakfast sandwich and what looked like a small bowl of fruit, yogurt and granola.

Did you learn how to cook?

Some things stay the same, some things change.

I don't think that's how the saying goes.

Matt sent him the eye-rolling emoji in response.

Hey...

Yeah?

I know it's been a while, and some of the guys knew when it was happening, but do you mind if I tell Gabe? I owe him an apology and an explanation.

It's fine.

Thanks, Matt.

Yeah. Okay, I have to go to the gym.

Aiden felt a little better after he finished the coffee and ate his toast. He texted Gabe, Do you want to get lunch today?

yes, Gabe responded, almost immediately. u can come over if u want.

Aiden sighed. He wasn't looking forward to this conversation, but he should probably pull the Band-Aid off sooner rather than later. He also wasn't looking forward to lunch; any deviations from the Routine made him feel a little sweaty and nauseous, and it had only gotten worse since his retirement, without any external impetus to make him do things he normally wouldn't. He went to the gym and lifted weights in silence about it for a few hours, but he didn't feel any better after.

Aiden paid for and picked up the ramen Gabe had ordered from a place not far from his apartment, made his way back to the building and headed up the elevator. It was a modern, shining edifice, something that would have been unthinkable in this neighborhood when Aiden was a rookie. There was a doorman and everything.

"Hey, buddy," he said, when Gabe opened the door for him.

"Hi!" Gabe took the bag. "Come on in, Soupy. I even cleaned up for you so, like, you should feel pretty special."

"I already do," Aiden said solemnly and followed him into the kitchen. If it hadn't had Gabe in it, Gabe's apartment would have been almost as soulless as Aiden's house. But Gabe had personalized it with pictures of his family and colorful prints hung everywhere, and the couch was covered with so many pillows you could barely even sit on it.

He watched as Gabe bustled around, opening the take-out containers and pouring the soups into bowls set up on his kitchen island, spooning the sesame salad and gyoza onto plates, very carefully not looking Aiden in the eye. They sat down at the stools and ate in silence, Aiden mostly pushing the food around on his plate and Gabe stealing glances up at him when he thought Aiden wasn't looking. Aiden tried to stop his leg from bouncing, but he couldn't.

"Look, Gabe, I did want to apologize to you for my behavior that night."

"You don't have to."

"Yes, I do. It wasn't fair to you, especially since I know you were just concerned for a friend." Gabe flushed, like he was about to say something else, but Aiden pushed onward before Gabe could get it out. "I did want to offer you an apology, because I was an asshole and you didn't deserve it, but I also wanted to, uh, give you an explanation because I know that wasn't in character for me."

"Okay," Gabe said, his chopsticks frozen in midair.

"I don't know if you remember the conversation we had last year, when you asked me if I'd ever dated another player."

"Of course I do." The tips of Gabe's ears were flushed darker, and he couldn't look Aiden in the eye.

"And I told you that I had, and it hadn't ended well?"

"Yeah? Oh, shit, you were talking about *him*?"

"Yeah. We used to…well. We were together for almost five years."

"*What*—I'm—" Gabe stared at him, speechless for the first time since Aiden had known him. "*What?*"

"It was the first time I've really seen him off the ice in over a decade. I'm sorry. Like I said, it wasn't fair to you. It was just a shock, and I wasn't prepared for any of it, especially not after drinking."

Gabe looked down at his ramen again. "I mean, I guess, if it was still that bad after all this time. It must have been really serious."

Aiden had one of those memories he wished wouldn't surface at such inopportune times but that he couldn't seem to stop having. Matt in bed with him, rolling over with his stupidly determined expression. Taking Aiden's chin in his hand, forcing him to look. *Well, why* shouldn't *we get married?*

"Yes. But I was young and stupid, and I fucked it up, and now here we are. But I still shouldn't have taken it out on you. I won't do that again, I promise."

"I forgive you, obviously," Gabe said, still a bit flushed. "Especially since you bought me lunch."

No matter how Aiden tried to change the subject, the

conversation was still awkward after that, Gabe obviously wanting to ask more but holding back out of either embarrassment or respect. Twisting the wrapper from his chopsticks in a tight spiral, he looked from the half-eaten food to Aiden and back. "But it was ten years ago, right, you don't still have, like, *feelings* for him, right?"

Aiden shrugged, uneasy, his fingernails digging into his palm. "Not that kind of feeling. Okay. Let me help you clean up."

He could feel Gabe's eyes on him the entire time.

Later that evening, alone in his home again, Matt asked, "So what the hell do you even do in your spare time these days?"

Aiden had known it was a bad idea, but after leaving Gabe's apartment, he had been seized with the unaccountable, intrusive thought that he *needed* to talk to Matt. He spent most of the afternoon trying to talk himself out of it, but after he made dinner and cleaned up, he finally gave in. He'd called and Matt had picked up almost immediately. They had talked about mostly nothing for the last half an hour. Aiden hadn't *exactly* forgotten how much he liked just talking to Matt, but it was strange to be reminded of it as he was actually doing it.

Aiden, sitting on his roof deck, stared out at the horizon and its riot of oranges and pinks. "It's all spare time. Absolutely nothing. Today I walked home from Gabe's just because I had nothing else to do. It was five miles? I don't know. Took me an hour twenty."

"So retirement's *not* going well."

"Fuck, no. Try to sign somewhere if you can, because it's just *mind*-numbing."

"You know…about that."

"What?"

"I'm not sure if our GM is really interested in bringing me back after this season. We're tight on cap space, and I guess the optics of paying me a league minimum and shoving me on the fourth line after everything I've done for them—it's easier to let me go."

"Matt..."

"It's fine. I was prepared for it. I was even thinking that maybe they'd try to flip me at the trade deadline, if I'd agree to waive my no-move clause. The thing I wanted to tell you is that my agent said that at the last deadline, anyway, the only team that really seemed seriously interested were the Libs. And obviously, there's the NMC, but I told him that either way, I'd retire before that happened."

Aiden had to take a minute to process that. The last and only time he'd played with Matt was the Winter Olympics after they'd broken up, and they hadn't been talking at that point. "This was—"

"Before we—all of this. Yeah. But I still... I don't know. It wouldn't feel right playing there if you weren't. New York's *yours*."

"Not anymore." It wasn't sad or bitter, it just was.

"It'll always be yours, Aiden."

Aiden wanted to tell him that it wasn't his anymore, no matter how softly Matt said it; that the worst thing about retirement was the feeling that a city that used to bring him so much joy mostly felt like a prison, when he missed playing so much it felt like a cramp in his entire body. But he was already in over his head.

He thought about his own father, a former professional hockey player who'd never really been the same after *his* retirement. Dad had only ever come alive when they were watching games on TV, when he accompanied

Aiden to the rink and watched him battling his way onto rosters and, eventually, into what was probably going to be a Hall of Fame career. Aiden had always had a memory of coming down the stairs silently one night, of Dad's morose face, lit by the blue light of the television in the dark, staring longingly at something he could no longer access. Aiden had always pushed that memory down, in the box of things he chose not to look at too closely. The things he couldn't avoid anymore now.

Instead, he said, "It's really just not the same right now. Maybe you'll understand what that means one day. I hope you don't."

Matt was silent for a while, and finally said, "I'm sorry."

"It's fine." The sun had dipped below the skyline, although the diffused orange glow remained for those few moments. "Not your problem."

Matt laughed. More than a little rueful. "No, I guess you're right."

Aiden didn't say anything for a bit, just watched the fading light and listened to the sound of Matt's breath on the other line, then the faint noise of water running and the clink of dishes, the strange shift between the normalcy of some parts of the conversation—like they were picking up where they'd left off, no time in between—and the surreal quality of talking about the ends of both of their careers. And studiously not talking about the way other things had ended.

"I should go," Aiden said, reluctantly.

"Okay. Night, b—buddy."

The more Matt thought about Aiden retiring, the more it fucked him up. Obviously, he'd known retirement was in the cards for him. For both of them. It was the inevitability of hockey. You couldn't play forever. But when you were young it was easy to pretend that it would never happen, or that it was so far in the distant future that it didn't actually seem real. You couldn't play forever, but you could basically pretend. Even with his knee the way it had been, Matt hadn't liked to think about it too much. It was better to think *I can always sign another contract, of course they'll want me back,* or even, *I guess I could test free agency if I really had to.*

Aiden retiring felt a little like a friend dying.

Even after they'd broken up, Matt liked knowing that Aiden was out there still. It made the matchups with the Libs more intense, even if they'd never spoken during them the way they had when they were dating.

Even if it was mostly spite, Matt had always made it a mission to get on the scoreboard during those games. It was worth it to watch Aiden's frown behind the cage on the Jumbotron, the way he'd pull off his helmet to shake out his sweaty hair and the bitchy little twist of his mouth he'd make during stoppages in play, the way he'd work through his water bottle visualization exercise, watching the droplets arc and fall in an attempt to get his mind back into the game.

And now it was just Matt and his bum knee, leading a team of aging vets and baby rookies back out onto the ice. A reminder that retirement loomed ahead of him too, whether it was next season, or a few seasons after that. He was only thirty-five, but hockey years were like dog years, and he was an old man now. And he hadn't *really* thought about not playing, or what he'd do if he wasn't playing, until Aiden's situation made him do it.

By now, development camp had started, and the kids were all on the ice, kids who were still playing in juniors, some who were still in college and hadn't even signed entry-level contracts yet. Technically Matt didn't need to be there, but he showed up anyway. It was a good chance to get to know the new kids, to figure out who would be making the roster and who wouldn't.

"What do you think of the boys?" Jammer asked, standing at his side. They were watching the group running through their drills with the coach.

"Pretty solid this year. I bet Jack Crane's a lock," Matt said, watching Crane roofing the puck over the goalie's shoulder. They'd been lucky for him to fall to tenth overall because of his size, but he'd shown his last season in juniors that there wasn't any more for him to learn. Some of the others, like Rémi Cormier or Joel Koskinen, were a little more of a gamble. "I like Cormier's grit. Doesn't lose a board battle often."

"Koskinen's got a good eye down the middle," Jammer said, as they watched the ebb and flow of the exercise.

They were kids, though. All of them looked so fucking young, goofing off on the ice, chirping each other for missed shots in the drills, pushing and shoving with mock seriousness when the coaches weren't looking. They hadn't noticed him watching in the stands of the practice facility.

Hockey in Montreal was a religion, and people showed the fuck up for church, even when it was just to watch rookies who might not even sniff the roster for a few years yet. It was easy to blend in at first, until the fans noticed and started asking him for autographs.

Matt didn't want to be a distraction. He went down to the boards, Jammer tagging along, and greeted all of the rookies, wished them good luck, told them they should feel free to text him if they had any questions or concerns. They all looked at him, wide-eyed, when he said that. He knew from experience there would be only one or two of them brave enough to do it.

And then, because he didn't want to be a distraction, Matt beat a retreat for the steps. It was still good to get back into the practice facility at Brossard. There, he knew so clearly who he was and what his role was. It was hard to think about what he'd do when he didn't have that option.

What Aiden was doing now that he didn't have that option.

But the thing was…now, he could ask.

After the initial hesitance faded, it was like a dam had broken. Aiden found it surprisingly easy to fall back into their old pattern of texting all the time and sending pictures throughout the day. It was mostly innocuous, random observations, sending photos of interesting things they'd come across or Matt teasing Aiden in a way that felt comfortable and familiar, almost like he was on a hockey team again.

Sometimes it wasn't.

Aiden sent Matt a picture from the gym, one of approximately four places he ever went to anymore. It wasn't a suggestive picture, just his legs where he was sitting on the edge of the deadlift platform, next to the bar and weights. Even though he wasn't playing hockey anymore, he still found himself following his preseason lifting regime, like that would somehow provide some kind of a structure and purpose to his life.

He added, Back to work, I guess.

Matt said, You should move the camera up a little.

Aiden snorted. I see you haven't changed.

He did wonder about that, how easy it was to shift back into casual flirtation with someone who'd broken his heart so resoundingly. The strange thing was that the more they talked, the more he was starting to realize he wasn't bitter and angry at *Matt*. When it had actually happened, it wasn't like they'd been cruel to each other. He'd been gutted after finding about Emily, how quickly Matt had moved on, but it wasn't like Matt had tried to hurt him on purpose or make it worse than it already was. Aiden had been the one to ruin things. The more time that had gone by, the more Aiden was starting to realize the person he was really furious with was himself.

And now, a decade later, Matt was saying, I used to lose my fucking mind when you'd send me pictures like this. Especially at the beginning when you never seemed to realize that when I was sending you a gym selfie, it was because I wanted to give you a boner.

Well, it worked.

Yeah?

Are you working out, or...?

Well, now I'm just thinking about you at the gym. So thanks, for that.

Aiden said, Anytime.

In response, Matt sent him a picture, too. He sat on the bench facing the wall of mirrors, legs spread a little on either side of it, in the mostly empty gym. The thick thighs and solid core that had always driven Aiden completely insane. Every single muscle on display, sweaty in his tank top and shorts. He was close enough to the wall that Aiden could make out the outline of his dick, half-erect, under the fabric.

Aiden stared at it for a very long time, trying to figure out what to say. Every nerve was on fire. Well, he said finally, now I'm thinking about you at the gym.

Matt sent him a smirking emoji in response.

Distractions aside, Aiden had to admit he was still not doing very well in retirement. He had made schedules to get through each day—down to the minute with chores, guitar playing, reading a book, even bathroom breaks—and he knew that it was probably a little crazy. Even for him. But if he kept to the schedules, at least he was doing *something*. At least he wasn't just sitting around, staring at a wall.

He spent a lot of time avoiding calls and texts from his parents and Hannah, all increasingly worried about him. He spent a lot of time avoiding invitations to go out from Pears and Gabe.

Although his days were well regimented, Aiden was starting to realize that he could schedule his time down to the minute and it wouldn't matter. If he didn't do something else soon, something was going to break. Or he would. No matter how intensely he tried to fill his days, without the Routine, it was meaningless.

Slouching out of the gym toward his car, he thought, not for the first time, about his old mentor, Ward.

Hey, Wardo, he texted. Ward was almost fifty now, with an entire house full of kids and a steady job as an accountant. He was probably busy, but he never seemed to mind when Aiden bothered him. How's Wisconsin?

Hey, Soupy. It's going. How are you doing?

Aiden hesitated. He missed Wardo, missed the sense of security that came with having someone older and more responsible around to tell him to chill the fuck out when he was too deep in his head, missed the way Wardo used to look at him like he was very fond of Aiden but also very aware that Aiden was dumb as hell. It was reassuring to have someone around who knew your limitations and didn't treat you like the savior of a city.

Oh, you know.

Everything OK?

Yeah. Sure. Can I ask how you knew what to do after you were done?

Well, I already had the business degree, it was just the next logical choice to figure out a way to use it. Just kind of fell back into accounting.

Aiden, who only had a high school diploma because his mother would have killed him if he didn't, frowned. Thanks.

You know, you don't have to figure out a career path right away. You can enjoy a hobby, or travel, or do pretty much anything you want. Why don't you take some time to enjoy life?

But I don't really have any hobbies except hockey. And the guitar, but there's only so long during each day that you can play before your neighbors start complaining.

Oh, Soupy...look, there's nothing to stop you from picking up a new one, you know. Go golfing. Learn to paint. The only limit is your imagination.

Imagination's the problem, though. Wardo, I'm a hockey player.

You always had a warped sense of humor. But seriously, bud—don't stress so much. You have the rest of your life to figure it out.

Thanks. Hope Wisconsin's treating you okay.

They spent a few minutes chatting about Wardo's wife and the kids, about Wardo's accounting business, about their summer plans. Wardo was planning an extended fishing trip, which Aiden dutifully said sounded nice, even though he hated fishing.

Eventually, Wardo had to get back to work, and Aiden had to sit with the knowledge that there was a whole world of possibilities out there that he just could not, for whatever reason, see himself reaching for.

Matt was playing with fire, in danger of burning his hands every time he flirted with Aiden, every time he sent a gym selfie, every time he reached out at an odd hour of the night just to see if Aiden would respond. Even if Aiden was flirting back—Matt thought he was, anyway, sometimes it was hard to tell—even if Aiden was responding like he was waiting for it every time, Matt was playing with fire.

He tried to think about what his longest-serving winger, Eero Saarinen, would have said if he were here to see it.

What are you actually hoping to accomplish, buddy?

No, don't do it.

Don't you remember how things were, how you fucking imploded?

Matti, you fucking idiot.

He deserved it.

He was a fucking idiot.

In his condo, alone, Matt went about his day-to-day. It had been their little inside joke, when he'd first hooked up with Aiden, that Matt couldn't cook. Aiden used to tease him about it, used to delight in making *him* food, partially because Aiden had liked to take care of him but also just to rub his nose in it.

After they broke up, Matt had taught himself some basics over the years and thought about what Aiden would have said if he could have seen it. Probably some dry remark about how boring and easy the recipes were. It wasn't like he was relying on a meal service, at least, even if he usually kept it simple and planned ahead so he would have leftovers.

He made his dinner.

He folded his laundry and put it away in the drawers immediately, even though he hated doing that.

He kept everything in order because if everything was in order, that meant his life was in order.

It was a quiet little existence.

Even with making sure all of the rookies were settling in properly, that the team was all on the same page about the upcoming training camp, and all of the responsibilities of the captaincy, Matt was starting to realize that his quiet little existence wasn't just quiet. It was fucking *lonely*.

He ate by himself. He came home by himself. He got into bed by himself. He hadn't really dated anyone seriously since the divorce. It hadn't seemed worth it. Anyone coming back to the condo was just a one-night stand, or at most, a two-week stand. And in the end, he'd discovered that that was almost lonelier than just not hooking up.

He thought about Aiden, alone in New York.

He thought about Aiden saying, *It's really just not the same right now. Maybe you'll understand what that means one day. I hope you don't.*

He thought about watching Aiden on the ice, the grace and power and beauty that made him immediately recognizable even if you couldn't see his face under the cage. He thought about how, even now, he could remember exactly the way Aiden's face looked when he woke up in the morning, the slow, sleepy smile that had only ever been Matt's. He could remember the way Aiden's pulse felt under his fingers pressing down on his throat, beating fast as a rabbit's, the way his head tilted back in an invitation. He could remember the way Aiden's face would get so fucking red when Matt slapped him, eyes watering, desperate for more. He could remember Aiden, sitting on a private beach and watching the sun set blood orange over the water, his shoulders hunched forward, a serious look on his face. His voice, equally serious: *I don't want to go home, Matty. Let's stay here forever.*

He could remember all of it, a million snapshot memories of Aiden he'd never been able to purge from his brain.

He thought about Saari saying, *Matti, you fucking idiot.*

Maybe so.

Aiden was taking his chicken out of the oven and prepping his salad and grains to go with it when Matt FaceTimed him. He propped his phone up against the toaster while he worked, watching Matt from the corner of his eye.

It hadn't been a great day. Aiden had gone grocery shopping after the gym and his conversation with Ward and had gotten stopped several times on the way and in the store. He'd signed the autographs and hated it every time. It felt like committing fraud, somehow, even though they were legitimately fans of his, and he had done the things that had made them love him. He wasn't that guy anymore, and the knowledge rattled around in his head, too loudly. Even the mantras couldn't drown it out. The house seemed especially quiet when he got home and unpacked, and he'd jumped in both surprise and eagerness to answer when he heard the phone ring.

"What's up?" Matt asked, during a lull in the conversation.

"I'm making dinner."

"No, I mean…something's up with you. You're really jumpy tonight. Or sad. I don't know."

"I've just—" Aiden set the knife down. "Matt, I just don't know what the fuck I'm doing with my life, you know? It's been bad this week. Worse than usual. I even texted Ward for advice, and he told me that I don't *need* to do anything."

"I mean, do you really need to do anything? Maybe Ward's right."

"Matt… I *do*. I have to do something different. I'm fucking losing it. I really feel like I'm losing my mind, you know?"

"Come to Montreal," Matt said, the words falling out all in a rush, like he needed to get them out before he could bite them back.

"What?"

Matt took a deep breath, and said, slower: "Come to Montreal."

"Are you serious?"

"Yes. I don't know, maybe a change of scenery would do you some good."

"I… Matt… Montreal is kind of a… There's a lot of people who would recognize me. And you."

Matt's face was inscrutable as he shrugged. "You need to get out of New York for a bit, I think. My life's in Montreal right now. I have a spare bedroom and the rest of the summer. Come for as long as you want. We'll figure the rest of it out."

"This is a terrible idea," Aiden said, slowly.

"When has that ever stopped us, Aiden?"

The arc of their relationship flashed behind his eyes, compressed to a ten-second movie, scenes he couldn't have burned from his memory even if he'd wanted to. The first time they'd locked eyes in the handshake line. The first time he'd met Matt in an airport in the offseason and saw his entire serious face light up. The last time they'd slept together and Aiden had looked down at him and known it was the end and could feel the grief choking his throat. The last time Matt had shut a door in his face and said, *Fuck you, Campbell*, tired and so, so sad.

Aiden rubbed his hand over his eyes, suddenly very tired. Tired of his current life, of fighting it, of throwing himself against the walls. The weight of those quiet days, the lack of routine, the meaningless of it all crushed down on him. For a second, he couldn't breathe. He had to close his eyes and think, again, *There are no thoughts. There is no future. There are no thoughts. There is no future.* The words, usually a comforting mantra, did nothing to quell the queasy tide of panic.

You have the rest of your life to figure it out, Ward had said.

He was so fucking tired. And here was Matt, offering him an out. It might have been a terrible idea, but—how was it any worse than what he was doing right now?

"Okay," he said. "I'll look at flights."

Aiden bought a one-way ticket to Montreal. He packed a week's worth of clothes and his travel kit.

want 2 get lunch tmrw? Gabe texted while Aiden was in a cab to the airport.

I'll be out of town for a bit.

ok.

We can meet up when I get back, I just don't know when that will be.

Gabe didn't ask where he was going, and Aiden didn't offer an answer.

It was raining in Montreal when his plane touched

down that night, the kind of steady, misty drizzle that had the smell of hot concrete and asphalt lingering in the air for hours after. It was still raining by the time he caught a cab to Matt's Mile End condo; it was still raining by the time the cab driver dropped him off a few blocks away, and it was still raining by the time Matt came down to collect him.

"Hey, you made it," Matt said.

They stood there, frozen in place: even if there wasn't a doorman watching, Aiden wouldn't have known what to do. Whether he wanted to throw his arms around Matt and squeeze him until he could hear his bones crack or whether he wanted to punch him in the face.

"One useless houseguest, at your service," Aiden said, finally.

Matt punched him hard in the shoulder. It stung, and that, at least, felt right. "None of that, Campbell."

Aiden didn't argue. He still felt strange, like he was moving in a dream. To be doing this after so long, like it was just easy to pick up and go, even if it was probably all going to blow up in his face.

He wondered what their lives could have been like if he'd done this sooner. But Matt had been married for most of that time, so it probably wouldn't have happened anyway. He could only imagine what Emily would have thought if Aiden had shown up on their doorstep, some random hockey player from a rival team, bedraggled and soaked with rain.

They were quiet in the elevator up; quiet when Matt opened the door and Aiden followed him in. It had a similar vibe to his old place, a kind of lived-in clutter but still more put together than Aiden could ever have managed without assistance. It felt homier than Aiden's house, despite all of the concrete and exposed pipes in the ceiling, because Matt had probably picked out everything himself instead of throwing a lot of money at someone and telling them to go nuts.

"Well, this is it," Matt said, gesturing to the living area and kitchen. Aiden had seen them both in video chats before. "It's nothing spectacular, but it's mine. You can put your stuff down in the spare bedroom."

"Thanks."

Matt took the bag from him. "This is really all you brought?" he asked, eyebrows going up.

"I wasn't—I didn't want to presume—"

"I was just teasing."

"Don't? *Fuck*, Matt, it's already as weird as hell without that."

"Yeah. Yeah, you're right. Sorry."

The second bedroom had a bed, shoved in next to Matt's desk and a desktop computer, presumably doing double duty as an office. Like the main room, it was airy and comfortable even if it was small. Matt set the bag down on the bed and shrugged. "Well, that's the grand condo tour. Very exciting, eh?"

"I like it. It feels like you."

Instead of answering directly, Matt looked away. "Hey, you hungry? I'll order dinner if you want to change into some dry clothes."

"Sure. Whatever you want; I'll leave it to you."

While Matt went to take care of dinner, Aiden stripped off everything he was wearing, still damp from the walk to the apartment. He changed into house clothes: comfortable, worn athletic leggings and an equally beat-up T-shirt. He fluffed his hand through his hair, shaking the extra moisture out of it, looked at himself in the mirror and wondered, again, what the hell he was doing. His hair and beard were shaggy and longer than they'd ever been before. He hadn't really seen much of a reason to keep them in line. There were dark circles under his eyes.

He looked, to put it bluntly, like shit. Nothing like the kid Matt had fallen in love with.

Nothing to do about that now.

They made awkward small talk about the flight, about Matt's training. Aiden's skin buzzed with the prickly awareness of what they'd done the last time they were in the same room together, his head buzzed with just being here, talking again, like maybe this wasn't over. He was relieved when Matt went downstairs to get the food, exhaled a breath he had been holding in for some time.

The anxiety of not knowing what it was, of departing from the Routine, gripped him again. He took a few deep breaths and reminded himself that he was in fucking Montreal. He'd taken the Routine and dropped a bomb on it.

And despite the anxiety, he found that Matt had remembered his dietary preferences. He had ordered an assortment of dishes to share from a Lebanese restaurant in the neighborhood, and it was all without dairy. Matt had always been like that. Fucking thoughtful. Better to Aiden than he'd ever deserved.

The food was good, and they split it standing across from each other at the kitchen island. Aiden was careful as they talked, not wanting to say too much. Every time they reached for the same thing, or Matt's fingers accidentally touched his, he could feel his entire body lock up.

"Thanks," Aiden said, afterward, as he helped clear

away the paper plates and take-out containers. "What do I owe you?"

"Man, *nothing*, this is a welcome-to-Montreal meal, okay?"

Aiden eyed him a little suspiciously but didn't argue.

They spent the rest of the night watching a movie on either end of Matt's living room couch, which was, Aiden admitted to himself, a lot more comfortable than his own. It was overstuffed soft leather, easy to sink into and prop your feet up on the coffee table.

Aiden was a little surprised how, in some ways, it was easy to slide back into Matt's life like that, on the couch watching a movie like any other summer they had spent together. Except for the fact that he was hyperaware of his promise to himself that he wasn't going to fuck this up and make it weird.

The thing was: Aiden was always going to make it weird.

It was impossible not to make it weird when you had almost five years of memories built up of someone, ten years on top of that to turn them over and over in your head until they were polished like sea glass. It was impossible not to make it weird when every time you looked at him, you noticed that when he laughed his eyes crinkled up and the one dimple emerged the same way they always had, or when you knew exactly the way he was going to finish a sentence.

Ten years had gone by, but Matt was still the same, and Aiden was always going to make it weird, because all he could think about was that he broke Matt's heart and fucked things up for both of them. That Matt broke his too…well. That was incidental at this point to the monumental regret he felt, the knowledge he didn't really deserve to be here. Shouldn't really be here.

Aiden could barely pay attention to the movie, but finally, it was late enough that both of them were yawning and exhausted.

Matt said, "I have to get up to go to the gym early tomorrow, so I'm gonna crash. You can stay up and watch something if you want to, don't worry about it."

"Okay."

Matt reached out and his hand rested against the side of Aiden's face, thumb pressing lightly right below his jaw. "Thank you."

"For what?"

"For taking the offer seriously."

Aiden couldn't quite look him in the eye, but there was nowhere else to look. It had always been hard to turn away from Matt when he got like this: so intense and so sincere it was overwhelming. "Yeah, well. A change of scenery, right?"

"Yeah," Matt said, then patted him sharply on the cheek. "Okay. Uh. Good night."

Matt's spare bed was objectively comfortable, like everything else in his condo, but Aiden tossed and turned for an hour or so, staring at the ceiling. Tried one side of the bed and then the other. As nice as the bed was, it wasn't right. He couldn't get his body to calm down. Like any other night at home, it was loud as hell in his head, all of the thoughts he'd been able to meditate away during the seasons he played back in full force and at top volume. The same problem that had driven so much of his New York misery.

But he wasn't in New York anymore.

Aiden sat up and got out of the bed. He walked to

the other side of the condo and into Matt's bedroom. Matt was asleep, sprawled out and taking up most of the bed like he always did, tangled in blankets he had mostly kicked off already.

Aiden took a deep breath and slipped into the bed next to him. Matt's eyes half-opened, blearily. "…Aidy?"

"Sorry," he mumbled, "couldn't sleep."

Without answering, Matt closed his eyes, threw an arm over Aiden's side and shoved one of his knees between Aiden's legs. He was broader and harder than he used to be, but he still smelled the same; his face still had the same soft look in sleep.

Aiden fell asleep like that, under the weight of Matt's arm, listening to the sound of Matt breathing.

He didn't dream.

Matt slowly opened his eyes, groggy and out of it, and for a second, he wondered at the fucked up dream he'd had yesterday. Aiden in Montreal. Aiden in his condo. Aiden climbing into bed with him.

And then he realized that it was real, and he was still in bed, curled up against Aiden's warm back. His eyes flew open, and he sat up, slowly, so he wouldn't disturb him. For a second, he couldn't breathe.

In sleep, Aiden looked almost like Matt remembered him: serene in a way he never was awake. The long, proud line of his nose. The curve of his lip. The thick, black eyelashes against his cheek, the dark circles under his eyes. His hair hung into his face and his face rested on his arm. His mouth hung open a little and he was breathing the slow, even rhythm of sleep.

Matt stared down at him. It was fucking surreal. He'd woken up like this countless times over the years. Back then he would've woken Aiden up, too, with a blowie or a hand on his cock, enjoyed the sleepy way he always leaned into the touch. Matt wanted more than anything to touch him. Just to run his hand down Aiden's arms, his back, the line of his face. Like if Matt could trace his entire body, somehow it would make it more solid, make it more real.

It was stupid. *He* was stupid. He had to be normal about this, because if he couldn't, Aiden would flee again. That would be it. Matt would lose him for the second time, and there wouldn't be any way in the universe that he could possibly fix *that* again. No: he just had to be patient. Let Aiden rest and recover and do whatever he needed to do to feel more like himself, and then—well, he'd worry about what came after that, when it happened.

He couldn't help it. He leaned down and pressed his mouth against Aiden's shoulder, the barest hint of a kiss. Aiden smiled in his sleep, shifted a little to turn over, tucked himself around Matt's body.

Jesus.

It was a tempting thought. To stay in bed, to wake Aiden up with a deeper kiss, to see if he would be this needy when he wasn't sleeping.

But also, Matt had his training: the gym, meetings with the coaching staff and specifically the skills coach and the head trainer to discuss his knee and how they were going to manage it over an eighty-two-game season. He didn't have the time to stay in bed with his ex-boyfriend, however soft his hair was against Matt's skin, however snuggly he was with his eyes closed.

Matt took a deep breath.

This whole idea had been insane. The fact that it had

worked wasn't the point. It could explode in his face, spectacularly, at any second. He was really treading the tightrope here, no net underneath. But he couldn't regret what he'd done, even if things were—weird. Even if he was caught in this limbo of Aiden's sad eyes and hesitance, and Aiden's warm body in his bed at night.

He gently disentangled himself from the half-embrace and slid out of the bed. After a second, he pulled the blankets back up over Aiden, still asleep in the rumpled sheets. He squared his shoulders. He went to get dressed. He grabbed a receipt from the top of his bureau to scribble a note on the back.

He went to the gym.

Aiden woke up later than normal, unusually well-rested but alone in Matt's bed. Blinking, he sat up to find that Matt had left him a handwritten note on the side table, next to a small brass key. It was the same sharp, slanted handwriting he'd always had. Aiden could picture it, the scrawled MS4 that made up his signature.

I'm at the gym. Be back around 11. There's coffee, bread and cashew butter in the kitchen. If you want to go out there's a spare key that's yours too.

Aiden stared at the note, then set it back down on the table.

He drank some coffee and made his toast and wandered around the condo, like he could gather some kind of idea about Matt's life through context clues. The fridge was covered in family pictures of Matt's parents and his brother, Miles, and Miles' wife and their two adorable children. Teammates from various events:

Matt and the Royal during their first Cup celebration, Matt shirtless and drenched in beer in the locker room, screaming with triumphant joy, Eero Saarinen riding on Matt's broad shoulders.

There was some art hanging on the walls, but Aiden couldn't tell if he liked it or not. It was modern and minimalist and reminded him, a little, of the times they'd gone to the MoMA together. Even now, those were bittersweet memories, ones he wasn't sure if he wanted to revisit. He poked around in the kitchen, and it seemed like Matt wasn't lying about learning to cook—even if he was, there was a good variety of equipment.

By the time Matt made it home, sweaty and disheveled from the gym, Aiden had unpacked his clothes. He had showered and trimmed his beard back into something resembling normal length, the closer shave he wore during his later playing seasons. It didn't make him feel any better, really, but it did make Matt smile when he saw it.

"Got tired of the mountain man look?"

"Just wanted to feel a little more human."

"Good."

While Matt showered, Aiden put together a lunch for both of them, mostly leftovers. It struck him again how this was something he'd done a hundred times over the summer in the past, without even thinking about it. Even though Matt could've eaten at the practice facilities, he had always liked that Aiden cared enough to feed him at home. He looked down at the plates, frowning, and wondered what the hell he was trying to accomplish here.

It turned out that what Matt was trying to accomplish, at least, was to distract Aiden. To some extent, it worked. Although he was still training for the season, he folded Aiden into his life seamlessly with a guest pass to the gym owned by his personal trainer and a standing invitation to work out together.

After a day or two of balancing his concerns about the Montreal media and stir-craziness from being stuck inside, Aiden gave in and went. That would end, of course, once Matt started going back to Brossard full-time when the season started. But it would do for now. It felt good to lift again, felt good to have his muscles aching. As far as he could tell, no one really noticed him there, which was a relief. But he was so awfully aware of Matt that it was also the opposite of a relief.

Every time he spotted Matt on the bench, or waited to trade off on the deadlift platform, Aiden had to try not to look at the way the muscles shifted under Matt's skin, the frown of intense concentration he had when he was reaching the end of a set and hitting his limits and forcing his way through them. Every time Matt gave him that same heated look, from the corner of his eye, Aiden had to pretend it didn't affect him.

Don't make it fucking weird, Aiden admonished himself, repeatedly, and every time, he made it weird. His thoughts rattling around inside his own head, screaming.

Aiden tried to find ways to keep himself busy. While Matt was on a call with his agent, Aiden went out and wandered around the neighborhood, found a grocery store and picked up a few things for the fridge and pantry.

He made Matt dinner, pan-seared salmon and farro and vegetables, ignoring the teasing *wow, is this five meals you can do now?* It was an earned jibe: during their first relationship, Aiden had taught himself to cook, but had often eaten the same thing, over and over again.

It had been easier. Comforting. Matt, of course, hadn't seen it that way, but he'd accepted it the same way he'd accepted all of Aiden's little quirks. Because Aiden had always been luckier than he'd deserved.

The situation in Montreal was sometimes nice. Aiden could pretend his life wasn't a disaster, at least for small segments of the day. The other times he was just as aware of the mess he had made of it as ever. It was worse because he wanted to touch Matt so badly he almost felt nauseous about it. Wanted to shake him and ask, *what are you thinking, what do you want from me* so badly that he could scream it.

Aiden started to settle into a holding pattern of life in Montreal. He got tired of repeatedly having to wash his one or two shirts and bought some more clothes, which ended up in Matt's closet instead of the guest room. Matt glanced sideways at him when he hung the first shirt but didn't say anything.

Aiden finished reading the books he'd intended to read before his attention span vacated the premises. He cooked and cleaned. His body started to feel like it used to right before a season started, rested and exercised and ready for anything, except there was nowhere to turn that energy *toward.*

In the beginning, before anything had gone wrong, Aiden had found the long silences he shared with Matt comforting. They hadn't needed to say anything; it was enough to know Matt was there and if they wanted to speak, there would be the time to do it. It was enough to spend time in the same space together and know neither of them felt like they had to fill it. The same pauses now just made him anxious, fidgety. Wondering what the hell he was doing here.

Sometimes he caught Matt watching him, during those silences, from the corner of his eye.

"What?" Aiden asked one night as he washed the dishes from dinner.

"It's you—you're just different."

"Yeah, well, that happens when you get old." Aiden put the bowl he'd been washing into the rack to dry. He wiped his hands on the towel.

"That's not what I meant. You're just more… I don't know."

Aiden sighed, the force of his breath flipping a hanging strand of hair up into the air. "Well, you haven't changed at all. Still trying to figure me out?"

Matt looked away. There was a flush of red on his cheekbones. "I could never figure you out. I spent years trying, and it wasn't—Jesus, never mind."

"I mean, what *are* you trying to find? The cheat code?"

"No, I just… Aiden, we haven't talked in years. You know? It's like I can still see *some* of the boy I knew, but you're not the same, and it's just gotten so complicated."

"I'm not complicated. The same as I've always been," Aiden said, unable to quite keep the bitterness from his voice. "Except I'm not a goalie anymore."

"Oh, no. That's one thing that's never going to change, even if you're not playing in the show. You're *always* going to be a goalie."

Aiden exhaled, sharply, and said, in a rush, "Matt, I've fucking *missed* you. I've really fucking missed you."

"Yeah," Matt said, softly. "Well. That's how it goes."

Even though they hadn't hooked up since New York, Aiden slept in Matt's bed every night.

It would have been a lie to say it wasn't torture every time he woke up with Matt's furnace of a body draped over his back, Matt's arm wrapped around him, Matt's erection pressed against his ass. He didn't want to ruin the fragile peace of whatever he had here, but it was also hard to ignore how his body responded, hard to ignore how his heart responded.

It was torture and yet he slept better than he'd slept in his own bed in longer than he could remember.

You could talk to him about it, the reasonable part of Aiden's brain said.

Don't fucking ruin it, said the part of Aiden's brain that had gotten him to Montreal without clarifying this beforehand.

Aiden didn't say anything.

cap, Jammer texted Matt in the morning, what's up?

Matt frowned at his phone. What do you mean, what's up?

u've been acting a lil cagey recently. just not like u. if it's contract stuff or w/e u can talk to us u know

He could feel himself smiling, just a little, lopsided. If it was only the contract stuff, that would have been easy to handle. Not easy. Manageable. Something he could make lists for. Pros and cons. Something he could think through logically, even if thinking about it made him want to scream and take off running down the hall.

Matt couldn't explain to Jammer that he had thrown caution to the wind, invited his ex to stay with him for the summer and had promptly realized two things: his ex was fucking *depressed* and also, that Matt was still as stupidly in love with him as he had ever been.

Neither realization happened all at once. They snuck up on him, gradually. Aiden had always been tightly wound, a perfectionist, compulsive in the way that goalies often were. But around Matt, he'd learned how to smile easily, flash a goofy sense of humor. Not to mention the wild shit that came out of his mouth in bed, the insanely filthy things he asked Matt to do to him. The complete opposite of the calm, serious face he presented to the media.

Matt couldn't see any of that in him now. Aiden was quiet and withdrawn, watching Matt with sad eyes, barely saying anything. There was a bitterness to his words that hadn't ever been there before. He ate mechanically, without any of the enjoyment Matt remembered. He'd told Matt that he'd mostly been eating the same thing every day for the last few years which was—Aiden had always been a creature of habit, but that seemed a *lot*.

When Matt caught him unaware, he would often just be sitting there, legs folded in some kind of ridiculous way underneath him, frowning into space like he was thinking about something. Was it retirement? Was it something else? Matt, who had always been good at getting reads on guys and had spent years of his life intimately attuned to the tiniest shifts in Aiden's mood, found that for once, he just couldn't figure it out.

Matt woke up every morning with Aiden wrapped up in his arms, partially underneath Matt's body. Matt still knew Aiden's tells well enough to know he was awake, that he could definitely feel Matt's morning wood pressed up against his ass.

Every time, Aiden said nothing. He barely breathed.

It was like he was afraid to move and ruin the moment, and Matt could absolutely sympathize.

Every morning he thought about rolling Aiden over and kissing the haunted look off of his face. Every morning he thought about what would happen if he did it, if he slipped his hand down between them to take Aiden in hand the way he used to do. By this point in the week it was a given that Aiden was coming to bed with him.

But something held Matt back. It seemed wrong, somehow, to try anything when Aiden *looked* like that, like Aiden might kiss him back not because he wanted Matt, still felt anything for Matt except the desire to feel any differently than he was feeling then.

Matt had thought about this a lot of ways over the years, how things would go if he had the chance to talk to Aiden again. Sometimes he imagined punching him in the face and telling him to fuck off. Sometimes he imagined holding out his arms, Aiden falling into them gratefully.

He'd never really thought about what he would do if Aiden turned up on his doorstep, bedraggled and shaggy and sad as fuck, and just *stayed* with him, clinging like a koala at night, moping around during the day.

Matt realized, horrified, that as much as it was physically painful to wake up every morning and have to hold himself back from the reactions that still felt automatic after all of these years, he was holding himself back because of Aiden. Because he wanted to do the right thing. Because he was *still*—

It's not really anything I can explain, Matt said to Jammer. I'll feel more like myself once camp starts.

ok.

I promise, Jams.

On Saturday night, Aiden picked the movies, and they watched a double-header of *Venom* and *Let There Be Carnage* on the couch. Aiden found himself trying to explain to Matt why Carnage was really the superior comic book villain, especially considering Venom was more of an anti-hero at this point. He could feel himself rambling, the way he sometimes did about things he'd been so interested in for so long, the way that had always embarrassed his sister when they were kids. But he couldn't stop it now any more than he could have done then.

"You know, the bond with the symbiote is stronger, and it's fused with Kasady's blood, so the body doesn't really need to rest the same way Brock does."

Matt leaned forward, took Aiden's face in his hands and shoved his tongue in Aiden's mouth. Aiden's muffled noise of surprise got lost in it; it took him a second to react beyond that exclamation. Then he was all in, breathless by the time they broke apart, his heart thumping in his chest like the bass of a particularly intense breakdown.

"Matt, *what*—?"

"You fucking *nerd*," Matt said, and kissed him again. Softer, this time. Fondly. "You and your goddamn comic books."

And then they stopped talking at all. It was easy to give in when Matt kissed him like this, like he was the only thing Matt had ever wanted.

"I wasn't sure we were—" Aiden gasped, a little

later, seated on Matt's hips, Matt's fingers wrapped just this side of too loosely around his dick "—you know, doing this."

"Are you kidding me? I've been holding myself back all week."

"*Why?*"

"I didn't want to push you when you were in a bad place."

"Matt, I've been sleeping in your fucking bed for—"

"Well why didn't *you*—"

"I didn't know you wanted this, I didn't want to assume things were still going to be like this, even after New York."

"I just didn't want to take advantage of anything, Aiden."

"Advantage? I'm fucking up my life, that doesn't mean I can't… I want this, I want *you*."

"Look," Matt said, his hands twisted in Aiden's shirt, pulling him down. Their eyes met, Matt's searching, like he was looking for something in Aiden's face but still couldn't find it. "If we're both here and we're both on the same page, I want you every way I can have you."

Aiden exhaled. It would be easy to hear it, easy to accept it. Easy to pretend there wasn't ten years of bitterness behind it, that they could start over again or that they never really stopped in the first place. Like everything else he had done recently, it was a terrible idea. But for the first time since Matt showed up on his doorstep and left New York again, Aiden felt something beyond the dread of knowing he was going to have to live through the exact same day again when he woke up in the morning.

Couldn't he let himself have this?

"You've always had me."

Matt looked amused. And a little rueful. "Liar."

Aiden wanted to say *no, that was the one thing that wasn't a lie*, but instead he managed, "So do you want to fuck me on the living room floor, or…?"

There was probably a time they would have just kept it going right there, but they weren't getting any younger and his knees and hip and back wouldn't thank him for it in the morning. They went to the bedroom.

It was different than in New York. There they had been frantic and desperate, both certain every time was going to be the last time. Now, Aiden took the time to undress Matt, slowly, carefully, touching each part of him as he exposed it, enjoying the increasing impatience with which Matt submitted to his exploration. Took the time to admire Matt's body naked: how solid he was, the trail of hair from his chest to his stomach, the twitches of muscle in Matt's abs and thighs and arms betraying how much he was holding himself back. Aiden, still fully clothed, rocked against him; Matt's breath hissed, like he couldn't hold it back if he wanted to.

"Aiden…"

"Yeah?" Aiden asked, his mouth trailing the line right under Matt's jaw.

"Are you going to let me touch you?"

"I thought I'd make you wait," he started, but then he was on his back in the bed, unceremoniously lifted and dumped down again in a movement too fast to track.

"I don't want to wait," Matt said, grinning down at him.

"Then make me, coward."

A little later, Aiden was naked, too, trying desperately to catch his breath. The struggle for his own clothes had been perfunctory, slid easily into something else by the time Matt slammed his wrists against the headboard. It felt *right* to be here, in Matt's bed, trapped under the weight of Matt's body, one of Matt's slick fingers a little too roughly crooked inside of him.

"Fuck," he gasped. "Fuck, Matt, I don't want to do it like this—come on, I don't want to wait, fuck me *now*, you *have* to—"

"Oh? I thought you were all about dragging this out."

Aiden had thought so, too, thought he was going to make it last, torture both of them, but now that he was here, he could see how wrong he had been. Felt almost frantic with the intensity of what he wanted, how badly he wanted Matt, how badly he wanted to feel *anything*. "No—I need, I need you, I need this, I don't want to think—"

He watched with that almost nauseous sense of anticipation while Matt fumbled with the condom and the lube, tried not to think of anyone else Matt might've fucked in the same bed, tried not to think of anything except Matt, except the way Aiden knew it was going to feel. It was easy when watching Matt do this was pornographic all on its own, when Matt looked up at him suddenly, stricken, and Aiden knew he was just as fucked up by the whole thing.

And then Matt was crouched over him, leaning down for one last, messy kiss before he pressed against Aiden's body, slowly pushing forward.

Aiden exhaled one long gasp of breath. It felt different like this. Uncomfortable, but not in a bad way. Matt went slowly, centimeter by centimeter, but steadily and without pause, and it was the best kind of agony. Not pain, just an awareness of the way Matt was deliberately opening him. The way his body had to struggle to adjust. How full he was and how sensitive every part of him was and—

Aiden opened his eyes to look at Matt's face. His eyes were closed, mouth slightly open, almost like he was in pain, or a concentration so intense he couldn't bear it. Aiden couldn't help himself; he reached up to push a stray piece of hair away from Matt's eyes and Matt tilted his face into Aiden's hand.

When Matt finally bottomed out, they paused, frozen like that. Matt stared down at him and Aiden was the one who had to look away.

"Matt, come on, come *on*—"

Matt didn't say anything, but Aiden could hear his labored breathing, feel how much effort it took to hold himself back as he moved, sliding out and then in again. It was slow, still, slower than Aiden wanted, and he forced himself to wait, to let Matt set the pace. It was so fucking deliberate, *patient*, that he was practically shaking out of his own skin anyway. The occasional rough push had him gasping and whining. His fingers dug into the muscle of Matt's shoulders, half for leverage, half to pull him closer. Matt's head dipped down, his forehead bumping against Aiden's.

"Fuck," Aiden could hear himself saying, as if from a distance, "fuck, Matt, ten fucking, fucking *years*—I need—harder, *please*—"

When Matt started fucking him in earnest, finally, Aiden threw his legs around Matt's waist and his head back against the pillow and gave himself permission to stop fucking *thinking*. He lost track of time, lost track of everything except the way it felt now that they finally had the rhythm of it, now that every thrust and every drag and every teasing swivel of Matt's hips, every slow, dirty grind, drove him out of himself. It was what he wanted—needed. Even if it was going to destroy him, he would say *thank you* for it.

He was saying *thank you*, the words ragged and crazed, over and over again. "Thank you—thank you, thank you, *thank you*, thank—"

Matt groaned, "Aiden, *Aidy*," and stopped the *thank yous* with his mouth, his teeth digging at Aiden's lip.

An interminable time later, Aiden came without Matt's hands anywhere except his wrist and his throat, fingers pressed against the throbbing pulse at Aiden's neck. And for a time, he was free—floating somewhere blissfully outside of his own skull.

For a time.

A little later Matt, on his back, his chest still heaving, said, "Jesus *Christ*, Aiden."

Aiden exhaled. His hands were shaking. His mouth wasn't cooperating with his brain. It was fine. They lay in silence for a time, sweat cooling, goose bumps rising in the air-conditioning.

It wasn't fine.

Matt watched Aiden stumble out of the bed and into the bathroom and couldn't bring himself to get up. If he thought too much about the absolute disaster of a situation he'd just created it made his head and chest ache. If he thought too much about how irresistible Aiden had been, talking about his stupid comic books so seriously and with such passion, it made his head and chest ache. If he thought too much about the glimpse of the boy Aiden had used to be, the hyperfixations that he'd seemingly set to the side in the fog of depression, it made his head and chest ache. If he thought about

Aiden falling apart underneath him, begging first and then saying *thank you*, it made his head and chest ache.

Ten fucking years, Aiden had said, and Matt felt every single one of them. It was surreal how they had fallen right back into it like nothing had changed. How Aiden's body still felt the same, how he still liked the same things, how fucked up he got just from Matt touching him, how easy he was for every single touch.

Not easy. *Greedy.*

Matt listened to the water running behind the closed door and thought about how intense it had been to be inside Aiden again, how hot and tight and eager he was. To hold his wrists down and feel Aiden's pulse thudding against his fingers. To look down and see Aiden's wide light brown eyes, dreamy and unfocused, his mouth hanging open, unselfconscious in a way he only ever was around Matt.

Ten fucking years. Ten fucking years.

Ten fucking years they'd been apart.

In that instant he knew that as much progress as he thought he'd made, as much as he'd assumed that he had moved on with his life and gotten it together—being with Aiden like that made it clear that he had never really moved from the starting line. He was right back there again, like a time loop, the wound as fresh and painful as it had been when he fell in love the first time.

But was it really such a bad thing, if he was?

Aiden was here now.

Aiden slept in his bed.

Aiden had fucked him again.

Aiden had moved all of his shit into Matt's closet; he wasn't going anywhere anytime soon.

Matt was a responsible guy. He put the team before

himself. He put his duty before himself. When Emily left him, he'd still been the first one at the practice facility and the last one to leave, the one everyone had come to for advice and for anything they'd needed. The one playing twenty-five minutes a night without a complaint.

Did he have to be the responsible one forever? Couldn't he make a stupid, impulsive decision again, even knowing how disastrously his last one had ended? If it was ten years or ten months or ten weeks or ten minutes they'd been apart. What did it matter? Why couldn't he just let himself have this? Hockey and being the captain and Aiden, who for whatever weird twist of fate, happened to be here *now*?

He was so tired, so fucked up, that he didn't even realize when his eyes started drooping.

Aiden looked at himself in the bathroom mirror. Same dark circles under his eyes, same lines at the corner of his mouth. His hair wet from the shower, hanging beyond the nape of his neck, almost brushed his shoulders.

I want you every way I can have you.

He wasn't sure what he was expecting to get out of this. Now that the high had faded the reality of the situation set in. Here he was, in Montreal, almost thirty-seven, making the same mistakes he'd made in his twenties. Except back then, he still had his entire future ahead of him. Now he had—what?

Aiden turned the sink on, leaned down and stuck his face under the cold running water.

If this was the only way he could have Matt, he'd take it.

By the time he collected himself and went back into the bedroom, Matt had already fallen asleep, still on his back, his arm thrown over his eyes. Aiden stopped and just stared at him for a second, the gentle rise and fall of his chest, the line of his stomach, his arm slowly dropping to rest against the blanket, the way his dark eyelashes looked against his skin, the dumb half-smile tugging his mouth up.

He did his best to clean Matt up without waking him, thought, *you fucking moron*, and got back into bed.

When Matt woke up, Aiden was still asleep. It was like he hadn't slept in so long that now that he'd made his way back to Matt's bed again, he was making up for lost time. Matt looked down at him, the dark bruised eyelids and slack mouth, and brushed a strand of hair away from his face. It was insane how different he looked with long hair. Not worse, just so different.

Whenever Matt used to think about him, in the long years they'd been apart, he pictured Aiden the same way he'd looked when they'd first met: his pretty baby face and his perfect hair and his pouty mouth. It was difficult wrapping his head around the fact that he'd broken up with a boy and Aiden was a man, with a history of years Matt didn't know, habits he hadn't become familiar with and sad eyes he couldn't change.

Well. Aiden hadn't looked like that last night. Aiden had looked—

Okay.

Matt had to stop doing this, or he was never going to get up and go to practice. He showered, even though he'd have to do it again after the skate, because if he showed up in Brossard smelling like *that* the guys would never let him live it down. And he didn't want to set a bad example for the rookies. But he was distracted, his brain turning over and over the way Aiden had sounded, gasping *thank you*, knowing that sex was a fucking stupid idea, unable to turn the car around before it went off the cliff.

Rookie camp wouldn't start for a few weeks, but a lot of the kids who would be there had stayed in Montreal after dev camp, and were coming to the practice facility to skate with the major league regulars and get their reps in. When Matt was younger, he had done that too, and even participated in exhibition games and a summer three-on-three league for fun. Now that he was older and his knee was fucked up, he had to conserve his energy and ligaments, but he still liked to work with the kids.

He remembered when he had first gotten called up, how much it had meant to him when Gavin Weaver, the longtime captain of the Royal, had immediately introduced himself and invited Matt out for dinner. He made sure to fill that same role for the new kids, even if he was already aching a few games into the preseason.

Aiden was still sleeping when Matt came out of the bathroom. He dressed as quietly as possible. Passing by the bed on his way out, he paused, a stupid instinct gripping him. He leaned down and kissed Aiden's temple. Barely a touch. But it was just—after the night before, it felt wrong to leave without *anything*, even if Aiden didn't know he'd done it.

It felt good to get back on the ice, even though Jammer immediately saw the hickey Aiden had left on his collarbone, red and tender, and made a loud noise of amusement that really sounded more like a hoot.

"Damn, Cap!" he said, his usually expressionless eyes dancing with laughter. "Sowing your wild oats before the season starts, huh?"

The rookies stared at them, unsure of how to proceed. There was always the regular chirping you'd get in the locker room, but Matt was the *captain*. Matt had brought *Cups* home to Montreal. That was different, right?

Matt knew how he was supposed to respond—laughing or bragging or making a joke out of it—but he couldn't. Sleeping with Aiden felt fragile and new and like something he desperately needed to protect. He *couldn't* laugh about it. But not saying anything was making this more awkward and weird than a hookup had any right to be.

"Yeah," he said, pulling his Under Armour over his head, "your mom was pretty great last night."

"Hey," Jammer said, hurt. "I didn't mean anything by it. I just thought it was cute you're finally getting out there after Emily."

For a second, Matt had to bite down the urge to laugh hysterically—after Emily, like that had done anywhere near the kind of damage that Aiden had done to him, that Aiden continued to wreak. Maybe he'd tell Jammer one day, when the rookies weren't staring at them like they weren't sure if they should say something or jump in or pretend they hadn't heard any of it at all. For now, he sighed. "*Cute?* Really, Jams?"

"Hey," Jammer said, wriggling into his pads—he was one of the few guys who didn't play with any kind of underlayer at all. "I'm at ease with my masculinity. If you're cute, I'm gonna tell you you're cute."

"Thanks," Matt said, dryly. "Huge boost to my ego, bud."

"Anytime," Jammer said, reaching over to knuckle his fist against Matt's head, before they both went back to dressing, Matt pulling his socks and pants on, and Jammer adjusting his straps. "That's what you keep me around for."

"That, and to quarterback the power play."

Jammer waved his hand, unconcerned. "Priorities, Cap."

Matt threw himself into the practice, making sure that Cormier and Crane were settled in, making sure that he wasn't pushing his knee too hard. But the whole time, he was aware of his clothes and gear rubbing against the bite, of Aiden at home, waiting for him.

If he was a little off his game, who could really blame him?

Aiden had woken up when Matt was in the shower, but stayed with his eyes closed just because he didn't trust himself to say anything. When Matt leaned down and pressed his lips against his head, Aiden's chest lurched like he'd been in some kind of centrifuge. It was such a stupid, tender gesture, and Aiden didn't *deserve it*.

When Matt left for the rink, Aiden spent about thirty minutes lying in their bed, until the warmth Matt's body had left had definitely faded. The sheets were still rumpled, still smelled like sex, and every time he closed his eyes, he could feel the ghosts of Matt's hands on him.

It was fucked up.

He was fucked up, mooning around over his ex like sleeping with him would make anything he'd done in the past any better. Like sleeping with him would change the fact that Aiden was turning thirty-seven soon and was basically freeloading in Matt's condo because he had nothing better to do with his life.

The more he thought about it the more he could feel

the old feelings rising up, like the room was suddenly too small, like the walls were closing in on him and crushing his lungs. He breathed through the sweaty, sick feeling until it passed, and then rolled over to grab his phone.

Aiden Googled *therapist montreal*, wrote down a few names and made some phone calls.

It was awkward and uncomfortable making the calls. Part of him didn't even know how to explain his situation. He wasn't *depressed*, he was just having a hard time with retirement, with the situation with Matt. It wasn't something he needed medication for either, because…what would that even do? Medication wasn't going to stop him from making stupid decisions about Matt. Medication wasn't going to unretire him. He just had to get his head sorted out. That was all.

The therapist he ended up picking had immediate availability, more immediate than he'd expected. *In fact,* she'd said, *I have some time today following a cancellation,* and he'd had to make a last-minute leap of faith by saying *yes*. Dr. Gauthier turned out to be a stocky, muscular woman maybe ten years older than he was, with the kind of thousand-yard stare and brusque, no-nonsense manner that instantly put him at ease. Like she would be completely unimpressed with whatever embarrassing thing he had to tell her.

She had a heavy Quebecois accent and had a laconic way of speaking that reminded him of every goalie coach he'd ever had.

It was awkward and uncomfortable, too, going to that first appointment, but it was a start. He felt shaky and anxious when he said goodbye and headed back, on his own, to Matt's condo. But it was a start.

* * *

"Any news on the contract front, Cap?" Adam Morin asked.

They were in the locker room after practice, stripping down. Even though they'd won a Cup together, Matt couldn't honestly say the Morin twins were his favorite teammates. They were both a bit full of themselves and tended to have an unerring big-sibling instinct for poking their noses exactly where they shouldn't. Matt hadn't envied their younger sister, Beatrice, having to grow up in their shadow, though she had just won a Cup herself and was doing quite well, far away from their judgment.

"No," Matt said, "and there probably won't be for the rest of the season. I'd appreciate if you didn't bring it up. The last thing I want is for my situation to be a distraction."

"Always a team player," Adam drawled.

"Leave him alone," Fournier said, in French.

"I'm just asking," Adam replied in the same language, wounded look on his face.

"Well, don't ask. Tabarnak, not everything is your business."

After so many years in Montreal, Matt could easily understand the conversation. Technically he could respond in kind, but he still felt uncomfortable speaking. No matter how often he practiced his French, he still had a pronounced Ontario accent in it. He said, in English, "Thanks, Fourns. I got it from here."

He tested out his knee again: it was aching a bit, but not enough that he worried about it just yet. Still, it was kind of a relief to get out of the practice facility and head home, knowing Aiden would be waiting for him.

For a second, Matt had the brief, stupid idea of surprising him with something: nice beer or takeout or a dessert, but Aiden didn't drink much, and he was almost religious about eating healthily. Maybe Matt could… buy him a new yoga mat. Something, anything, that would show Aiden how much Matt wanted to fit him back into his life, make him comfortable in the condo.

In the end, all he had to give was himself, but judging from the way Aiden's mouth gave underneath the eager kiss, that was enough.

"Hi," Aiden said, a little breathlessly. He had pulled back a little so he could talk, but he was still close enough that all Matt could see were his eyes, huge and intent. Eyes you could drown in. "What was that for?"

"It's just—nice to come home to someone," Matt mumbled against the corner of his mouth. "It's nice to come home to *you*."

"You're going to get tired of me eventually." Aiden swatted at Matt's hands before he apparently changed his mind, grabbed Matt's ass and pulled him into a closer embrace.

"I'm pretty sure that could never happen," Matt said, and winced inwardly. Too honest too early. "What've you been up to today?"

Aiden went still in his arms and Matt wondered, yet again, if he'd said the wrong thing. Then he swallowed and took a deep breath, like he was gearing up to say something difficult. "I, uh…made an appointment with a therapist."

"Yeah? That's great, Aiden."

"Yeah. Um. I had the intake appointment today. I don't know how it's going to go, but it felt bad just sitting around doing nothing, so at least I'm…taking steps. Right?"

"It's awesome. I'm really proud of you."

"Let's wait and see how it goes before you go that far," Aiden said, and Matt couldn't help laughing. "Anyway, are you hungry? I made lunch."

Matt leaned up on the tips of his toes so he could press his mouth briefly against Aiden's forehead. This whole thing was stupid—it was too much like the way he'd have greeted a boyfriend, and Aiden was—he didn't know what Aiden was. But it was worth it, watching the flush slowly color Aiden's cheeks darker. "Could get used to this, eh?"

"Stop," Aiden said, embarrassed, and finally pulled himself free. "Come on. Let me show you what I've done."

It was difficult to let him go, but somehow Matt managed.

They spent a lot of their spare time exploring Montreal. It wasn't as big a city as New York, but there was still a lot to see. In a way it felt like making up for lost time. Although Aiden had spent some time during the summers with Matt there, they hadn't gone out much. Both of them had been too paranoid about the Montreal media fishbowl sniffing out a story. He still felt a little paranoid, but no one seemed to have paid him any attention so far and it wasn't like he had a career to worry about anymore.

"Come on," Matt said, one afternoon. "You loved that mountain near New York, right? Come see Mont-Royal with me."

And Aiden agreed.

It wasn't quite the same kind of place as Storm King; there were no dirt hiking trails or rocky creeks. It was a hill. But there was an abundance of green trees, and there were paths through them. It was only about a twenty-minute walk from home to the Park Avenue entrance. They mostly walked in silence, up the trails through the green-canopied trees to the summit. It was a beautiful day, and the trails were crowded with pedestrians and tourists and families, and Aiden was pretty sure that more than a few people had recognized Matt.

No one bothered them, which was nice.

They made their way up to the summit, mostly in silence, and Aiden looked up at the huge LED cross, lights out, then out over the city spread below them, the way it stretched out into the distance across the river. Matt stood next to him as they observed in silence, watching below them as more people climbed toward the summit.

"Let's go to the lake," Matt said. "There's skating on the rink in the winter, but—"

"Yeah, even if it wasn't the middle of August I, ah, haven't skated since the last game. You know."

"Well, you don't have to worry about that now."

Aiden watched a kid below them, throwing a ball off the edge of the summit and crying when it vanished into the distance.

"It won't be too long before winter," he said, but what he meant was: *it won't be too long until the season starts.* He didn't want to think too long about that, what he would do when Matt was playing, what Aiden would do when he would normally be back on the ice.

From the time he started playing hockey, there was never a September he didn't lace up his skates. *You can still skate,* he argued with himself, but he responded, *It won't be the same.*

Matt's hand on his arm, shaking him out of it. "Come on," he said, and Aiden sighed and followed him.

It was a clover-shaped artificial lake, but that didn't mean there weren't hundreds of people sitting around it on picnic blankets or sprawled in the grass, piled onto boats, running and kicking soccer balls, flying kites. Aiden and Matt found a spot that didn't seem as crowded and sat. Matt leaned back and lay down on the hill, his hands resting under his head as he looked up at the sky.

At first, they didn't really talk, just people-watched. Aiden ran a hand through the soft grass, absentmindedly pulling at individual strands until he had a small pile. Frowning, he brushed his fingers off on his shorts and looked out at the water again.

"It's weird," Matt said, finally, "doing this again with you. Being here with you." He was still looking anywhere but Aiden, his eyes focused on the fluffy clouds drifting over them. "Kind of doing my head in, a little. You know?"

Aiden blew a breath out of his nose. "Yeah… I don't really know what I'm doing, either."

"I just never thought we'd ever have the chance again. I thought about you a lot, over the years. Not all of the time, but sometimes it would hit me, and I'd wonder how you were doing. What you were doing. If you were happy. Whether you were dating."

Aiden's shoulders hunched forward. He didn't look sideways. Didn't want to see what Matt's face looked like right now. Matt was usually the only person he never minded looking at directly, but he couldn't do it. "I thought about you, too. But it was my fault, so.

I didn't feel like I had the right. You never…you never said you still…"

"I *couldn't*. I was married, and even before Emily, it wouldn't have been a good thing for me."

There was a long, quiet pausc. Aiden turned the words over and over again in his head. "What do you mean?"

Matt made a noise that wasn't quite a laugh, although it had the outline of one. "There's a lot you don't know about my life. We have a lot of catching up to do, you know?"

"What did you mean, though, that it wouldn't have been a good thing for you?"

Matt's face, so familiar and so different at the same time, was carefully expressionless. He was still looking up at the sky, squinting as the sun shifted. "Had a bad couple of years after things…you know. I did the player assistance program the summer after."

"You what?"

"Yeah. I don't think…well, I couldn't have talked to you. Not for a long time, even if I always thought about what I'd want to say if we did."

"Matt, I'm—*Jesus*. I'm sorry. I didn't know."

"Of course you didn't. It wasn't your problem," Matt said, without rancor. He was still on his back, perfectly motionless, like a statue toppled into the green. "It's fine. I got my shit sorted. Had a pretty good run of it since."

"It wasn't my…but I…"

"Aiden, it's really…well, it's not *fine*, but I get it, man. You were right. No, don't look at me like that, you were. It wasn't the right time. I don't blame you for not wanting to be the first ones to come out, especially not that way, especially when it wasn't like either of us were leaving our teams anytime soon."

"I never wanted to hurt you. I just wanted to do the right thing."

"Yeah, well. You did. You did hurt me. But I don't know. I've thought about it a lot. Maybe it's better things ended when they did. Before we really started hating each other."

"I thought I did hate you. I hated you for a long time, after I saw the wedding photos."

"I thought I hated you, too," Matt said. The corner of his mouth tipped up in one of those familiar smiles, one of the ones that showed the dimple. "Not the best reason to get married, but I had a decent run of that, too."

"I don't hate you, though. I haven't—"

"I know, Aidy. I know."

They sat in silence for a while and Aiden watched two kites tangled in the air, owners trying to tug them apart as they fell. "What happened? With Emily?"

"Same thing that always happens when you marry someone for the wrong reasons, I guess. One day she got tired of the fact that we had nothing in common and she couldn't come up with a good enough reason to stick around. The money only goes so far when you're that lonely."

He was smiling, again, rueful, and so sad that Aiden wanted to reach out to touch him, but stopped when he noticed a small kid coming toward them, snapback in one hand and a pen in the other. "Ah—you got a fan," he said, pointing.

Matt sat up and signed the hat. Smiled his warm smile, made small talk, told the kid he'd have a great season in mites, while Aiden pretended that he didn't exist, imagined melting into the grass and disappearing.

He couldn't stop thinking about Matt, whether player assistance had been for alcohol or drugs or mental health, or any combination of the three. Whether Aiden had done that to him, even unintentionally. He didn't know how to feel about it. Like many of the other things he'd felt the last six months, it was too fluid to get his hands around.

Instead of boxing it up, this time, he let it wash over him. Like he used to do, except it was so much larger a feeling than he'd had in a long time.

"How about you?" Matt asked, as they watched the kid running back to his parents, eagerly waving the hat. "Has there been anyone in your life?"

"A few," Aiden said. He shrugged. "Kind of a serial monogamist, I guess. Never more than a year or two, though. Nothing that really lasted. I wasn't what they wanted, I think. I couldn't ever...really be that."

"Yes."

What Aiden didn't say was *you ruined me for other men.*

They sat in silence for an interminable amount of time; Aiden didn't want to check his phone to put a boundary on it. All around them, kids ran and screamed and played. Couples made out on picnic blankets. Boaters on the lake cut through the water. Artists painted the crowd. An entire park's worth of people streamed around them, going about their lives, unaware that something in Aiden's chest had eased, minutely, for the first time in a decade.

"Oh, I missed this," Matt said, laughing, startling Aiden out of his thoughts.

"What?"

"That good old Aiden Campbell dissociation face, the one where you go hang out in your mind palace in the middle of a sentence."

Aiden made a face at him. "You're lucky we're in public, or—"

"Or what?"

He leaned sideways to whisper in Matt's ear, in itemized detail, the things he would do.

"Oh," Matt said, after taking a moment to process them. His face slowly flushed red, from the neck up. Aiden kept going and he said, "Well. *Oh.*"

On the walk back home, Aiden thought again about the therapist. It had been five or six sessions now, and he'd watched her long enough to recognize her habit of looking at him like she could see right through him or saying, "Oh, ouais?" in her soft voice. It made him shift uneasily, especially when he was specifically trying not to answer a direct question she had asked him right before that.

There were certain things she kept bringing up that he didn't want to talk about at all, like the way he could consider beginning to separate his own personal identity from his role or function to a team or pointing out that some of the explanations he provided to her regarding his behavior—which he felt were reasonable, even logical—were rationalizing maladaptive actions.

He was really trying to take it seriously, but there were more than a few sessions where he was so frustrated and uneasy about trying to put into words all of the shit that had been knocking around in his head for years that he considered not going back.

He kept going back, anyway, and every week, Dr. Gauthier smiled like he had done something admirable and said, "Welcome back, Aiden."

It shouldn't have felt so encouraging, but there he was, still crossing the threshold. And here he was, still walking shoulder to shoulder with Matt.

Later that day, Pears sent him a link to an Instagram story. It was some random girl's profile, a little video of Aiden and Matt sitting by the lake in Mont-Royal. In it, Aiden leaned forward, right at the end of their time there, when he'd rendered Matt speechless. Aiden stared at it before it minimized back into the chat window.

He could barely recognize himself in the picture, with the hair and beard and sunglasses. Jesus, he needed a haircut.

Pears added, Soup, what the fuck are you doing?

I needed a change of scenery.

You really think this is a good idea?

No, but it's not the worst idea I've ever had, either.

It's pretty close, buddy.

Yeah. Probably. But I'm here.

You okay? Do I need to get my passport and come up there and give him a talk about your tender feelings?

No. It's been a little weird, but it's fine.

OK.

I know you're worried.

You're an adult, Soup. You gotta do what's best for you. But I'm your friend, so I'll be here to pick up the pieces.

Thanks, Pears.

And just know that I will kick his ass if I have to.

You don't have to.

OK.

Every time Matt thought that he was starting to get used to having Aiden back in his life, something happened to throw him off and remind him that actually, it was a precarious position, and that any second the house of cards could come tumbling down. This time it came in the form of a phone call from his mother after dinner.

He'd been mostly avoiding his family since he got home from the trip. It was cowardly, but he hadn't really wanted to try to explain Aiden to them. He hadn't been lying when he'd told Aiden that he'd had a bad couple of years after their breakup. If anything, he'd been downplaying what had actually happened. He'd shut his parents out then, too, until he couldn't anymore. They hadn't judged, they'd done all of the right things, but it had been almost as hard for them to see him in that state.

He'd been avoiding the phone calls, mostly, but there was a limit to the number of concerned voice mails he could scroll through transcripts for and ignore. Eventually, he had to pick up. "Uh, hey, Mom."

"What's going on, Matthew?" she demanded, blunt as always.

"What do you mean, what's going on?"

"It's not like you to avoid us like this. What's going on? Are you okay?"

"I'm fine," he said, which wasn't entirely a lie.

There was a delicate silence, like she was trying to decide how to phrase it. "Matthew, be honest with me. Miles told me about what happened in New York."

"Jesus, Mom. It's no one's business but mine."

"Is it?" she said. "It's the same as it was back then. The secrecy. The lies. I know you're a grown man and you can make your own decisions, but I'm your mother. I was there when you were struggling. And I have to look out for your best interests, too. And I have to tell you that whatever you think you're doing is a terrible idea."

Matt counted to ten and exhaled a deep breath. Years ago, when he'd seen a therapist regularly, they'd done a lot of work about boundaries and controlling your reactions to things people said. They'd done a lot of work about boundaries and controlling your reactions to things *your parents* said. There was only so much he could do about the way his parents saw his life, especially because he still wanted them in *his* life. The options were limited.

"Mom, maybe you could back up to knowing that I'm a grown man who can make his own decisions, huh?"

Mom snorted. "I knew this wouldn't go well. You've always been stubborn, especially about that…" She trailed off, like she wanted to say something worse. "About that man."

"His name is Aiden, Mom."

"I *know* what his name is. That doesn't mean I have to…acknowledge him."

Matt rubbed his fingers over his eyes. If things kept going the way they'd gone, he'd have to figure out what he was going to do about his family and the way they felt about Aiden. It was still early to force things, but he couldn't put that off forever, either. "Look, Mom. I hear you. I understand your concerns. You just have to trust me that I know what I'm doing and that things are different this time. I don't want to talk about this right now."

"Fine," Mom said, but she wasn't happy about it, and he knew it wasn't going to be the end.

The rest of the conversation was strained and stilted: she pretended to have an interest in the way his training was going and how his knee was feeling, but the fact was that she had only really called because of Aiden. When they hung up, it was with the uneasy feeling of issues unresolved.

And Matt, left with the uneasy knowledge that even as he was approaching middle age, his parents still treated him like a child. Maybe it was deserved. The bad years had been really fucking bad, and he'd almost lost everything because of it. It had been nearly a decade since, and he'd changed. But he wasn't sure if his family realized it.

It was hard to describe the feelings. The frustration and the unease and the worry. All of it was knocking around in his head like a maelstrom. Matt needed to get his fucking head on straight, get it calm before the season started. He couldn't afford to fuck things up for the boys. He'd dealt with this over the years, learned how to force himself to be even-keeled even when he didn't feel it.

The difference now was that Aiden was here, and Aiden looked up when Matt came out of the bedroom with a concerned expression.

"Matt? Are you all right?"

Matt thought about telling him, but he didn't want to burden Aiden further by reminding him of the negative opinions of his family. Aiden had enough on his shoulders. Instead, he sat down on the couch next to Aiden and leaned forward. Aiden's mouth melted under Matt's, and he gasped, the sweetest little noise of surprise that Matt swallowed down.

He wasn't sure if he'd ever get used to this.

It had always been like this between them, that electric chemistry, like their bodies knew how to communicate better than their mouths ever had. Even now, Aiden's big hands were gripping his biceps, an anchor. Even now, Aiden's body against his was a comforting weight.

"What's wrong, hey?" Aiden mumbled into Matt's mouth. He had shifted so he straddled Matt's thighs. "You've been acting weird since that phone call."

Matt looked up at him, the familiar face that had morphed into something unfamiliar and was slowly shifting back to something he knew intimately again. He lifted his hand, cupped it around Aiden's cheek. Let Aiden turn his head into the touch. His beard was so soft under Matt's fingers. "You know. It was my mom."

"And...?"

"My parents, ah, they've been a little worried about me. Just in general. It's just, it's just, it makes me feel pretty shitty sometimes."

"Do you want to...talk about it?"

"No. God, no."

Aiden's eyes crinkled in a smile, one of the few Matt had been able to coax out of him recently. "Okay. So we don't have to talk about it. But what can I do?"

"Fuck me," Matt said, before he could stop himself. "Fuck me until I can stop thinking about this."

Aiden laughed and kissed Matt's forehead, one of those affectionate little gestures he'd done so casually a decade ago, and Matt's heart clenched a little when he did it now. "I can do that, Matty."

"Yeah?"

"Yes," Aiden said, and slid off of his lap. He held out his hand, and Matt took it.

Aiden thought that Matt was probably going to drive him completely insane, one of these days. It was like he had regressed to a younger version of himself, a raw kid with an obscene refractory period and the desire to just fuck Matt up and be fucked up in turn, constantly, continually.

Like if he was otherwise occupied, Matt wouldn't stop to think too long about whether Aiden should still be there, taking up space and time in his life, an ugly shadow lurking at the edges of his neat existence. It was hard not to feel at least a little shitty about it, when he was still consumed with the uncertainty of what exactly he was doing in Montreal.

But that didn't mean he was going to stop.

Aiden, on his knees, pulled back to take a deep breath and look down at his work. Matt sprawled on his back, chest heaving as he tried to catch his breath, blotchy red and damp with sweat and his own come. He still looked a little dazed as Aiden reached out to rub his thumb under the head of his dick, shuddering and flinching away from the touch.

"Aiden, I'm not twenty-one anymore, I *can't—*"

"Let me try?"

"I—I can go down on you, I just, I don't think I can come again."

Aiden leaned forward and scraped Matt's thigh with his teeth, lips pressing against the same spot. Kissed his way farther up Matt's torso, licking the come off of his stomach. His hand twisted and Matt groaned, shivering underneath him.

"Let me," Aiden begged, not even sure exactly what he wanted to do, just wanted to—needed to—wreck him. "Matty."

Matt didn't answer immediately. His eyes were closed, and his mouth hung open as Aiden stroked his finger over Matt's rim, still wet from his tongue. Matt's entire body jolted as Aiden slid his finger back in, but his legs fell open, sensitive but unresisting, at least for the moment.

He clutched at Aiden's hair, grip tightening as Aiden teased him with his fingers, ignoring the gasps and the trembling of Matt's thighs when Aiden twisted them up, the yelp when Aiden licked his way up the length of Matt's cock. Aiden could barely think, half of his attention focused on making Matt feel as insane as Aiden felt right now, half on holding himself back.

"Aiden," Matt managed. "It's too much."

He pulled away. "Do you want me to stop?"

"No, no, please—"

Aiden lost track of time, of how long they'd been doing this, subsumed in the feedback loop of the ragged noises Matt made and the way he felt when Matt made them. Matt shook underneath him, alternating between trying to push himself onto Aiden's fingers and squirm away. His eyes were still screwed shut and his hair plastered sweatily on his forehead, and he was hot and achingly hard again in Aiden's hand.

"Matt," Aiden said, and his voice sounded like he was the one who'd been getting fucked this whole time. Matt had come twice already and looked and sounded like it and Aiden was holding himself back. It felt like his entire body was one tingling nerve, so intense it hurt. "Matt, what, what do you want?"

Matt didn't really answer right away, just kept rolling his hips up and grabbing blindly at Aiden's head and shoulders. He gasped, "*Anything.*"

Aiden gently pushed his hands away, shifted farther up the bed so he could settle between Matt's legs, push them apart and line himself up. He couldn't remember when exactly they stopped using condoms again or why and it wasn't really anything to get poetic about, but the heat and friction of it almost ended him right there. Aiden already felt raw and exposed, and fucking Matt like this made him feel like he'd ripped his skin off.

Matt said, "Oh," very quietly, when Aiden was fully inside and still mindlessly trying to push deeper. Matt's eyes finally opened to look up, although they were still hazy and unfocused, almost dreamy, and Aiden thought, *I did that, that's because of me,* I *made him feel like that.*

Aiden moved, a slow, agonizing motion first, and then faster, harder.

He didn't want to think anymore, so he didn't.

"Shit," Matt said, much later. He kept trying to sit up and not quite managing it. Eventually, he gave up, lay back in the crevice between the disarrayed pillows. "Where the fuck did *that* come from?"

"Fuck off," Aiden mumbled, sprawled on his stomach next to him.

"Seriously, what's—what the hell got into you?"

Aiden looked over at him, sticky and sweaty, his body marked with the imprints of Aiden's mouth and teeth, his face bemused, dark eyes flicking from Aiden's face to his lips, and thought, *I'm still in love with you.*

He said, instead, "Well, I can rule out 'you,' huh?"

Matt managed to punch him in the arm, and in response, Aiden waggled his eyebrows, and then Matt was rolling on top of him pinning him down and trying to kiss him, even though the angle was awkward. Aiden managed a squawk of shock before Matt's insistence killed his token protest.

Later, while Matt was in the shower, Aiden buried his face in the pillow and wondered whether he could just smother himself that way and end it all.

I'm still in love with you.

He'd never really stopped.

It didn't feel any better, admitting it.

It wasn't like Aiden was going to *stop* fucking him. It just felt worse to know that the end of the summer was coming, and Matt was going to be back on the road, and Aiden was going back to New York, doing absolutely nothing with his life, still in love with his ex, like a fucking idiot.

Dr. Gauthier asked why he found it so hard to envision a future for himself.

"It's just that I've never done anything except hockey.

I've never wanted to do anything except hockey. And now I don't have hockey anymore."

"You don't do anything except hockey, or you won't let yourself do anything except hockey?"

"Isn't that the same thing?"

"Not really, Aiden."

Some of the stuff he was supposed to work on at home was making lists of things he could see himself doing with the rest of his life, but he usually spent most of the time he forced himself to do it staring at a blank piece of paper, pen in hand.

"What are you doing?" Matt asked him, one night, as he glared in frustration at the empty page, screaming internally at his equally empty brain.

"Trying to—think of shit to do with the rest of my life. Something that doesn't have anything to do with hockey."

Matt sat down on the couch next to him, shifted closer so he could force his arm behind Aiden's back, set his hand on Aiden's waist, rested his chin on Aiden's shoulder. It shouldn't have felt as comforting as it did. He shouldn't lean back into it. He did anyway.

"Why can't it involve hockey?" Matt asked, so close Aiden could feel the heat of Matt's breath against his ear.

"It just—I don't know. I can't play for a living anymore and I don't want to keep looking at what I can't have, every day. It, uh, it just hurts too much." The words were falling out of his mouth before he could stop them. His neck felt red and hot, his hands clammy, because it wasn't just hockey, it wasn't just—

Matt's hand on the side of his face, turning Aiden's head toward him. "Baby," he said, kissing the corner of Aiden's mouth, "it's okay, it's okay."

It wasn't, of course, but Aiden let himself pretend for another night.

He woke up at midnight and checked his phone to find a text from Hannah. Aiden, please answer me this time. I'm really worried about you.

I'm fine, Hannah. You can tell Mom and Dad too.

Are you coming home for Raksha Bandhan?

Probably not. I've been busy. I'm sorry. I'll mail you a check.

I don't want a check, asshole, I want to tie a rakhi on my brother. I want to actually see you for a change.

I'm sorry, Hannah. Things have just been a little hectic.

ARE you in Montreal?

Yeah. I have been for a few weeks now.

Aiden, seriously? Are you sure that this is a good idea?

Can you please stop asking? I wish you guys wouldn't keep treating me like I'm a little kid who needs his hand held.

It's just if this doesn't work out, how are you going to handle it? I was there for the aftermath of the first time, you know.

I KNOW, Hannah.

You were such a mess for such a long time.

Aiden thought about telling her what a disaster his retirement had been, in general, even without Matt, that Matt was the only thing that had made him feel much of anything since he hung up his skates, but he didn't think Hannah would appreciate hearing that. Especially not when they had been trying so hard to be supportive, trying so hard to bring him back home.

Instead, he said, I know. Thank you for being there for me.

And I know you're an adult.

You should've been the older sibling.

Yeah, well. Life happens. I'm not.

How are Ankit and the kids?

Everyone's fine. We miss you.

I miss you too.

Come visit soon, okay?

I will.

He must have been shifting around too much because he woke Matt, who blinked at him for a second before reaching for his own phone. He opened up the Notes app and said, "Okay, look, if you can't think of anything, I'm just going to keep a running list for you."

"I don't—"

Matt ignored him. "Bean counter?"

"That's Ward…"

"Bean farmer?"

"*Matt.*"

"Juggler? You are pretty good at that; you could always take it on the road."

"Matt—"

"Mime?" Matt typed the words with his thumb, without looking at the screen; his full attention was on Aiden, torn between horror and laughter. "Mime could work, you're handsome enough people would probably give you a pass for being creepy."

"Oh my god—"

"Yoga teacher?"

Aiden actually thought about that one for a second. "I mean, I *could.*"

"You walked my inflexible ass through it, you could probably teach anyone."

"I don't think I, uh, want to do that with anyone else, you know…" Aiden had a momentary mental image of how yoga with Matt had usually ended—in bed or on the floor—and of the kinds of people who'd be in a yoga class he taught, the way he'd had to turn down people's numbers in the yoga classes he attended on his own throughout the years. He shuddered.

"Sex therapist?"

"*Excuse me?*"

"It was just a thought," Matt said, the corner of his mouth tipped up. "Again, it works for me…"

"*No.*"

"Personal trainer?"

"I mean, same problem with yoga, really."

"Real estate?"

"I hate talking to people I don't know—"

"Phlebotomist?"

"Is that even a real word?"

Matt set the phone down, took Aiden's face in both hands and said, "Baby, that's the person who draws your blood."

"I didn't—uh—" Aiden started to say, but then Matt licked his lower lip, sucked it gently into his mouth, and Aiden stopped arguing. Matt's mouth was so soft under his, so fucking tender that it almost killed him. Matt's eyelashes fluttered, eyes closing. After a few minutes, though, he pressed his hand against Matt's chest, pushing him back. "I…thanks, you know?"

"For what?"

"For not treating me like I'm fucking dying, or with kid gloves. I don't know. Thank you. This is the first time I could laugh about this, even a little bit."

"Gonna be right there with you in a few years, bud," Matt said, patting Aiden's thigh. "Better we both figure it out now. Come on…it's late as hell. Try to sleep, huh?"

None of the suggestions were any good. It didn't matter. Aiden settled himself back down into the bed. They fell asleep not long after, and Aiden didn't dream.

CHAPTER FOUR

August

Matt's thirty-sixth birthday—and Aiden's thirty-seventh, a few days later—snuck up on him before he realized it.

When they were younger, since the birthdays fell right before training camp started, they usually tried to make a week out of it, wherever they happened to be. They'd managed a few trips out of the country without anyone noticing. Once it had been to Amsterdam and they'd spent most of it either exploring the city or stoned out of their minds in their hotel room. Even with that particular memory, a damn good one, Aiden had never managed to top the high of skating together during the first summer they'd been together in New York: he'd gotten them private ice time, a chance to play one-on-one without interruptions or teammates or spectators.

Even though he'd peaked early, he still tried to pick out a thoughtful gift anyway. It was harder now, because while Matt was the same in many ways, in others, he was also a complete stranger. Aiden didn't know what he liked anymore, besides hockey, although he had done some work piecing it together after spending the last few weeks living in the same close quarters.

Present-day Matt cooked more, played less video games and had a small shelf that held mostly books about hockey, but also some other topics like philosophy, for some reason, and some actual novels. Aiden didn't know enough about modern literature, or really literature at all, to pick anything like that out.

He had plans anyway, but they were derailed when Matt said, "Oh shit, Miles and Jessica are going to be here tomorrow."

"Seriously? You just forgot?" Aiden asked. His mouth felt dry.

"Come on, man, I wasn't expecting *you* to be here when I made those plans."

"Okay, well, I can get a hotel room or something and we can just meet up again after they go home, we can figure it out."

"No. No, you came all the way here and I'm not… I'm not hiding you."

Aiden rubbed his eyes. "Are you sure? I mean…it's going to be awkward as hell. Worse than the first time you met the team. Miles hates me. He really, *really* hates me, and I don't blame him."

"He's going to have to get used to it. At least for now."

"Well. It's your birthday, Matt. Whatever you want."

"I want *you* there."

Aiden exhaled. "Okay. I'll stay."

Beyond the brief encounter over the summer, Aiden hadn't seen Miles Safaryan for any length of time in over ten years, even though Miles was good friends with Noah Brooks, one of the Libs who had made the team early in Aiden's tenure there. He would have preferred to keep it that way.

He still remembered the last time they had spoken in any meaningful manner, about three months after Aiden and Matt had broken up. It was after the first Libs/Scouts game of the season and Miles cornered him in the hallway after everyone had showered and most of them were on their way home already. He'd shoved Aiden into the wall, hard enough to show he wasn't joking, but not hard enough to really hurt.

Aiden still remembered the way Miles' arm felt pressed against his chest, elbow digging in, so forcefully that Aiden's ribs creaked under it. And what he'd said: a warning and a threat, to stay away from Matt. Aiden hadn't argued, hadn't fought back, just stared and nodded and said, *I'm sorry, I'm so sorry, I never meant to hurt him,* over and over again, until Brooksy saw them and came over to break it up.

It wasn't like he could even reassure himself that it would be fine. It was definitely not going to be fine. He couldn't blame Miles for being protective, especially now that he knew what Matt had gone through after they'd broken up.

Aiden wondered whether he would have been better off if *he'd* tried to talk to someone about it when it happened, how his life would have been different if he hadn't just boxed everything away and kept it with him for the next ten years, but—

"I said, they're bringing Ellie and Theo."

"The kids?"

"Yeah."

"Okay, well, again, I can get a hotel room."

"*They're* getting a hotel room. I've got a tiny condo

and they've got two small kids. Like I said before. I'm *not* hiding you. Aiden—you'll be fine. It'll be fine."

Aiden exhaled, remembering the way he had tried to reassure Matt the afternoon he'd met Hannah for the first time. Matt was probably about as convincing today as Aiden had been then. He thought, *There are no thoughts. There is no future.* He thought it, over and over again, until he had calmed down a little.

"Okay," he said, finally, because it was easier not to argue.

On the morning of Matt's birthday, Aiden stuck with tradition and woke him up with a blowjob. Even after all of these years, he still felt the lurch in his chest when he saw Matt's face shift from sleep to awareness, the smile that tugged the corner of his mouth up when he realized what Aiden was doing. At the trust in it. At the way Matt buried his face in Aiden's neck after he'd come, mouth pressed against Aiden's pulse, and Aiden had moved up to hold him close.

After Aiden finished cleaning himself up and while Matt was in the shower, he went into the kitchen to make breakfast. It was just pancakes, albeit fancy pancakes with the buckwheat flour he found in Matt's pantry and some strawberries he cut up and tossed in sugar so they started to break down a little.

Matt's face softened almost imperceptibly when he walked out of the bedroom and found Aiden flipping them in the pan. He came up behind Aiden and slid his arms around Aiden's waist. His mouth was warm, breath humid against Aiden's shoulder. "You know, you were making me pancakes when I first realized I was in *love* in love with you."

"Really?"

"Yeah," Matt said, looking around Aiden's arm at the stack of pancakes on the plate. "It was that first summer when I came out to visit you in Winnipeg, and you were flipping them shirtless just like this in that shitty apartment we had, and I asked you if you finally learned how to make a new breakfast, and you said someone had to feed me and you were taking one for the team and I just… I just knew. Now that was a mortifying way to figure it out, huh?"

"I dunno about that," Aiden said. He flipped the last pancake onto the top of the stack. "I'm a pretty great cook, so I understand the impulse."

Matt groaned, and half-heartedly headbutted him in the shoulder. "So that's what, like six dishes you can make now?"

It devolved into a mock fight that ended in heated kisses on the kitchen floor, Aiden sticking the tip of his tongue into the space between Matt's teeth, just to tease a reaction out of him, but they both sobered rapidly when Matt's phone buzzed.

Matt took his hand away from Aiden's throat, hitched his hips up so he could pull it out of his pocket without rolling off of Aiden, who was still on his back, shirt rucked up and exposed skin cold against the tile, watching while Matt answered the call.

"Oh, you're downstairs? Okay, let me come down and let you in." He hung up, looked down at Aiden. His hand cupped Aiden's cheek. "Hey, they're here."

Aiden had spent years working on controlling his emotions and anxiety, practicing meditation and mindfulness and breathing exercises. It was difficult to manage in situations like this, even with practice, even with breathing exercises. It was one thing to get into the crease in front of a stadium full of twenty thousand people, of fans from opposing teams who hated the insignia on his sweater. Another thing entirely to face one family who had every reason to hate him personally.

He made himself smile, and said, "Okay."

"Thank you," Matt said, very seriously. He looked down at Aiden with the same kind of intensity in his voice. "I know it's not going to be…fun."

"Yeah, well. It's *your* birthday, so."

Matt leaned forward and kissed him, quickly, affectionately, before he slid off of Aiden's hips and stood. "All right. Let me get them before he starts texting me about how old and slow I am."

Miles Safaryan looked exactly the same as Aiden remembered him, except, if possible, even more pissed off than he usually did. He looked like Matt, but a little skewed: the same dark eyes and thick eyelashes, the same prominent nose and sharp features, a thinner face; taller and slimmer. Where Matt's face had always seemed inherently kind, Miles looked like an angry hawk.

Miles' wife and children were new to Aiden, though. The kids came barreling through the door, pushing past their parents to throw themselves at Matt. He immediately crouched down to their level.

"Uncle Matt!" the little girl shrieked, as Matt gathered both of them into a hug.

Miles and his wife both looked at Aiden. Dr. Jessica Zhang cut a striking figure: beautiful, slim and almost as tall as Miles. Her long black hair was pulled back severely from her face. She wore a loose gray linen jumpsuit, a nondescript outfit that nevertheless looked like she had just stepped off a runway. Maybe that was because she had the kind of vibe that would be intimidating, if it weren't for the smile tugging at the corner of her mouth and the crinkle at the corner of her eye when Miles introduced her.

Miles sounded like he was in the process of scraping a piece of dog shit from the bottom of his shoe. "Jess, this is Aiden Campbell."

"It's so nice to finally meet you," Jessica said, like a completely normal person, and held out her hand to Aiden, who shook it. She had a firm, strong handshake and looked him directly in the eye. "I've heard a lot about you."

Aiden could feel the heat creeping up the back of his neck as she kept smiling at him, steady and bland. "I'm, uh, I'm sure you have."

Matt stood up, holding one child in each arm, although they were both technically too big for that and it was only Matt's size and strength that made it possible. They shrieked with joy—apparently, this was a habit for them. Matt was smiling, too, unguardedly happy in a way that he only looked around Aiden lately when they were in bed together. "It's really good to see you guys. How was the flight?"

"It was fine," Miles said, steadfastly ignoring Aiden now that he had done his duty and introduced him. The kids were busy grabbing Matt's hair and pulling it, talking over each other in their eagerness to tell Matt exactly how the flight had gone. "Theo was getting a little antsy toward the end, but we survived without any major meltdowns."

"Here, come in," Matt said, "you guys can use the bathroom and the kids can calm down a little before we head out."

They made awkward small talk while Ellie and Theo tore around the kitchen until Matt opened the cabinets and gave of them a bag of cookies to share. Once they'd gotten what they wanted, they huddled in the corner, arguing over the fact that there was an odd number in there and Ellie thought she deserved more, because she was older.

Miles cornered Matt at the far end of the apartment, talking to him in a low voice and making some emphatic gestures while he did. Aiden sighed, watching them.

"He's very protective of Matthew," Jessica said, from a few inches behind Aiden, startling the shit out of him.

Once he got his heartbeat back under control, he said, "I know. I don't blame him for it."

"Of course not. But, you know, if you're going to be sticking around for a while, do you want my advice?"

Aiden had the feeling that his answer wouldn't make a difference either way, so he lied, "Yes, I'd appreciate it."

"Don't let Miles walk all over you, yeah? Because if you let him, he will."

"I—"

"Just think about it." Jessica had a way of talking, precise and pointedly cheerful, that reminded him a little of Hannah. It was just as terrifying on her, especially when she smiled. "Ten years is a long time to grow up, Aiden. And I'm sure you have. Miles needs to move on, too."

"What kind of medicine do you practice again?"

"Oh, me? Ortho." She smiled at him again, all teeth. "Comes in handy when Miles needs a second opinion."

Miles looked up from his discussion with Matt. "What are you two talking about?"

"Just getting to know Aiden, honey."

"We're, um, ready to head out, I think," Matt said, sounding more hopeful than sure, and Aiden had never been so thankful to leave a room in his life.

Later that morning, in the Contemporary Art gallery of the MMFA, Ellie announced, "My dad says you're a bad person."

Ellie was almost six years old, tall for her age, with Coke-bottle glasses, a black eye and a line of stitches parallel to her lower lip. She wore a custom Scouts jersey that said SAFARYAN-ZHANG on the back—the letters barely fit between her tiny shoulders—and it shouldn't have been as cute as it was.

"He does think that," Aiden agreed.

"You don't seem that bad to me."

"I've been on my best behavior today."

That seemed to please her. She smiled, revealing her missing front teeth. Aiden was reminded, briefly, of some of his former teammates. "I'm on my best behavior, too. Mom said I'm not allowed to fight with Theo. *Or* anyone else."

They walked slowly, a little behind the rest of the group. Miles didn't seem to have noticed that Aiden and Ellie were back there, otherwise occupied talking to Matt and Theo, who was crying because he wasn't allowed to eat in the gallery.

"Do you get in a lot of fights?"

"Well, yeah," she said, like it was completely obvious. "I play on a boys' team. Even with Bee Morin, some of them are *jerks* about me being there."

Aiden thought about his own mites teams, and said, "You know, that's fair."

"I won the last one," Ellie said, with immense satisfaction.

"Is that where—"

"The eye, yeah. But the stitches are 'cause I tried to go down the stairs in a cardboard box and my teeth went through my *skin*."

Aiden managed to bite back a startled laugh at the mental image, because he had the distinct impression that Ellie wasn't the kind of kid who appreciated being laughed at. "Why were you going down the stairs in a cardboard box?"

"I want to be a goalie, so I was working on balance. But it *didn't* work."

"Yeah, ah, there are maybe some safer ways to do that."

"You were a goalie," Ellie said, looking at him sidelong, with the kind of obvious cunning that only small children could manage. "You should tell me some things about being a goalie."

"You mean to work on balance, right?"

"Yeah," Ellie said, her arms crossed over her chest like she wasn't sure if he was making fun of her after all. "What about it?"

They walked past some truly spectacular examples of modern art, the kinds of things that Aiden and Matt would have had private jokes about if they'd been alone. Aiden wasn't looking at any of it, attention absorbed by his small, intense private audience.

"Well, there are a few you can do without any equipment at all. A simple one is, you can kind of do a half-squat, like this—" he demonstrated, briefly "—with your arms extended like that, and have someone tap and push on various parts of your body without letting them move you at all, and you can do that same exercise, with a lower and more staggered stance, like this—"

"*Eleanor Safaryan-Zhang,*" Jessica called over her shoulder, "what did we say about bothering Dad and Uncle Matt's friends about hockey?"

"Not outside the home and not in places you can't normally play hockey." A mulish frown twisted Ellie's mouth. "But he *wanted* to help me, Mom." She glanced sideways at Aiden and whispered, "Okay, but will you? I wanna be the best, and if you have Cups, you must be pretty good."

Aiden said, "Yes, of course."

Ellie flashed her tooth gap at him again. "I'm going to be your best student."

"You're going to be the only student," Aiden said, thinking about the long stretch of hours during the day where he had nothing to do except arbitrarily created tasks.

Ellie just beamed, and then looked up and frowned, like she was seeing the paintings for the very first time. "Wow, this art is so bad."

"You know, your uncle and I used to think stuff like that, but it's actually just a matter of perspective..."

The stretch of birthdays that Matt had experienced over the last decade were mostly unremarkable, blending together in a long, lonely stretch. They had even been pretty lonely when Emily was around to host the parties, which mostly teammates attended. There had been a few years after player assistance when he had been completely sober, and the gatherings had been awkward and stiff, no one quite knowing how to treat him, whether they were allowed to drink, too.

Those were the worst kinds of parties, and this birthday had the same exact feeling. Everyone was on edge except for Jess, who was never on edge anywhere, no matter how tense the atmosphere was. That probably was a side effect of being an orthopedic trauma surgeon, but Matt didn't have the benefit of years of working under crisis conditions.

He felt like at any minute he was going to have to lunge sideways and separate Miles and Aiden. Miles was usually a pretty chill guy, on and off of the ice, but he did have his protective instincts. And he was watching Aiden like a hawk, just waiting for him to step out of line, so he could swoop in and bite his head off.

Instead, Miles cornered Matt in the MMFA while Aiden was busy talking to Ellie. "I'm serious, Matthew, what the hell are you doing?"

"I told you this morning," Matt said patiently. "Aiden's recently retired, he was having a hard time, and we both agreed that it would be good for him to get out of New York for a little bit."

"I meant about *you*."

"Miles," Matt said, surprised by the flicker of anger that lanced through him, tamped down again. It wasn't fair to get upset with Miles: Matt knew what he'd put the family through. No one had ever let him forget it. "I'm an adult. I can make my own choices. I'm not the same kid I was back then. I'm not—"

"But you don't *know*," Miles was saying urgently. "Campbell's...he's unreliable, Matt. He's just going to chew you up and spit you out again, like he did the last time, and then we're all going to have to pick up the pieces and—"

"Hey," Matt said, surprised by how loud his voice sounded in the echoing halls of the gallery. Everyone turned to look at him, and he smiled awkwardly and turned back to Miles. He lowered his voice. "Listen to me, Miles. I know how you feel. I understand why you feel that way. But it doesn't matter. Don't talk about him like that. Not to me. We were both young and stupid back then, and I—I had a really hard time accepting that things were over. But this is different."

"*How?*" Miles demanded, looking like he was about two seconds away from putting his hands in his hair and pulling it out in frustration. "How the hell is it different?"

"I'm older," Matt said, slowly. "He's older. I'm not going into this with any expectations. It's just been so good to have him back. It's just… Miles, how would you feel if you hadn't seen Jess in ten years, and then all of a sudden, she was back in your life again?"

"That's different! We've been married for years. We've got two kids. Jess never *dumped* me."

"And if she had?"

Miles deflated, suddenly. They'd never liked fighting off of the ice, outside of the direct competition of sports. His voice was still a low whisper, but it had all of the urgency as if he'd been yelling. "I don't know, man. It's hard to imagine my life without her in it. I can't even picture it. But it's not the same. She's my *wife*."

"And I'd gone as far as buying a fucking ring, Miles. It didn't work out. That doesn't change the fact that…" Matt couldn't quite bring himself to say what he'd been thinking about saying. He didn't fully think that Miles would understand. "Listen. All I'm asking is that you try to be a *little* more open-minded about it. Whether you like it or not, he's part of my life, in the past and right now."

"Yeah?" Miles asked, a little bitterly. "For how long?"

Matt exhaled. It felt a bit like a punch in the gut. "I don't know. And honestly, I don't care. This is enough."

Miles just looked at him, sad and a little resigned. "Okay… I guess you know best, yeah? I just… I love you so much, Matt. And I'm really fucking worried about you."

"It's different this time," Matt said. *I'm different this time.*

"Okay," Miles said, but it didn't sound like he believed it.

It was a busy day, especially for Aiden, who was starting to realize how few busy days he'd had since his retirement.

They hit most of the major tourist attractions, and by the end the kids were yawning and sleepy. Miles spent the last bit of the walk carrying Theo over his shoulder. It could have been worse: Miles mostly pretended Aiden didn't exist, and Aiden obliged him by not getting in the way.

Matt spent most of the time trying to bridge the gap between his family and Aiden, which functionally meant talking to either Miles or Aiden but not both at the same time. There were more than a few times that Aiden had gestured for Matt to go ahead and not worry about him.

It could have been worse, really—Aiden was surprised to find that he legitimately enjoyed spending time with Ellie, who did seem to be serious about the goalie thing. She had been playing wing, but Jessica promised she could try switching positions if she did all of her chores every single day for three months to help earn money for the pads.

It reminded Aiden, a little bit, of when he'd been younger and told his own father he wanted to play goal. Dad had marched him right outside to start firing orange street hockey balls at him to see if he'd flinch. He hadn't, even when they'd bruised him. Dad hadn't been a goalie when he'd played, but he'd certainly done his best to dissuade him anyway. Aiden had just been even more stubborn. It had been his mother, eventually, who broke Dad down.

Ellie said, "I've got twenty-three days to go, because the vacation doesn't count," with the kind of weird, slightly manic intensity beyond her years, that reminded Aiden more than a little of himself at that age.

Obviously, he had done a lot of work with kids over the years—from charity skates to visiting them in the wards at Mount Sinai to spending one-on-one time with a young fan who'd been with him since juniors—but with a few exceptions, this was the longest he'd talked to a kid this young that he could remember. He wasn't sure if all of them had this much personality, or whether that was just Ellie. She asked focused questions, listened to his answers and seemed to process everything at a level far beyond her age.

When they finally said their goodbyes to Miles and his family, Ellie came up to Aiden and tugged at the hem of his shirt.

"Soup," she said, having decided that because they were both goalies, that made them colleagues, and she could call him by his nickname, "if my mom lets me, can I send you some questions?"

"Of course."

"Cool," she said, beaming.

"Cool," Aiden repeated, and ruffled her hair.

She punched him in the hand and ran back to her parents.

Aiden felt—something. *Huh.*

"Thanks," Matt said, when they were finally alone, "it meant a lot to me to be able to see them today, even though I'm fucking exhausted." He had his arms wrapped around Aiden's waist, head resting right under Aiden's chin. "And you were *amazing*. I know it wasn't ideal, but you were—Ellie loved you. She couldn't stop talking about you."

"Of course," Aiden said. He was completely exhausted, a bit overwhelmed, and his brain wasn't working properly. One of his hands traced the line of Matt's shoulder blade. It was the kind of casual affection that he never would even have noticed doing ten years ago but felt significant now. It grounded him in a way that he had really fucking needed. "I enjoyed getting to know her. She's a good kid. And—hey, you know, your birthday's not over yet. I still owe you a homemade dinner."

"Oh, we can just order something, it's not a big deal."

"No, I wasn't really able to get you a present, so this is it, okay? If you want to take a nap or something while I work, that's fine."

"That's actually not a bad idea," Matt said, stifling a yawn. "You sure you'll be okay?"

"Yeah, yeah. Go on."

He watched Matt head into the bedroom, took a deep breath and went to the fridge. He had been slowly gathering ingredients over the last few days, preparing things that could be made ahead when Matt wasn't home. He hid them in the back of the shelves and hoped Matt wouldn't look too closely and figure out his plans.

He had learned years ago that Matt enjoyed meals with a lot of different options, so he planned something similar: chicken shawarma that could be eaten either as a sandwich or a salad plate. He had homemade pickles, homemade hummus and dough for pitas. It was more ambitious a meal than he usually attempted, but it wasn't like any of it was that hard, especially considering Matt's kitchen actually had things like grill pans now.

He spent a couple hours shaping the pita into balls and keeping a careful eye on it puffing up in the oven, making sure all of the extras were arranged in little bowls and throwing the marinated chicken on the stove.

Even though he didn't do this often at home, it wasn't because he *couldn't*, there was just no point in cooking like this when it was just him. When he was alone, food and eating was more about the efficiency of getting the appropriate nutrients into his body, as simply and healthily as possible. Food was part of the Routine, something else he could use to impose order on his day, and it was comforting to just eat the same thing, every day, to not have any worries or expectations or surprises.

When it was Matt…well, Aiden would do pretty much anything for him, and this was no exception. It wasn't like it was a hardship, though. There was something calming about slicing tomatoes and onions and lettuce, something satisfying about seeing tangible results of his hard work.

The sun had gone down and Aiden was almost done carving the chicken by the time Matt slouched out of the bedroom. His hair was still messy from where it had been smashed into the pillow and he wore only a pair of threadbare sweatpants and his sleepy eyes snapped wide open when he saw the kitchen.

"Aiden—what is this?"

"Dinner," Aiden said, a little smug. It *was* impressive.

"What the *fuck*?" Matt had made his way over to the kitchen island to examine the spread. "You did all of this?"

"Yes."

"You learned *how* many recipes?"

"Come on, it's been over a decade since I really cooked for you, I've learned a lot you didn't get to try."

"Aiden, this is amazing," Matt said, pushing one of the fluffy pitas in with one finger. "I really can't believe how much time you must have spent on this? Like fuck, man, at this rate, you should just open a restaurant."

"Too stressful," Aiden said, starting to put together a plate for him. "This is just for you. Happy birthday, Matt."

"Thank you." Matt took the first bite and closed his eyes, a lopsided smile on his face as he chewed. That was good enough for Aiden.

When he checked his phone later, Pears had sent him a playlist. It was called *shacking up with your ex in montreal*.

Aiden opened the playlist, but it was just the *Amélie* soundtrack three times in a row.

Thanks, Isaac.

Anytime, bud.

Aiden did not play the playlist.

You good, though? Pears asked.

Aiden said, yeah, surprised to find he almost meant it.

Matt had gotten the impression that Aiden had been dreading his birthday: he was morose and quiet after Matt's, and it didn't get better over the next few days. He'd never been like that when they were younger, but Matt had the general idea that getting older complicated things. His own birthday had been a minefield he hadn't entirely recovered from.

Aiden, asleep, was absent the quiet fog of despair that seemed to have settled in around him that week. Matt ran his hand down Aiden's flank. It was still insane he had a body like he did, without one extra ounce of body fat, more abs than anyone needed. He'd always had dark body hair, and Matt remembered the one time he'd waxed it because a bunch of his teammates were taking an island vacation together, and Matt had almost choked himself laughing when he'd seen it up close. Remembered the dark blush that would rise up Aiden's whole chest to his ears, the way he'd covered himself up, even though Matt had seen every single embarrassing part of him already.

"Hey," Matt murmured, mouth against Aiden's thigh. "Good morning, baby."

He could feel Aiden shifting into wakefulness, though his eyes didn't open. He was still limp and boneless and relaxed, sighing a little when Matt kissed his way along the line of muscle.

"What do you want for your birthday?"

Aiden's voice was an exhale more than a word. "You."

The sex was sleepy and sloppy and lazy, Matt barely

moving inside of him, the barest shift of his hips here and there to listen to the way Aiden's breath hitched when he did it. It was enough just to be close to him, hungry kisses and desperate hands and the tiny, broken noises Aiden made when Matt took charge.

After it was over, Aiden sat cradled in Matt's lap, trying to catch his breath as Matt shifted so that his softening cock slipped out. It was messy and both of them desperately needed to shower, but Matt held Aiden down when he tried to get up, brushed a thumb across his cheek.

"What's wrong?"

At first, Aiden didn't want to answer, like he was afraid of ruining the moment. Matt shifted again so that Aiden could settle more comfortably straddling his thighs, and Aiden shook his head.

"I just…this is closer to forty than thirty. The first one since retirement. Just feels, you know, really fucking weird. Not myself. I'm sorry, I fucking—I hate that I keep doing this. Not what you signed up for when you asked me up here, I know."

Matt exhaled. "It kind of was, Aidy. I signed up for *you*, anyway."

"Matt—"

"Aiden, let me do nice shit for you today, okay? We can…talk about it later."

In the shower, Aiden got down on his knees, like he was trying to show Matt exactly how grateful he was. Maybe neither of their mouths could form the proper words, but they could do this. And Jesus, could Aiden's mouth do this.

"It's *your* birthday, Aiden," Matt gasped.

Aiden pulled away, looked up at him from the shower

floor. It had to have been hell on his knees, those little tiles, but he didn't seem bothered by it. "It's just—this whole *time* in Montreal you've been doing nice shit for me. And you haven't been getting anything in return. I'm just—I don't know, a shell—"

"Aidy." Even now, he was still so hard it was almost painful, looking down at the way Aiden's soft mouth parted, at his eyes, the pupils wide, darker with desire. It didn't matter if he couldn't get the point across, but he didn't know what to say to make Aiden believe him. "I'm getting you. I'm getting *you*."

Aiden didn't say anything, just indicated *shut up* with his hand and his tongue, his warm, clever mouth on Matt's cock again.

Eventually, Matt gave in.

By the time they got outside, Aiden found a fittingly gray and overcast day, unseasonably chilly for August. Although he was starting to have a working knowledge of how to get around downtown Montreal, he was still unfamiliar with the surrounding suburbs. So when Matt drove them east and over the Samuel De Champlain Bridge, it took him a second to figure out where they were going.

When he did, he contemplated opening the door and rolling out onto the road.

Matt glanced sideways and said, not quite a warning, "Aiden."

"You didn't—"

"Give it a chance."

"I haven't—I don't even have skates, I don't have pads, I don't have anything."

"We're not doing goalie stuff, we're just gonna go out on the ice. And I got you skates."

"You *what*?"

"I mean, not like your regular skates," Matt said, a tiny smile tugging at the corner of his mouth. "These probably aren't quite as nice as what you'd order for yourself during the season, and they're not goalie skates, but they're better than anything you can rent around here, and they'll do for now."

"Matt?"

"Give it a chance."

It was the voice he used when they were fooling around, when Aiden wanted to be told what to do and Matt was willing to do that for him, and he wilted a little in the seat and didn't say anything else.

The Sports Complex looked like any other practice facility, a boring rectangular box of white walls and wide windows. He had done this so many times for so many years. He never loved anything as much as he loved being on the ice, except maybe Matt. There was no reason Aiden's heart should be knocking around in his chest like that, no reason his breathing should feel like something had pressed hard against his ribs. Therapist aside, it was pretty clear to him, in that moment, exactly how fucked up retiring had gotten him. And here was Matt, still trying to help in whatever way he could manage. Aiden felt like he was floating outside of his own brain.

"Hey," Matt said, when they had parked. "We don't have to if you really don't want to. I just thought it might be good for you."

"No, I…have to get back on the ice at some point, I might as well, I might as—"

"It doesn't have to be anything except fun." Matt's hand rested on top of Aiden's; his fingers were warm and Aiden's felt like ice underneath them. "It's always been good when we can skate together, right?"

"Yeah, except the Olympics," Aiden said, with the sudden, perverse urge to lash out. "I don't know if you remember, but fuckin' Captain Canada had to ask me what was going on because it was that awkward."

"Oh, I got the talk, too." Matt grinned, for a second, adopting an approximation of the serious, concerned face that Henri Jean-Phillipe Lévesque must have made during that talk. "'Now, Safaryan, I don't know what happened with Campbell, but for the good of the team and the country, we have to put our personal differences aside—'"

"Don't do the voice, don't do the voice," Aiden begged, a slightly hysterical laugh bubbling up before he could stop it.

"'—and concentrate on the important thing here, which is playing hockey and bringing home the *gold*, for Canada,'" Matt finished, the concerned frown fading back into a smile.

"God. We were—"

"—fucking awful. Just horrendous little shits. Insufferable."

"Yeah," Aiden said, and looked at the door of the complex. He remembered again how miserable he'd been during that Olympic tournament, so careful to avoid being in the same room with Matt when he could, barely talking to him even on the ice, so painfully aware of him anyway. Even taking home the gold had felt empty after that. He also remembered the way that, even though they hadn't been talking, Matt had made sure to place Aiden's towel on the boards exactly the way he had always liked it, so it was available for him to wipe his face during the TV timeouts. At the time, that little attention had felt mocking, cut deeply into his chest. But now, knowing that Matt had been thinking about him all of this time—

He took a deep breath. "Okay. Let's go skate."

Traditionally, when they had had the opportunity to skate together, Aiden let Matt have the first blade on the ice. This time, after they had both laced up their skates and Aiden spent a moment getting his breathing and heartbeat back under control, Matt gestured for Aiden to go out before him.

He hesitated at the edge, wondering what the hell he was so afraid of. That it would drive home how much he missed hockey? He already knew that; he was already living with that. The longer he groped for a reason, the dumber it seemed. He had just been keeping himself from doing something he loved. Taking one deep, steadying breath, Aiden pushed himself out on the ice.

Regular skates were a different experience than goalie skates, and it wasn't just because they were cut higher and didn't have the protective shell. The blades were curved and angled deeply, while Aiden was used to straight, flat blades that allowed for quick lateral movement. He was a professional hockey player, though, and he had been skating since he was a toddler, so it was easy enough to adjust. Aiden tested the fit of the skates and the feel of the rink, pushing off with one foot and streaking down toward home ice.

It felt surprisingly good, to just go as fast as he could, letting the practice complex fade into the background around him. Obviously, he didn't have the speed or explosiveness a regular skater would build up, and obviously he wasn't getting any younger, and obviously, he hadn't been on the ice in months, but it still felt so fucking good.

He almost didn't realize that Matt had skated out to join him until a dark blur streaked by at the corner of his vision. Matt, showing off exactly how much faster than Aiden he was.

Aiden concentrated his weight on the one knee, pushing his edge outward against the ice into the extension. He couldn't really keep up. His training and work didn't involve the same kinds of muscles that Matt's did; he didn't have eighty-two games' worth of practicing his stride every year to develop it. But he did a pretty good job of trying, and although Matt never went easy on him, Aiden wasn't that far behind.

They chased each other around the ice, and Matt whooped when Aiden managed to get close enough to grab him by the sleeve of his hoodie, tugging him almost off his skates. He didn't fall, though: Matt caught himself on Aiden's arm and then it was Aiden's turn to flail for balance.

The speed they were moving, the pull of his hands, drew them together with centrifugal force, and all of a sudden, their faces were very close as Matt whirled him around in a circle. Matt's eyes were wide and dark, and his cheeks were pink, and he was a little breathless from exertion, and he looked up at Aiden's mouth. For one long, insane second, Aiden thought Matt was going to kiss him, right there in the middle of the rink where anyone could see. His heart was beating so fast it felt like it was going to flutter up through his throat like a hummingbird. Part of him wouldn't have even minded. Part of him would have melted into it, surrendered to the magic of the moment.

Matt didn't do it, of course, just reached up to scrub his hand over Aiden's face and, laughing at his splutter of dismay, took off toward the other end of the ice again before Aiden could even react.

Aiden pushed off in pursuit, forgetting, for the moment, any reason he'd had to dread this.

In the car on the ride home, Matt couldn't stop looking sideways at Aiden to make sure he was okay. He'd been so happy on the ice, smile so wide that for a second Matt felt like the old Aiden had time-traveled into this Aiden's body. It had been worth every second of the anxiety leading up to the reveal. It had been the happiest Matt had been in years, probably. Just getting to skate with Aiden like that again—like a weight had been lifted from his shoulders.

But now, Aiden kept trying to say something, like he wanted to explain, but every time he opened his mouth he got too choked up with emotion and couldn't finish.

Not for the last time, Matt wished he had the power to read minds, to figure out what the hell was going on in there. "It's okay, Aidy," he said, merging back on the highway and not looking at Aiden directly, "I know."

Instead of answering, Aiden pressed his forehead silently against the glass, and didn't say anything else.

Aiden had been dreading the day but overall, it had been—good. It felt a little like having his skin ripped off and his nerves exposed to the open air, but it was fine. He could get on the ice again, and the world wouldn't end.

He kept going over and over it in his head, even after they got back to Matt's, ordered dinner and ate it. He kept going over and over it in his head while they watched *Goon*. Aiden spent most of the movie tucked under Matt's arm, his cheek smashed against Matt's chest, sinking into the solid, comforting presence that Matt always was. And he was still going over and over it in his head when Matt asked him what was wrong, and Aiden said, "I just can't get out of my fucking head today."

He wasn't going over and over it in his head when Matt said, "Well, I can help you with *that*, anyway."

And that was just—even after all of this time, Matt knew when he needed that.

That was how Aiden ended up on his back in the bed, watching Matt fumble through his closet for his game-day ties. He wasn't sure how this was going to work, exactly. It wasn't like they hadn't done this before, but it had been a while, and he wasn't sure how Matt's preferences had changed.

They had been so young the first time around. Aiden still remembered that first Cup day. He'd done the usual charity and family visits while the sun was still shining. And then, when everyone was gone, Matt had come over and they got completely fucked up on ridiculously expensive champagne, half of which had ended up dripping all over Aiden's naked body, and Matt had tied Aiden's hands backward behind the Cup and fucked him against it.

It would probably have been one of his favorite memories of all time, except the details were fuzzy. He'd been *really* drunk. He remembered the cold metal digging into his back, the sticky champagne between his and

Matt's skin, the rope pressing hard into his wrists, trembling on the uncomfortable edge of pain and pleasure.

But the important thing, the thing about Matt, was that whatever Aiden had asked for, he was always enthusiastically all in. And a decade later, here was Matt, looking at the ties and at his bed, a rustic industrial monstrosity with an iron rail bolted into the wooden headboard, like he was gauging the distance and angles.

Aiden shivered with involuntary anticipation as Matt straddled his thighs and said, "You're not allowed to move."

"That's the point of tying me up, isn't it?" Aiden asked, a little mean, frustrated he couldn't hide just how into this he was. He was already naked, already so fucking hard.

Matt pressed his hand over Aiden's mouth. "If I wanted to make it easy for you. I'm only tying your arms, but don't move your legs, either. Just stay as still as you can until I say so."

Instead of answering, Aiden licked Matt's palm, tongue teasing the tender web of skin between his thumb and pointer finger. Matt swore and jerked his hand away. He took Aiden's left wrist first, then his right, and pulled them over Aiden's head, thumb pressed a little painfully against the nerve.

Aiden couldn't move to see exactly what Matt was doing, but he could feel Matt wrapping the tie around both of his wrists and slipping it into some kind of knot. He wanted to crane his head to look, but he forced himself to stay still. There was a little pressure as Matt looped the tie around the rail. He couldn't really see anything except Matt's abs in front of his eyes. He wasn't cut the same way Aiden was, but Aiden had dreamed about his body for years after they'd broken up, how solid and broad he was, hard as iron under the softer cushion of his stomach, and it was almost overwhelming seeing it right in front of him now. He leaned forward to try to press a kiss against Matt's torso.

Foiled when Matt immediately pulled away.

"Aiden."

"Yeah?"

"I told you not to move."

"Mm, sorry, I couldn't—wait, what are you doing?"

What Matt was doing was wrapping a second tie around Aiden's eyes and knotting it behind his head and Aiden's dick gave another traitorous little jump.

"If you can't listen, then I'm going to have to make it more difficult."

Aiden couldn't see what he was doing but he could feel the pressure of Matt's body on his thighs for another second or two before Matt moved away. Maybe he was admiring the view. Maybe he was plotting some other kind of torture. Maybe he was laughing at Aiden, and the idea of that, of Matt's judgment of Aiden's exposed body, *exactly* how much he *needed* this so easy to see. He could feel the deep flush starting at his chest and rising. Along with his dick, straining up, bobbing and leaving a sticky streak on his stomach.

"Spread your legs," Matt said, somewhere above him, and Aiden took a deep breath and spread them in a V, his feet pointing to the corners of the bed. Matt's voice again: "Raise your knees."

It was awkward and exposed, and he could feel the flush deepening, even though Matt had already seen every part of him, in pretty much every way there was to see it. "Is this good?"

"Yes—*Jesus*, you look—"

Aiden's cock twitched again, just from the rough edge to Matt's voice, from the force of his regard, which he could feel even if he couldn't see it. He wanted to turn, wanted to look at Matt so fucking badly, but he forced himself to stay still. "*How* do I look?"

"Eager," Matt murmured, and laughed.

"Oh fuck *off*."

The first thing Aiden felt was Matt's finger featherlight against the curve of his foot. He twitched, ticklish and sensitive, and Matt said, "No, Aiden, no," and kept touching him, barely brushing the skin. Aiden held his breath, shivering, as Matt leaned forward again.

It was his mouth, this time, hot and wet against Aiden's calf, the muscles bunched and tense. He moved slowly up the line of Aiden's leg. Aiden gasped, trying to hold back, but it was hard when Matt pressed his teeth along the inside of Aiden's thigh, the tender places that made him want to jerk away. When he switched from one leg to the other and Aiden couldn't predict where he was going to touch next. Matt's mouth where Aiden's leg met his torso. The sensitive skin on the underside of his dick. Aiden squirmed, legs falling before he could stop them.

Matt immediately pulled back and Aiden whined a strangled noise of protest.

"Matt—"

"What did I tell you?" His voice wasn't steady at all, the only consolation in this. The kind of even that could shake apart at any moment.

"You said not to move, but…"

"No *buts*. Maybe I'll just, just leave you here."

"No—I won't move, I promise—"

Matt let him stew anyway. Aiden couldn't accurately

gauge how long it was; when you couldn't see, any amount of time felt like ages. All he knew was Matt wasn't touching him and Matt could have done *anything*: left him tied, walked away, even left the condo or invited someone else inside, and Aiden would have been completely helpless. He tried not to twist too restlessly, thinking about that, about all of the ways Matt could have made him sorry.

Then: Matt's hand, thumb stroking Aiden's lip. Aiden's mouth opened under it, tonguing it the same way he would have tongued Matt's cock, rewarded by the ragged groan that still did nothing to settle the bone-deep ache inside of him.

Matt's mouth on one of Aiden's nipples, gentle at first and then a sharp bite, an electric shock that had him straining against the tie, muscles screaming as he desperately tried to keep still. Matt tortured him that way, mouth and hands a shock and surprise each time, until Aiden could barely contain himself. He jerked his leg to the side, instinctively trying to get away. Matt's hand came down hard on the inside of his thigh, the crack of a hand against skin, and the groan that tore itself from Aiden's mouth was embarrassing but couldn't be helped.

He was so hard it hurt, only the sheer force of his own will holding him back from coming.

"Forgot how much you like that," Matt muttered, and did it again, slapping Aiden's other thigh, palm flat, fingers spread. Not as hard as Aiden knew he could do it, but it still stung.

"Matty—*please*."

"Do you want me to stop?"

"No—come on, do it again, do it again, harder—"

Matt kept slapping him, his hand slamming against

the same area of Aiden's thigh—twice, then three times—until his skin was flushed and stinging and Aiden was straining against the tie again. The breath hissed from his mouth, muscles trembling, holding himself back.

"Do you want me to stop?" Matt asked, voice completely wrecked. Like Aiden, tied and helpless and sweaty, his skin red from Matt's hands, was somehow taking him apart the same way.

"Matt—"

"Do you want me to stop? *God*, look at you."

"Please—"

"Tell me, you have to say it."

"*Hit me*, come *on*—"

The blows rained down, shifting so he wouldn't know where they'd fall, harder and harder. He couldn't help whimpering: it *hurt*, even if he had never liked to admit it. His legs were on fire with the force of trying to keep himself still, with Matt's relentless hands hitting parts of him that already burned. He burned with the way Matt talked to him, a constant stream of nonsensical words and endearments, and then the wet heat of Matt's mouth on his dick, knocking the breath from his chest. The way Matt's fingers pressed inexorably inside of him. The noise Aiden made was obscene, but he couldn't care.

It was all too much: the effort of holding himself back, the effort of trying not to come. At this rate, Aiden was going to shake himself apart despite the anchor of Matt on top of him, trembling in counterforce.

"Matt, I *can't*."

"You can, I know you can, you always do—do you really want me to stop?"

He was beyond words at this point, making desperate noises every time Matt touched him, every time his mouth moved or his fingers twisted. He was outside of himself, beyond himself, the only way he'd ever found to get there.

"I'm going to fuck you now," Matt managed, "you can move for that, you can come, you can come whenever—"

Aiden was still restrained and blind but that didn't matter. The only thing that mattered was how good it felt when Matt was inside of him, when Aiden rocked up to meet him, when Matt alternately stroked and slapped him and he never knew where Matt's hands would fall, whether it would be a caress or a sting.

Matt's hands on his stomach and biceps, softer places where it didn't hurt as much; harder places where the muscles were already straining, where Aiden cried out, overwhelmed. Matt's hands gentled him, soothing down the ache, a tenderness that was almost more painful than anything else. Matt, relentless, driving up into him. And eventually it didn't matter whether it was a slap or not, it all felt the same, it all rolled through him like an inexorable tide, blanking out everything else.

Matt was saying something, again, voice small and strained and pained, but Aiden couldn't understand him at first. Matt's hand on Aiden's cock, and then Matt's voice: "Come on, *come on*, Aiden, baby—please?"

The entire length of his body bowed in on itself, or it would have, if he weren't pinned between the tie digging into his wrists and Matt's weight on top of him. And then Matt: more of a gasp than anything, his head dropping so suddenly that his forehead bumped painfully against Aiden's. They lay together like that for what seemed like a long time; Aiden still shaking, the aftershocks sparking all over his skin.

Eventually, Matt pulled out and sat up, started to untie the restraint. Aiden still couldn't see him, just felt the shift of his bodyweight and the sting and burn as he could finally lay his arms down and the blood started recirculating. Matt tugged the blindfold away, too, revealing Aiden's face. It must have been blotchy from exertion, his eyes watering, lip red where he'd bitten it.

He felt lightheaded, brain empty, didn't even bother moving as Matt dropped back down on the bed next to him, breathing hard. This is what he'd been looking for: just a time of quiet. It would be over soon enough.

"Thank you," he said, still shivering. Matt rolled over on top of him and the weight was welcome. Aiden's wrists ached, but his body slowly stilled as Matt rubbed the circulation back into his arms.

"Your birthday," Matt murmured into Aiden's ear. "Not that I'm complaining. You're—god, you're something fucking else."

Aiden was too tired to say anything, just rubbed his face against Matt's cheek.

"Don't fall asleep yet, Aidy."

"Mm," Aiden agreed, already drifting off.

Matt came home from practice to find Aiden frowning at his phone. "Hey, you okay?"

"It's fine. It's just Gabe asked me how Montreal was."

"What'd you tell him?"

"The truth. It's okay."

Matt snorted. "I hope I'm doing better than okay, huh?"

"Sometimes," Aiden said, with a brief, sly smile that

reminded Matt of the early days again. It faded to a creased frown again. "It's just that he misses me."

"Do you miss him?" Matt asked carefully. Aiden had said he and Walker weren't romantically involved, and Matt believed him, but it wasn't… Aiden had been here a few weeks now, and he hadn't seemed to really talk to anyone else except for Matt. He had spent a year seeing Gabe almost every day, had taken him under his wing.

"I mean, yes," Aiden said. "He's a good kid. Training him was kind of the only thing that kept me sane that last season."

"How do you mean?"

"It was something else to focus on. I didn't have to think about retirement. All I had to do was make sure Gabe was doing okay. It was always easier, you know? With a distraction."

Matt had the brief, uncomfortable realization that he was in the same place: preparing for what could be his last season, focused solely on the rookies. "And then when you retired anyway?"

"He still wanted to see me all the time anyway, so that never changed. We were really close, Matt. Closer than Wardo and I ever were, but that was probably because Wardo had his kids, and I had…well, nothing."

Matt held out his arms, and Aiden came to him easily. Matt inhaled, the familiar smell of him, the familiar way he could just barely tuck his chin against Matt's head. "Why did you have nothing, Aiden?"

"You know me. I've never been very good at people."

Matt wanted to laugh, but it was true. The beginning of their relationship had been full of stops and starts: it was amazing they'd ever been able to make it work in the first place.

The first time had started after that handshake line, when Matt had gotten Aiden's number from Duncs and spent the next three months pulling his pigtails over text until things had started to shift into something more companionable. And as soon as it did, Aiden had immediately pulled away and told Matt they had to stop talking because it was a distraction.

Matt hadn't even known he *was* queer yet, and still remembered how weirdly, inappropriately crushed he'd been by the sudden end of something that hadn't even really started, something he couldn't have even begun to label. How relieved he'd been when Aiden approached him at the All-Star Game a few months later and told him, *it's not working, not talking to you, I'm* still *distracted.*

"You were better than you think, baby. We made it work for almost five years, huh? And Gabe clearly loves the shit out of you."

"Gabe looks up to me as a mentor," Aiden mumbled into Matt's hair. "The same way your rookies look up to you. But outside of the rink, it's just been…since you, I haven't really had anyone. Not the same way. Eventually it was just easier to stop trying to look for that."

Matt's head was spinning. That they'd each spent all of this time suffering, and now that Aiden was here again, in his arms, he couldn't help wondering if they could have avoided all of this altogether. Was it insane to think that maybe Aiden was just meant for him, that all of this time apart had just been time they'd spent growing up, so they could find their way back to each other?

He had to get it together.

"What are you thinking about doing once the season starts?"

"I… I don't know," Aiden mumbled. "I don't want to think about it now, Matty. Please?"

Matt sighed—this was just pushing off the inevitable, the same way they'd done back when they were trying to figure out what the future looked like for them. But Aiden was so fragile, he just didn't know how else to handle it. "Whatever you need, Aiden."

"Thank you," Aiden said, and looked down at him with those big brown eyes, and Matt realized he was still just as much of a fool as he'd ever been.

The end of August came to Aiden with a series of punches to the gut.

"Let's try something else," Dr. Gauthier said, "let's not even consider your profession. If you could have any life that you wanted, right now, what would it look like?"

"I'd be playing—"

"If you *weren't* playing."

"I—I don't know."

"Why do you think you can't picture even this? Is it that you aren't comfortable admitting to yourself the things you do want? Or do you feel that you don't deserve them?"

His mouth felt dry. "I don't know."

"You can think about it," Dr. Gauthier said, firmly, and Aiden knew he probably spent the rest of the appointment both unable to participate the same way he had been, and unable to look Dr. Gauthier in the eye. Instead, he spent it staring at a spot on the wall a few feet to the left of her head, and mumbled stuff like, *I don't know* and *I don't really have anything else to say about this today.*

Later that day, Ellie emailed him. The message was a little difficult to parse, between a five-year-old's spelling and what was presumably Jessica's autocorrect, but Ellie told him that she had been allowed to pick out her pads and try the position if that was what she really wanted. Would Aiden still be interested in talking to her and answering questions?

He wrote back, of course, whenever you'd like, and Ellie replied with a smiley-face emoji.

The Royal's training camp was due to open soon.

Aiden woke up early so he could run from Matt's condo to the summit of Mont-Royal and back. It wasn't the most challenging run, but it was long enough to clear his head a little before they went to the gym together. Sometimes Matt was awake by the time he got back, and he came home to find coffee and toast already made; sometimes he wasn't and then Aiden could get back into bed and laugh at Matt's sleepy, disgusted protests when Aiden got sweat all over him, spooning up against his back.

Aiden went running.

His hair was long enough now that he had to pull it up in an awkward ponytail or topknot, so it didn't stick to his face once it got sweaty. His feet pounding the pavement felt good. A tangible accomplishment. The park, this early, before the sun had even come up, was quiet and peaceful. No tourists, no families, just Aiden's sneakers on the asphalt and the completely empty feeling in his head. He could pretend he was the only man in the entire world. He could forget anything except the burn in his lungs.

At the summit, he paused to catch his breath and look down at Montreal. The building lights were still on, picking out the windows like stars against the midnight blue sky. Matt was in one of those houses, probably still tangled up in the blankets and sprawled out over three-fourths of the bed where Aiden had left him.

Aiden exhaled. If he was being honest with himself, alone in the thin sliver of time when night hadn't quite shifted into sunrise, this was the scaffolding of his ideal life. However he thought about it, it ended up coming back to this: Matt waiting for him when he ran home.

Aiden still didn't know what he could really do with that, especially with the season starting, especially when there was only so long he was going to be able to fool Matt into believing Aiden was getting his shit together.

Aiden ran from the summit.

Training camp was right around the corner, and Matt's teammates were finally all back in one place. The group chat buzzed as guys made plans to catch up, talked about how their summers had been, compared personal records they'd hit in the gym. It was nice to see it, even if he was distracted and distant himself. He'd built a good culture here over the years, and if this was the last season, it was a good legacy to leave behind.

Instead of texting, Saari called him the way he always did. It wasn't a request: "Get lunch with me."

"Sure, when?"

"Tomorrow. Today I have to finish helping Aino unpack all of our shit for the season, but I wanna catch up before camp."

"Yeah, sure," Matt said, and then hesitated.

Saari immediately knew something was up. "Safy?"

"So…there's something I have to tell you." There

was a long silence, as Saari let him figure out how to say what he was trying to say. "Aiden's been staying with me this summer."

The answer was quick and decisive, exactly the thing Matt had predicted he'd say. "Safy, the fuck you *doing*?"

"I know. I know, it sounds bad. But it's different this time. We've been—we've been reconnecting, and it's been really, really nice."

Saari was silcnt a long timc. "You'rc a big boy, Safy. And I trust you know what you're doing. You've probably heard it from everyone else, anyway."

"Jesus Christ, have I," Matt said, and he must have sounded so exasperated that Saari started laughing.

"You know we all just want the best for you. Your family, me, the team. I'll be here for you no matter what."

Matt's throat felt thick, clogged with too much emotion. The two of them had had each other's backs on and off the ice for years now, and maybe he wouldn't have Saari at his side next season, if the team didn't want to re-sign him, or decided to trade him. It was strange to think about, having to start all over again on a different team, with guys who didn't know him at all.

"So yeah," he said, instead of what he was thinking. "Wherever you want to meet, tell me the time."

"And…you know, you can bring him if you want, huh?"

"Yeah?"

"Yeah," Saari said, and then laughed again. "Haven't seen that prissy little asshole in years, anyway. Be good to catch up, I guess."

"Hey," Matt said, warning.

"Ohh," Saari drawled, "you got it this bad already?"

Matt hung up on him.

* * *

"Saari's back in town," Matt said, as he helped Aiden with the dishes after dinner, "he wants to get lunch."

"Okay," Aiden said, blinking. He set his dish in the rack and thought, *focus on the things you can control.* "I mean, I can keep myself busy, it's not a problem."

"You should come. I told him you're here."

"You…you did? How did he…"

Matt laughed. "Well, first he said, 'Safy, the fuck you *doing*,' but that's pretty much everyone, right?"

Saarinen was one of the first teammates Matt had let in on the secret, back during their first go at this thing. It had been McCall first, of course, and then Saarinen and Grenier, all four of them inseparable back then. But McCall was playing in San Jose now and Grenier had retired.

Still, Matt's closest teammates had been surprisingly chill about the idea of their friend falling in love with a rival goalie and it had been fine when he'd come to Montreal, although Aiden had to assume that after things flamed out, their loyalty to Matt had won out over any positive feelings they may or may not have had toward Aiden. Of course, not everyone could hold a grudge like Miles Safaryan. He hoped.

"Are you sure?" Aiden asked, still skeptical.

"Yeah."

Which was how Aiden ended up at a crowded bar on Saint-Laurent, seated across from Eero Saarinen. He still looked exactly the same, huge and broad-shouldered but baby-faced as hell. There were laugh lines at the corners of his eyes and mouth, but that was really the only discernible difference; on the ice, the only discernible difference was that he wore an A.

Matt stood at the bar putting in their drink order.

Saarinen and Aiden looked at each other for brief seconds from the corners of their eyes, and the rest of the time, literally anywhere else.

"Soooo…" Saarinen said, drawing out the word into multiple syllables.

"So," Aiden agreed.

"Here we are."

"Yes."

"Sorry about the concussion."

"Water under the bridge," Aiden said, although he had an immediate flash of memory at the words. Saarinen crashing the net and into him; opening his eyes and realizing he was on the ice and had lost at least a couple of seconds unconscious. "Sorry about knocking you out of the playoffs four times."

"Water under bridges." They both glanced down at their hands. Then Saarinen looked up at him slyly. "You going for the peikko look, buddy? You don't have the Amirov charisma to really pull it off."

Aiden didn't know what a peikko was, but he could guess from context. His old teammate had had the wild hair and beard of a mountain recluse, a little like some sort of supernatural forest demon. Aiden managed to keep from touching his own hair, although he was suddenly conscious of it in a way he usually wasn't. The table was shaking a little, the plates and glasses rattling in time with his bouncing knee.

"I haven't had time to get it cut," he lied. He had nothing but time.

Saarinen glanced over at Matt at the bar and sighed. His English was fluent at this point in his life, barely a hint of an accent. "Look, I'm just gonna ask you,

Campbell, like, whatever you're doing here, to please don't fuck it up for Safy. This is maybe his last season here, and I want to make it a good one."

"I'm not—I'm not trying to fuck it up. I'm going to be gone by the time the season starts, anyway. He'll be fine."

Saarinen's eyebrows shot up and his mouth opened, but whatever he was about to say was cut off when Matt came back, a pint glass in each hand and another one balanced precariously in the crook of his arm.

"Safy," Saarinen said brightly, "what you drinking?"

"Oh, I don't know, whatever Dieu du ciel they had on tap." Matt set the glasses down on the table. He looked from Saarinen to Aiden, who both looked back at him, studiously expressionless. "How're you boys doing?"

"One hundred percent," Saarinen said. "Totally sick."

Aiden wasn't entirely sure what that meant, but he didn't argue. He took a deep breath and settled in for at least an hour of trying to act normal for Matt's sake, smiling when he didn't feel like smiling, and trying not to think about the fact that Saarinen probably hated him.

As they walked home later that afternoon, Matt said, "It was really good to see Saari again." It wasn't a short walk, but Montreal summers weren't as humid as New York, and it wasn't uncomfortable. "Makes the season feel real, you know?"

"Yeah," Aiden mumbled.

They were both full from lunch and a little buzzed: Saarinen had had a lot to say about training in Lappeenranta over the summer. He and Matt had almost sixteen years' worth of history and in-jokes built up between them. Aiden had felt strange watching them talk, the easy way Matt smiled, the way they had that casual trust and camaraderie a captain and his alternate had. Lunch took them almost to dinner, drinking the whole time.

It hadn't been as awkward as Aiden had thought, although he would sometimes catch Saarinen looking at him when he thought Aiden wasn't paying attention, like he was trying really hard to figure something out.

Aiden was quiet on the walk home, thinking about Matt going back to camp, with his team, with purpose, and how it was going to feel on that plane ride home.

"What's up?"

"Just thinking," Aiden said.

"Don't do that, come on."

Maybe it was just because they were both a little drunk, but Matt reached out and brushed a strand of hair away from Aiden's eyes, and Aiden didn't stop him. After a second, Matt dropped his hand like Aiden burned him, and started walking a little faster. "Come on. It's getting late."

"Right behind you."

Aiden blinked when he received a text from Allison Kuhn, the Libs' beat reporter at the *Times.* She wasn't so bad as far as reporters went, but he hadn't spoken to her since she had done the long piece on his retirement.

It had been a career-spanning retrospective interview that was so difficult to get through he'd had to excuse himself in the middle of their conversation, go into the restaurant bathroom and puke up the lunch they'd been sharing. Stared at himself in the mirror for a long time before tilting his mouth down to the sink to try to rinse the taste out before going back out.

He unlocked his phone to see what she wanted.

Hello, Aiden, I hope retirement is treating you well. Do you have a moment?

I've got nothing but moments.

Would you care to confirm a story for me?

What do you mean?

Sources say you've been living in Montreal. I'd love to talk if you have time for a phone call.

Aiden set the phone down on the table. He felt—not as bad as he thought he'd feel, given everything. He was honestly surprised it had taken this long, given the nature of social media and the Montreal hockey market and the fact that he had just been going about his business like everything was normal, when it wasn't.

Ten years ago, he would've panicked.

Today, he thought, *Nobody cares. Nothing really matters. We're all going to die one day.* The thoughts he had always had in the net, during a bad game, when he'd let in too many bad goals and needed to reset himself so he wouldn't get pulled. The thoughts he'd had after he had ended things with Matt, when he was searching fruitlessly for something he had never been able to find with anyone else.

Today, he just felt tired.

He had to talk to Matt.

When Matt got home, Aiden told him what had happened, asked, "What do you want to do?"

Matt shrugged. "She's your beat reporter. It's your life. It's up to you, buddy."

"I mean—" Aiden wasn't sure how to phrase it appropriately. "You're the one who's still playing; it's your city. I don't know what she's planning to write, but if you don't—uh—want everyone to know about us, or to make assumptions..."

Matt just looked at him for a very long moment. If you didn't know him as well as Aiden did, it looked like a very bland, unreadable expression. But Aiden did know him. He knew him well enough to immediately recognize that Matt looked tired and a little annoyed.

"Aiden, I never cared about anyone knowing. The fact that you did is at least half of the reason we broke up the first time."

"I—" Aiden started to protest. But Matt was right, of course. He looked down. "I'm sorry."

"Like I said. I understand why you weren't ready. But I would have done it. And I don't really care if you do it now."

"You're still going to get so much shit on the ice—"

"Baby, you really think I can't handle that? I'm thirty-six fucking years old—some kids chirping me isn't going to be the end of the world. It never was."

"It's not always just chirping," Aiden said, thinking about some of Gabe's stories about juniors, about the way he'd been ready to fight anyone and everyone when he'd first come up to the show. "Even now, it's not."

"I'm a grown-ass man. I can handle it."

"So you want me to—?"

"I'm saying, Aidy, you can do whatever you want about it. Confirm, deny, I don't care. The puck's always been in your zone on this one."

"Okay," Aiden said, and exhaled a breath that felt shakier than he was expecting.

"So think about it."

He watched Matt, still in only his basketball shorts, folding laundry on the couch. It was one of those weird moments where Aiden could see how life could be, if he just let it keep going like this, if he didn't fuck it up.

The kind of life where he could come home to someone folding laundry on the couch, half-naked, completely at ease with Aiden's presence there during this mundane moment. The kind of life where he'd have clothes to fold, too. The kind of life where he wouldn't have to worry about someone getting the wrong idea if, when they went out for dinner after, he wanted to touch Matt in public. The weight off of his shoulders that would be. To be able to live the kind of life that he actually wanted to live.

He was retired. He wasn't playing anymore.

He had nothing to lose except Matt.

Again.

I think I'm going to come out, he said to Gabe, a little later.

uh what? now? i mean congrats but. wow?

I mean, I think there's probably going to be an article no matter what I do. So I wanted to do it first. And I guess I wanted to tell you first.

oh...so this IS about safaryan then.

Aiden stared at his phone. He always had trouble interpreting tone, and it was worse when it came to text messages. Yes. Indirectly.

Gabe took a while to respond, but finally said, lmk

if u want advice on how to *handle* it. ive been doing this for like 7 years.

Thanks, Gabe.

yeah. ur welcome. tell safaryan he better not fuck this up.

I'm not sure what there is to fuck up. The season's starting soon and I don't think he'll want me to stick around, so I'll probably be back in New York by then anyway.

soupyyyyyyyyyy...jesus fucking christ man

Aiden didn't know how to answer that. So he didn't.

The phone call with Allison wasn't as awkward as he thought it would be. Unlike some of the Libs' old beat reporters, she'd always had a way of phrasing her questions that didn't sound antagonistic, and she knew when to stop pushing when it was too much.

Aiden was honest about living in Montreal with Matt, although he was vague about their actual relationship. He still didn't know what to call it, and the last thing he needed was to humiliate himself in the local paper. He said something like, "Now that I'm retired, it's a good opportunity to see friends I haven't caught up with in a while and warn them off of retirement, you know?"

"You're *friends* with Safaryan? I wouldn't have guessed."

Aiden hesitated. "We started off on the wrong foot, back in that first playoff series, but we've been good friends for a long time. He was at my first Cup day."

Allison paused but didn't push back too hard against that explanation. They chatted a little bit about Montreal, about various things Matt and Aiden had done and seen together, how much he liked running in Mont-Royal and the Lebanese bakery. About skating again. They talked about retirement, and how it was difficult to feel like you had a purpose, and that Aiden still didn't know what he was going to do with the next chapter of his life. The entire conversation only lasted about half an hour.

Aiden felt jittery during the whole thing, wondering if and when it would come up, but it didn't. He could probably just let it go, end up with a puff piece about how he was spending his retirement puttering uselessly around Montreal, doing the sad major junior reunion tour with various buddies from the past.

He thought about how tired Matt had looked when he'd said, *The puck's always been in your zone.*

Nobody cares. Nothing really matters. We're all going to die.

"Uh, Allison…"

"Yes?"

"So there is something else, uh, I should probably tell you."

He'd done this a number of times throughout the years. First to one of his teammates, accidentally; then to his parents and Hannah, on purpose; then to various other teammates, as the need arose. He hadn't realized, when he was a kid, that it was going to be such a continual process. And when he'd started coming out, he'd thought it would get easier each time, but that hadn't been the case at all. Sometimes it was pretty easy but mostly it just *sucked.* This was one of those times. He'd always hated being the center of attention, even though by nature of his position, he ended up there anyway.

Aiden cleared his throat. He could feel his leg practically vibrating, the hand that wasn't holding his phone clenched in a fist, his fingers twisting together. "Because I'm retired now, and I'm kind of tired of, you know, keeping that aspect of my life secret, especially since I'm fairly sure that it's why you reached out to me about this in the first place." Allison, true to form, waited for him to continue. "I'm gay, and, ah, if you want to include that in your article, you can."

"Thank you for sharing that with me," Allison said, in her pleasant, nonjudgmental reporter voice, and immediately pivoted into follow-up questions.

Aiden wiped his sweaty palms on his shorts and did his best to answer them.

She didn't ask for details about his relationship with Matt, and he didn't offer any. People could assume what they wanted to assume. And they probably would.

II.
FALL

CHAPTER FIVE

September

Matt had known Aiden had done the interview, but he didn't realize when it was published until a September morning right before camp was due to start, when both of them were woken up by Aiden's phone buzzing non-stop. Even after Aiden turned off the notifications and sound, they both knew they were still coming.

Matt gave him some space to answer the ones he needed to—telling his parents no one had forced him to do it, responding to congratulations from Gabe—but hung around as long as he could, just in case.

"Is it okay?" Matt asked.

"Well, it's mostly just family right now. And friends. Just heard from a few guys from my juniors team I haven't spoken to in years." Aiden looked down at his phone, like he couldn't entirely believe it. "Almost all of that's been…really nice. And my social media's been mostly fine, but there's a lot of 'why can't they just play hockey' sort of shit starting to pop up."

"Ignore it."

"Honestly, if that's the worst it gets, I'll be satisfied."

Eventually, Matt had to get out the door and start the

drive to Brossard if he wanted to hit the ice for practice in time. Aiden hovered in the living room as Matt was packing his bag, and Matt looked up at him. He wanted to say something that would accurately convey the tightness in his chest, but he couldn't. "I still can't believe you actually did it."

"You can't? Because I *did*."

"I know, it's just…we spent so much time arguing about what this would look like the first time around. It's just weird as fuck, you know?"

"Yeah," Aiden said, dry as anything. "Fucking tell me about it."

"Sorry," Matt said, softening. He stood, and Aiden bent down to grab his bag, follow him to the door. "Are you okay, Aidy?"

"I'm fine. I think. It just feels weird."

"It *is* weird."

"It's not as weird as it would've been if I did it while I was still playing, I think."

"Probably not. You don't mind that I'm not saying anything official yet?"

"No," Aiden said, so quickly that it actually startled him. "I don't want things to be worse for you than they're probably already going to be. I'm sure people will speculate anyway. You don't…there's no reason to stick your neck out for *me*."

He looked at Aiden again, trying to gauge how he was feeling, what was going on. But Aiden looked the same as ever, in his oversize hoodie and worn-out leggings, the arms of the sweater hanging over his hands. It looked a little bit like he was trying to retreat into his clothes, and Matt couldn't entirely blame him, even if it wouldn't have protected him from what would probably be a shitstorm of both supportive and unpleasant comments. Aiden had always been like that: when things got too much, he just sort of…shut down.

Aiden looked back at him, brown eyes unreadable, and finally said, "Hey, you're going to be late if you don't get out of the door soon. I'll have shit ready for you when you come back."

"Okay," Matt said. "Thanks."

He wasn't sure what it was going to be like, heading into camp. He was fairly sure that his teammates would put two and two together, even the ones who hadn't been in on the secret the first time around. Whether or not they'd have the balls to bring it up to him was another story altogether.

In the end, Fourns was the one to do it, cornered Matt in the locker room as they were all pulling on the last bits of their gear. "Cap? Got a pretty interesting notification from the *Times* this morning."

Matt exhaled. "Yeah."

"So it didn't say it exactly, but I can read between the lines. This guy's living with you?"

"For now."

Fourns' eyes crinkled at the corners in the way they often did when he was making a joke. "Man, an *American*? I thought you had better taste than that."

"He's from Winnipeg," Matt said mildly.

"Yeah, but he played in America for years. He's got a house there. It's basically like being American. Also the amount of times we've met them in the playoffs… esti de câlisse de tabarnak."

"Is it going to be a problem with the guys, Fourns?"

The goalie shrugged. "Doubt the younger ones have figured it out. I'm not even sure if Jammer figured it out, or whether he's just letting you tell him on your own time. I just had some thoughts and I wanted confirmation. Is it gonna be a distraction this year?"

"Not if I can help it."

"Then we're good."

Matt thought about telling him that the knee was probably going to be a worse distraction than Aiden could ever be, but he didn't want to freak anyone out. He just had to take it slow, stretch before the games and not push himself too hard at practice. Maybe he'd be able to get through the season unscathed.

Out on the ice, he felt a little more at ease. Jammer waggled his eyebrows at him under the visor, but didn't say anything, and Matt was grateful for the ambiguity. The thought of the whole team getting into his business before he was even truly sure what he wanted to say about it, how he wanted to handle it on his own terms—it was a little overwhelming.

It felt better to skate hard, to listen to the short, barked instructions from the coaching staff. By now, the drills and exercises were familiar to him, and he was able to do them almost in his sleep, do them with half of his attention and enough left over to correct the rookies if any of them got out of step. It helped that the three new forwards were focused and competitive, even with Manny Singh buzzing and chirping around them.

"Manny, go easy on the rooks," Matt said, during a break in the drills.

"Hey, I'm just making sure they have what it takes," Manny replied, "especially if the line rushes are any indication of how things are gonna shake out during the season. Looks like I'm gonna have Koski as a center and Cormier on the wing, huh?"

"Looks like it."

"I just have to make sure they can hang," he said, his eyes wounded. "If I'm out there talking shit, they're gonna get it back, you know?"

Matt would have pinched the bridge of his nose if he wasn't wearing gloves. "Go easy on Cormier. That kid is *shy.*"

"Throwing him into the water's the best way to get him to swim," Manny said, with a little sniff. "That's what my dad did to me when I was a kid."

"You know, this explains an awful lot about you, Manny."

Manny shot him another wounded look. "Low blow, Safy."

"Don't dish it if you can't take it, eh?"

Manny made an exaggerated face, nose wrinkled. "*Fine*, I'll go easy on Cormier. Koski's fair game, though."

Koskinen, who'd been skating by, came to a sharp stop and looked from Matt to Manny, a little suspiciously. He had very pale gray eyes that were a little unsettling when he looked at you directly. "Are you talking about me?"

"I've been telling Manny to go easy on you and Cormier," Matt said. "He likes to talk. You don't have to listen unless it's about on-ice stuff."

"I have three older brothers, Cap. Nothing he says will bother me."

"See?" Manny said, smiling his toothless smile. "A perfect match."

Matt shook his head—even this made him feel more settled, more like himself—and said, "Enough. Any more time chatting, and Coach Roy will be on all of our asses. Come on. Back to work."

* * *

Aiden had told Matt that he was fine, and strangely, he was. The world didn't feel any different, he was still breathing the same, sitting in Matt's condo the same, feeling a little rudderless the same.

Well, this was definitely something he would have to talk about with Dr. Gauthier.

To keep himself busy while Matt was at camp, Aiden started meal prepping, which he had generally taken over as his responsibility.

Today he was making a definitely not Jain-approved version of the comfort food his mom used to cook at home, particularly on days he'd not been feeling well, or was coming home from after time away in his billet. Dal bhat, the fluffy rice perfect in its steamer pan, the dal liberally spiced but sweet with jaggery; bateta nu shaak, with the addition of chicken for extra protein, even though Aiden could feel his mother's anguish across the entire continent. Wheat rotli, carefully rolled into perfect circles every time. That mechanical ability was also thanks to his mother, who'd hovered like a hawk over his and Hannah's shoulders so many times to correct their motions.

They weren't finicky recipes, especially because he'd made them so many times, but it was time-consuming. It was something to do, at least.

It helped that Ellie had been emailing him, so while he waited for the timer to go off and put the pot into the oven, he wrote back to answer her questions about positioning and which skates she should get for her sixth birthday.

The correspondence had been a little halting but rewarding: she obviously needed help with some of the writing. Sometimes Jess sent him a picture of Ellie during her practices, small and determined in her pads and cage, and Aiden smiled and saved them to his phone. She had picked 31 as her number for the new team. Aiden's old number.

Aiden felt—something—about it.

By the time Matt returned from Brossard, the condo smelled like home in Winnipeg and Aiden was chopping up the vegetables for kachumber. Matt's eyes widened, briefly, when he breathed in. He sighed happily, slouching up behind Aiden to rest his chin on his shoulder.

"Did you read it?"

"Probably won't," Aiden said, pausing mid-chop so his shoulder didn't send Matt's teeth through his lip. The guy just had *no* sense of self-preservation.

"Why not?"

"Don't want to know what she's got to say about it. Don't want to see the comments."

"Fair," Matt murmured, and pressed his mouth against Aiden's neck. It wasn't really a kiss, just a light touch, a declaration of his presence. "You know you can read the article without reading the comments. It was a good one. Thoughtful. Circumspect about certain things. I know she was interested in the Montreal angle, and *me*, but she didn't really go into it as much as I thought she would have."

Aiden shivered anyway. "She probably got the juicier angle from me coming out. Either way, I *know*, but if the comments are there, it's hard not to look. So I just avoid the whole thing altogether. Anyway—how's camp?"

"Fucking weird, knowing it's maybe the last one. Can only imagine what it was like for you."

"I didn't really know it was the last one at the time. I wasn't… I was focusing on the things I could control."

"Jesus, baby, you really *haven't* changed."

"I have, though, I came out—"

"You have, you have, I didn't mean—fuck, Aidy, I'm sorry. Are you okay? With that."

"I guess so. It's kind of a relief, in a way, to…not have to tell anyone anymore because everyone will just know. But also I just *really* hate people paying that much attention to me for things that aren't hockey."

"Yeah," Matt said. He nuzzled his face into Aiden's neck again, and Aiden's skin prickled at the sensation of Matt's beard against it. He had to fight the urge to tip his head back, lean against the solid weight of Matt's body. "Well, I'm proud of you. Anyway."

"Thanks," Aiden said, a weird, swooping feeling rushing through his stomach. The timer went off. "You should, uh, let go of me. I need to finish making the rotli."

While he waited for Aiden to finish, Matt helped out by washing the accumulated dishes that had built up in the sink. Aiden thought, again, how nice it was to have this: working together in the kitchen, knowing where Matt was going to be so he could pivot around him. The synergy of not needing to tell Matt what to do to help or ask him to move out of the way. It was almost like being on the ice again, knowing where the defender would be waiting for the pass when Aiden scooped the puck up from behind the net. It was almost like it was years ago, but better, because it felt more grounded. Real.

And it was worse because it had to end so soon.

Aiden sighed. "It's going to be weird going back to New York when—"

"What?" Matt cut him off, and his hands stilled where they had been scrubbing the sauté pan.

"Uh, when I go back to New York, when the season starts?"

Matt turned away from the sink to take Aiden's arms in his hands, holding tight right above the elbow. His palms and fingers were still wet and soapy, and Aiden's shirt slowly absorbed the water. The sensation was so uncomfortable against his skin that Aiden almost couldn't pay attention to what Matt was saying, which was, "Why would you—why, do you *want* to go back?"

"Wasn't that the arrangement? I would come for the summer? Well…the offseason's almost over."

"No, you should stay, if you want to."

Aiden stared at him. But Matt didn't look like he was joking, his hands still digging into the muscle of Aiden's arm. Aiden said, slowly, "I won't have much to do when you go on the road. I'm just going to be in your condo, you know. Taking up space. You're going to be busy with hockey, you won't want me around."

"Yeah, but I won't be on the road the whole season, right? You're still figuring your shit out, so there's no rush—you don't have to go, right?"

Aiden felt, for the first time in a long time, like maybe he was missing something. "I mean… I guess?"

"Okay. Okay."

And then Matt's mouth against his, the kiss insistent, the kind of fervor Aiden hadn't been expecting at all after the quiet night in they'd been having. A surprised noise escaped before he could stop it, but as always, it was easy to give in, easy to allow himself to not think too hard or look too long at anything in front of him. Matt started tugging Aiden's wet shirt over his head, and he forgot, for a moment, about dinner, about the fall, about anything else except Matt's hands on him.

welcome to the club officially, Gabe said. it wasn't a bad article right? allison's been pretty cool to me too. so if u had to do it that was a good way to go.

Aiden was in bed, aggressively spooned by Matt, who was fast asleep, his hot breath condensed in the space between Aiden's shoulder blades, half of his body folded on top of Aiden's. The weight was comforting. Thanks, bud. I still haven't read it. Probably won't.

ur so weird. i love reading news abt myself.

That's because you're vain as hell.

i know it's part of my charm. r u gonna be back in nyc anytime soon?

I don't know.

i can get home opener tix for u. itd mean a lot to me if u could make it.

I haven't been to a game since I retired and I don't know how it's going to feel, but I'll do my best.

thx, soupy. i miss u. its not the same practicing with knighter.

You got this, buddy.

In response, Gabe sent him back a litany of heart emojis in the Royal's blue, white, and red.

In the end Aiden was both surprised and not surprised that things died down quickly after the article came out. There had been a bit of a stir when it was first published because there were so few players, active *or* retired, who were out. It wasn't as notable now as it would have been if he'd done it at twenty-six and still an All-Star; and he didn't look himself up on the internet anyway. He got an occasional shitty comment on his social media, but he had gotten used to those anyway after an off night and a hard loss.

Easy to ignore.

It was strange when Matt started playing the preseason games. It was the first time in a long time that Aiden was actually at home watching a game solely as a spectator and not as a child hoping to get there one day or a potential competitor observing his opponents.

The Royal usually played most of their exhibition games at home, but Aiden couldn't bring himself to go. It was one thing to get out on the ice himself, another thing entirely to watch Matt on it, to hear the bite of skates on the ice and the players shouting to each other, and to have to watch it from the stands with plexiglass between him and the thing he'd loved most in life. He still had to make up his mind about whether he was going to the Liberty's home opener, but that was a problem for another Aiden.

"I'm sorry," Aiden said, as Matt got ready to drive over to l'Arène and Aiden helped him grab the shit he had lost track of last minute: his keys and phone and wallet. "I'm, uh, not ready to go to a game."

"It's fine," Matt said, distracted, as Aiden handed

him his keys; pressed a quick kiss at the corner of Aiden's mouth. "You have a standing invite."

And then he was gone, and Aiden was left alone to figure out what to do until game time. He tried to read one of Matt's books, because the title was *Meditations*, which sounded like something he would be into after years of mindfulness and meditation to keep himself on an even keel for games. But it turned out that the book wasn't about meditations as much as it was some Roman emperor going on and on about the things his family had taught him and things he was thankful the gods had given him. Aiden found himself reading the first page about ten times before giving up. It was hard to imagine meditating going very well with this guy; that was an awful lot of fucking words. He put the book back on the shelf.

But he still felt restless and unsettled. Instead of trying to read more of the book, he decided to work on actual meditation. Aiden put down his yoga mat and stretched his legs out. By the end of his exercise, he was loose and marginally relaxed, although he immediately tensed up when he realized it was almost game time. He had an intense internal debate about whether he was actually going to watch it, but ultimately, he ended up fumbling for the remote.

Aiden watched most of the game from the floor, alternately draped over the coffee table to get a better view of the TV, or fully prone, like he was when Fournier let in a goal and the Royal fell behind. He felt overwhelmed: there was the anxiety of his personal investment in Matt doing well, the anxiety of watching the game, thinking about the way he'd have positioned himself when they showed shots of the goalies, missing the way he could just shift into that calm zone with no thoughts, just reaction. Now it was like the worst of both worlds, with his brain screaming at him about rebounds, and he wasn't even in the same building to do anything about it.

During the intermission, he lay down on his back between the couch and the table, closed his eyes, and worked on an actual meditation, no thanks to Marcus fucking Aurelius. The rest of the game was less exciting. Matt tied it up about fifteen seconds into the second period. One of the Morin twins slammed home a rebound for the insurance goal five minutes later, and the Justice couldn't get it back.

Aiden still felt like he couldn't entirely breathe until the time ticked down and the final horn sounded, and the win song played over the rink speakers.

He hadn't watched Matt in a postgame interview in years, and only a few since he got the C in his fourth season with the Royal. It was a little surreal. Aiden could see the same person in him, the way Matt always talked about hockey back when they were kids, but now he had a little gray at his temples and his beard, now he had the added weight of responsibility when he answered questions.

There was no smile when he said the necessary things, just that familiar intent look in his dark eyes and a curious angle to the way he cocked his head to better hear the reporters. It was just an exhibition game, but it was also a reminder that the season would be starting in earnest.

Aiden hauled himself to his feet. Matt would be home in a few hours. He should get his head together.

And the rest of him.

CHAPTER SIX

October

Matt didn't play all of the preseason games, generally. He was as much of a sure thing as the Royal had: at this point, he was their longest-tenured player. It wasn't a responsibility that he took lightly, though, so when he was in the games, he gave it his all.

This year was different. The knee was going to be an issue going into it, he knew that already. An entire summer of rehabbing it after the last injury hadn't seemed to have made much of a difference. If he said something to the trainers, that would lead to more tests and potentially to more time out, which he couldn't afford, especially so early in the season itself. No: he was just going to have to play and manage it as best he could and lean on Toradol if it got unbearable and ask for Percocet if it got worse than that. There would be time for tests later on and maybe another arthroscopic procedure in the offseason if he needed it.

And in the meantime, it was good to get back on the ice.

"Man, you fucking love playing Toronto, don't you,"

Jammer said, as they were dressing for the fourth game against the Justice. "Kind of a traitor to Ontario, huh?"

Jammer was American, so he hadn't been raised around the cult-like atmosphere that surrounded the Justice even when you lived over an hour's drive away from Toronto. Matt *had* been raised watching their games, but as soon as he'd been drafted by the Royal it hadn't even taken him a second thought before he folded up all of the jerseys he'd worn as a child, packed them away at his parents' house, and embraced a new side of the rivalry.

"Jesus, Jams. Do I give you this hard of a time when we play in California?"

"*I* don't have any childhood loyalties," Jammer said, with a little sniff. "My parents mostly watched football."

Matt surveyed the room: Manny, teasing Rémi Cormier about the game last night, where his skate blade had snapped and Matt had had to drag him like a drowned kitten by the neck of his jersey across the ice to the boards; Jack Crane, deep in concentration in a pre-game meditative routine that reminded Matt of nothing so much as Aiden in his youth even though Jack wasn't a goalie; Saari, taping his stick with the single-minded, repetitive movement that looked almost robotic. It hit him again how much he was going to miss them when he had to retire. And again, thinking about Aiden, at home, how much he probably missed this, too.

It wasn't an easy loss: sometimes, Matt thought the ones that they lost by only one goal were worse than the blowouts, just because they'd been so close to winning. Matt pushed himself too hard and by the end of the game, he was feeling it. Tested out the knee as he hopped over the boards and felt the ache.

"You good, Safy?" Saari asked, because of course he'd noticed.

"Fine," Matt said. "Just have to give it some time, I think."

It had been years since he'd felt so eager to go home after a game. When he had still been married to Emily, especially toward the end, there'd always been the vague feeling of dread, knowing she'd be upset about something, knowing it was one more thing he'd have to manage. And after Emily, it had just been quiet night after quiet night, not even admitting to himself how lonely it had been.

And now there was Aiden, waiting for Matt when he got home, like he'd been lurking by the doorway and trying to seem like he hadn't actually been doing that.

"Hey," Matt said, unable to keep the slightly goofy smile off of his face. "Were you lonely, baby?"

Aiden's face flushed darker, and he looked down. "Uh, no, it's just—sometimes it's not easy watching you playing and wishing I could be out there, too."

Matt couldn't help wrapping Aiden in his arms immediately. "I'm sorry. I wish—I don't know. Is it weird to think that maybe it would have been nice if we could've played together, that last year?"

"We would've been miserable," Aiden mumbled into Matt's hair.

"Maybe we would've reconnected then, too. Maybe it would've worked out. I wouldn't have been able to resist you."

"Do you ever think about that?" Aiden pulled back a little, so he could look down at Matt. "How long it's been. How I still feel exactly the same goddamn butterflies in my stomach when I look at you now as I did that first handshake line."

Aching knee and bruises and exhausted body aside, despite the fact that it was close to one in the morning, he felt himself stirring. It was impossible not to, when Aiden was looking at him like that, when Aiden's lean body was pressed against his, when Aiden's eyes were hot and intent and needing. Matt pressed his mouth against Aiden's neck, savoring the little sigh it earned him.

"We don't have to…it's late, I know you're exhausted…"

"You could fuck me," Matt suggested, "I could make you do all of the work this time, eh?"

Aiden sounded like he had surprised himself into laughing, short and wheezy. "If that's what you want."

"Yes," Matt said, "please."

Sometimes, when Matt thought about the way sex with Aiden had evolved over the years of their relationship, it did his head in a little. When they'd first started hooking up, it had been a surprise to both of them for different reasons. Matt because he'd assumed he was straight; Aiden because he hadn't ever met anyone who could compare to hockey. But the attraction had been electric and undeniable. It had been awkward at first, figuring out what they liked and what was comfortable, before Matt had cracked the code and learned the two most important things about Aiden: he was kind of a freak, and he was incredibly flexible.

By the time they'd broken up, they'd tried pretty much everything together. Matt had learned things he'd never thought he'd learn about himself, like the fact that even though he had never intended to *hurt* Aiden, Aiden really, really liked it when Matt hurt him. That was the thing: it hadn't just been about sex, it was about the way Aiden was so vulnerable and cracked open when he let Matt do those things to him, the way that Matt could be the same way with him. The way he couldn't be with anyone else, for so many fucking reasons, not the least of which was because he was the captain of the Montreal Royal.

They might not ever have been good at talking about their feelings, but their bodies could do it for them.

And now that they were back together, Aiden still sounded and felt the same underneath and on top of him, around him or inside of him, but there was that ache in Matt's chest, the thought of all of the other men over the years who'd been able to see Aiden like this, who'd been able to look up in bed and see his huge brown eyes focused only on them.

It was so fucked up. It wasn't like Matt to be that possessive. Aiden wasn't a *thing*, wasn't something he could own. But it was like now that Matt had Aiden back in his life after so long, now that Matt had Aiden back in his bed, focused on taking Matt apart, piece by piece, everything was all mixed up in his head, a combination of joy and pain so intense he couldn't even begin to untangle the mess.

It didn't help that Aiden was deep inside of him now, slow, even thrusts driving all logical thought out of his head. All he could think about was how much he had missed this, all he could think about was how good Aiden felt, draped over his back, like he couldn't bear to put even an inch between them. Matt was so intensely aware of every little sensation: the slick sweat between them, Aiden's hands wrapped around Matt's wrists, pressing them down into the bed, his short, bitten-off fingernails digging into Matt's skin. They were barely moving and Matt's whole body was on fire anyway, building up to the climax.

"Matty," Aiden mumbled into his neck. His mouth was hot and humid, barely coherent. "Matty..."

"I'm so close, please, Aiden, come on—"

Aiden gave him what he wanted—he had always been good at taking direction—a slow, inexorable grind of his hips, and it was like Matt's whole body was enveloped and penetrated and covered, and all of his senses, everything around him, were just *Aiden*. And then Matt was crying out, unable to even feel embarrassed about how desperate he sounded. It took him a while to collect his thoughts after, flat on his stomach in the sticky spot on the bed.

Aiden pulled out and sat back on his legs, but Matt couldn't move, rolled over onto his back and threw his arm over his eyes because looking at Aiden, just then, was almost too much for him to bear. The only sound was his own ragged breathing, panting and short, and Aiden's, just as breathless.

"Gabe wants me to go to the home opener," Aiden blurted out all at once, like he was trying to stop himself and failing.

"Oh—okay?" Matt managed, still gasping and disoriented. He blinked, trying to process Aiden's words.

Aiden was saying, "I'm going to go. I bought tickets."

Matt pushed himself up onto his elbows. It felt a little like Aiden had slammed him in the head with a two-by-four. He wasn't entirely sure whether it was the orgasm and the aftershocks, or because of what Aiden had just said. "I...okay. Are you coming back?"

"It's a round-trip ticket?" Aiden said, slowly.

Matt covered his eyes with his hand, couldn't even look at him again, for an entirely different reason this time. His fingers rubbed at his temples. "Aiden, I sometimes wonder if—"

"If?"

If you ever think about what you're saying. If you ever know how deeply you've fucked me up. If you know how much I fucking love you, if you know how terrified I am of losing you again.

Like he could ever say any of that. He'd chase Aiden right back to New York, like he'd bought the plane ticket himself. He hadn't had a plan when he'd invited Aiden to come to Montreal, but he'd hoped—he'd *hoped* that once Aiden was here, once he was reminded how good he and Matt were together, that he'd understand. That he'd want to stay. That they could build something new here, just the two of them. Matt was remembering that no matter what he thought, Aiden's mind never worked the way his did. "Never mind. I'm going to shower."

He could feel Aiden's eyes on him as he got out of the bed and went into the bathroom.

Aiden never thought it would be strange to be back in New York. Even after spending an entire summer in Winnipeg, it always felt like coming home the minute the plane's wheels hit the tarmac at JFK.

Aiden had been in Montreal for two and a half, almost three months. New York didn't *not* feel like home now, but he was conscious of the difference in temperature from Montreal, the familiar New York smells that weren't present there, the way even the crowd of people walking toward the cars from the baggage claim had a different feel and tempo than it did in Montreal.

New York had an attitude that no other city had: it just couldn't be replicated.

Aiden didn't need to collect his bag; he had only brought enough clothes for an overnight stay. He went outside to catch a cab. He frowned, a little, thinking about the way Matt had reacted to this trip. Maybe it was because Aiden was going to one of Gabe's games but hadn't gone to any of the Royal's? He sighed. He'd probably have to end up getting over himself and getting into the rink again with Matt, one way or another. The thought made him feel a little nauseous, so he tried not to think about it.

He focused on the things he could control: the rest of his day.

He stopped at home first, but everything was exactly the way it was when he'd left it. The plants in the kitchen were all dead, but that wasn't surprising since he'd forgotten to ask anyone to check in on them. They were withered and rotting, shriveled pathetically in their pots. He dumped them, soil and all, into the trash, and texted Gabe, I'm home.

yaaaaay, Gabe wrote back. wasnt sure if u were actually gonna make it.

Aiden sighed and didn't answer immediately. Eventually, he said, I got tickets, so you don't have to worry about that. See you after the game?

yes!!!!! its a date!

Aiden got to the arena early enough that he could go down to the lower bowl to watch the team warming up before the game. All of the guys crowded around to put their gloves up to the glass and say hello, and Aiden waved back, smiling like a crazy person but unable to stop it. Even if he couldn't play, it was just—good to see them all again.

Pears made a big show out of throwing his stick over the glass, like Aiden was a fan who was actually begging for it. Aiden, grinning, rolled his eyes and handed the stick over to a kid standing next to him instead.

They didn't look any different warming up than they did the last season he was playing: the way the cycles of cap and contracts had been going, the team was on the young side again. With the exception of Amirov, who would probably be playing well into his forties and consistently took contracts below his worth just to stay with the team, and Pears and Brooksy and Simmer, there were a few guys in their mid-twenties and a lot of guys who were either rookies or close enough to it that it functionally didn't matter. It reminded him a little of his own first few seasons, when it seemed like the majority of the team had never actually been to the playoffs.

Before Aiden was about to head up to his seat, Gabe skated over and pressed his glove up against the glass. It was his first season where he'd started on opening day as the official number one, and he'd stepped up admirably to the challenge. Aiden could see him grinning behind the cage, confident and happy and with his whole life ahead of him.

"Fuck 'em up," Aiden said, using the pregame encouragement that had always seemed to help Gabe the most.

Gabe smiled even wider, if that was possible, and punched the glass. Aiden punched back.

Aiden watched the game from center ice, near the top of the bowl. He wanted to have a good eye on everything that happened, and usually the fans willing to pay for those seats were at least fairly serious. The couple on his right side kept glancing sideways at him with wide eyes, like they couldn't really believe he was there, but they let him watch in peace, which was all he cared about. The older man on Aiden's other side probably didn't even recognize him, which was even better.

Matt was probably in the air by now, but Aiden texted him anyway. Call me tonight? He didn't get a reply, but he wasn't too worried about that.

It was a good game. They were playing the Seals, and it was one of those nights where everything clicked. The crowd energy was good, roaring at the right parts, booing San Jose when they managed to get a good shot on goal, mocking applause when Brooksy drew a penalty and the Libs went on the power play. Aiden had even missed hearing people yelling *shoooooot*. The passes connected and the shots might have been hitting the post, but the Libs outshot the Seals by a good margin. It wasn't a heavy workload for Gabe, but he made the saves he needed to make, calm as ever, never out of position.

Maybe it was the nature of the game, but Aiden felt less anxious than he thought he'd be. He could let himself get swept up in screaming for his teammates, in being one fan of eighteen thousand. It didn't feel as bad as he'd thought it would feel, and that was at once a strange thing and a relief.

That was, at least, until someone in the broadcast operations room realized he was there, and they showed him on the Jumbotron at least three times. The little caption underneath said *Aiden Campbell, won two Cups for New York*. Aiden waved, awkwardly, and then tried to pretend he didn't see it at all.

Gabe stole the team a shutout, and after the horn sounded, he came out to do a quick loop to acknowledge being awarded first star.

Aiden made his way down to the dressing room, ready to say hello to all of the guys and congratulate Gabe, but paused outside when he realized that they were still in the middle of the press scrum. He definitely didn't want to step in the middle of *that*. Instead, he lurked in the doorway, accepted some hearty back-pats from the trainers and equipment guys as they milled in and out, and hung back to listen to Gabe taking his moment in the sun.

Gabe was, of course, incandescent. He hadn't had a chance to shower yet, and his curly hair was damp, the flush of exertion still visible on his cheeks and throat, the imprint of his helmet in his forehead. He was beaming; it was a magnetic smile that made you want to return it.

"Yeah," he was saying, "I mean, of course it's always great to win a home opener, even better to do it with a shuttie. I always try my best, but it feels great when it works out."

Someone asked a question that Aiden couldn't hear, and Gabe's smile broadened, if such a thing were even possible.

"Well, yeah. I asked Soupy to come, because it means a lot to me to be able to share these moments with him, and I was really glad he was able to make it. I told him this summer; I wouldn't be half the goalie I am today without his mentorship. You know. Both on the ice and off. I learned how to keep my focus and control my emotions on the ice from him and—"

He paused to listen to the reporter's question, cocked his head to the side.

"Yeah, so I'm sure you've read the news. This might be the first you've heard of it, but Soupy was open with me from the beginning. And when I say it meant a lot to me, I don't know if I—you know as a gay kid in juniors, it was really hard growing up being one of the only ones there, and without that many role models in the show, wondering how it was going to be when I finally made it. I came up ready to fight and Soupy told me I didn't have to, because he'd already done a lot of that work for me. And it was just like this huge weight off of my shoulders, not having to worry about my teammates and whether they'd be cool or not, and to just finally have that guy I could look up to, who *knew* what I was going through and who I could talk to about, um, anything. It meant the world to me. I hope one day I can be that guy for some kid who needs it, you know?"

Aiden's throat felt tight, thinking about the hours he'd spent with Gabe, how rewarding it was to see the results of that mentorship before him, but before he could fully appreciate the moment for what it was, Pears slid his arms around Aiden's waist and pressed the entire length of his body, still damp and stinking from game sweat, against Aiden's back and his clean clothes.

"Hi, Pears."

"Buddyyyyyy," Pears crowed. "You made it."

"Wouldn't miss it."

"Oh boy, young Gabriel's gonna be beside himself," Pear said, nuzzling his cheek against Aiden's shoulder.

"You're, uh, kind of beside yourself."

"Well, we all miss you, bud. Especially me, your intrepid captain. Viens à la maison!"

"Did you Google translate that just so you could use it tonight?"

"So what if I did?" Pears asked, and he finally released Aiden, only to whirl him around and hug him again. "You knew what I was saying. And we *do* miss you."

"Yeah," Aiden mumbled. "Well. Good game, bud."

Pears patted him on the shoulder. "Well, we had two goalies to play for today. All right, I gotta hit the showers, but I'm sure Gabe will be thrilled to talk to you. You sticking around?"

"Flying back tomorrow."

"Right, right," Pears said, waggling his eyebrows suggestively and then holding out his fist to bump. Aiden obliged, but didn't say anything encouraging; eventually, he seemed to give up on waiting. "Okay, bud. See you around."

Aiden watched him go and lurked by the door, waiting for the hero of the hour. He made small talk with Amirov and Simmer, then with some of the younger guys as they filed in and out. And then Gabe, showered, fresh-faced, and beaming.

"Soupy," Gabe said, "I'm so happy you made it."

"I'm really happy I came." Aiden was surprised to find it was true. "You were lights out tonight, buddy."

"Thanks." Gabe smiled his dimpled smile. He rolled a knot out of his shoulders, pointed down the tunnels, and asked, "Walk with me?"

It was a walk Aiden had done over a thousand times before, from the depths of the Square out and down the street to the parking lot the players used, not too far away. He could probably make it in his sleep. He still let Gabe lead, followed behind him and tried to put together his thoughts into some kind of a coherent sentence. He kept replaying in his head Gabe's little talk to the reporters, the warmth in his stomach fighting the way his head immediately countered it with *you don't deserve any of that praise, you haven't been here for him at all—*

They were outside now. Most of the other Libs were already gone; the Seals' bus was gone, too. It was a crisp October evening, the ones Aiden always used to love because it meant a break in the humidity of New York summers, because it meant the season was well and truly underway. You couldn't see any stars with the lights shining all over the city, but sometimes he used to pretend.

Gabe turned to him and said, "Soupy—Aiden—" and although Aiden waited for him to say something, instead of going on, Gabe just threw his arms around Aiden in a hug that was so tight he could hear his own ribs creak. He returned the hug, looser, his hand patting Gabe's back.

Gabe said, "I saw you standing there during media. I meant everything I said, you know, you mean *so much* to me. I couldn't have done any of this without you."

"You would have," Aiden assured him. "You're Gabe Walker, bud, you can do anything."

"No. I mean, I would have won games. I would have figured it out eventually, you know? But it wouldn't be the same."

"Really, kid, you were great. And you would have been great with or without me. Brave with or without me."

"Stop calling me a kid," Gabe mumbled into Aiden's chest. His hand smoothed over the bunched muscle of

Aiden's shoulder. "I'm not a *kid*. I'm twenty-two, I'm the starting goalie, I'm an *adult*."

Aiden thought about what he was doing at twenty-two—the starting goalie, winning his first playoff series against his childhood idol, completely failing to live alone and cook for himself, fucking things up so badly when he'd first gotten called up that Ward had had to explain to him *again* that friendships were relationships too and that he couldn't hold himself apart from the team like that even if he *was* the goalie, accidentally falling in love with Matt and not knowing what to do with all of those feelings—and thought, *oh, kid.*

Instead, he said, "No, you're not a kid."

"I just wanted to... Soupy, I love you, like, I really do—"

"I love you too, buddy," Aiden interrupted him, taking a step back and putting a little distance between them.

"No—Aiden, I'm—"

"Gabe, come on, don't say anything you can't take back—"

"No! I'm not going to be a *coward*, okay? I just got a fucking shutout on home opener night, and I'm in love with you, okay? I *am*. And I have been for a long time. And I know you're living in Montreal now, but you never said exactly what's going on with that whole thing, and you're really important to me, and I couldn't fucking live with myself if I didn't at least *try*."

"Gabe, I..." Aiden rubbed his eyes with the heel of his hand. "I'm sorry, I don't—that's not—that's not love."

Gabe took another step back. He did look very young in that moment, mouth turned down in a frown, his eyes sad and furious, his arms folded over his chest. “Don’t tell me I don’t know, because I do. I mean, I understand if you don’t feel that way about me, but, but I know what I feel, and you can’t fucking tell me otherwise.”

Aiden wondered what it must be like, to be that young and that sure of yourself. He was nearing forty and hadn’t managed to develop an ounce of that confidence. “You’ve always been that way. I’ve always envied that about you.”

“But you don’t—you don’t love me.”

“I *do*, it’s meant so much to me to be able to teach you, help you ease into the starting spot, to watch you grow up—”

Gabe made a rude noise, somewhere between a snort of disdain and spitting. “I didn’t mean like *that*. That doesn’t count. *Grow up,*” he said, and rolled his eyes. “Grow up. Jesus Christ, grow *up*. Aiden, I’m a *man*, what will it take for you to realize that?”

“Gabe—”

“Are you still in love with him?” Gabe demanded, looking up at Aiden with his furious brown eyes and his full mouth pressed into a thinner line. “Are you?”

Aiden took a deep breath. “Yes.” It was the first time he had said it out loud. Admitted it to anyone else. “I just don’t know…if he loves me, too.”

Gabe visibly deflated. He was still close enough that Aiden could almost feel the heat of his body, like all of the frustration and fury was just radiating off of him into the cool night air. Aiden was surprised he wasn’t steaming.

"You love him, but what are you, like, hoping to accomplish up there? Are you going to *say* anything?"

Aiden stared at him. "What?"

"Are you going to say anything? Do anything? About it?"

"Uh…"

"Oh, my god," Gabe said, horrified. "Are you seriously just gonna let things *go*?"

"I hadn't thought about it."

Gabe took two steps forward. His warm, soft mouth pressed firmly against Aiden's. He was close enough that Aiden could feel Gabe's long eyelashes brush his face, like the ghost of a kiss there, too. It was fairly innocent, as far as kisses went. It was a declaration, or some kind of benediction, more than anything romantic.

Aiden was too surprised to respond, but it was over almost as soon as it started, and then Gabe was patting the side of his face.

"Soupy, I love you, and so I'm gonna tell you this: you need to figure your fucking shit *out*. Like ASAP. The rest of the world can't wait for you forever. Even Safaryan can't wait for you forever."

"Gabe, I'm sorry, I didn't mean for this to end this way."

Gabe smiled, rueful and not a little sad. "Don't be. It's not the end. I knew what I was doing. Nothing ventured, nothing gained, you know? Think about that when it comes to your boy in Montreal. Ugh, it's fucking late as hell now. You need a ride?"

"No, I'm gonna catch a cab."

"Okay. Well. Thanks for coming to my game, Soupy. That shutout was for you. I *do* love you."

"I love you, too."

Gabe threw his arms around Aiden in another one of those bone-crushing hugs, ran his hand through the hair at the nape of Aiden's neck and tugged. "And get a fucking haircut, you know you're not *actually* Jesus, bud."

And then he was gone, leaving Aiden alone in the middle of the street, wondering, not for the first time, what the hell just happened to him.

Aiden spent most of the night tossing and turning in his bed, which was usually comfortable but currently felt both foreign and unusually empty, like a hotel bed. It was like without Matt, even his home wasn't home anymore.

He gave up around four in the morning and just got up, ended up spending the rest of his time going through his closet and picking out a few cold-weather items to bring back to Montreal with him. When that was done, he threw the clothes he was wearing yesterday in the washing machine, because they still smelled like Pears' game-day sweat and it was making Aiden feel itchy and anxious.

Pears showed up along with the sunrise, bearing breakfast sandwiches and coffee from the bodega around the corner from Aiden's house, and a small carton of oat milk. Aiden, who had no food in his house anymore, accepted it, even if it was decidedly *not* what he usually ate in the mornings. They mostly ate in silence, because the combination of soft egg and bacon and toasted bagel meant that if you weren't careful your breakfast ended up squirting all over the plate. Pears licked his fingers when they were done, heaving a huge sigh of satisfaction. They talked a bit about the Libs' preseason so far, how the new kids were settling in, how the new coach had been in the offseason.

Pears adjusted his snapback, rubbed his eyes a little sleepily. "It's good to have you back in New York, bro, even if it's just for a day."

"It's good to be back."

"Really? Seems like you're pretty settled in up there."

"No… I don't know. I thought it was only for the summer, but now it's just… I don't really know."

Pears poured some oat milk into his coffee, tasted it, made a face and then dumped another large spoonful of sugar in. "Okay," he said, and took another sip. "But why don't you know?"

"I don't want to, you know. Ruin what I've got right now."

"If you don't, you're gonna make it worse."

Aiden pushed his own coffee mug back and forth between his hands. "I did start going to therapy, you know."

"Huh. Are you, like, actually paying attention? Are you actually trying?"

"*Yes*, Isaac."

"Okay, okay. But I'm just wondering, like, what are you actually afraid of?"

Aiden shrugged. "If I fuck it up again, I come back here, and then I'm just…right back where I started. Right now in Montreal, it's not easy, but I have kind of a life, and I'm helping Matt's niece with goalie things, and Matt is—Matt. It's just easier dealing with everything else when I have that—when I have him."

"You can still have all of that shit, man. What's actually stopping you from making it real?"

"Me?"

Pears laughed his honking laugh. "Now there's that therapy insight, buddy. But what are you gonna *do* about it?"

"Thanks," Aiden said, sourly, put the oat milk back in the fridge and did not answer the question. Mom had texted him a few times—she must have been watching the home opener and saw him on the Jumbotron—but he didn't answer. He wasn't sure what he was going to tell her. He had gone home, and it was good, but also a mistake. A huge, huge fucking mistake. And no, he wasn't coming back to Winnipeg.

That'd go over really well.

He took a cab to JFK.

sorry abt the whole last night thing, Gabe said, while Aiden was waiting to board. if it made u uncomfortable.

Nothing to apologize for, buddy. And I'm sorry too. About everything else.

ok. just as long as were clear.

Aiden sent him a thumbs-up emoji.

When he deplaned at YUL and slouched his way through the terminal, the first thing he really saw was Matt waiting for him by the baggage claim, texting someone, a little frown knitting his eyebrows together. When he looked up and saw Aiden coming toward him, his face immediately changed: a broad, open smile.

Aiden had a moment of vertigo when he realized that it *did* feel like coming home.

Except it wasn't his home, and he was too chickenshit to make it his home, and he didn't even know if Matt would want that, anyway, and—

"You okay?" Matt asked.

"Yeah," Aiden lied.

CHAPTER SEVEN

October

Ever since Aiden had gone to New York and then come home again, he'd been acting funny. Matt had watched the media availabilities the Libs had posted after the game, seen everything Gabe Walker had said about Aiden.

Whatever Aiden had said or thought about his relationship with Gabe, it was pretty clear that the kid was in love with him. To be honest, Matt couldn't really blame him. He'd known Aiden when he was young and dumb and pretty; Gabe had gotten to know him when he was old and sad and hot. And basically his teacher. So it wasn't really surprising.

But whatever had happened there, it had really messed Aiden up, like all of the progress he'd made with Matt had just evaporated into thin air. He was quiet for most of that night, didn't even say anything when they got into bed together. Instead he lay still on his side of the mattress for a few minutes before he rolled over and wormed his way into Matt's arms, a worried little frown creasing his forehead.

"Are you okay?" Matt asked.

Aiden mumbled into his chest, “I’m fine,” and shuddered a little when Matt ran his fingers through Aiden’s hair.

They fell asleep like that, and every time Matt woke up overnight, Aiden was still clinging to him, like a particularly anxious koala.

“Everything cool?” Matt asked, over breakfast the next morning. Aiden usually cooked for them, but he had taken a while to get out of bed, so eventually Matt put together bowls of coconut yogurt and fruit and granola and scrambled some eggs. And then Matt had had to go back into the bedroom, haul him out of bed and drag him into the kitchen.

“It’s fine,” Aiden said, but he was clearly still a million miles away. He swept his spoon through the yogurt, frowning.

“I have to go to Brossard for morning skate,” Matt said, after a bit. “You gonna be okay here?”

“Yeah.”

It wasn’t convincing, but Matt had to go to practice, so he left it there. By the time he came home, Aiden was still on the couch, head tucked low against his chest, the TV blaring in the background while he scrolled through something on his phone. He looked fucking terrible, that sad downturn at the corner of his mouth, dark circles under his eyes. The fingers of his free hand twisted around each other, one of the anxious, repetitive motions he made sometimes and were a clue that he was either upset or overwhelmed.

“Aiden,” Matt said, pausing the TV, “seriously, what’s going on?”

“What’s going on?” Aiden’s mouth seemed frozen halfway between a smile and a grimace. “Nothing.”

"You've been in kind of a strange mood since you got home from New York, and I was... I don't know, I was just worried." When Matt looked down at Aiden, Aiden licked his lips, and Matt had a second where he thought briefly about kissing him and just forgetting the line of questioning. It was easy to do that, but he needed to stop doing the easy thing.

Aiden laughed, although there wasn't much humor in the noise. "You really don't need to be concerned, all right? Not really your business, I'm totally fine, just, you know. In case you didn't notice. Not exactly the world's most cheerful person one hundred percent of the time."

"So it's okay for my business to be yours but not the other way around?"

"Matty...that's not fair."

"What happened to *talking* to me?"

"Yeah, well, I don't want to talk about this."

"Clearly something's wrong and I—don't want you to be unhappy."

"News flash, Matt, you really don't have much control over that."

"All right," Matt said, and pulled himself away.

They sat on the couch, watching each other. Aiden still had that deer-in-the-headlights wariness in his eyes and Matt knew that even though it wasn't visible, he was frowning. His mouth twitched. There was something strange happening on Aiden's face, worry that flickered across before he could stop it, and Matt wondered whether the other shoe would finally drop.

Whether the thing he was waiting for all of this time would happen and Aiden would finally say, *I'm going back to New York for good.* He wondered whether Aiden was feeling that same strange combination of worry and sick relief. But Aiden was just curled in on himself, looking miserable, and Matt thought about all of the times Aiden had freaked out on him when he'd really just needed—

"Aiden."

"*What*, Matt?"

"Get up."

"What?"

"You heard me. Get. Up."

Aiden stood, as gracefully as he ever did, and it was only the way his mouth twitched that really betrayed how nervous and upset he was. "Look, Matt, I'm—"

"No. Don't say anything."

Aiden stared at him, wordlessly. He looked ridiculous, his face stricken and his cheeks red, still in his bare feet and boxers, muscles tense like he was trying to decide whether he wanted to fight or flee. He looked down at Matt, still on the couch, and swallowed hard. He crossed his arms over his chest like he was trying to cover his nipples, and Matt thought about saying *no, move them*, but this stuff was always a delicate balance, not doing too much too soon.

"Kneel on the floor."

Aiden blanched, head whipping back like Matt had slapped him. "What?"

"I told you not to say anything, Aiden."

Aiden's face flushed darker, and he hesitated for a second before his body did what Matt had told him to do. He moved so gracefully, even now, years of goalie training and acrobatics on the ice in every easy line of his body. Aiden knelt on the floor, next to the coffee table, awkward and embarrassed. His eyes flickered from Matt's face and back down: if he was a prey animal you would've been able to see the whites. But Matt could see the line of his dick, slowly getting hard under his boxers.

"Spread your legs a little wider. And sit up with your back straight. Balls of your feet on the ground. Don't let your weight rest on your heels." He felt like his voice was admirably steady, considering the way his hands were clenched in fists, the way he was so fucking nervous about doing the wrong thing and making something worse. The way he was always so undone by Aiden's easiness, his malleability, that his skin felt like it was already prickling with goose bumps.

Aiden shifted. He did what he was told, eyes turned demurely down to the floor. In that position, he couldn't just rest his weight on the ground, but had to actively brace himself up. If Matt made him stay there for a long time, it would probably get a little painful. He licked his lips, a bit nervously, and said, "How long…?"

"Until I tell you to get up."

"Or you'll what?" Aiden asked. He looked up suddenly, unable to look away from Matt's face. His eyes were very wide and darker than usual. Fishing, now, trying to rile Matt up.

"Stop asking questions, Aiden."

Something about the way that Matt had said it sank in, because Aiden didn't ask or say anything else, just knelt on the floor where Matt had left him and watched. Matt turned the TV on and sat back against the couch, propping his feet up on the coffee table, very carefully not looking at Aiden even though he was so aware of him that he felt like an electric current ran between them. He couldn't keep from looking sometimes, checking from the corner of his eye every now and then to see how he was doing.

Aiden was admirably still, like this was just another hockey exercise. The position had to have been awkward, knees bruising against the cold hardwood floor. Matt admired the visible strain in his thigh muscles. He had muscular legs, not as thick as a skater's, but defined in a way that Matt could see every line of them. Aiden might have been in fantastic shape, but human beings weren't made for this kind of sitting. Not without cushioning. Not for this long.

But he kept at it, his posture ramrod-straight, and Matt could hear the way his breathing slowly calmed, got deeper and slower even while his face flushed red. Knowing how Aiden must have felt all twisted up inside, the pain of the position and the humiliation of it, of the desire to please—it was fucking heady, almost a little like being drunk. It took almost everything he had in him not to look, not to stare like a beggar at a feast, to keep focused on the TV.

Aiden wasn't any better. Matt could see him, every little movement of his hands, every sideways flick of his eyes. Waiting. Watching.

Matt realized he hadn't even been paying attention to what had been on the TV, but the episode was over. He turned it off and went back into the kitchen to wash the dishes Aiden had accumulated across the course of the day and didn't look back. Didn't tell Aiden he could get up; didn't tell him it was over. He chanced a look over his shoulder and Aiden still knelt there, head bowed, just breathing.

He poured himself a drink of water. He considered dumping it over his head. He settled for splashing it into his face, blinking. It didn't do much to get his head together.

By the time Matt went back into the living room and sat down on the couch, Aiden was shivering a little. Matt said, "Come here," and then when Aiden started to stand, "I didn't say you could walk."

"Matty—"

"I didn't say you could talk."

The way Aiden looked at him, anguished and full of desire, eyes huge and dark, almost undid him right then and there. Aiden wasn't thinking about whatever had been bothering him anymore. All he was thinking about was Matt, all he was thinking about was what they were doing together. On his hands and knees, he crawled across the floor. It wasn't far, but he did it slowly, like every movement was at once a humiliation and an excitement, head bowed. The tension in his shoulders was fucking amazing, and when he was finally sitting at Matt's feet, Matt couldn't help himself.

"Aiden…" He reached out to touch Aiden's face, hand gentle on his cheek, fingers dragging over his lips, and Aiden made a little whine, unembarrassed, shaking with the force of trying to hold himself back until he was given permission.

"You're so good," he said, before he could stop himself. He sounded like he'd been bag-skated, breathless and clipped. "Not at the beginning, you never are, but you're…*god*, you're so—what do you want, Aidy?"

There was the unspoken question in the words: *Is this okay? Are* you *okay?*

Aiden licked his lips again. He was still almost naked, cock straining against his boxers, a little damp patch visible where it rubbed against the fabric. He looked tortured, like it pained him to say it. It was always this moment that Matt had fucking lived for, both figuring out what Aiden had wanted when he was too worried to say it or too fucked up to untangle it, and making him admit it.

"Can I take off your belt?" Aiden said, after a long quiet, and Matt could feel the breath between them, ragged but somehow at the same speed, like he was breathing in the air Aiden exhaled.

"My belt?"

"Please?"

"Yes."

With another one of those graceful movements, Aiden leaned forward carefully, deliberately. He unbuckled Matt's belt and started to tug it from the loops as Matt canted his hips up to help. It was just a regular leather belt, not particularly thick or wide, but it would do. Aiden folded it in half, tested the pull of it between his right hand holding the buckle and his left slipped through the loop, and then held it out to Matt. Nervous. Waiting.

Matt took it from him, slowly, not entirely sure about it but still wanting it so fucking badly. "Why do you want this?" he asked, his voice rough-edged even to his own ears. He wasn't sure, at this point, if he was asking Aiden or himself.

Aiden swallowed. "I want you to hurt me."

Matt knew it wasn't the whole truth. He'd spent literal years trying to figure out the whole truth. What it came down to was that Aiden wanted this and maybe needed it sometimes. And maybe he should have been working out his shit in other ways. But this would do for the moment.

"That's not really an answer." Matt traced the line of

Aiden's face again, this time with the edge of the belt. Aiden looked at him, shuddering, tormented with need and hesitation and a strange kind of affection. "Why do you want this?"

"I… I don't know. I just… I do."

Matt didn't know either, but he just did. Aiden was still watching him, all of the hesitation gone. He was kneeling between Matt's legs, his arms resting on Matt's thighs. "Will you, Matty? Please?"

The word rocked through him like *he* was the one who'd been hit, and he gave up on waiting. "Stand up," Matt said, and Aiden stood, stumbling a little at the rush of blood to his legs and toes. And Matt was on his feet too, arm held out to Aiden to lean on as he shifted back and forth, trying to get rid of the pins and needles. His hand gripped too tight, bitten-down fingernails digging into Matt's skin. It was kind of painful, but also kind of nice.

"Where do you want me?" Aiden asked, and Matt couldn't help it, learned forward and kissed him, messy and passionate, on the mouth. Aiden sighed into it, eyes slipping shut, and let Matt take him apart bit by bit, one hand tangled in Aiden's hair, pulling hard enough to make him hiss, the other still gripping the belt.

"The wall," Matt said, when he finally pulled away.

He felt in control and out of it, voice sandpaper raw as he watched Aiden stumble to the living room wall, found a little space between the tasteful prints that Matt had hung to make it seem less lifeless when he had been living here alone. Braced his forearms against the wall and bent forward so his forehead pressed against the green paint. Matt's hands fit like they belonged in the waistband of his boxers, tugging them down. Aiden was completely naked now, every inch of that ridiculous body exposed, and he was shivering.

"Aidy," Matt said, and Aiden shuddered again. Matt wondered desperately what the fuck he was thinking, but instead of asking, traced the edge of the belt over Aiden's skin. First carefully and gently, pulling away and touching him again. He could feel Aiden forcing himself to hold still, the muscles in his back so tense and his fists clenched with such anticipation that Matt thought he might actually break apart.

The first blow caught him on the left shoulder, hard and sure, and he gasped. The noise was loud, ragged, almost obscene. Matt knew he was good at taking it, especially when the belt was folded like this, didn't even have the full power of his arm behind it. Aiden shook under the force of it, the force of everything else he probably wanted.

When they were doing this, it was easy to fall into a kind of fugue state, arm moving on instinct. The second blow. The third. He was moving his arm, fast, so Aiden wouldn't know where to expect them, so the blows would fall from all sides. On Aiden's shoulders, his ass, his thighs, his biceps.

Matt felt him cringe underneath the force, his hands screwed into fists, his eyes squeezed shut. His body flinched, but he didn't move, just took the blows in silence, at first. It felt so goddamn good to do this, knowing that for whatever reason, this was what Aiden wanted and needed, and Matt could give it to him.

He focused on particular areas, the belt licking again and again on already tender parts of Aiden's body, drinking in the noises Aiden couldn't quite keep himself from making, gasps and whines and groans, stupid words, pure nonsense falling out of his mouth. Matt's name, over and over again, stupid endearments, a litany of nonsense about how good it felt, please, keep going, please, more, how much he wanted Matt to fuck him.

Matt should have been in control. He *should* have been, but it was impossible to do it when Aiden reacted like that, when Aiden was losing it under him, when his skin was straining and singing under Matt's hands, hot to the touch. Matt couldn't stop running them over and over the muscles of Aiden's back, tracing the thing he'd created with the belt and his hands alone.

"Matt…oh, *Matt*, I need…"

And somehow, he had already turned and fallen into Matt's arms, face buried in Matt's chest, every piece of him burning, beyond embarrassment, beyond almost anything. Aiden probably didn't even know what he needed, and Matt could barely get his head straight long enough to figure it out.

But when he shoved his hand down between them to wrap his palm around Aiden's dick, Aiden came immediately, just like that, from being forced to kneel and be flogged and then touched tenderly. He looked up and his face was an echo of what Matt felt: completely lost, felled by desire and stupid fucking feelings. Somehow, that made it a little better. Knowing he wasn't alone.

Fucking him after that was almost an anticlimax. They ended up on the couch, half-collapsed because Aiden's legs could barely hold him up anymore, Aiden on top of Matt, the two of them struggling to get him out of his pants. Aiden was like a drunk person, fucked up and clumsy as he leaned over Matt, who couldn't do anything except stare at him to see if he was okay, the only thing he could feel a maelstrom of need and terrible, painful fondness.

"Thank you," Aiden breathed, and in response, Matt dragged his fingers down the abused flesh of Aiden's back, and then they weren't talking anymore.

After it was over, Aiden lay on top of Matt, half-asleep. His weight felt completely relaxed, boneless and satisfied. Matt stroked his back gently, knowing it was probably still burning.

"Ugh, Matty," Aiden mumbled. "For someone who says he doesn't like hurting anyone, you're really good at hurting me."

"Unfortunately."

"No-o, not for…not for me."

Matt was quiet for a while after that, as their breathing slowed, sweat cooling to an uncomfortable chill. He said, "So do you want to tell me what was wrong?"

Aiden was silent too, before he said, finally, "I… I had a hard time going back to New York. It—it didn't really feel like home anymore. Too many things are changing. I'm just…not really where I wanted to be? In a lot of ways. And I'm just…frustrated, and I want to be better, and I don't know *how* to."

"You're doing pretty good as far as I can tell, Aiden."

"Thanks." He sounded frustrated still, like whatever he was saying wasn't enough. "I know I'm trying, it's just…"

"Aidy," Matt said, and rolled Aiden off of him so they were lying side by side on the couch instead. He knew his face probably looked stupid as hell. Way too fucking soft. Aiden couldn't meet his eyes. "Really, you're…doing just fine. From my vantage point. From one person who should probably have it figured out by now to another."

"Thanks. Matt. Thank you. I—really."

He didn't say anything, just looked down again and tried not to think about how badly Aiden was going to break his heart, when the time came. It'd have to be enough that he had him now.

The first roadie that the Royal went on after Aiden got back to Montreal was only to Toronto. An hour plane ride was barely even a road game, particularly when it was a matinee; Matt would be back at the condo by seven p.m.

Functionally, the day wasn't even really that different from a home game. The second roadie was to Vegas and Utah and St. Louis; Matt would be gone almost three days. Aiden helped him pack, even though it was the last thing he wanted to do.

He visualized the things he would do during the time Matt was gone: reorganize his clothes in Matt's closet, clean Matt's condo, rearrange Matt's entire library, go to the gym almost every day, run, work on getting his bread recipe to rise properly.

He *could* make this a positive experience. He *could* be alone with his own brain, and it would be absolutely fine.

Eventually it was time for Matt to leave for the airport. He crowded Aiden against the door, kissing him until the goodbye Aiden had wanted to say was completely forgotten. When Matt pulled away, Aiden looked down at him, his intent dark eyes, his familiar features, and he felt—whatever the feeling was when your heart jumped into your throat and choked you.

"You going to be okay?" Matt asked.

"Oh, yeah. Be nice to have some time alone."

Matt just looked at him, even-keeled and so kind that Aiden wanted to facewash him. "Good. Hey, I'll call you when we land, okay?"

"Sounds good," Aiden said, and took a step back so Matt could actually open the door.

And then it was just him, alone with his thoughts.

It wasn't so bad, at first.

Aiden killed time watching a movie and throwing together some dough for an overnight rise. Matt actually had a stand mixer, surprisingly. He'd said it was a wedding gift, but Emily never used it and didn't want to take it with her when she left. Aiden still preferred to knead the dough manually, just because it was calming to force it into shape with only his hands. To feel the roll of his muscles as he pushed it into existence.

His mother texted him to ask how he was doing, and what he was doing, and he guiltily muted their message thread. It was funny: he and his dad had bonded over hockey, and they were able to spend time together in that context, without ever talking about anything beyond those careful parameters. It was as real as anything else, but it was safe. His mom had been different, always eager to talk about his plans for the future and his personal life and how he was *feeling*. And now he didn't have hockey and couldn't talk to his dad about that, and he couldn't tell his mom anything about how bad that made him feel. *Funny* indeed.

By that time Matt had landed in Missouri, so that text conversation killed another couple of minutes as the team headed to the hotel before they went to the rink. Once that was done, Aiden made himself dinner.

There was still time to go before the game, so Aiden went out for a long run. He got back in time, aching and exhausted, to flip on the TV and watch the Royal lose in overtime.

"Sorry, Matty," he said to Matt, sometime around midnight, after Matt had gone through the usual post-game routine of exercise and shower and was safely back in the hotel. His eyes were already drooping, exhausted, and Aiden had a brief, sharp stab of wishing he was there in the hotel room, too.

"Win some, lose some," Matt said, yawning.

"Okay, you need to sleep. I'll let you go."

"G'night," he mumbled, out almost before Aiden ended the call.

Aiden spent most of that night awake, staring at the ceiling.

The next day was harder. He burned the bottom of the bread in the Dutch oven, and it was a rest day, so he couldn't even push his body beyond exhaustion at the gym or on a run. By the end of it he felt like he was practically vibrating out of his skin, furious and frustrated with his inability to keep himself occupied, with his inability to ignore the noise in his head.

By the time Matt came through the door, after two a.m., Aiden just happened to be awake, rolling out of bed as soon as he heard the key in the lock. He felt a momentary sense of disgust with himself—waiting for the door, like some kind of eager dog. Another moment after, the bone-deep relief when he went to greet Matt, who dropped his bags to take Aiden in his arms instead.

Disgust aside, he had the first good night of sleep since Matt left. And that had to be enough.

* * *

Matt had been playing games at l'Arène for a decade and a half. Even now, he hadn't gotten tired of it. The routine was the same every time: he got to the rink several hours before the game, worked out with the boys, made sure the rookies were doing what they needed to do and that he was there to answer any questions if they had them, made sure his knee wasn't going to give out on him in the middle of the game. Even though the equipment managers made sure that his gear was ready for him, he still checked all of it anyway, cut down his sticks the way he liked them, taped them to his specifications.

By the time he was ready to go out onto the ice for warm-ups, he'd been there, focused on hockey, for long enough that it was easy to drown out the rest of the noise in his head. But even with that focus he would always look up at the banners hanging over the ice: the numbers the team had retired, the banners from the twenty-six times the Royal had won the Cup. It was impossible not to play here and feel the weight of history.

He always stayed behind after the team filed off of the ice when they were done, heading back to the room to run through their final pregame routines. Another last moment to take in the atmosphere of l'Arène and the smudgy blur of fans in the stands. Usually he was the last one out here, but he had the little tingle at the back of his neck, the sense of someone behind him.

"Cap?"

"Jack," Matt said, without turning. "Everything good?"

"Yeah," Jack Crane said. "I was just thinking about how you always stay out here. I guess I should've asked why you do it sooner, huh?"

Matt glanced over his shoulder at the future hope of the Montreal Royal. "Well, you didn't really need to."

Jack's serious brown eyes crinkled a little at the edges. It wasn't quite a smile. He had made the team out of camp this year after being sent back for another year in juniors last year, but he hadn't quite gotten used to the major leagues yet, and it showed. "I'm going to need to learn all of the ins and outs eventually."

Matt looked back out at the stands. He couldn't see much from this distance, with the glare of the lights in his eyes. "What do you know about the Colisée?"

"I know it was where the Royal played from the beginning, until sometime in the mid-nineties when we moved to l'Arène."

"It was, and it was more than that. There was a history in the Colisée that you could feel. It wasn't just the building itself, it was on the ice, too. Teams used to say that when you played in the Colisée, you weren't just playing the men on the ice, you were playing the crowd, and the ghosts of all of those who'd come before them."

"Yeah?" Jack asked, skeptical, as he stared up at the lights. "More than *here*?"

"It wasn't just atmosphere or vibes, you know? They used to say that it was almost magic. A stick lift when you really needed it. That extra bit of a push when you were rushing for the puck. The referee's eye turned at just the right moment. It was the ghosts, giving that last small extra bit that they had, for us." Matt exhaled. Even now, talking about it, he got the little shivery chill, the joy of that history and the part he'd played in it. Not everyone got the opportunity to play in Montreal, and he had done it for so long.

"I didn't know you were so superstitious, Cap."

"It's hard not to be when you play here long enough. You see enough shit that it really...sinks in."

"So—the Colisée? The ghosts?"

"Right. The Colisée, and the history. So they say that when the Colisée shut down, got converted to shops and a theater and we moved to the new facilities, the ghosts didn't come with us."

"I heard about the curse. I never put much stock into it."

"The curse isn't just about the building—it was moving from the Colisée, trading Belanger out of Montreal, too—but they used to say that we'd never win a Cup until things were made right, one way or another. Either we made peace with him, or we brought the ghosts to l'Arène again with us somehow."

Around them, the bustle of the pregame routine: some of the guys were coming back out into the tunnel to work through their exercises; the equipment staff were rushing back and forth to handle problems and requests; the coaches were deep in conversation outside of their office. Above them, the hum of the crowd as people streamed toward their seats from outside and from below, where they'd been watching the team warm up at the glass.

"But *you* won a Cup," Jack said. "You won *two*. So what does that mean—the ghosts, the curse? It wasn't real after all?"

"I don't know. Before that season, it had been decades since the Royal had won a Cup. Since any Canadian team had won a Cup. I think... I don't know. I think about it sometimes. Was that enough? Are the ghosts still restless, or will they finally follow us home?

Did I do enough to cement my legacy here? Did I do enough for the city, when I'm gone…?"

It wasn't a thought that he could articulate well. Matt had thought about this, obsessively, over the years. The Royal weren't just a team, they were a history, a religion. The captains who had come before him hadn't just won one Cup or two Cups, some of them had won ten. The captains who had come before him were *legends*, men who'd made the sport what it was, men whose nicknames were still household names in Montreal. Matt had won the Cups, but it was just a drop in the ocean of history that made up the Royal's bloodline. He was reminded of it every time he went into the dressing room and looked up at their pictures above the stalls. He was reminded of it every time he walked through the halls of the arena or stood by the statues outside. He'd brought the Cup home, but what did it mean for the city, *really*? What did it even mean for him?

He'd always felt like he could or should do more. But he was running out of time.

Jack slanted a sideways look at him. He was slight for a hockey player, young enough that he was still growing into his lanky body, with the kind of posture that said "recalcitrant teenager" more than "superstar hockey player in the making." The posture didn't go with his attitude at all, serious and solemn like he knew what it meant that Matt was taking the time to talk about it with him. "This is the shit you have going through your head every time you're standing out here looking at the lights?"

"Sometimes. Not exactly this. But I think about legacy a lot. The history of the team and what that means to the city. And what I've built here, and what I'm leaving behind when I'm gone."

"You've built a good culture, at least." Jack's arms crossed over his chest, like he was shielding himself from the fans. "Even I could tell that, just coming in. And you had the Cup."

"It's important. The culture, I mean. Not just what you're doing with the team, and with the boys. But knowing about the men who came before you. The history of it. It matters to the city and to the fans, the same way that working at your French will take you a long way. I'm always...conscious of it, to some extent. It's a heavy weight. But it's an honor, Jack."

"You sound like you're trying to, uh, set up a will or something."

Matt exhaled again. He was conscious of the weight again, on his shoulders, on his knee. "I'm not going to be here forever. You and the rest of the rookies are going to have to carry the torch, you know?"

"But you're not...you're not retiring?"

"No. Not yet. I just don't know what the trade deadline's going to bring. That's something else you'll learn the longer you play. That a no-move clause is worth negotiating. Or you never really know your future."

"It's really hard to imagine you playing anywhere else," Jack said, with another one of those sideways looks.

"It's hard to imagine playing anywhere else," Matt admitted. "I've been here my whole career. I really thought I'd retire here."

"Well. You're not retiring yet, Cap. We need you out there on the ice."

Matt rubbed the back of his neck, looking again at

the white stretch of ice, the blur of red and blue and white in the stands, the glare of the lights. He dreamed that image, sometimes, he'd seen it so many times. "Maybe you do. Maybe you don't."

But he couldn't afford to be melancholy: it was time for the game.

Even this early in the season, Aiden was still punched in the face repeatedly by reminders that neither of them was getting younger. Every time Matt came home from a game, favoring his left leg, Aiden worried about it. Every time Matt mentioned, offhandedly, that he'd had an injection either during or before a game, Aiden *worried* about it. Every time Matt brushed off his concern, Aiden was only determined to figure out exactly what the hell was going on with him.

He remembered that Matt, like Aiden himself had during his playing years, tended to downplay his own discomfort. The knee was part of another series of injuries Aiden had missed over the decade of their separation. First a sprained MCL, then a tear, then a surgical repair. And then Matt pushing himself to get back on the ice a little too fast.

Aiden and his own shitty right knee could relate.

One night, Matt came home and winced when he sat down on the bed, not quite ready to fall asleep, body still amped up from the game.

"Are you okay?" Aiden asked, more because he wanted to know what Matt would say than because he didn't already know the answer.

"It's not great today." Matt grimaced. "The game and then the weather..."

"You're old enough that you have a bad-weather knee?"

"Always going to be younger than you, though," Matt said, and winced again when he pushed the heel of his hand against the knee.

Aiden frowned and slid out of bed, walked around to settle on the floor between Matt's legs. "Can I try something? This helps sometimes, when my knee's bad."

"What, a blowjob?" Matt asked, dryly. "I knew you were flexible, but…"

"Oh, you've got jokes tonight, eh?" Aiden's fingers were on Matt's knee, rubbing gently across it. "It's just a massage the trainers showed me. For scars and shit. And ligaments. Can I try?"

"Couldn't hurt," Matt said, finally. He let Aiden rearrange his leg for better access, clenched his teeth a little as Aiden started, but slowly, steadily relaxed under his hands.

Aiden didn't work around the knee for too long—the trainers had said five minutes at most—but he moved his hands to press against Matt's thighs instead, his calves. When he started, he could feel how tense Matt was, how knotted up every single muscle happened to be. His skin was hot and tight. By the time Aiden finished Matt had sunk into the pillows, liquid under his hands.

Matt's eyes were closed, and when Aiden paused, for a minute, he mumbled, "Jesus, that's good."

"Yeah?"

"Yeah, I mean—it's different than at the rink because it's…it's you."

"Did you tell them it's still bothering you this much, Matty?"

"No, I don't want it to be a thing, because of next season, my contract…"

Aiden looked down at him in the bed, his solid body, usually so strong and full of tension, completely relaxed. Aiden rested his head on Matt's thigh and rubbed his cheek against it. "I could do this for you more often. If you want."

"Yeah?"

"Yeah."

"I'd… I'd like that.

"But you should—we should—sleep."

"Get up here, then."

And he did, and as he drifted off to sleep bracketed by Matt's body, he did not think about next season.

It was a Saturday night at l'Arène, and the Royal had dropped a trap game against Utah. It had been the kind of game where nothing had seemed to go right: not Matt's passes, not his judgment, not anyone else's shots. Even Jack, with his normally lethal wrister and deceptive release, had been firing muffins into the Utah goalie's chest pads. The kind of game where Coach Roy came into the locker room immediately during the intermission rather than waiting.

Matt took the lashing stoically, the way he always did, but no matter how they tried to rally in the third, it was just too late. Afterward he rounded up Crane and Koskinen and Cormier, gave them a little chat about every team having a few bad games in the season. How you had to leave them behind and move on to the next one. They would have to internalize the lesson, particularly because they *were* playing the next night, a back-to-back before they had a break and then a travel day. In the major league, you couldn't afford to let a previous night's failures follow you to the next game. He thought about one of the sentences from *Meditations* and shared that with them, too: that time's a river, glimpsed once and already carried past us, but he wasn't sure if they really appreciated it for what it was.

By the time he was finished with everything, it was getting late, and Matt knew Aiden was probably waiting up for him at home. He was seized by the almost feral need to just get out of the building. To go home. To bury his face in Aiden's hair and close his eyes and not think about the loss or the next game or his aching knee or the contract he hadn't been offered or signed yet.

"Cap," Jammer said from behind him, "can we talk?"

"Yeah," Matt said, blinking. "Anytime, of course. You know I'm here for all of you."

"That's actually kind of the problem," Jammer said. His usually serene face was creased a little bit with a frown. "Let's walk and talk, huh?"

"Sure," Matt said, and followed him toward the players' exit to the garage level. They walked in silence: it was one of those cool October nights where he could feel winter trembling in the air already. Some of the guys complained about the harshness of the Montreal winters, but Matt had always liked them. They were bracing. Down here, they were sheltered from the worst of it.

"I was just thinking, you know?" Jammer said. "That you've been kind of, ah, disconnected. Is it the contract stuff? What's the deal?"

The only reason Matt didn't bolt immediately was because his car was right here. He could easily end the conversation whenever he wanted to by opening the door and getting in, no matter how rude it would be. "I don't know what you mean," he lied.

"Come on," Jammer said. He extended one heavy hand to rest on Matt's shoulder. Matt, who wasn't a small guy, was still dwarfed by Jammer's height and width. "I've noticed. Fourns has noticed. We're just concerned about you, you know?"

Matt didn't push his hand away, but he had to push down the sting of bile in his throat. "It's kind of complicated, Jams. A personal-life thing."

"Okay?" Jammer said. "I thought we were friends, though. If there's something I can do to make this season easier for you, I wanna know." *So you'll stay* was the unspoken undercurrent to the words.

"All right," Matt said. "You want to know? My ex-boyfriend who I hadn't spoken to in a decade moved in with me a few months ago and came out publicly even though that was pretty much at least half of the reason we broke up in the first place and I haven't fully gotten used to the idea that he's back and we haven't talked about the future at all and I was hoping he'd be feeling better by now but it doesn't seem like that's the case and I'm half expecting at any minute that he's going to bolt right back to New York."

Jammer blinked. "Well. That would explain things, certainly."

"I was trying not to let it affect my play. I don't think it *is*. Or at least, it's not the only thing. The contract negotiations are…"

"Not fun," Jammer agreed. He'd been to arbitration before, back when he was an RFA, and in a lot of ways that experience was even worse than what Matt was going through right now. In arb, you had the team laying out all of the reasons you sucked, and they didn't want to pay you before a judge. This was just a GM stonewalling Matt's agent. Jammer's dark eyes looked Matt up and down, like he was considering both the contract and the ex-boyfriend information. "Came out… you don't mean…"

"Yeah. Aiden," Matt said. "And he's not dealing with retirement very well. I was thinking about inviting him to karaoke night. Not that I have any idea if he'd like that. Not that I have any idea if the team would be okay with that."

Jammer's eyes crinkled at the edges in a little smile. "Cap, if it makes you happy? You know the team would roll out the goddamn red carpet for this guy."

Matt snorted. "Probably not the ones who were around for the first time. You think?"

"I don't know how to explain it to you, Safy, but all of these guys would go to war for you. I'm pretty sure they'll be chill if you want to bring your boyfriend to a team night."

They stood awkwardly, Matt's arms folded over his chest. "Ex-boyfriend."

Jammer rolled his eyes. "Come on. The guy's been living with you for *months*? This isn't a roommate situation, really, is it?"

"No."

"Then that's not your *ex*-boyfriend, man."

Matt wondered whether Aiden had realized this, or would agree with it, and thought that the chance was probably pretty slim. He sighed and ran his hand through his damp hair, pushing it away from his forehead. "I mean, maybe not. I guess that's part of why I've been so distracted. It's great. It's been…great. But it's also… I don't know. The whole thing is kind of overwhelming if I stop to look at it too long."

"My solution is usually to look at it as long as necessary, until it ceases to become overwhelming and merely becomes a fact of my life," Jammer said, his eyes crinkling up into a smile.

"Thanks. Very useful help. Will be implementing this one shortly."

"But seriously, Safy. If you were worrying about the team, I'll help make sure it's not an issue. Because it's not."

"Thank you." Matt was struck momentarily by an almost physical pain at the thought of having to play somewhere else, without the team he'd built up around himself over the years. "It means a lot more to me than I can really say, Jams."

"You don't need to. That's not why I said that shit. It's because we love you, you idiot."

Matt hugged him, briefly, one of those bro-type hugs where you pounded the other guy on the back. It was easier than trying to further discuss his feelings, even with someone as generally tuned into feelings as Jammer was. But Jammer didn't let him go when it was over, and Matt was forced to mumble into his shoulder, "Okay. Thanks. Listen—I'm fucking wiped, okay? I gotta go before I fall asleep at the wheel."

"See you at the rink tomorrow," Jammer said, and released him from the hug.

Aiden was asleep when Matt got home, and he took a second to look at him in the bed, peacefully asleep and illuminated only by the sporadic lights from outside. Some of the dark circles under his eyes and the hollow shadows in his face had started to fill in, and he was just so fucking beautiful, long eyelashes fanned out against his cheek. Matt stripped as quietly as possible in the dark, trying not to wake him, but Aiden's eyes opened groggily when he got into the bed and peeled the covers back so he could get under them, too.

"Matt?"

"Sorry, baby," Matt mumbled, pulling the covers back over both of them, "I was trying not to wake you."

"Mm, don't apologize," Aiden said, still half-asleep, shifting in the bed so he could wrap his arms around Matt's body, tuck his head into the hollow of Matt's throat. "I was trying to wait up for you, but..."

"I'm here now."

"Yes." It was more a sigh than a word, the heat of his breath against Matt's neck.

Matt did what he'd wanted to do so badly earlier: bury his face in Aiden's hair, inhale the familiar, comforting smell of him. It didn't matter whether his knee fucking hurt, whether he was probably going to have to do another injection before practice tomorrow, whether the contract situation was uncertain or whether he was going to broach the topic of introducing Aiden back into team activities. All that mattered was Aiden in his bed, a warm, comforting body against his, the only anchor he'd ever needed.

He was asleep before he even realized it.

One of Aiden's promises to Dr. Gauthier was that he would try to give things a chance without immediately dismissing them, which was probably at least three-quarters of the reason he ended up outside of a karaoke bar on the Main, his hands shoved in the pockets of his jacket like that alone could protect him from the awkwardness he could already feel heavy on his shoulders.

The other reason was that Matt had looked at him,

with an expression so hopeful it was almost sweet, and asked, "Will you please come?"

And Aiden, even though his brain was yelling, *no! no! absolutely not!* had nodded, dumb, and said, "Sure."

"Thanks for coming with me," Matt said, as he tried to blow some warmth into his hands. "It means a lot to be able to, you know, bring you to team stuff again."

"Yeah, of course," Aiden said. He was still staring at the door like it was the barrier to a pit of lions. In some ways, it was. The one positive note was that Saarinen was one of the few guys still on the roster who knew Aiden back before he and Matt broke up, before they had to deal with the aftermath. So most of them probably didn't want to kill him on sight the same way the majority of Matt's teammates *that* year probably still did. That didn't mean he was looking forward to it.

"All right," Matt said, "it's just a team bonding night, no pressure."

"Of course. Do your thing, Matt. Don't worry about me."

It was dive-y inside, dark with only paper lanterns above the grimy tables to illuminate the space. The tables themselves were sort of crowded in the small space left between the bar, the wall and the fairly large stage in the background.

Matt squeezed Aiden's shoulder, and murmured, just loudly enough for him to hear over the din of the crowd, "Thanks, baby."

Aiden waved him away and wandered a little deeper into the bar itself as Matt went to greet a crowd of the rookies, lurking awkwardly near one of the tables.

Aiden looked around. He never thought he'd be glad to see Eero Saarinen, but his life had taken him to such weird places that it was almost a relief when he caught sight of him by the bar. He nudged his way through a crowd of regular bar patrons and Royal. He recognized a few of the older guys—Morozov, Lee, Fournier, Singh, Ayer, the Morin twins—and their young superstar in the making, Jack Crane. He didn't know any of them as well as he knew Saarinen, though, so that was where he made his beeline.

"Buddy," Saarinen said, and pushed a shot glass toward Aiden. "Here, take this. I can order another one. You look like you need it more than me."

It was clear liquid. Aiden took it and drank. Just vodka, neat. "Thanks. I got the next round for you."

Saarinen raised his fist and tapped it gently against Aiden's. "Deal."

"Whose idea was this?"

"Oh, it was all Safy. We do this every year, around the beginning. It's not as expensive as the rookie dinner, but same thing, you know? Humiliate the rookies, let some of the old guys have their day with the songs of their youth. If you can get Fourns to stop singing Backstreet Boys, I'll buy your drinks for the rest of the night."

"*You're* an old guy."

"Yeah, it's pretty sick. Just wait 'til Safy and I take our turn."

Aiden tried to imagine Matt doing karaoke every year. "*Does* he sing?"

"Not until the end of the night when we bully him into it."

"I don't think I'm drunk enough for this."

"There's still time, buddy."

Aiden ordered them another round and slid one of the glasses across the bar to Saarinen.

"Hölökynkölökyn," Saarinen said, lifting the glass to him.

"Hol—"

"It's like cheers. Hölökynkölökyn."

"Hölo—"

"*Hölökynkölökyn.*"

Aiden lifted his glass, too. "Hölö—hölö—fuck it," he said, and did the shot.

Saarinen laughed and drank one, too.

Aiden could do this. Aiden could definitely do this. He just needed to drink more.

By the time Aiden was drunk enough to process the fact that he was at a karaoke night with Matt's teammates, everyone had loosened up a bit. True to Saarinen's warning, Fournier had been monopolizing the mic. His voice wasn't bad, exactly, it was just—a lot. But it was at least the kind of music everyone could dance to. There was a drunk couple in the crowd singing along, and Fournier directed his attention toward them, serenading them from the stage, dipping the mic forward.

The nice thing about being drunk at a karaoke night with a bunch of Royal was that Aiden could mostly lurk on the fringes and watch, and no one really bothered him too much. He did shots with Morozov. He did shots with Lee. He avoided the Morin twins as much as possible.

He tried not to think about all of the places he'd rather be right now. He watched Matt and the rookies, three of them in addition to Crane, all huddled around him—three on chairs and Crane sitting on the table—hanging on every word he said. Aiden sidled a little closer to try to hear what he was saying over the din of Saarinen attempting to forcibly take the mic from Fournier. He could only catch fragments.

"…you know, the first playoffs is, you really can't prepare yourself for it."

"What's more difficult, the mental or the physical aspect, because I hear the grind—"

"I'd say both equally, although my first playoffs were unusual—"

"Oh, yours were—"

"Yeah, although it wasn't that bad, really, I was just excited to be there, but the grind is real—"

It was kind of cute, the way all of their big, rangy bodies, still not quite done growing, angled in, their faces turned toward him, like sunflowers. Just soaking in everything he had to say. It was nice watching Matt in his element, although it did make Aiden miss his own team and the way he used to be able to talk to Gabe during team events like this.

Matt looked up and smiled when he saw Aiden, like Aiden wasn't lurking at the edges of the bar like some sort of serial killer. "Aiden," he said, raising his voice, "think it's time for the rooks to take their turn, eh?"

"Oh no," one of them—Cormier?—said. "Cap, I don't think I can—"

"You can do it in a group," Matt told him, kindly but firmly, a smile on his face that reminded Aiden more than a little of some of his old captains, "but unfortunately, you gotta do it. It's the rules."

Cormier looked a little green, but Crane slung an arm over his shoulder and said, "No worries, bud. We'll all go, eh?"

"That's the spirit," Matt said, "knock 'em dead, boys,"

and as they headed en masse for the stage, Matt gestured for Aiden to come to him.

Aiden didn't even think about not following the instruction; he weaved his way around a few of the Royal defensemen, and slid into the seat Cormier had vacated. On the stage, the rookies staggered their way through some Top 40 radio hit that Aiden vaguely recognized from hearing it everywhere over the summer but couldn't name. Crane was in the front, letting Cormier hang behind him. One of the other children—Koskinen?—hit the falsetto part with an exaggerated gusto that set the hair rising on the back of Aiden's neck. Like hearing dogs howling in the distance at night.

Aiden glanced back at Matt, who might have looked completely sober to someone who didn't know him well. Aiden could tell from context clues, like the flush high on his cheeks and the easy smile and the little slump to his shoulders, that he was *shitfaced.* Matt slid a shot glass sideways across the table to him and then his arm over Aiden's shoulders.

"Oh, very smooth," Aiden said, and rolled his eyes.

Matt grinned, his fingers squeezing Aiden's bicep. "Having fun?"

"Uh—yeah," Aiden lied.

It wasn't as bad as he had thought it would be, but *fun* might have been a step too far. It was just a reminder of the things he had lost; the things Matt had that Aiden had given up, the reminder that he was holding Matt back just by being here. The knowledge that Matt belonged here, with these guys, and that Aiden was at best an interloper. He leaned into Matt's side anyway, and Matt shifted in the chair to accommodate Aiden's weight against him. It felt so fucking good that Aiden almost pushed him away on reflex.

Aiden added, "Not entirely drunk enough to appreciate Fournier's singing."

"No one is, really. Take the shot, then."

"Hölökynkölökyn," Aiden said, lifting the glass. It was easier to get the entire word out, drunk.

"Bless you?"

"No—hölökynkölökyn. It's like cheers."

"Oh, you've been talking to Saari? Good, I'm happy." Matt beamed at him, incandescent and so handsome that it felt like a punch in the chest, before he knocked back his own drink.

Aiden looked at him from the corner of his eye, watched him swallow, the movement of his throat.

Matt caught him at it, grinned slow and lazy: "Aidy, *you* haven't gone yet."

The thing was: Aiden might have been introverted and quiet, but he wasn't *shy*. He didn't care if he was in the net in front of twenty thousand fans or playing guitar in front of an entire team. Hobey used to make fun of him for it, egg him on if they were in a hotel lobby in some shitty city and the guys were bored, knowing Aiden didn't really give a shit about who heard him. Aiden had always shrugged and just gone for it, even if he knew that Hobey was laughing both at him and with him. It was fine being the butt of the joke when it was *your* team. Drunkenly singing in front of a bunch of Royal was no different, really, but—

"You're the captain, Matthew," Aiden said, digging his elbow into Matt's side. "Think you should go first."

Saarinen dropped into the table across from them,

eyebrows up. "Well, you two look comfortable, but Safy, you're up. We're gonna do a duet."

Aiden let him go, not sure what to expect.

The two of them stumbled up onto the stage. It was a study in contrasts: Saarinen was the kind of guy who was a natural entertainer, unafraid to make a fool out of himself, anytime, anywhere. Matt was reserved and earnest, but willing to take one for the team.

Together, they managed a truly terrible rendition of some pop song Aiden didn't really recognize but must have been popular, considering the crowd reaction it got. Watching Matt singing was surreal enough, considering Aiden had never seen it before this. His voice was not very good, and he knew it, but he belted it out anyway with such a serious, almost martyred expression.

Saarinen was also not very good, but he was doing an improvised, exaggerated dance, completely uncaring that he looked ridiculous. The rookies were laughing; Morozov and Singh wolf whistled as Saarinen finished with a flourish, down on his knees, arms thrust out toward the audience.

Matt half-jumped and half-slithered off the stage when they were done, loped over to where Aiden was sitting still and hauled him bodily from the seat. "Your turn" was the only thing he said.

"Fine, fine," Aiden grumbled, pulling himself up on the stage. He flipped through the selections, some of which he recognized and some of which were foreign to him. Finally he picked an easy one, something he could do in his sleep or, in this case, swaying-on-his-feet drunk. An old standard, one of the first songs he'd ever learned how to play on the guitar: the Foo Fighters' "Everlong."

Aiden took a breath and launched into the song.

About a verse in he realized it was a huge mistake, because the lyrics were a little too on the nose for him to handle right now, and the mood was not a party mood, and all he could think about was how he didn't want this to end but that it was going to, one way or another. He couldn't really see much beyond the spotlight shining in his face, couldn't see what Matt was doing, kept pushing through the lump in his throat.

This whole thing was a mistake, really, that he thought he could do this and then, finally: the song was winding down and he was done. Aiden carefully set the mic down on the stool and made a break for it.

"Buddy," Saarinen said, when Aiden stumbled back to the table. "*Buddy.* I didn't know you could sing?"

"Like—a limited amount of things," Aiden mumbled, embarrassed.

"That was kind of a bummer of a choice, though. Wow, man, you got some stuff you need to talk about?"

Maybe it was just the drinking catching up with him, but Aiden was suddenly very tired, and he put his head down on the table while he watched Morozov and Singh butchering "Livin' on a Prayer."

This wasn't *his* team. This was Matt's team. Matt belonged here, with them, whether that was this season, or next season, or any season after that.

"Hey," Matt said, hand between Aiden's shoulder blades, "you wanna get out of here?"

He did. So they went.

CHAPTER EIGHT

November

November was early enough in the season that Matt shouldn't have been having this much trouble with his knee, but he had accepted it as a new fact of life this year. No matter how carefully he tended to it with foam rollers and stretching and cold/hot soaks and diclofenac gel, it was just going to ache after every game. And during every game. By now, the Toradol injections were frequently part of his pregame routine, even though he knew he shouldn't have been using it that often. In the short term, he needed to be able to *play*. He thought, *nothing happens to anyone that they can't endure.* Philosophers aside, he had been enduring it for several seasons now.

In his youth he'd had one of the longest active Iron Man streaks in the league and it had been something he'd been proud of. His surgeries had cut that abruptly short, but in between, he worked at regaining it. He knew it was kind of fucked up, especially because he didn't have anything he needed to prove, but that was always the kind of guy he was. He hadn't even missed a game the time he'd needed seventy stitches after getting cut with a skate: he'd just worn a cage for the third period.

Today, the team was in Columbus, before heading south for another game in Raleigh, and a flight back to Montreal. The Battery were one of those perennial bottom-scraping teams that couldn't seem to ever get it together, unlike the Royal, who were on the cusp of maybe a rebuild, maybe transitioning straight into the next wave of kids successfully taking the reins. The kind of team where the lack of success ground down on the players, made them mean. Matt always prepared to get cross-checked in the back of the neck more often than usual, especially if he was in the blue paint.

He took the opening face-off anyway, used his shoulder to push the Battery center out of the way and shove the puck back to where Alex Morin was waiting for it. This late in his career the face-offs were almost automatic, nothing like the struggle they'd been when he was a kid, before he'd built up enough muscle and the experience to know where and when to move.

The knee wasn't an issue *while* he was playing, particularly if he'd taken care of it beforehand—it was like being able to concentrate on the developing play, anticipating the open areas of the ice and the movements of his teammates, even going up and over the boards were enough of a distraction that he didn't feel it until after, when the adrenaline had worn off and he started to regain sensation in his limbs again. That was why he'd loved hockey so much, as a kid: playing was all-consuming, a way to shut out the rest of the world. When he was playing, nothing mattered except the win.

Tonight was the kind of night where everything was

connecting: Morin anticipated his passes, Fourns was locked in and Jammer was a menace on the blue line, his rocket of a shot a constant danger during the power play. By the time the horn sounded for the first intermission, the Royal were up two, thanks to timely goals by Crane and Jammer.

Matt took the time during the break to ice his knee and test it out gingerly. He could probably go a little longer without the heavy meds, which was always good. Too much Toradol could cause nasty stomach issues, and he only used opioids when there was breakthrough pain even with NSAIDs. Too many horror stories and former colleagues who'd had their lives ruined. His own experience after Aiden had left the first time was a personal illustration of how quickly you could slide down into the depths of something very fucking dark.

Back out on the ice, he threw himself into the game in earnest.

"Hey, Safaryan," Morgan Wright said, as they battled along the boards for control of the puck. When Matt didn't respond, Wright kept going, "Hey, Safaryan, you fag," the slur falling easily from his mouth as he slammed Matt against the glass. "How about I take out your knee, and then you can go home crying to your boyfriend."

Matt didn't ask *what did you say*, because he didn't like talking to opposing players on the ice, even when he was trying to get under their skin. He preferred to let his body do the talking. He dug in with all of his weight and *shoved*, and Wright lost control of his stick. That half-second was all Matt needed to get the passing lane, and the puck was on Morin's stick and safely out of the zone.

It wasn't a close game. Matt widened the lead with a goal late in the second, and by the time the third rolled around, the Royal had a comfortable 4-1 margin to protect. Matt was pushing himself a little too hard, maybe—this was a win he really wanted to earn.

He thought about Aiden saying that it wasn't just chirping, and he thought about Morgan Wright and what he'd said in the middle of the third. Matt wasn't as fast as he used to be. He'd never been that strong a skater. But he turned on the jets for this one, streaking after Wright through the neutral zone. Wright had his head down, eye on the puck, and Matt had him lined up.

If it had been anyone else, he probably would have let it go. The team was up three goals, and he could have poke-checked the puck away, probably, could have cut Wright off with his body and forced a turnover. If it had been anyone else, he would have.

He didn't.

Matt leveled his shoulder down and braced himself for the impact. It was lined up so perfectly that Wright basically skated right into him, and it took only a little extra force from Matt to send him flying, bouncing off of his body and down to the ice. He could hear the roar of the arena around him, the fury of the Columbus faithful, the boos that followed.

Matt was moving fast enough that he couldn't tell whether Wright was slow to get up or not. To be quite honest, he didn't care. He had the puck on his stick, and the play had gone from the neutral zone to the offensive zone, and he was setting up a scoring chance for Crane, who'd come out in the middle of a line change, and then it was Matt's turn to get off of the ice. It had been petty. The character and actions of another player shouldn't have affected him. But it had been satisfying, to give in to that nasty impulse, anyway.

On the bench, breathing hard, he took a second to collect himself.

"Câlisse, what the hell got into you, Cap?" Alex Morin asked.

"Wright likes to talk. I don't think he'll be talking so much after this."

He regretted it later on, of course, once he got back to the hotel and his knee felt like it was on fire. He weighed his options and took two Percocet and FaceTimed Aiden, who was still awake and sitting on the couch in Matt's living room.

"Hey, baby," Matt said, and it was like all of the anger and frustration he'd felt in the moment during the game were gone.

"Hey," Aiden said. He looked concerned. "What the hell was that hit in the third period? That's not like you at all, Matty. I know you like to get physical sometimes but it's never out of the blue like that."

"You know how you told me that it wasn't just chirping? Someone was chirping. I shut him up."

Aiden pushed his hair out of his eyes. "I'm sorry. I shouldn't have—the article? He put two and two together?"

"I'm sure even if you hadn't, he probably would've said something shitty, just because people know you're here now. It wouldn't have mattered if they knew you were gay or not. It's fine. I was prepared for it, and I took care of it."

"I'm just worried about your knee. I don't want you to hurt yourself—"

"Hey," Matt said softly. "It's okay, you know? I know

what I'm doing. I'll be careful. The sooner you shut one of those assholes up, the less you have to do it in the future."

"Okay," Aiden said doubtfully, because he was a goalie, and Matt was the only fight he'd ever had.

"Don't worry, Aidy. I'll be home soon, eh?"

"Not soon enough," he muttered, and then: "You must be exhausted. Let me let you sleep."

"I love you—" Matt started, but Aiden was already hanging up.

Hello! an unknown number texted Aiden. The greeting was followed by several smiley-face emojis.

Hi?

Sorry, I should have introduced myself first!! This is Aino Saarinen, Eero's wife.

Nice to meet you?

Nice to meet you too!! Now that things are a little more official, I wanted to reach out and on behalf of the rest of us, welcome you to Montreal!!

Aiden stared at his phone and tried to remember if he'd ever seen a picture of Aino Saarinen. He couldn't bring her face to mind. Right now, he was mostly picturing the smiley-face emoji, which she used almost like another form of punctuation. He wondered if she'd asked Matt for his number, or if Saarinen still had it saved from the last time. Thanks, he said, that's very kind.

Please feel free to ask me if you need anything! Or if you'd like to hang out!

Thanks? I'm okay, though. Mostly settled in.

Okay, well, the offer stands! And you should come and watch a game with me!! We can get to know each other, we have pretty good seats reserved for the girls!! And I promise you I don't bite!!

Aiden stared at the phone again. He drafted several potential texts in his head, but ultimately said, That sounds nice. Thank you.

Great!!! Let's pick a home game sometime soon! Can't wait! I'll add you to the group!

Aiden sighed and put his phone back into his pocket. He looked at the condo. There wasn't much to do at this point in the day, so he wasted a few hours reading the book about Jacques Plante he had downloaded on his phone last week, and then got up to start getting dinner together. When Matt was on the road, Aiden reverted to his old habits of making the same thing for every meal. This week it was bison burgers, but the sooner he could eat, the sooner he didn't have to think about it anymore. Just another monotonous detail in the day.

Matt FaceTimed him later, after Aiden had eaten and cleaned up, in the middle of doing hundreds of push-ups in the living room. The repetitive physical activity was painful but mindless and it kept him occupied, at the very least. There was no game tonight between Matt's games in Florida and Texas. Aiden flopped down out of the position and answered the phone.

"Hey, Aidy," Matt said, eyes flicking from Aiden's face to his sweaty hair and back down. He looked vaguely amused. "You working out?"

"I was bored, so I just did some push-ups. How's the trip going?"

"Just lost three hundred to the rookies in a poker game," Matt said, grinning a little sheepishly. "I couldn't take their money, so…that's about how it's going."

"You lost on purpose? Oh, Matty, now *that's* some captain shit, eh?"

"Ah, shut up. You really think I'd take some kid's ELC money? But they're never going to let me live it down."

"That's why you don't play poker with the rookies," Aiden said, the smile fading as he remembered that he didn't have rookies anymore. "You can't win, no matter what you do."

"Yeah, well. Too late for that now, eh? But enough about that…what've you been doing today?"

Aiden sighed. It was a gustier sigh than he was intending. "I kind of got invited to sit with the WAGs for a game."

A variety of expressions shifted over Matt's face in the five seconds it took him to get it under control, most of them somewhere on the spectrum between amusement and horror. He smoothed it out into a carefully expressionless mask. "You…what?"

"Saarinen's wife said we should watch a game together and get to know each other."

"Oh, Jesus. She's very friendly, and I'm sure she didn't mean to offend you."

"I'm not offended, I mean… I kind of…well, it's not totally off base right now, is it?"

"I wouldn't say that."

"It doesn't matter."

"Are you going to take her up on it?"

Aiden sighed again. "I think I kind of have to, don't I?"

"You don't have to do anything you don't want to do."

"She was really nice about it. I don't want to be an asshole, you know?"

"Aino is—ah—kind of aggressively nice. I'm sorry. I'll make it up to you."

"It's fine, Matt. Let's, uh—talk about something else, eh?"

Matt somehow managed to hold it in, but his eyes danced. "I'm sorry, I'm just picturing you in there. They're going to eat you *alive*, baby."

"Not *helping*," Aiden groaned, and hung up. He'd call back in a minute, once Matt had gotten it out of his system. Aiden sighed again. These were not the problems he'd expected to have back in June.

Aiden texted Aino Saarinen to tell her that he could come to any of the games within the next week. It seemed better to rip the Band-Aid off and get it over with.

Great! How about the Cons game on Tuesday?

Sure.

Perfect!

"You really don't have to do it if you don't want to," Matt attempted to reassure him, on their next call.

"It's fine. Really."

Tuesday rolled around, Matt left for the rink and Aiden spent the rest of his time staring at his phone, half-hoping that Aino would tell him she couldn't make it, for whatever reason.

It was weird dressing for hockey games, now—he never had to think about it before. He couldn't really wear his own jerseys there, and he couldn't wear Matt's jersey in public without making more of a statement than he was really comfortable making while he still felt the future dropping like pebbles off the edge of a cliff as his toes tried to grab purchase. A suit was too formal when he wasn't even playing or sitting in the press box.

He usually ended up settling for one of ten Libs hoodies he had brought with him and the kind of joggers that cost more than he ever would have felt comfortable paying as a rookie.

Then he had no more excuses, and it was time to drive to l'Arène. It was a building where, even though it was relatively new in the grand scheme of things, you could feel the history and weight of it as soon as you approached. It didn't hurt that all of the Royal legends were represented in statues outside, their metal faces stoic and determined, a reminder of just how many giants had carried this team over the years. He felt a little self-conscious walking through the crowd of people streaming in the doors, like they probably would know or recognize him. No one stopped him, though, and some of the tightness in his chest faded.

Aino waited for him in the lobby. He knew it was her because she was holding a sign, like she was in an airport or something, that said *CAMPBELL* surrounded by hearts in the Royal's blue, white and red. She was a small woman, probably only five feet and six inches even in the towering heeled boots she wore, with a mane of ashy blonde hair flowing loose over her shoulders and framing a freckled face that could only be described as elfin. She beamed at him, and he realized his earlier mental image of her—the smiling emoji—wasn't entirely far off. It took up her whole face.

"Aiden! Welcome to l'Arène!"

"Aino?" It turned out the caution was unnecessary, because she immediately threw her arms around his waist in a hug. Aiden patted her on the back, awkward. "It's nice to meet you."

"Lovely to meet you, too," she said, released him and winked. "Eero says you have a very nice voice; I'm sorry I missed karaoke night."

"He's, uh, being generous."

"I'm sure he wasn't! Well, come on up! Everyone is mostly here already, so I can introduce you!"

Aiden followed her down the halls to the elevator or, more accurately, allowed her to lead him, since she had hooked her elbow casually through his, like they were old friends who had reunited after years apart rather than relative strangers.

She didn't stop talking the entire way: she jumped from topic to topic, from things she loved about Montreal, to things the other women loved about Montreal and that she was sure he would also love about Montreal, to asking him about his own last season. She was cheerful enough that he found himself answering, even though he hated talking about it.

Sometimes, for special occasions, the WAGs might reserve a box. But Aiden knew that most of them usually sat in the stands, with a row of seats reserved so they could all hang out and talk. Even without the pressure of being in an enclosed box area, he wanted to run as soon as they all turned their eerily similar faces to look at him, like the moment before they'd start speaking in tongues, or levitating, or climbing up the walls with their heads at the wrong angle.

It was unfair of him. He was sure they were all perfectly nice.

Aino pulled him forward by the arm, surprisingly strong for such a tiny person, as they awkwardly squeezed their way around the other WAGs, who were all standing as they went. "This is Maddy and Mia and Maya and Avery and Daria and Chloe and Sophia—"

Most of them were tall and slim and white, with blonde hair, natural or dyed, and they were all wearing very similar clothes, the kind of casual look that spoke of way more effort than they ever would have admitted to. He shook hands awkwardly as he went, before he finally got to sit down in the seat they had reserved for him.

"We're so happy you came," Aino was saying, "definitely make yourself at home, we'll probably go and get food during the intermissions, and Eero did tell me you don't eat dairy, so there will be something for you—"

"Thank you," Aiden cut in hastily, a little overwhelmed. He took ten deep breaths, and then ten more, and then ten more.

"Hey," Saari had asked, as they were getting ready to head out for warm-ups. "By the way, Aino asked me if you want me to add Campbell to the group chat. He never gave her a clear answer."

Matt had exhaled. The WAG group chat was one of those constants of hockey life, the kind of thing that you always knew was going on in the background, but usually tried to stay out of. It had its own rules and customs and histories. It was basically the same no matter where you were playing: there was one WAG in charge, usually the captain's wife, and you needed approval from the player before she'd add you to all the official shit. If Aino had asked, that was as good as saying that she wanted to know if things were *official*. And that, at least from the women, was an endorsement.

But he didn't have time to think about it, because it *was* time for warm-ups. Matt had been playing in the league for a long time, long enough that he knew guys on pretty much every team. Either he'd played with them in juniors, or they'd spent some time on the Royal and been traded, or he'd played with them during international competitions representing Canada. It was one of the things he'd always loved about hockey: what a small world it really was, when it came down to it.

That was no different now that the Philadelphia Constitution were in town, the ice filled with red, white and blue jerseys in clashing shades. It had been a few years since he'd won a Cup with Zachary Reed and subsequently watched his tailspin and trade. There were no hard feelings, though. Matt had been relieved to see a player he still thought of as one of his rookies pick himself up out of the gutter and work himself into a position of responsibility and win another Cup with his new team.

"Hey," Matt said, casually, skating by Reed during warm-ups. "The A looks good on you, buddy."

Reed grinned. He had a cheerful, handsome face, with curly brown hair and warm brown eyes, the kind that were best described as twinkling. Some of that light had dimmed, that last season in Montreal, but it was back in full force now. "Everything looks good on me," he said, and extended his glove to bump fists with Matt. "How're you doing, old man?"

"Well enough," Matt said, with a shrug.

"The knee?"

"Not talking about that with a rival right before a game, come on."

"Aw, Safy, you're gonna hurt my feelings, talking like that," Reed said, pushing his lower lip out. "I was asking from a legitimate place of concern."

Matt didn't answer immediately. They watched their teammates going through their various pregame routines: Sakari Mäkelä, the Cons' goalie, tapping his posts with his stick and whispering something to them; Manny Singh slamming his entire weight into Jammer's bulky body and bouncing right off; Bee Morin shooting a sneaky puck at the Royal's net, much to the displeasure of her brothers, who immediately skated up to try to intimidate her. She didn't back down.

"Thank you," Matt said, and left it at that.

"And, uh, I wanted to ask…" Reed trailed off. He lowered his voice, so that Matt had to lean forward to hear him. Things carried on the ice, but Reed spoke quietly enough that it didn't. "You don't have to say anything if you don't want to, I know it's not *really* my business. I'm just asking because I…well, I heard through the grapevine that Campbell's in Montreal. And maybe staying with *you*. I know it wasn't in the article, but…"

Matt looked levelly at him, unsure of what to say. Reed, on the Royal, had been a mess. He'd fucked his way indiscriminately through Montreal, and even if he'd never really *come out* to the team, they'd certainly figured it out quick enough on their own. He hadn't been particularly discreet. Of course, Reed had grown up since then. He wore an A now, Singer's loyal right hand. Matt remembered the photographs of Singer handing him the Cup, the way they'd looked at each other like nothing else existed.

Ah.

"You don't have to tell me," Reed was saying hurriedly, "it's just, there's not a lot of us out there, you know?"

The moment stretched between them, fraught and awkward. He could shut it down, right now. He could say, *I don't know what you're talking about.* He could say, *it* is *none of your business.* He said, finally, "It's been nice to have him back in my life."

Reed's golden retriever face scrunched up almost comically, processing the implications. Matt was old enough that his first relationship with Aiden had ended before Reed had even been drafted, which was a depressing thought. Reed got himself back under control and shot a bright smile Matt's way, the kind of smile he'd often given to the media, one of the ones that didn't quite reach his eyes. He was *nervous.* "Well, you know, if you guys are ever in Philly…you're welcome to stop by our place. We could hang out, shoot the shit, that kinda thing."

"'Our place'?"

"Mine and Nate's," Reed clarified. "I sold my house last season."

"Ah," Matt said, and wondered if this would ever get less awkward. On the one hand it was—nice, to know that he wasn't alone. Even if the first interaction he'd had about it, in this new world where Aiden had been *public* about things, hadn't exactly been positive, it was still something. On the other hand, he tried to imagine Aiden's face when he told him about the invite, the horrified wince it probably would've brought out, and almost couldn't bite back the laugh.

"What's so funny?" Reed asked, a little wary.

"Just the way you said *you guys*—you're really going full-on Philly, huh?"

"Fuck you," Reed said, but he was smiling as he shoved at Matt's bicep.

"Careful. Don't push the guy who's gonna kick your ass in about twenty minutes."

"Hey!" Manny yelled, careening toward them. "No fraternizing with the enemy, Safy."

"Fuck *you*, Manny," Reed said, still just as cheerfully as he said anything. He glanced over his shoulder as he skated away. His eyebrows went up. "Well—Safy—the invite's open."

"I know. Merci," Matt said, surprised to find he meant it.

Once the game actually started, it got a little easier. Aino knew quite a lot about hockey—and used to play defense in a women's league in Lappeenranta—and when they only talked about the game, it wasn't that bad. It was almost like watching from the bench back in New York, with the way she would occasionally break off what she was saying to mutter a curse word in Finnish when Philadelphia got possession or lurch out of her seat in disgust and frustration when the refs made a bad call. As much as he would have liked to talk only to her, that was impossible when he was the curiosity of the evening to the rest of the women.

They kept leaning in to pepper him with questions about when he had met Matt and when he came to Montreal and whether he was planning to stay long and whether… Aiden didn't really answer beyond one-word replies or short sentences: they had known each other since their first playoff series, July, he didn't know.

And then he had to be content to simply listen to the chatter while keeping one eye on the game. No matter how he sat in his seat or how unapproachable he looked or how deeply he slouched into the cushions, someone was *always* talking to him.

It was overwhelming. On his immediate right, Mia whispered to him quick little introductions about some of the other women, the kind of quirky little anecdotes you wouldn't find out except from someone who had been friends with them a long time. From behind him, Sophia offered, generously and with the most innocent wide eyes, to cut his hair for him, because she had a salon on Sherbrooke Ouest. Daria, next to Sophia, told him that Montreal was an interesting city, but the locals were such snobs especially if you didn't speak French—oh, call her Dasha, by the way. Avery, one extra seat down, wanted to know if he was going to be interested in *organizing*, because although Aino mostly did it now, after all, Matt was the *captain*. Maya, a nurse, and Maddy, the owner of a small, trendy bakery, seemed fairly normal, but they were farther away down the row, and he couldn't talk to them.

Unfortunately, he didn't know what to tell *any* of the women.

This happened sometimes when he was dealing with social situations where he didn't have a script. He'd freeze up and choke, and either start rambling on about something unrelated or shut down completely. It had been easier at the team night because he'd had Matt there as a safety net, and he'd had alcohol to make it a little easier to turn his brain off, but he didn't have either of those things right now.

The thing about all of this was: however well-meaning they were, Aiden could barely think of anything to say to any of them. Could barely string together coherent sentences. He could feel the sweat soaking through the thin underlayer he had thrown on beneath the jersey, the kind of cold chill that went deeper than the skin.

The thought of spending forty-one nights a year like this made him want to gouge out his own eyes. Even by the end of one night, he had to excuse himself to go into the bathroom, wet his hands with cold water and slap himself in the face several times. The sharp sensation helped jolt him out of the panic, but it didn't help him feel any better, really. A guy finishing up at the urinal looked at him oddly and Aiden beat an even hastier retreat.

How was he going to do this? In Montreal or anywhere else. It would be exactly like this anywhere. Rows of arena seats full of perfectly nice women who were going out of their way to include him, to make him feel welcome, even though the situation was undoubtedly pretty fucking unusual for all of them. Rows of arena seats full of perfectly nice women he had nothing to talk to about. He wondered whether any of them would be willing to listen to him do the things he normally did when he was panicking, which was either recite a little mantra to himself, or talk about goaltending technique. Aino, at least, would probably be amenable to it.

He exhaled. That was a problem for future Aiden. Right now, he had to get through the rest of the game.

By the time the clock had ticked down and the horn sounded for the end of the period, the Royal had eked out a win. The players went through the little routine that they always did for home wins: after the line to bonk Fournier on the helmet and give him a hug, they circled back to center ice, skating in slow circles with their sticks raised in a salute to the crowd. Matt faced the section of the arena where the WAGs were sitting and waved one hand. Aiden watched Matt on the Jumbotron as he skated toward the tunnel, looking up at the upper levels again. Maybe for Aiden. Maybe it was a coincidence.

It shouldn't matter, but it did.

Matt felt unexpectedly emotional about the whole evening—the chat, the conversation with Reed—even after the win. He'd looked up into the stands, knowing he wouldn't be able to see Aiden in such a crowd with the lights shining in his eyes, looking for him anyway. He wondered what Aiden would say if Matt told him he'd said yes.

But then he had to worry about changing and showering and media. He didn't have time to think about how he felt about it. He didn't have time to think about how Aiden felt about it. He hoped he didn't mind too much. Matt would have to tell him that it was okay to mute it if he wanted to. That it was just for organizational and logistical purposes.

But it wasn't. It was Matt telling the team what Aiden was to him.

"How was it?" Matt asked, when he got home later that night. For the last few years, he'd always been exhausted after games, eager to fall into bed. It was different now that he had Aiden in his life again, curled up against his side. He still felt exhausted, but his body was insistent about the fact that it wasn't ready to sleep yet, that it wanted other things first.

Aiden looked up from under his eyelashes at him. It was the look that had really done him in, fifteen years ago. They were just such pretty eyelashes, thick and dark and a little curled. It was absurd, really, that Aiden looked like that still.

Aiden said, "I don't think I ever want to do that again."

"Sorry. I had hoped you wouldn't be uncomfortable. Were they okay?"

"They were all friendly. It's fine. It was fine. I'm just so fucking awkward, Matt. Just not cut out to be a WAG, I guess."

Matt slipped his hand beneath the waistband of Aiden's boxer briefs. It was cheating, kind of, to do that. "I dunno, it's pretty nice coming home to you here. You do all of the WAG stuff already, except the socializing."

"Oh, fuck off," Aiden muttered, but he was already getting hard in Matt's hand, teeth digging into his lower lip as he trembled with the force of trying not to push his hips up into Matt's grip.

"Can I fuck *you*?"

"Yes—okay—*fuck*, Matt, Jesus *Christ*—" Aiden's voice broke on the last word, jumping up an octave. It was funny: Matt hadn't done anything except stroke his dry, calloused hand up the length of Aiden's cock and he was already falling apart under Matt's hands and the weight of Matt's body, rolled half on top of him.

"I think about you all of the time when I'm playing," Matt said. Their mouths were so close together, not quite a kiss. Close enough that Matt could feel the words vibrating against Aiden's lips.

"What do you think about?" Aiden asked, a little breathless. He had his hands in Matt's hair, running them through it even though Matt kept things pretty short during the season. His mouth was hanging open, a little dumb, a sigh escaping when Matt took his hand away.

"You, waiting for me at home." He spat in his hand and took Aiden in his grip again. "Sometimes I think about you waiting for me naked in bed at home."

"I did that for you already, basically," Aiden said, a little arch. His light brown eyes were intent on Matt's face when Matt pulled away, crinkled a bit at the edges in a smile. It made Matt feel a little crazy, knowing that Aiden rarely met anyone's eyes directly, but always looked at *him* like that.

It was like Matt could get glimpses of the way he'd used to be, before everything went sideways, before they vanished again. Mostly just in bed. Maybe that was all he needed to know: if things weren't going well out of it, he could just use his body to let Aiden know how much he meant to Matt. "It's never enough," Matt said. "Take these off."

He helped Aiden squirm and kick the underwear away, even though it was difficult, because Matt didn't want to move and Aiden didn't seem to want him to, either. He still had one hand gripping Matt's hair, like if he would let go, Matt might get up and vanish, too. As if he could ever fucking do that. Aiden was painfully hard in his hand now, even harder when he moved his free hand to Aiden's throat. He didn't grip or press, just let it rest there, watched Aiden struggling not to push himself up into that, too.

It was objectively kind of insane, how easy Aiden was.

"What else do you think about?" Aiden blinked rapidly, like he couldn't control it, couldn't focus on anything and was desperately trying to anyway. Matt moved his hand again so he could touch Aiden's eyelashes with one hand, feel the feathery movement against his skin. Aiden didn't flinch away, just lay still under Matt's fingers, gentle against his eyelids, his cheekbone, the line of his jaw.

"Just—you. Everything about you. The way your voice cracks when you're turned on. Your pretty eyelashes, the smell of your hair, the way you taste—"

Aiden tilted his head up, his stupid needy little way of asking for a kiss without having to say it. Matt couldn't help but give him what he wanted, remembering as he leaned down and drowned in Aiden's mouth all of the other times he'd kissed Aiden like this, hundreds of thousands of kisses over the years they'd been together. He still felt as insane, doing it, as he'd done the first time, like he couldn't believe this was his life, that it was happening to him.

"What else?" Aiden asked breathlessly.

"I think about—about how fucking easy you are, baby, how bad you always want it."

"You just *do* something to me," Aiden managed, in between kisses, "it makes me insane. You always have."

"And I was thinking—I was thinking about some of the shit we used to do, back when we were kids."

"Yeah?"

Even if his mind was in a million places at once, memory layered on top of physical reality, his body knew Aiden's well enough to move on instinct, grinding against him, free hand back at his throat, the other one stroking, insistent and a little rough. The way Aiden had always liked it. It was working, if the way Aiden's fingers were digging into Matt's shoulders was any indication.

"I was thinking about the time you bought my jersey."

Aiden didn't answer at first, just swallowed so hard Matt could feel his Adam's apple bob against Matt's palm. His eyes were heavy-lidded when he looked up and said, "I only bought it so you'd fuck me in it."

"It worked," Matt said, and twisted his hand, a little mean, just hard enough that Aiden winced and groaned. "It fucking worked, baby."

"You *ruined* it, though."

"Like you could have worn it outside anyway. And we got enough use out of it, anyway, you wore it a few times, and I took those pictures—"

Aiden was laughing, now. "Jesus, those pictures. I don't know how you ever convinced me to do that."

"Didn't need a whole lot of convincing, from what I remember." He shifted his weight, ignoring Aiden's noise of dismay and his grasping hands, moved a little farther down his body, pressing his ear against Aiden's chest so he could listen to his heart for a second, the wild *thump thump thump* of it, ignoring the increasingly desperate way Aiden squirmed under him. "From what

I remember you were pretty eager to show me whatever I wanted, huh?"

He'd saved those, on his phone, for a long time after, pulled them out to look at them when he was jerking off on the road. Aiden, on his knees in the bed with his back to Matt, so you could see the name and number so clearly. Aiden, legs spread wide, hand wrapped around his dick, the jersey rumpled up around his wrist, eyes hooded. Matt's hand fisted in the jersey, almost sacrilegiously twisting the logo, as he pulled Aiden's unresisting body up toward him. Aiden, bent over, from behind, with Matt's hand splayed on his lower back. Aiden, with Matt's dick—

"Something about having your name on my back," Aiden mumbled, trying to push him farther down, "just made me kind of crazy."

"You know." Matt mouthed his way along the line of Aiden's stomach, digging in his teeth just to make Aiden shudder. "Since you're part of the WAG group officially, I could probably get you a playoff jacket."

"Have to make the playoffs first," Aiden muttered, his hands in Matt's hair again. "*Please*, Matty, I need—"

Face-to-face with Aiden's dick, Matt couldn't help smiling, lips pressed against the head, where he could feel and taste exactly how badly Aiden needed him. "We're going to make the playoffs this year. And then I'll get you your jacket. It's been a while since you've worn my name, huh? I bet you'd look so fucking good wearing it—"

Aiden was propped up on his elbows now, staring down at him, eyes wide, pupils huge. For a second, it was like he couldn't think of *anything* to say, like he was transfixed by Matt's face, by Matt's words. Matt could probably look at him like that for ages and never get tired of it.

Finally, he managed, "Matt, *please*."

Matt pushed him back down again, took a second to give him what he wanted, the suction of his mouth and the swirl of his tongue around the head. He lost himself for a few minutes in the groan of relief that Aiden made, the sharp tug of his hands in Matt's hair. Sometimes Matt thought he could do this forever, just listening to Aiden losing it underneath him, knowing how much he needed Matt to touch him. He stopped, pulling away and wiping the spit with the back of his hand.

Aiden gasped, "Matty, *really*?"

"I was just thinking about the jacket—you'd like it? Wouldn't you?"

Aiden was doing the thing he did sometimes, where Matt knew what the answer was, but he was being stubborn about it. He shook his head, even though his face was flushed and he was squirming underneath Matt, trying to get him to touch, to take him in his mouth, to do *anything*. "I—I don't know," he said, looking down at Matt again, almost sly.

"What do you mean, you don't know?" Matt said, and went down on him again. Aiden didn't answer, just thrust up a little too roughly into Matt's mouth, needy, desperate.

"I just—I just—"

"But you *would*? Everyone knowing you're mine?" His voice sounded wrecked already, and it wasn't because Aiden had been especially rough. The idea of Aiden wearing one of those ridiculous jackets with *Safaryan* across the shoulders in rhinestones or fluorescent paint or whatever Aino had picked out for that year's theme was really—it was a really good mental image. Thinking about Aiden, after the games, naked in only the jacket, the way he'd worn Matt's jersey a decade ago—that was overwhelming, too.

He went back down, savoring the sigh that Aiden made when he did it. Held Aiden's hip down with one hand, the other wrapped around the base of his dick. Aiden was twisting between the points of contact, his eyes closed and his head thrown back against the pillow, one arm over his eyes, just as overwhelmed as Matt felt.

When Matt pulled away again, Aiden actually whined, an almost animal noise of dismay. *Good,* Matt thought, the weird, savage part of him that Aiden had woken up oddly satisfied.

"Maybe I'll fuck you while you're wearing it," Matt said, jerking Aiden off, too slow for Aiden's liking. He was panting, now, trying to set the pace, until Matt shoved him down again. "Maybe I'll fuck you while you're wearing it, and nothing else, and then I'll make you wear it to the game the next day."

"*Oh,*" Aiden was saying, and Matt could feel every flinch of his body, every shiver that wracked it, every shift of muscle underneath him, skin so warm it practically burned him. Matt, trapping him with his own weight, thought that maybe—"Oh, Jesus, if—if it's anything like the jersey, everyone's going to *know.*"

"Know what?"

"Please, Matt, I'm so close—"

"Know *what*?"

It was a knife's edge, here, pushing him but not pushing him too hard. Aiden was capable of insane self-control when he wanted to show it. It was a side effect of being a goalie, of years of mental strength practices and meditation. And of Aiden's own peculiar personality. But sometimes, when Matt did this to him—practically choked himself on him, fingers teasing his rim, ruthlessly using every single trick he'd learned about Aiden's body over the years—it was almost too much. Aiden liked to suffer, and Matt liked to watch him suffer, but it was the balancing act on the precipice that was the hardest part. Aiden was sweating, moisture beading his forehead, and he was biting down hard on his finger to keep from crying out.

"Please," he said, his voice very small.

Matt took his mouth and his hands away, shook his head. "Aiden. Know *what*?"

Aiden was stubborn, hated crying even in the intense moments during sex, but his voice was practically sobbing when he gasped, "That I'm yours, that I'm yours, that I want to fucking—I want you to cover me with it, I want everyone to *see* it—please, Matt, I have to *come*—"

They hadn't been messing around very long today, but something about the idea of it had always lit a fire in Aiden, an answering flame in Matt. Aiden *was* close, and Matt couldn't deny him that. He stopped talking and took Aiden in his mouth again, pushed right up against his fist gripping Aiden's cock, mean and merciless.

Aiden's thighs clenched around his head, and all Matt could hear was the roar in his ears. All he could smell was Aiden's skin. All he could see was Aiden's body, close up in flashes. All he knew was how good it felt to do this to him, to figure out the puzzle, the pins of the lock to slot into place to turn Aiden into this, a groaning, pleading, shifting mess of a man underneath him.

When Aiden came, he yanked Matt's hair so hard that his eyes watered, made a strangled noise that was half a sob and half a groan. It took Matt a second or two to swallow and finally lift his head up, and he took the quiet moment to stare down at Aiden. He was still breathing hard, rumpled and loose and vulnerable, face still flushed.

"Matty," he managed, "what do you want me to—"

"Just stay there," Matt said. His voice was unsteady, strained. "We might not have the jacket, but I want—let me give you what you wanted."

"Yeah?" Aiden might have looked languid, relaxed, but his whole body tensed again when Matt said it. "What are you…oh," he said, when Matt moved up to straddle his thighs, hand wrapped around his own dick. "Yeah. *Fuck*, yes."

Matt was so exhausted from the game and so worked up from getting Aiden off that he knew it wasn't going to take long, especially when Aiden was looking up at him like that, eyes huge and dark, like he both wanted to devour Matt and be devoured by him.

Matt wanted that. Matt wanted to devour him, wanted to keep him here forever, wanted to take him everywhere and show him off so everyone who saw him knew he was Matt's, that he got *off* on being Matt's, that he wanted—that he wanted—

He had to grab the headboard to brace himself when he came, the force of it almost knocking him off-balance. It wasn't a shiver as much as a punch in the face, so sudden and intense it was almost painful. When he opened his eyes again, Aiden was still staring up at him, except he had come striping his chest and a little splattered on his cheek. He took one finger and wiped it across his face. Then he put his finger in his mouth, meeting Matt's gaze directly as he licked the come away, and Matt's dick gave a pained little jerk, like it was trying to do it all over again.

Aiden sat up again and leaned forward to kiss him, so different from the hungry, desperate kisses they'd shared just a few minutes ago. It was a sweet press of his lips against Matt's, almost grateful. "I don't need a jacket."

"I know," Matt mumbled into his mouth, "but if we do make the playoffs, I'm going to make sure you get one."

"Okay." Something brief and strange shifted across Aiden's face, a shadow Matt didn't understand and didn't want to see. "Look. I'm going to go use the bathroom and get cleaned up. I'll be right back."

"I'll be right in after you," Matt said, but then he lay down and, before he knew it, was asleep.

It seemed like every time Aiden started to get used to things, Matt went on another roadie. This one was to Winnipeg, Minnesota and Chicago. He would be gone almost a week, and as the day of the first flight approached, Aiden could already feel the dread building up in the pit of his stomach.

The problem was, no matter how well things were going, until Aiden figured out how he needed to shape the rest of his life, it was always going to be like this. The problem wasn't Matt, whether Matt was there or not: it was that Aiden was drifting through the water without any direction or anchor.

He got through the first few days just fine. He met Aino for coffee, and they went for a walk in Mont-Royal, sipping their drinks. She looked cute as a button, wrapped up in her huge parka with a beanie hiding most of her lion's mane of hair. Aiden, on the other hand, was constantly swearing and shaking out his hand as hot coffee leaked out from under the lid and fell on the web of his fingers.

"I'm glad you decided to come!" Aino said, politely ignoring his problems. "I was worried about you, you know. You don't often answer on the group chat."

His phone had started buzzing not long after he'd attended that first game with Aino and he realized that he'd been officially added to the WAG chat. At first he'd scrolled through the messages—it was mostly welcomes from numbers he didn't recognize. Aiden exhaled, and said, *Thanks, everyone, it's great to be here*, and muted the chat. Saving their contacts seemed overwhelming. He hadn't even re-saved Matt's number yet. So he didn't do anything else with that chat.

"I'm sorry," Aiden said, unable to meet her eye. "It's not that you all haven't been incredibly nice and welcoming. It's just I… I get a little weird with social stuff sometimes. I'm not very good at it."

"You did just fine at the game. I especially liked getting a goalie's perspective on some of the game."

Aiden surprised himself by laughing. "It's good to hear it from a defenseman too, I suppose."

She glanced sideways at him, her blue eyes shrewd. "I don't want to pressure you into doing anything, you know. I just know it can be lonely in a new city where you don't know anyone, and these girls are really a good group. I know it's not the same as what you're used to, probably, but we're more than happy to be a resource or company for you. Whatever you need. And it's pretty busy. Matt hasn't had a partner for a long time, so I'm the one who does a lot of the charity events and parties and organizing."

"Please don't expect me to do that," Aiden said, gripped by a sudden chill of terror.

Aino laughed, surprisingly loud for such a small woman. "Absolutely not. I mean, if you wanted to, you could. But somehow, I get the feeling you aren't really up for that."

"No," Aiden said, and shuddered.

She nudged him with her elbow. "Well, I am just saying. I am more than happy to meet for coffee or lunch whenever you want, if it's too much to see everyone at once. We can even mostly talk about hockey."

"Thank you." It was sincere, even if he couldn't see himself taking her up on it. She'd get sick of his shitty conversation and foul moods soon enough, anyway. No need to overdo it too early and drive off the entire group of wives and girlfriends as a result.

He went to the gym; he went for a run. He successfully baked a loaf of bread without burning it. He read a book and watched a movie. He made himself an unremarkable dinner.

On the second day he wandered around Montreal doing something he had tried to do since coming up there, which was find small things for the apartment that he could sneak in, things Matt wouldn't notice but would appreciate when he saw them—a piece of art that reminded him of Matt and the Royal, or a small kitchen appliance Aiden thought he'd be able to appreciate, or a book Matt mentioned but didn't own—but he had trouble finding anything that outing.

By the third day he was going a little stir-crazy and ended up taking apart the kitchen and deep cleaning it and reorganizing all of Matt's cabinets. Then he tackled the living room. Then the bathrooms. By the time he was done, Aiden felt a little worn out but mostly frustrated with himself. As far as productive uses of his time, it could be worse, but ultimately, it was meaningless.

By the fourth day, he had run out of things to organize and ways to occupy himself, but he had an appointment with Dr. Gauthier. During that appointment he studiously did not mention the way he felt like he was slowly losing his mind. Whether she could pick up on that anyway was anyone's best guess.

By the fifth day, he did push-ups until he ended up in a sweaty puddle on the floor, arms too sore to move. Then he did some more.

Aiden spent most of the sixth day curled up on the couch, flipping through various sports channels, not really paying attention to much of anything. He tried to make a list of things he could see himself doing with his life. He crossed off most of them, but he kept coming back to one option.

He crossed it out.

Wrote it down again.

On the seventh day, Aiden thought, *I can't do this.* He thought: *If I'm here for Matt, I have to do this.*

The Royal were on the road again, to Winnipeg, Minnesota and Chicago. Matt wondered idly whether Aiden's family would be at the Winnipeg game: Aiden's father might have been a former professional player, but he'd never really made it beyond the minor leagues, and both he and Aiden's sister were Falcons fanatics. During Aiden and Matt's first relationship, Aiden's parents had had season tickets, although he had no idea whether they still did. Aiden's mom had never really warmed up to hockey and only went when Aiden was playing at home. Matt doubted they would have made an exception for *him*, especially after things had ended.

In the plane, on thc way out to Manitoba, he realized that he'd never actually asked Aiden what he'd told his family about the breakup. He had always just assumed Aiden had just told the truth, but maybe that had been a bad idea. Maybe it didn't even matter if he had or hadn't—it was clear that even though Aiden had been the one to break things off, he'd been more messed up about it than Matt had realized originally.

Matt usually sat with Saari on the flights, and Saari usually slept on them. It worked out well because Matt had never been a big talker. Today, though, Saari was awake, frowning as he scrolled through something on his phone.

"You good?" Matt asked.

"Yeah, you know." Saari rolled his eyes. "You should never read the comments on the articles, right?"

"Buddy, you've been playing for almost twenty years, and you're breaking the rules *now*? What are you even looking for?"

"I don't know," Saari said, and shrugged. "It's just… you know, we have so many rookies this year, and we've been playing pretty well, but who knows about the playoffs. And then you, and the trade deadline…"

Matt felt his eyebrows go up. "It's months away, you know."

"I *know*. But you haven't signed an extension yet, man, and I'm worrying about it."

"Aw, you'd miss me, huh?" Matt asked. He could feel the smile tugging at the corner of his mouth, almost against his will.

"Of course I fucking would." Saari's face looked almost wounded. "Matti, we've played together for almost twenty years. You've been my captain for over a decade now. It's not gonna be the same without you."

"I haven't gotten traded yet," Matt pointed out. "And the deadline's not for another few months, anyway."

"Not if you look at any of these websites. *The Athletic*'s pretty much traded you to Edmonton already."

Matt leaned back in the seat and closed his eyes. "Try not to read them until at least January, eh?"

"Yeah," Saari said, a little darkly, and locked his phone. "But you...what *are* you thinking?"

"I don't know," Matt said honestly. "It's hard to think about *not* playing. It's hard to think about playing anywhere except Montreal. It's hard to think about retiring. I'm still pretty young, but the knee..."

"Yeah," Saari said. He had his own injury history and several surgeries, and he knew how the eighty-two-game season really wore down on you after a while. No matter how you prepared or tried to take preventative measures or treatments, the parts of your body that had been surgically repaired let you know. "Fuck, Matti, I'm sorry. You're probably stressed enough about this. I don't need to add to it."

"I mean...it's nice to know you'd miss me, I guess."

Instead of answering, Saari elbowed him in the side. "Fuck off, man. Do you really not understand how important you are to this team?"

Matt didn't answer, just shook his head and let it go. Being the captain of the team meant a lot of responsibilities, on ice and off, and he wondered how well he'd been doing at the off-ice responsibilities so far this year. He'd been distracted by Aiden falling back into his life, hadn't been as on top of things as he normally would have been. He made a resolution that he *needed* to spend more time away from home, as tempting as it was to just run back to Aiden as soon as the plane touched down at YUL. The rookies—especially Jack—needed to have him around.

Especially if he wouldn't be here next season.

It was funny, thinking about it: the idea of playing anywhere except Montreal turned his stomach. It still felt like he had unfinished business here, the drive to feel satisfied with what he'd done cemented. Maybe he would do what he'd threatened to do when they were talking about trading him to New York: just retire instead. Not that he *wanted* to retire. Not that he had any idea what he'd *do* if he retired. He was seeing the effects of it in his own home, Aiden sadly moping around the condo without anything to do. Not that Matt would be any better. His only hobbies were typical hockey player hobbies: golf, fishing, fantasy football. Nothing you could translate into a fucking *job*.

Matt rubbed his eyes and wondered, yet again, why they didn't fucking give you advice about this when you got drafted. To maybe try to take classes or something, to think about what was going to happen when your body gave out on you or your brain had been through one too many concussions. When he tried to think of what *he* would do, what he'd be good at, his brain just blanked out. A lot of guys went into business, or real estate, or shit like that, and Matt couldn't see himself enjoying any of it. It was one thing to jokingly suggest career paths to Aiden, another altogether to visualize it for himself.

Maybe enjoying it wasn't the point. Maybe you just had to *do* something, anything, to keep busy. He had enough money not to work, but the thought of just sitting around, with no purpose to the day, was vaguely terrifying.

Then again, he had Aiden. Maybe…they could just have a life together. A quiet, purposeless life. No responsibilities, nowhere to be, nothing to worry about except each other. The idea was strangely appealing, if unrealistic.

And then they were landing, and he was too busy to worry about anything else. He wondered whether or not he should ask Aiden about checking in on his family, whether they would be upset by it. Aiden himself seemed a little distant and sad that night, which Matt had just chalked up to the absence.

"I'll be home before you know it, baby," Matt said, already falling asleep: travel nights always did that to him.

"I know," Aiden said, and smiled. It was a weak smile, but sincere. "I just miss you when you're gone, kind of…a lot."

When he said shit like that it took almost everything Matt had in him not to call his general manager and tell him he couldn't play anymore, he had to go home, it was family business. He couldn't do any of that, obviously. But he thought about it. He wondered whether Aiden would think it was weird, if he told him. Probably. Probably it'd be too much. He didn't say it, just closed his eyes and said, "I'll be home soon, Aidy, I promise."

"Knee holding up?" Aiden asked, the way he had started doing every call.

"Yes, Mom."

Aiden smiled, a little sad, still. "I won't keep you, Matt. Sleep well?"

"You too, baby."

At morning skate the next day, Matt took the time to make sure that all of the rookies were on track with the drills, and that Coach Roy wasn't pushing them too hard in the process. He pushed *himself* too hard and was grateful by the time the practice ended and he could take a long, hot shower.

By the time he finished up and was headed out from the visitors' locker rooms and to the garage where the bus was waiting, ready to head back to the hotel for an afternoon nap before the game, he abruptly came to a halt, almost tripped over his own feet.

Aiden's mother, Shilpa, was standing outside of the door, lurking like she was an assassin about to pounce.

"Ms. Parekh," Matt said, shocked. "I—hello? What are you—*how* are you? Shouldn't you be in court?"

Considering Aiden was pretty tall—at least four inches taller than Matt—it had always amused him just how tiny his mother was. Shilpa Parekh stood a little over five feet tall, even in her short heels, although she had Aiden's slim build, his huge brown eyes and distinctive nose. Her wavy, salt-and-pepper hair was cut short in a bob, and she was still dressed in her usual work clothes, a severely cut pantsuit that made her look like she should have been starring in some kind of legal drama. She and Aiden's father—a sad man whose posture always looked vaguely defeated—were a strangely matched pair, but it had always been clear who was the driver of that particular bus.

She looked over the rim of her thick-framed glasses at him. "Hello, Matthew. Please, after all of this time, I'm still Shilpa to you. You don't need to stand on ceremony. And I took some time off to come and see you."

"I'm, ah, honored," he said, even though the more correct word was *terrified.* Around them, the rest of his teammates were headed out toward the garage as well. Some of them pretended not to see; a few of them shot curious glances in his direction. He might miss the bus, at this rate, but it would be worth it.

Shilpa raised one eyebrow. "Why don't we walk and talk, so we have a little privacy?"

"Sure," Matt said, because saying no to her wasn't an option.

They walked a little farther down the hall, in the opposite direction, and Matt waited for her to lead the conversation. It was strange, seeing her in person again; equally strange that she didn't seem upset to see him, after everything.

"This is very awkward," she said, after a pause. "I just wanted to—I wanted to check in. And see how *you* are doing. And see how Aiden is doing. He doesn't talk to us very much anymore, and I worry about him."

Matt's mouth went dry. "I, uh, I'm fine? Just getting through the season, you know. It's a grind, even this early."

"And my son?" Shilpa pressed. She had that hawk-like look on her face that probably terrified opposing counsel almost as much as it terrified Matt.

"I think maybe it's his place to tell you," Matt said,

as politely as he could. "I promise you that he's as comfortable and happy in Montreal as I can make him."

She softened, visibly. "I know. You were always good to him, even before things…"

"It wasn't his fault," Matt said, even though he wasn't sure what she was going to say after that. "It wasn't either of our faults. It was just a bad time for the things I wanted, and I didn't blame him at all for how he reacted when I made some really stupid choices after."

"I know." Shilpa shook her head. "That doesn't mean I'm not worried about him *now*. He hasn't taken retirement well, and you… I know how much he loved you. But sometimes, I don't think he knows what to do with all of those feelings. And the combination of things. I just… I worry."

Matt ran his hand through his hair, which was still damp from the shower. "I mean, I understand. I wish he'd talk to you himself. I don't want to overstep."

"You were always such a good boy, you know. I'm sorry things went like they did." Shilpa looked up at him, serious but fond.

"It's fine. It's—we both had a lot of growing up to do."

"That's for certain." She looked down the hallway, where a few of the rookies were lingering. "It's strange to see you now, all grown up, the veteran captain. I see you've got some gray hairs."

"That's all Aiden," Matt said, dryly, and she laughed.

"Mine, too, if I'm being quite honest. All right, Matthew. I won't keep you. I just wanted to…see you. To make sure you're still the same person Aiden fell in love with the first time. To tell you I'm worried about him. Just the small things, eh?"

"Only the small things," Matt agreed, and hesitated.

She did it for him, though, stepped forward with her arms open to hug him. She was small but quite strong, the embrace brief but fierce.

"I can't say I wish you luck tonight," Shilpa said, with a half-smile, "no matter what happens, I can't quite bring myself to root for Montreal, but Matthew—take care of yourself. And him."

"I will," he promised. "I am."

"Good," Shilpa said, and turned. He could hear the sound of her heels clicking as she walked away.

Matt took a deep breath, tried to settle his rattled nerves and picked up his pace so he wouldn't miss the bus.

When he got home, Aiden was waiting up for him again, and Matt had the little thrill in his stomach when he realized. "Hey, baby," he said, as he dropped his bags. It was becoming familiar: the drop, the eager step forward, the way Aiden would melt into his arms immediately after.

"Hi," Aiden said, his eyes crinkling a little in a smile. "I, um, got a few things for the condo while you were gone, this time. I hope you don't mind."

"Things?" Matt asked, blinking.

"Yeah. I upgraded the blender for breakfast stuff. And you were talking about that new book about that Roman philosopher you like, so I uh, bought a copy of that, too." He looked almost embarrassed by the gesture, although maybe that was Matt's imagination. It was pretty late.

Matt leaned up to kiss his forehead. "Thank you, Aiden. You didn't have to do that."

"I know," he said, his hand tracing over the lines of Matt's back, like if he didn't touch him constantly, relearn the shape constantly, he'd forget what it felt like.

"I just wanted to do something for *you.* And it's hard when you're on the road so often."

"Aiden," Matt said, seriously, "you do so much for me already. Just by being here. Do you understand?"

Aiden wouldn't meet his eyes. "Yeah, I do. But hey, come on, it's so late. Will you come to bed?"

Matt said, the way he always did: "Yes."

Adjusting to life in Montreal while Matt was on the road was a strange experience. They still FaceTimed after most of the games, although half of the time Matt was on the verge of falling asleep, but that was fine. It almost reminded him of when things first started, the little swoop of excitement he'd get when he realized Matt was calling.

But the day-to-day existence of living without a purpose, in a city that wasn't his, in a house that was partially his but only in a weird in-between way, in a place where Matt was really the only person he *knew,* was really starting to do his head in.

He was folding a load of laundry while Matt was at practice and he looked up at the calendar and realized that even though a lot of time had passed already, he was still going to have to make it through the rest of the season. And if he stayed for any length of time, the *whole eighty-two games* next season. At the thought of it, Aiden's skin started feeling a little itchy, the room too small.

It wasn't a full-blown panic attack, exactly, but he had to take some time in the bathroom, his head on the cold porcelain of the tub, eyes closed while he focused on the feeling of his breath, in and out, in and out, his lungs filling and emptying.

He could distract himself a little with emails to Ellie, who was the actual starting goalie on her mites team now, and who had specific questions about the angle she should be sharpening her skates for better lateral movement or what kinds of stretching exercises she should be doing before games, and who would occasionally send him a video of her doing drills to ask for his opinion on her form.

Aiden took his time to think about his responses and compose the best possible answers for her but at a certain point, he was emailing advice to a five-year-old, and as much as he enjoyed doing it, there was only so much time he could spend on that before the reality of his situation started to sink in.

When Matt was home, it was fine. They went for walks and watched movies and fucked and just existed in the same space. Aiden worked his way through yoga in the morning, and Matt watched him with huge eyes the whole time. Aiden made them dinner and Matt cleaned. Aiden made him laugh with dumb observations and stupid little jokes. Aiden accompanied him on walks in the park, shoulders bumping. Aiden went shopping for some new clothes and Matt teased him the whole time, offering a running commentary about how hot he looked in everything, just to make him blush. After Matt made it back from l'Arène after games or Brossard after practice, Aiden worked out the aches in his knee and legs and back for him.

All of it was—nice. Almost domestic. The kind of shit he'd been missing for so long it still felt like an aching wound inside. Aiden started to relax, a little, to let himself *enjoy* it. During those times, Aiden felt like his old self again, like a kid with the whole world in front of him, a life with a man who loved him so fucking much.

And then Matt *left*. And all of it—everything he was trying to ignore, everything he was trying not to look at directly—came rushing back in. Each time Matt left, it felt even worse.

He kept going to see Dr. Gauthier. It was just harder to pick apart his feelings when she asked him what he felt, because more often than not these days, it was like there was too much going on in his head, and to pull one bad feeling out of the knot of them was impossible.

"Hey," Matt said, "you've been kinda—not yourself tonight. What's up?"

Aiden said, "Nothing."

They'd had some form of that conversation several times over the last few weeks, and today wasn't any different. Matt sometimes wished that he could see into Aiden's head, that he could cut it open and put it under a microscope so he could figure out what the hell was going on in there. Trying to figure Aiden out had been a lifelong study, from the very beginning of their relationship to now, learning the code to crack when even Aiden didn't necessarily understand why he was reacting the way that he was. Matt had been good at it, during their first relationship, but the yawning gulf of years between them had obscured things, and he was still relearning Aiden from the inside out.

So he knew something was wrong, just not what it was.

They were sitting on the couch, watching a movie, the kind of quiet night that Matt had always treasured. The kind of night they hadn't had many of the first time around, when most of the year was spent apart. Aiden's head rested on Matt's thigh, and Matt had his hand twined in Aiden's hair. On a normal night, it would have been comforting, quiet and pleasant, the warmth of Aiden's body so close to him. The distance between was quiet, but palpable. Something was going on in Aiden's head, and Matt didn't know what it was.

He was curled in on himself, tense and miserable, and Matt couldn't reach him. He stared at the TV screen, but the movie wasn't really sinking in. It was a little like watching in a foreign language, even though it was all in English.

"Aiden?" he said, after a few longer moments of silence.

"What, Matt?"

"What have you been doing while I'm gone? Besides, like, the laundry and the cleaning and cooking, which I appreciate but—"

"It's a thank-you for letting me freeload in your apartment," Aiden mumbled into Matt's thigh. He didn't lift his head up to look at him.

"You *aren't* freeloading. You're here because—" *You're here because I love you. You're here because I never want to live without you again.* "You're here because we both want you to be here. Right?"

"There's nowhere else I'd rather be," Aiden said, although even Matt could pick the irony out of that.

"Is there anything you'd rather be doing? Do you want to look into skating again? Do you want suggestions about where to go? Aino said you guys have been hanging out a little, would that help if…?"

Aiden sat up, slowly. He'd been eating better since

he'd been staying with Matt, but his hair was still wild and shaggy, and he still had that haunted prey animal look in his eyes sometimes, like he was only a few steps away from bolting. "That's the problem, Matty... I just don't know what to do with myself, still. I'm trying. I'm *really* trying. But I just... I go through each day just waiting for you. You coming back here after games is the only thing that makes me feel *anything*."

Matt stared at him, unsure of what to say.

"It's bad, right? But I don't know how to fix it. It's just... I'm just fucked up, Matt, and I don't know how to fix it. I don't know what else to do that I haven't already tried. It feels pretty hopeless, sometimes, and at some point, you're going to realize—" He cut himself off there, and his eyes shuttered, all of the light in them dimmed.

"I'm going to realize *what*?" Matt asked.

Aiden didn't answer, or maybe couldn't answer. He ducked his head and wormed his way back into Matt's arms, an embrace that felt suddenly fragile. He didn't say anything, just let Matt hold him, and breathed in and out. It was the kind of rhythm that Matt recognized well, even all of these years later: he was doing a meditative breathing exercise, the kind of mindfulness practice that had helped propel him to incredibly successful heights as a goalie. The kind of blank acceptance of the present and exclusion of everything else that had destroyed their life together.

"Matty, please, I don't want to talk about it," Aiden mumbled into his shoulder.

"You know we can't just not talk about things forever, right?"

"I know. I *know*. But can you just…hold me? For now?"

"Yes," Matt said, although the sense of impending doom didn't abate, even when Aiden melted into his arms, almost shaking with relief that they weren't talking about it.

Sometimes Aiden was better at pretending than other times. Those days were better overall. If you could fake it until you made it, it was almost the same thing.

"Seriously, Aiden. What's going on? I thought we were doing better. I thought *you* were doing better, but you've just—"

"Everything's fine, Matty."

Matt eyed him suspiciously but didn't press.

? Gabe asked, later that day.

Everything's fine.

OK, buddy.

Matt left for roadies.

Aiden kept himself busy.

Matt returned from roadies and played home games.

Aiden went to most of them, sat in the stands alone, or sometimes with Aino and the rest of the WAGs, and watched. Now that he had ripped the bandage off, it wasn't as hard as he thought to watch them. Sometimes he could get into the game, sometimes he just let his mind drift. Pears sent him a meme someone made on r/NewYorkLiberty, a picture of Aiden sitting in the stands during a game the Royal had lost badly, with white impact font across his chest that said, when the royal are so bad u dissociate in self-defense.

Matt left for roadies.

Aiden kept himself busy.

Matt came home.

He did this for a few weeks.

III.
WINTER

CHAPTER NINE

December

By this point in his career, Matt could pack for a road trip with his eyes shut. The trick was bringing more than one suit jacket, but a shirt and pants that you could reuse in order to maximize suitcase space. The other trick was folding everything up into those little zipper cases so you could stack them like Tetris blocks. These days he'd rather travel light than anything else, give himself less work and dry cleaning to do when he got home. As he was packing, Aiden lurked in the doorway of their bedroom, arms crossed over his chest, watching Matt folding.

"What's going on in that head of yours?" Matt asked.

"Just thinking," Aiden said, light brown eyes distant, like he didn't want to, or couldn't bring himself to, look directly at Matt.

"About what?"

"I went on the road so many times as a kid and I just… I never even thought about how much time we actually end up spending away from home."

Matt looked up again, frowning. "It is a little crazy

when you think about it. How many days we've both probably spent in hotels over the last three decades."

"I didn't mind it so much when I was playing. It was part of the Routine, even the stuff that I had to adjust."

"You did have a really intense routine. I noticed you haven't been doing most of that stuff anymore."

"A lot of it was tied to the games," Aiden said slowly, "like, they were things I'd started doing when I was young, and then it made sense to keep doing them, because I'd played a good game after doing it. And having that many steps to go through made it easier to prepare for the mindset. And it helped me a lot after I lost you the first time, to focus on the steps even more. But now that I'm not playing…it just feels kind of hollow, and it doesn't bring me the sense of peace it used to. So I had to dial back. And then just stop it, at least the way it used to be. I don't even *have* the Routine anymore. And even that's hard. I've tried to find a new one, but it's not the same."

Matt thought about the times he and Aiden had been able to meet up before games, in New York or in Montreal, how tightly wound he had been. It was like if he adhered strictly to that routine, everything would be fine. If he couldn't, it would take him a while to settle into playing, flailing around, even letting in bad goals, until his brain focused in on what he needed to do. "Is that part of why you've been so unhappy? The lack of a routine?"

Aiden didn't answer, just came into the room and sat down on the bed next to Matt's open suitcase. He reached out with his thumb, ran his finger along the teeth of the zipper and shuddered like someone had slipped a cold hand down the back of his shirt. "It's hard when you're gone," he admitted. "I don't want it to be, but it is. When you're here, I can just think about you, but when you're gone…"

"I'll be home soon, though. And it's not healthy for you to rely so much on me, anyway, right?"

"I know it's not," Aiden said, and he did the thing where his entire face shut down, all expression wiped away.

"I didn't mean it like that," Matt said hastily. "I was just thinking, you know, wherever I end up playing next year—what are you going to do for a whole season?"

"That's what I've been having a hard time thinking about." Aiden looked down. "I don't… I don't know. I've tried to think about it, and I just don't know."

"Would you consider coming around more often with me? When I'm home? Maybe being around the guys would help."

Aiden was folded into himself now, the kind of shrunken misery that punched Matt right in the chest, the kind of thing he desperately hated to see, the kind of thing he had no idea how to begin fixing. "I don't know. I'd probably make things worse if I were there. I don't think your teammates would…"

"My teammates will deal with whatever I ask them to deal with." Matt extended his hand to rest on Aiden's knee. "It's just, Aidy, I want to help. I want to do something. Will you let me?"

"I appreciate you saying that," Aiden said, in the same dull tone he would have used with reporters after a bad loss, giving away nothing. "But you don't need to worry about me, Matty. I'll figure something out. I'll do *something*."

Matt leaned forward, pressed his mouth lightly

against Aiden's, and that at least seemed to jolt him out of the stupor. The kiss was as sweet as always, Aiden melting under the onslaught, and Matt wondered why he couldn't just stay home all of the time, keep Aiden in his bedroom, fuck the life back into his smile and his eyes. He couldn't do that, of course. He wasn't ready to retire. He wasn't ready to figure out the next chapter. But Aiden… Aiden was already there, and Aiden *needed* him.

"Aidy," he said, against Aiden's lips, "I'll be home before you know it. I promise."

"I know," Aiden said, but his eyes had dimmed again. "I know."

Matt didn't have time to do what he wanted to do—dump Aiden down in bed and make him smile again, make him gasp and shudder and come—because he had to get to the airport. He almost didn't make it, because it was hard to disentangle himself from Aiden's arm, from Aiden's mouth, from Aiden's sad eyes. He barely made it, limping a little as he rushed toward the tarmac where the rest of the team was waiting to board the plane.

"Safy," Jammer said, raising his eyebrows. "You good?"

"Yeah, uh, just got caught up at home."

Jammer looked at him again, head tilted a little. "Your *boy* good?"

"That's…another story altogether," Matt said, and sighed. "You ever think about retirement, Jams?"

They waited together as the rookies climbed the stairs, and it was clear Jammer gave the question some thought. His face was distant, and he rubbed his hand over his stubbled jaw. "I don't know," he said, after a moment. "Diya used to ask me about this. What the plan was. Especially since I've had more than my share of concussions over the years. Didn't know what to tell her, honestly."

"That's the problem, isn't it?" Matt watched Jack Crane nudging Rémi Cormier in the side as they laughed about some private little rookie joke. "When you're young, retirement seems so fucking far away. And then when it sneaks up on you… Aiden's having a really hard time with it, Jams. I don't know what to do about it. I don't know what I'm going to do when it's *my* time."

"Is it your time?" For someone usually so chill, there was an edge of concern to Jammer's words.

"No," Matt said, slowly. "I don't want it to be, at least. I don't think. I still have hockey in me, and the thought about trying to figure out what comes after… I just don't *know*."

"Knee and contract aside, buddy, you've been just as effective on both ends, even if you're slow as shit now."

"Lucky that my skating never relied on acceleration." It had been a common criticism, even when Matt was younger.

"Focusing on the wrong thing here, eh, Saf."

"I just don't like not knowing what to do. I don't know what to do about Aiden. I don't know what to do about *me*."

"Diya and I were never able to really come to an agreement about that, either. It's part of why we broke up."

"Sorry again, about that."

"It's fine," Jammer said, mouth twisting down. "All I'm saying is, maybe you should think about what you want for next season. Whether that's Campbell, or playing, or a new contract somewhere else. Before someone or something makes the decision for you. Because let me tell you, I know from experience. That one fucking sucks."

Matt thought about the last time he'd needed surgery, the way it had felt when his knee gave out. The audible *pop* of his muscle tearing, the immediate pain and the way his leg had crumpled under his own weight. He thought about Aiden turning down his proposal, which had somehow felt worse. "Yeah," he said, and moved forward onto the steps. "Thanks, Jams."

"For what? You didn't figure out shit."

"For being here while I didn't figure out shit," Matt said, and went up the stairs into the plane.

Aiden wondered if this was how the WAGs felt, caught in some kind of limbo in between games. He wondered if this was his own fault, because he hadn't figured out how to fill those spaces in between. He wondered if knowing how he wanted to form his life would make a difference or whether it was just the uncertainty of life in Montreal.

He wondered how long this thing with Matt would last if he couldn't figure out what he needed to do to not feel this way all of the time. He wondered what he would do if it did last and there were years of this. He wondered whether the things he was starting to think he might like to do with his future were even possible or whether he would screw that up, too. He wondered whether Matt would be better off—

He wondered whether therapy was worth it. He wondered whether it was even helping. He wondered if he'd feel like this in New York.

He wondered whether he should just go home.

Matt was washing dishes because Aiden had cooked. He was studiously not saying anything. His shoulders were tense and hunched forward as he scrubbed. It felt like Matt had been walking on eggshells around him in a way that he hadn't done since the first week Aiden fell back into his life, and Aiden wanted to punch something about it. Instead, he occupied himself with emptying the dishwasher and putting away the clean dishes. Sorting the cutlery. A repetitive exercise that was welcome and did a little bit to take the edge off whatever was going on in his head.

Matt was home for a few days and tomorrow was a day off. Normally Aiden would look forward to this: it was easier to ignore the shit swirling around in his head with a distraction, and Matt was as good a distraction as he could ever hope to have.

Aiden watched Matt washing the dishes. Matt kept looking back at him, a frown tilting the corner of his mouth, like he wanted to say something, but he was holding himself back.

Aiden did it for him. "What?"

"What?"

"You want to say something. You should just tell me what you want to say."

Matt set the pot down in the sink and turned around. "Aiden, I don't know what's going on in your head, but this isn't—this isn't working."

Aiden's brain, constantly screaming, quieted completely. This was what he had been waiting for, and now that it was actually happening, he felt almost serene. "Okay."

"What will it take for you to be satisfied? I'm doing

my best, but like—I can't *fix* you. You can't rely on me for that, and you're still—"

"I know you can't," Aiden said, short and clipped. "I know that really well. I never expected you to."

"It's just… I *want* to help. And I don't know how to help. Everything I try doesn't seem to be… And it feels like you're not even trying, sometimes."

"I am—*I am*—it's just *difficult*. There's too many things that feel *wrong*. I've been seeing someone about it, you know?"

"Well, do you think it's helping?"

"I don't know! I don't know. Things were easier when you were, before the season started, but now I'm just constantly thinking about it. I feel like until I can figure out some kind of *purpose* it's just going to keep going like this. I don't think I'm the kind of person who can just do nothing all day. It just feels like, like running out of time."

Matt's hand, still wet from the dishes, at the small of Aiden's back. His handprint soaked through Aiden's shirt. "What do you mean, running out of time? You've got all the time in the fucking world."

"It doesn't feel that way. Most of the time. It's like I knew who I was all of these years because I had hockey, because that's what I *did*, and now I don't do *anything*, and I just feel—I don't know. Lost."

"You're not," Matt said, insistently, "you're right here, with me," and Aiden didn't know how to tell him that as much as he wanted it to be true, it wasn't.

Later on, that night, Aiden murmured in Matt's ear, "Come on, touch me, please," because it was always easier in bed.

Maybe Aiden couldn't figure out what the hell to say

to make things better, couldn't say half of the things he wanted or needed to say. But in bed, naked in the dark, it was easy to show Matt how much he loved him, with his mouth or with his hands, with all of the ways he could offer himself, without ever having to say one single word.

He wondered if Matt understood.

Matt sometimes felt like his life was split into two: the time he spent on the ice, with the team, and the time he spent with Aiden, at home. When he got to l'Arène or the practice facility at Brossard, he could put his worries about Aiden out of his mind, at least temporarily. Focus instead on the game, on pushing himself through the pain in his legs, on the things he *needed* to be focused on.

They were finishing up a relatively long home stand before they would head out to the West Coast for the longest road trip of the year, and as Matt pulled on his gear in the locker room and looked up at the faces of all of the captains who had served before him, the players whose numbers were retired, he had the strange jolt of a reminder that maybe next year he wouldn't be doing this.

He watched Crane and Cormier, heads together in their side-by-side stalls; he watched Jammer, bobbing his head along with the music in his AirPods; he watched Fournier, silent and meditative in his own stall, a posture that reminded Matt of nothing so much as Aiden before a game, years and years ago.

He looked down at his knee, the scar tissue cutting through the hair of his leg, a thick pink line that hadn't really faded.

He took a deep breath and prepared to go out on the ice.

Today they were hosting the Boston Beacons, the Royal's perennial rival, though it wasn't much of a rivalry these days. The Beacons were in the beginning of a rebuild, even as the Royal were heading toward one themselves. It helped that their coach was Ryan Sullivan, a Hall of Famer who had some decidedly modern ideas about coaching, but even he could only do so much with a roster that was half veterans on expiring contracts and half young players who were still learning the ropes. The one thing that Matt could say about the Beacons was that they were never out of a game, no matter how badly they played. It wouldn't be an easy win, even if the team wasn't necessarily *good*.

At the very least, he wouldn't have to deal with any additional bullshit. It wasn't every game, but every few there was a player who thought about trying it, seeing whether they could antagonize Matt into doing something stupid by calling him slurs or chirping him about Aiden. Aiden, who came to home games more frequently than he didn't now, and was photographed occasionally by nosy fans, sitting with the rest of the Royal WAGs.

Matt responded the same way he always did: waiting to pick his spots, rarely taking a penalty unless he needed to. The Beacons weren't like that, though. You could see the work that Sullivan had done instituting a *culture*. The kids still took stupid penalties sometimes, but you never heard the players saying the kinds of things that had been common on the ice when Matt had started playing. The kinds of things that weren't even uncommon *now*. It was a nice reminder that, even if there was still a culture problem, the league was slowly starting to change.

Matt met Kai Williams, their best forward, a kid who was already carrying the entire team on his back, at center ice for the opening face-off. He was probably going to be their captain next year, and Matt made a mental note to reach out to offer him advice. It wasn't easy captaining an Original Six franchise, especially through a rebuild.

"Hey, kid," Matt said, as they lined up.

"Hey," Williams said, and smiled. It was weird, knowing that there were guys who were playing now who gave interviews about how they'd grown up watching and admiring and modeling their games after *him*. Williams was one of them, and he was in his second season now, confident and sure. They both wore number four, and the face-offs had a weird kind of symmetry that way, a guy at the end of his career and a guy just beginning it. "How's it going, Safaryan?"

"Been a while," he agreed, as they crouched.

"Knee holding up?"

"Yup. Team holding up?"

"Barely."

"All right, gentlemen," the linesman said, rolling his eyes. "When we're all done with the social call, we've got a hockey game to play."

"Yes, sir," they said, in unison, and Williams cracked another one of those smiles as the puck dropped and Matt put his shoulder into it, knocking Williams on his ass with the force of the push. He'd had that problem when he was younger, before he'd figured out his center of gravity.

"Sorry," Matt called over his shoulder, as he left Williams to pick himself up from the ice and went skating off to catch up with Adam Morin and the puck.

That was the thing: he could *still* do this. He was still doing this. Knee aside, Aiden's problems aside—Matt could *still do this*. He wasn't ready to give it up, not yet.

He wondered if Aiden was watching. He wondered if he would be there, with the WAGs, when Matt got off the ice. Matt shook his head again and ground his teeth together. He had to concentrate on the game. So he did.

Dr. Gauthier's office got a lot of natural sunlight, and she had a knack for plants. It reminded Aiden a little of Matt's condo, filled with green leaves curling eagerly toward the windows. He also, instinctively, turned toward the window, and her chair. Squinted a little against the sun.

"I think—maybe—I thought of something I might be interested in doing."

"That's wonderful. What is it?"

"Uh…coaching. But specifically coaching, teaching kids? I've been working with Matt's niece, and my rookie is…well, it was rewarding teaching him, too, but I think maybe it's easier to work with kids than young adults."

Now that it was out in the world, it was real. It felt more solid.

"You're certainly qualified to do this, Aiden. Is there something you're concerned about?"

"Just, uh, the logistics. You know."

"You can do research and figure all of this out.

The important thing is to allow yourself to envision the possibility."

Aiden knew a lot about envisioning things, although the efficacy of those visualizations over the years remained in doubt. The problem was allowing himself to go further, and he didn't know how to get around that.

Matt had started dreading the road trips, not just because they were long, but because Aiden looked so fucking sad when he went on them. This one was rough even in better times—through California and Seattle and up to Vancouver. The time zone difference was actual hell. And he'd be gone for ten days, and he wasn't looking forward to treatments from the medical staff on the road, outside of the familiar facilities in Montreal. It was exhausting to play, but it was even worse, now, knowing that Aiden was going to be waiting for him at home, and he wouldn't be there to do—well, anything.

"Hey," Matt said, "since I'm going to be gone for a while, how about we actually… I don't know. Let's have a date day."

"A what?" Aiden said, blinking.

"Just a day to spend together. No hockey. Just you and me, and Montreal."

"Matty, you don't have to…"

"Come on," Matt said firmly, "I'm not giving you an option. Get your coat, Aidy."

Although Aiden looked doubtful, he obeyed. Matt had run through his little mental list of places he had long ago thought about taking Aiden, and the Botanical Gardens were one of them. It didn't matter that it was winter, that there was snow on the ground: the gardens were open year-round, and even offered the option for cross-country skiing, if you were so inclined. Matt, who didn't want to risk hurting himself any worse on something that wasn't even hockey, opted for the walk instead.

Although a few other people had had the same idea, it was cold enough that it wasn't very crowded. The snow was still falling lightly, little flurries that stuck to the edges of Aiden's eyelashes before he blinked and they fell away or melted with the heat of his body. It was a fresh snow that hadn't been trampled yet, and the air trembled with the chilly snap, the sky still white and gray.

They walked in companionable silence through the park, and Matt watched Aiden's face slowly lose some of the anguish that it often had in moments where he thought Matt wasn't watching. It was enough just to enjoy the heavy silence of the morning, broken only by the noise of birds, the snap of branches, the crush of snow falling from them to the ground, his own breath in his ears.

Feeling a bit daring, he slipped his hand into Aiden's, both of their fingers freezing from the chill and slowly warming against each other. Aiden shot him a surprised look, a glance sideways that said, *are you sure?* Matt couldn't answer in words, just squeezed his hand, silent, and kept walking.

By the time they made their way through the Chinese Garden, enough snow had fallen and iced on the trees that it had the look of a toy box scene, the perfectly laden branches hanging over the impossibly clear water, atop the red roofs of the pagoda.

As they walked through the stone courtyard, Aiden looked up at the sky again, and for once, he didn't look anything except at peace, and something in Matt's chest eased infinitesimally.

"It's beautiful, isn't it?" Matt asked.

"It's lovely. And it's nice to get out into the fresh air. It's—I forgot how much I missed a real winter."

"Come on, you never got one in New York?"

"I mean, we had snows, but they'd get churned up into slush so quickly," Aiden said, as they walked through the portal door. "Even if I went to Central Park, it didn't really last long." He let go of Matt's hand for a brief second, ducking down to grab a handful of snow and toss it at him. It caught Matt right in the chest, splattering all over his parka, cold against his face.

"What the fuck," he gasped, and Aiden was laughing, ducking down for more snow. "Ohh, you're in for it now—"

It was a brief, brutal snowball fight, without much time to really form them into balls that would have any weight, but with enough snow flying that both of their hair, their coats, their clothes, were quickly sopping wet with it anyway. There was no one to judge them, no one to raise an eyebrow at two grown men acting like small children. Aiden looked a little like some kind of forest spirit with snow and ice crusted in his hair and eyelashes and beard, a wild look in his light brown eyes, like one of the foxes that hunted through the grounds.

Instead of lunging for more snow, Matt grabbed Aiden's wrists in icy fingers and backed him up against the stone wall. Aiden's eyes widened, but he didn't fight, trapped between the cold stone and Matt's warm body.

"Anyone could see," Aiden said, looking down at Matt's mouth. He licked his lips, a little nervously.

"This is what you were angling for with that snow, wasn't it?" Matt said quietly, just to feel Aiden shiver. Let go of one of his hands just briefly enough to brush some of the snow from his hair, to cup his jaw with one hand. "You always got excited, thinking about that, didn't you?"

"Matty..." Aiden's voice was breathy, nervous, excited, and he was so fucking irresistible that Matt couldn't help doing the reckless thing and kissing him. His mouth was hot but his lips were cold, frozen from the snow, and he was trembling under the force of it, his whole body shivering.

"Aiden," Matt said, "you know I'd do anything for you, don't you? Baby?"

Aiden didn't answer, just kissed him back, desperately, like if their mouths weren't tangled together, their bodies weren't touching, if Aiden's leg wasn't shoved between Matt's thighs, he might expire.

Eventually, reluctantly, Matt pulled away. As reckless and as open as they'd been, he didn't need anyone taking pictures and posting them online. Although they were technically in public, it was a moment that had felt precious and private and necessary. "Come on," he said, "I have a whole lot more planned for today."

They had a leisurely lunch at the garden's café, and by the time they'd dried off and warmed up, Matt decided to take Aiden back to the MMFA, where they could walk quietly together and enjoy the art without Miles yelling at Matt, or Ellie talking Aiden's ear off. Matt didn't hold his hand, there, but he thought about it, the way that Aiden had gripped him tightly like he was afraid of letting go.

They had an early dinner at a yakitori spot Matt had been meaning to try, split skewers of hearts and gizzards and octopus, knees bumping under the table. It was the kind of place that was loud and crowded and Matt only had to sign autographs a few times, ignore the curious eyes flicking to Aiden, who was shrinking again in the chair whenever anyone approached them.

"Was this a good day?" Matt asked him, as they were walking back to the car, full from dinner, warm even against the face of the cold winter chill.

"The best," Aiden admitted, and looked down at him, serious. "I hope you know how much I appreciate all of this."

"*Appreciate?*"

"Just—I know I'm not much fun to be around lately. I just…that you're still trying. That you still want to be with me."

"Of course I still want to be with you, Aiden, I—"

"Less talking, more going home and fucking me, I think," Aiden cut him off, and Matt couldn't argue with that.

Later that night, Aiden wrapped tightly around him, head thrown back and eyes wide open, an inexplicably melancholy look in his eyes. "Baby," Matt gasped, seated so deeply in Aiden's body that he felt like he could barely move, desperately needing to move anyway, "what's wrong? Am I hurting you? Do you want me to stop?"

"No," Aiden managed. "No, I just—I just—one day you're going to—you're going—" Instead of finishing, Aiden closed his eyes, like that would prevent Matt from asking any further questions. His hands stilled on Matt's back, his fingers gentle against the bunch of muscle at Matt's shoulder, where he was holding himself up above Aiden's body. When Aiden spoke, his voice was ragged, from sex but also an emotion so deep it seemed like it hurt him. "Matty, you're too good to me, you're too *good* to me, and I don't deserve it."

Mystified, Matt said, "I don't—I don't understand, Aiden. I love you. I *love* you, I—"

"Please, stop talking," Aiden said, his voice trembling, "please, just fuck me," and Matt, who could never say no to him, obliged.

Matt was on the last night of a roadie and Aiden was running to the summit of Mont-Royal for the second time that day.

There was nothing else to do except run, so he kept running.

He looked down at the city and thought about doing this, day after day, for the rest of the season.

He thought about doing this for years. He thought about what he was going to do if Matt signed somewhere else in free agency, whether Matt would even want to drag Aiden along, whether *he'd* even want to go and have to get used to another city. He thought about Matt saying *you know I'd do anything for you*, and what Aiden wanted anything to be was Matt, home with him, something he could never bring himself to ask for. He thought about Matt, pushing himself through the pain of his knee, because he—like Aiden years ago—loved hockey too much to give it up. He thought about how he couldn't ever ask that from Matt, that he didn't deserve to ask for it.

He thought about how it was going to feel when it ended, when Matt inevitably realized that Aiden wasn't the man he used to be and probably wouldn't ever be again, when Aiden had to pick up the pieces for the third time in his life. He thought about Matt, patient and kind and funny, and he thought about Matt, too fucking kind to let Aiden *go*.

He couldn't do this.

He couldn't.

Aiden ran back to Matt's apartment, didn't bother showering.

Packed his bag with only the things he couldn't afford to leave behind.

Left the spare key.

Bought a one-way flight to New York.

Called a cab.

After he landed, he texted Pears, I'm home.

Oh, buddy, what the fuck did you DO?

Everyone's better off if I just ended it now. I couldn't wait around for things to end. I couldn't wait around until I dragged him down to my level.

Oh, Soup...

No playlist?

I don't have one for shit like this, Soupy. You sure did that.

Aiden didn't know what to say to that, so he didn't answer.

Aiden knew exactly when Matt made it back to the condo because his phone rang.

It was slightly after two in the morning, and Aiden sat on his roof, nursing a glass of whiskey that he had been refilling for the last hour or so and looking out at the skyline and the half-moon over it. He contemplated not answering the call, but after more rings than he probably should have let it go, he did anyway.

He took a deep breath. “Hi.”

“Aiden, what the *hell*? Where are you? Are you okay?”

“New York. I’m fine.”

“I—you—New York? *What?*”

“I’m doing you a favor. It’s not going to work out, I—just pulled the Band-Aid off for both of us, you’re better off without having to—”

“Can you let *me* decide that?”

“No, because you’re clearly too fucking nice to admit you’d be happier without me and let me go. Look, you said yourself, you can’t fix me, and I’m not… I can’t stay at home waiting for you, I’m losing my fucking *mind*—”

“Aiden,” Matt said, quiet and very, very careful. “You couldn’t have just tried talking to me about it?”

Aiden said, “I’m sorry, Matty, you deserve a hell of a lot better than what I can give you right now,” and hung up before Matt could argue with him.

Matt set his cell phone down on the table.

It was almost three o’clock in the morning and the reality of what had just happened to him was really starting to sink in. Matt got up from the couch and stood there in the living room of his condo, empty for the first time in months, and took a deep breath.

Aiden was gone.

Aiden had left him again.

Aiden had—

He was exhausted the way he always was after a game and late-night travel, but he already knew there was no way that he was going to be able to sleep. He remembered how he'd felt the first time Aiden had dumped him. It had actually taken some time to sink in. He'd known, but he hadn't *known*. He'd thought, *I'm going to be so fucking normal about this*, and made a point of going in to work every day, working as hard as he always had, never letting on that anything had happened.

Of course, he hadn't been normal about it. He was never normal about it. Pushing it down and ignoring it had only let it fester.

This time, Matt took a deep breath again, counted to ten, and said, aloud, "What the *fuck*."

A million thoughts jostled around in his head, a million feelings in his chest. Anger at Aiden, for taking the decision away from him again; anger at himself, for not seeing the signs earlier. *Sad* didn't really describe the hollow feeling in his chest, not really. He'd never been great with words, but he'd have time to think of ways to describe that one.

Aiden had sounded pretty broken up about it on the phone, which was ironic, but not surprising. Aiden had always made choices that seemed logical on the surface but were ultimately driven by emotions he hadn't been capable of dealing with, and Matt had been the one left to pick up the pieces. He knew Aiden was probably gutted. He couldn't even bring himself to think *fuck him*.

He wasn't going to be able to sleep tonight, that was for sure. He was still wearing his coat and travel clothes, and so instead of taking them off, he just went back out into the hallway. Down the elevator. Outside.

Decembers in Montreal had the kind of bitter cold that cut right through you, no matter how warm your coat was. The punch in the face was welcome. Matt wasn't sure where he was going. He just started walking, first from the little side street that was his home, then to St.-Viateur. It was strange, walking down the streets this late at night. All of the businesses he'd spent fifteen years frequenting, shuttered and closed, the street illuminated by the lamps and nothing else. How many times on a rush to practice he'd stopped to grab a bagel, eaten it in the car on the drive to Brossard.

It was strange, how well he knew every single street of Montreal, how little of it he'd gotten to experience with Aiden, and how Aiden's presence in his life loomed over all of it anyway.

Matt cut through the smaller park at the intersection of Viateur and Outremont, the pond iced over. It was a lovely little area; he'd spent many summer days sitting on the benches, people-watching, or autumn days watching the leaves fall. Around the park rose rows of pleasant, well-kept, red-bricked Victorian homes. He kept walking. He knew the way quite well now: the path right up to the edge of Mont-Royal. It took him through the park and the cemetery, toward the trail that would lead to the summit, where the cross shone in white against the dark line of the sky.

Technically the park wasn't open this late at night, but no one stopped him. Matt would deal with it if anyone did. He wasn't sure why he was doing this. It had been some time since he'd been here alone; more recently, he'd been with Aiden. It was strange to come again, after him. *After him.* The thought twisted around and around in his head as he walked up the path toward the summit. Part of him had known it was coming. Part of him hadn't wanted to believe it was true.

Above him, the bare arms of the trees stretched up to the sky. He'd walked this trail in every season: the new green of spring, the full canopy of summer, the orange and yellow of the fall. It felt appropriate that he was here now, so close to the end of the year. The end of everything. He couldn't help laughing, breath escaping in a brief puff of steam in the cold air. It sounded melodramatic. It *was* melodramatic.

He felt a little better by the time he got to the summit and looked down over the city. The dark line of the trees first, and then the buildings beyond, the faint glowing lights in just a few windows as the earliest risers started getting up to get ready to make the city hum and whirr in its familiar patterns. This was the city he'd made his home for so long, the city he'd sacrificed his youth and his health and to some extent his personal life to. It had paid him back: he would never have to worry about money, he had the eternal adoration of a few million people in Quebec after bringing home the first Cup to Canada in decades.

Matt exhaled. His hands gripped the cold metal of the observation railing. It was so cold it was almost painful, but he welcomed it. He had to get it together. When everything came down to it, he had had a pretty damn good life. The uncertainty of the next few seasons was nothing. Aiden leaving him alone was nothing. He just had to put it in perspective.

He was older. He wasn't as weak as he had been as a child. Part of him had been preparing for this. Part of him had known it was going to happen. Part of him simply couldn't bear to have proved his parents and Miles *right*.

He flipped through his mental file of Marcus Aurelius, searching for something to focus on that would help him feel—something. Anything. He came to the mental image of the rock with the waves crashing over it. *"It stands unmoved and the raging of the sea falls still around it."* That was how Matt would have to be.

He was going to be okay.

He had to be okay—he didn't have much of a choice.

Whether or not that was just lying to himself again, he'd have to wait and see.

CHAPTER TEN

January

Even before player assistance, Matt had never been a big partier. It wasn't that he was shy, or even introverted—he was just quiet, and he liked to be in control of himself at all times. Hockey culture wasn't very friendly to that kind of personality, because most of the team bonding events involved alcohol or coke or both. There had been a time when he'd forced himself to participate. During the height of the worst of it, he hadn't been partying so much as trying to numb *everything*. And after it, he was usually pretty careful about how much he was drinking or why.

He was still careful, even though it had been a long time since he had had what he considered *a problem*. So normally, even on a New Year's, out with the team, Matt was pacing himself and keeping an eye on things. The last night he'd gone out with Aiden and the team—that had been the first time he'd really let himself loose, the first time he'd really relaxed in longer than he could remember. And now Aiden was gone, and Matt was…

Matt was out at a club in Vieux-Montreal, trying to

put a stoic face on things. Matt was in the middle of the party, chatting with Cormier about how he'd had to take a few face-offs after Koski got kicked out of the circle last night, giving him a few tips about ways to shift his weight so that he had a better chance of muscling the opposing center off of the puck. Matt was acting as a wingman for Jammer, who was chatting up the bartender. Matt was nursing drinks for longer than he really should have been, and Matt was maybe a little drunk, but nowhere near as drunk as he should have been, for a night like this.

"Happy New Year!" Jammer yelled in his face, and when the clock chimed, said, "Excuse me," to the bartender, and kissed Matt on the lips. It wasn't a real kiss: not with tongue, friendly and joking more than anything else. Jammer was a big guy, at least five inches taller than Matt, and having his hands on either side of Matt's face had only reminded Matt of all of the times Aiden had leaned down to kiss him like that.

Matt, blinking, said, "Happy New Year, Jams," as soon as he could breathe again, and then, "I'm gonna go outside for some fresh air."

It was a beautiful night, cold and clear, and for a second Matt wished that he could smoke. Something to do with his hands, something to burn the clenching pain out of his lungs. He leaned, instead, against the stone wall of the building and inhaled the crisp night air. He wondered what Aiden was doing and immediately shoved the thought ruthlessly down.

Whatever Aiden was doing, it had nothing to do with him. Not anymore.

That didn't make it any easier to bear. His knee was aching, too, so Matt sat down on the stairs leading up to the bar and put his head in his hands. It was stupid: his whole team was in there, having a fantastic time. The kids he'd been carefully watching through this whole year. The veterans who'd had his back for many long seasons. Matt knew he should go back in there and enjoy it. This could potentially be his last New Year's in Montreal, and if he *didn't* enjoy it, if he let Aiden ruin this for him too, he'd probably regret it forever. But somehow, he couldn't bring himself to do it.

Behind him, he heard the door open, soft footsteps on the stone. He didn't look up as someone sat down next to him and said, "Safy?"

"Hello, Jack," Matt said, with his head still in his hands.

"What are you doing out here?" Jack asked. He often sounded sarcastic, even when he was being serious. Tonight wasn't one of those nights. He sat down next to Matt, his lanky legs stretched out in front of him. "The party's inside, Cap."

"Yeah, well, I just… I don't know. I didn't want to bring down the mood."

They sat in silence for a while, although the streets were anything but. Montreal loved a party, especially in the winter, and the streets echoed with the sounds of music and fireworks and people laughing and yelling. It was probably a difficult thing to be so miserable in a city like Montreal on New Year's, but by god, Matt was managing.

It was *kind* of Jack to come out here. He had been having a strong rookie season so far, considering. He wasn't exactly a lock for the Rookie of the Year award, but he was in the conversation. He had a more than respectable forty-one points so far, and if he could avoid getting injured, would probably hit the sixty-point mark in his first season. His defensive numbers definitely could've used some work, but that would come as he put on a little more muscle. He was already going to be the 1C next year, whether Matt was there or not.

"What's the deal?" Jack said, after the silence started to get a little awkward.

Matt still hadn't picked his head up out of his hands. He wondered, if he looked hard enough at the ground, whether he could bore through the stone and escape into the sewers. It was something that might've happened in those stupid comic books Aiden was always reading. Jesus, he had to stop thinking about Aiden. "We've talked about the captaincy, right?"

"Right..."

"It's a lot. I don't know. Don't make the mistakes I did. There's a lot of things I haven't talked about and a lot of things I can't talk about. But... I don't know. Don't find yourself at thirty-six wondering what the hell you're going to do with your life after hockey. Don't let someone..."

He couldn't bring himself to look up, but he could feel Jack staring at him like he'd grown three heads. The kid really didn't look like a hockey player at all, out of his pads. He was tall and lanky and weedy, and his features were almost delicate, the kind of face that made him very popular with teenaged fans. The kind of face he'd have to grow into, the kind of face that definitely drew more than a little chirping on the ice.

"Don't let someone *what*?" Jack asked, mystified.

"Don't listen to me. I don't know. It's late, and I'm old as fuck, and I'm being...morose."

"Got it," Jack said, and Matt could see him from

the corner of his eye, making a check mark gesture. "Don't be morose. But Safy…why are you *telling* me this stuff?"

"I just… I've been here a long time, Jack. I've been the captain a long time. And I have a feeling that you're going to be the captain. Maybe not the next captain, if I'm gone next season, but at some point very soon."

Jack rocked back like Matt had slapped him. "What? No! You're not going anywhere. You can't."

"It might not be in my control." He finally picked his head up out of his hands. He *wasn't* drunk, but he almost felt like it, overwhelmed with the melancholy of the evening, of the weight of the legacy that he knew he'd have to pass on soon.

"You're not going *anywhere*, Safy," Jack said again, his eyes huge. He looked nothing like Aiden, and somehow, Matt was still reminded of him anyway, the same way that everything reminded him of Aiden, lately. Jesus, he had to get it together. Jack was saying, holding out his hand, "Come on, Cap. You can't just sit out here being sad all night. Not on New Year's."

"See?" Matt said, a little dry, but as seriously as he could manage it. "This is why you're going to be the captain one day."

Jack abruptly let go of his arm as he was pulling Matt to his feet, and Matt stumbled and caught himself. "Stop saying that," he said, as they both walked toward the door. "Seriously, Safy. We still need you here. *I* need you here. What am I going to do when we only have like one other line that's a real threat? I'm going to get murdered out there."

"You'll figure it out." Matt squared his shoulders, looking at the door. It might have been his last New

Year's with the team, it might not have. But he had to make the best of it. He had to be there for the team. "You'll gain the muscle, and you'll figure out how to deal with being the focus of everyone's checks, and you're gonna be fucking great, kid."

Jack was looking at him again, serious and strangely sad. "It means a lot to me that you think that. But also, if you keep being *this* sincere, I'm going to… I don't know. Come on, Safy, let's find Rémi. I bet he's hiding in a corner somewhere."

"Good plan," Matt said, and then he was once again enveloped by the noise of the club.

By the time he got home, it was almost three a.m. and Matt was a little drunk. Some of the guys had been planning to keep the party going at Manny's place, but Matt had begged off and caught a cab home. He'd considered walking, seeing whether the cold night air could knock some sense into him, but it would have taken him an hour and he was already exhausted. He was so fucking thankful that the driver didn't ask him any questions, but probably whatever Matt's face looked like had scared him off. He wasn't sure what that *was*, but considering the way he felt right now, it probably wasn't good. It didn't help that the driver had cranked the heat up all of the way, and Matt's face felt hot, his stomach nauseous.

The chill, as Matt stumbled from the steamy car to the stoop of his building, didn't help. Nor did taking the stairs instead of the elevator. He put one foot in front of the other, trying not to think about the rest of the team, probably having a great time without him; trying not to think about Aiden at all.

He shut the door of the condo behind him and leaned back against it, eyes closed. It had been a long time since he'd cried, and he wasn't going to do it now, but emotions were rising in his chest with the kind of intensity and fury that he wasn't used to anymore, after years of therapy and studied stoicism. It was just—it was so fucking quiet in here, so fucking lonely, and he hadn't even realized how much until Aiden had come back into his life and left it again.

Aiden. Aiden. Aiden, echoed in his head, over and over again, a cruel and mocking song. The empty rooms held a million stupid reminders of him. Aiden in the kitchen, melting into an embrace before half-heartedly pushing him away because a timer was going off. Aiden on the couch, curled up against Matt's side while they watched a movie. Aiden in the bedroom, naked and vulnerable and begging. What the fuck was wrong with him, that he couldn't *accept that this was over*?

His feet were moving without his brain's input, into the bedroom, where Aiden had taken over his closet and dressers. Before he could think about what he was doing, Matt was ripping Aiden's clothes off of their hangers, throwing them on the floor in a haphazard pile. He didn't know what he was going to do with them, and he didn't care. All he knew was that it was unbearable having them there.

He yanked open the drawers and banged his knuckles painfully on the edge of wood, abrading the skin, all of the things Aiden had left behind flying through the air. He didn't know why he was doing it or what he was hoping to accomplish, only that he was furious and felt the loss like a physical ache, and there was nowhere else for any of those feelings to go. But he could remove the remainders of Aiden—from the room. Even if he couldn't forget.

When he was done, he was breathing hard, shaking like he'd run a marathon. He was holding a singular sweater, a dark green cable-knit that made Aiden look like a lonely fisherman. Matt buried his face in it: it still smelled like Aiden, faintly but unmistakably, the sense memory like a punch to the side of Matt's head. He took another deep breath and the fury he'd felt bled slowly out of him, and all he was now was deeply sad and more than a little embarrassed at a display no one had even seen.

That was the thing: Matt would always know it happened. Matt was aware of his weakness, his grief.

Matt set Aiden's sweater down on his bed. He hadn't changed the sheets since Aiden had left. He would do the laundry tomorrow. That would be admitting that it was over, but maybe that was what he needed to do to grieve, to move *on*. Right now, he knelt on the floor and, slowly, started the process of folding the clothes, stacking them carefully. It didn't quite make up for the tantrum, but it made him feel a little more like himself, to put his life back in order.

It took him a longer time than it should have, and by the time he was done, he was so fucking tired that his whole body ached. He wanted nothing more than to fall into bed and sleep and not dream about Aiden. He couldn't bring himself, somehow, to get into the bed.

Matt exhaled, slowly, and went into the living room, curled up alone on the couch. It wasn't very comfortable, but it didn't matter. He was asleep before he could think any more.

The thing was: Aiden was always going to be miserable, whether it was in New York or Montreal.

The thing was: Aiden could make the choice about whether he was going to drag Matt down with him or not.

The thing was: that didn't make the next couple of weeks any easier to get through or make it any easier to stop thinking about Matt. Knowing he had done it *for* Matt didn't make it any easier, either.

The thing was: it was always going to be this bad, and he had been stupid to think that he could change it just by running away from New York.

Aiden settled back into life alone in retirement like he'd never left.

He wasn't expecting to hear from Matt, so it wasn't a surprise when he didn't. The Royal were still in the swing of the season, solidly in playoff contention. He did get emails from Ellie and felt even worse when he didn't answer. He just couldn't bring himself to do it. Couldn't bring himself to even open them. He wondered whether Matt had told Miles, whether Miles had told Ellie and whether she was just ignoring it anyway. It was what *he* would have done as a child. Heartbreak wouldn't have meant a single damn thing to him. Not when he was locked in on pursuing a goal.

A week went by, and another week.

It was just as bad as it sounded.

Someone knocked on the door. When Aiden ignored it, the knock came again. For a brief, stupid moment while he fumbled for his phone, he thought that maybe it was Matt. Instead, on the screen, he saw something far more terrifying: his mother.

Even if she hadn't been his mother, Shilpa Parekh cut an intimidating figure. All five feet two inches of her, shrunken even smaller on the phone screen. She said, into the camera, "*Aiden Suresh Campbell*, I know you're in there. Let me in."

"What are you doing in New York, Mammi?" Aiden asked, over the intercom. He winced: she had surprised him into saying it the way he'd used to call for her when he was a child.

"I'll tell you when, and only when, you let me inside," Mom said. Her voice had the tone that said *and I'm not going to argue with you any longer, young man*, so Aiden gave up and buzzed her in.

He couldn't hear or see her downstairs, but he knew that she would be doing the same thing she always did whenever she came into a home. Taking off her shoes, lining them up neatly by the door and hanging her coat up on the hook and taking the stairs two at a time like she was in a race to see who could get to the top of the landing first.

Aiden took a second to look around the room and determine whether there was anything he could do to avoid horrifying his mother once she got up here. She had always made sure that everyone in the family was pulling their weight to keep the home immaculate, and she was absolutely going to be horrified when she got up here and saw how he was living.

There wasn't anything he could do in this short a time. Aiden took a deep breath and turned to face the music.

She paused at the top of the stairs as she took in the wreck of his home and his person. She'd always had good control over her facial expressions, so the fact that she couldn't seem to prevent the look of horror and sadness probably said more about the sorry state he was in than anything about her own self-control. Aiden tried to remember the last time he'd taken a shower, and realized it was probably a couple of weeks ago.

"Beta," she said, and held out her arms.

It was strange that even though he was approaching forty and he was over a foot taller than she was, it still felt like being a kid again. At once comforting and eviscerating. Aiden hadn't cried in longer than he could remember, and he wasn't about to do it *now*, but his eyes were burning the longer Mom kept him trapped there.

"Mammi," he said, after what seemed like ages and was probably only a minute or two, "I'm fine, Mom, you can let me go."

She pulled back and gestured one hand at the living room and kitchen, at the dishes piled in the sink and the take-out containers overflowing in the trash can. "Are you really, Aiden?"

He exhaled. "Probably not."

"What *happened*? He didn't—"

"No. Um. It was me, again," he managed. He couldn't look her in the eye. "Please, Mom, I don't—I can't—"

"I didn't come here to give you a lecture," Mom said, and sighed. "Aiden, I'm here to help. Let's clean up the dishes and the room, and then you can take a shower and I'll make you something to eat. Have you actually been eating? You look like you lost weight."

Aiden had been ordering takeout, but once it got there, he hadn't had much of an appetite. Of course Mom would have been able to tell. He said, "It's just been too overwhelming to start."

"That's why you have me," she said, jaw set. It was the look opposing counsel saw in the courtroom, men who underestimated her because she was a woman, because she was small, and because she had an accent.

"We'll start on one side and work our way across. Come, it will go much faster with me here."

The worst part was that she was right. It did go faster when she was here. Specifically: when she was here to tell Aiden what to do, to turn sharp and disapproving eyes on him when he flagged. After a little while he fell into the rhythm of it, scrubbing the dishes she handed him and loading the dishwasher in the careful way he'd learned as a child, a kind of Tetris-block of plates and pots. Mostly cups, if he was being quite honest.

Mom was in the thick of it, too. She'd rolled up her sleeves almost immediately and dived right in, her hair neatly clipped so it wouldn't fall into her eyes. Aiden was briefly and violently grateful that she didn't try to talk to him about anything while they were doing this, or at least, not anything real. The only words exchanged were questions about whether something could go into the trash bag she'd shaken open with a *snap* of plastic, and orders when he lagged behind.

It seemed like hours that they worked, but when Aiden looked at the microwave clock, it had only been about ninety minutes. He still felt exhausted, but his living room and kitchen looked habitable for the first time in months. He tried not to look at the couch, leaned instead against the kitchen island.

"Go upstairs and take a shower," Mom said, her voice a little softer. She looked at him, dark brown eyes warm and concerned instead of stern. "I'll be down here deep cleaning."

"I can help—"

"Aiden," she said firmly. "Go and take a shower. You desperately need it."

He opened his mouth to argue, but she was shifting

toward the other end of the comforting/stern continuum, so he decided to cut his losses and do what she told him. He nodded silently and retreated up the stairs.

It was ridiculous, really, that sometimes something as simple as taking a shower seemed so insurmountable. He had been taking showers in a professional setting, multiple times a day, for years of his life. He had taken them frequently at home, too, because his brain had all kinds of weird rules about what was clean and what wasn't, what was an outside piece of clothing and what was safe. But sometimes there were periods, like this one, where it seemed like even trying to muster up the energy to throw his dirty clothes in the laundry or stand under the warm spray of water just seemed impossible to consider.

He stood there now, naked, and shivered. He probably wouldn't be doing this if he'd been any less frightened of his mother's disapproval. But now that he was here, he was going to have to see it through. Mechanically, he scrubbed his body; mechanically, he washed his hair. It was getting really long now, and it had been so tangled and greasy that even the conditioner was kind of a job to get done. It took so much energy, and he was exhausted by the time he was finished. He took a deep breath and wondered what the hell was wrong with him.

Finally clean, he went back into his bedroom to get dressed. He chose one of the dresser drawers full of identical sweatpants and hoodies, all in varying shades of gray or black. It had been a long time since life had had color in it, really. It hadn't again since Montreal.

By the time he came back downstairs, Mom was already heating up oat milk for cha. He'd had the spices and the tea at home, but he rarely made it for himself, because it was never as good as she made it. Seeing her in his kitchen, aggressively grating ginger and unpacking a Tupperware container of handvo from her tote bag, made him feel for a second like maybe everything might be okay after all. And then he remembered why he was feeling like this and sighed. It wasn't.

She looked up at the noise, her serious face still concerned. She had a permanent frown line creasing her forehead, the way she worried about him and Hannah. Not that she needed to worry about Hannah, who'd never done anything once in her life to need to be worried about. "Aiden," she said, "you're feeling a little better, yes?"

"Yeah," he said. It wasn't entirely a lie. Physically, anyway, the shower had helped. Wearing clean clothes had helped. The rest of it? There wasn't a solution for that.

"Take a plate. The cha will be done soon. And then we will talk. You still have moong dal and rice? Yogurt in the fridge? I'll make you khichdi and kadhi for dinner."

"Yes, Mom," Aiden said, resisting the urge to roll his eyes. There were certain pantry staples that he always had in bulk. And even though he was barely leaving the house these days, some things went automatically on the delivery list. She'd drilled that into his head from a young age, too. He took the plate anyway and went over to the table, pulled out one of the chairs and slid into it.

"I can see you're not feeling *too* bad if you can still take an attitude with me," she said dryly, and poured the cha through a strainer into the mug she'd taken down from the shelf.

"I'm really fine," he tried to insist, poking at the handvo with a fork. Handvo was a light but satisfying meal, and his mother's version of it was spicy but not overwhelmingly so, and it took his stomach twisting unpleasantly at the thought of it to realize just how bad not eating had fucked him up.

She didn't even dignify that with an answer. Instead, she poured her own cup, and took the seat directly across from him at the table. "All right. Now you're going to tell me what, exactly, is going on over here."

"Well," Aiden said, a little lamely. "You know Matt and I reconnected over the summer."

"Yes," Mom said, drawing the word out long enough that, if Matt had been in the room, he probably would have been preemptively ducking for cover.

"Don't be upset with him. It wasn't his fault. I just—well, things were going well, overall, but the longer the season went the more I just... I wasn't getting any better. In my head, Mom. It's been a mess in there since I retired, and I wasn't getting any better. I was trying, but I just... I wasn't. And I didn't want to drag him down with me. I didn't want to ruin his life, not for the second time."

"Aiden..."

"It's just like since I retired, everything is so fucked up. I don't have hockey. I don't have my routine. I don't have a purpose. I don't have *me*. Not really."

She just looked at him, contemplative and sad. She extended her arm and took Aiden's hands in her own. His fingers felt like ice, and hers were warm. "My poor boy," she said, after a moment. "It's never been easy for you, has it?"

"I don't know what you mean," he said, and his tongue felt too thick in his mouth.

"I don't know how much you remember about your childhood," Mom said, "but you were always...we always knew that you were a little different from the other children. You never wanted to play the same kinds of games that they did. Your favorite thing to do as a toddler was to sort things into even stacks. You were so particular about what you ate and how it was prepared. And then when you decided that you wanted to play hockey, that's *all* you thought about after. It was almost like the other children didn't really exist to you, except in relation to the team."

Aiden didn't remember, *really*. He had vague memories of other children, mostly in hockey rinks, but he'd been so focused on being the best at hockey, first at skating, and then when he'd finally convinced Dad to let him play goalie, he was shifted off into a whole other world by himself. It hadn't really mattered—what had mattered was learning how to play goalie. Learning how to be the *best*.

It wasn't until later on that a coach had taken him aside and told him that if he wanted the boys to play for him—*really* play for him—he couldn't be a mountain, or a world apart. He'd made a conscious effort at that too, running a little mental checklist where he'd force himself to talk or to make jokes with the other players a certain amount of times per practice. After a certain point, it became a little more natural, but he still often had to remind himself how to act or how often he needed to speak to someone to keep up a relationship. After his retirement, it was like all of that had fallen apart, too.

"You were always different, and that's just one of the reasons we loved Matthew so much, when he was around the first time. It was so clear that he saw that about you and loved it. Loved you *for it*. For a while, the worry I'd had about you being lonely, well. I could set it aside. I understood why things ended. I understood why it was so hard for you. But Aiden…it's so hard to watch you struggling like this. What can *I* do to help?"

Aiden realized he was gripping her hands too hard, hard enough that he'd probably hurt her, even if her face never reflected it. Neither Mom *or* Dad had ever made him feel weird or different as a kid. They'd never taken him to a doctor. They'd just let him put his head down and focus on goaltending with the kind of single-minded drive that had taken him to a probable Hall of Fame career. But they'd always known… "Mom, why didn't you *do* anything about this? About me?"

She looked, for the first time, a little guilty. "What would we have done about you? You always seemed happy, or whatever happy meant for you, and you were so successful, we never wanted to upset things. I wonder now whether we shouldn't have…but you're almost middle-aged now, and it's far beyond second-guessing that."

Aiden let go of her hands. His own palms and fingers felt disgustingly sweaty, and he wiped them on his pants. "I was seeing a therapist in Montreal. Before I left."

"Was it helping?"

"I don't know. Not really. I could tell her about some of this stuff, but I still felt…the same."

"Depressed?"

"I guess so," Aiden said slowly. Dr. Gauthier hadn't put labels on the way he was feeling, but he was, well, pretty depressed. It had been bad even with Matt, the only light in his life at that time, and it had only gotten worse since he'd left. "I've been pretty depressed after retiring."

"That's to be expected even for someone—someone who wasn't as intense about playing as you were. I'm glad you were seeing someone, even if it wasn't helping the way you would have wanted it to."

"It's just," Aiden said. Sometimes when he tried to explain things like this, he couldn't think of the appropriate words. It was hard to look at his own emotions from a distance. He'd never found it easy to understand them. Would it have helped if his parents had taken him to a doctor? If he could have had a framework for understanding his own brain? It was too late now. "It's just that I really feel like without hockey, I'm just not the same *person.* Almost like I'm not even a person. And I don't know whether therapy can even help that."

Mom sighed and held out her arms. He accepted the hug, even though the only person he ever truly felt comfortable hugging was Matt. Her arms were tight around him when she said, "We don't have to figure this out right now. Let's just get you eating and some of your house in order. We've got all the time in the world."

"Mom?"

"Yes."

"Thanks. For coming. For not being…" He wasn't even sure what he had meant to say. He was ashamed, when she saw how he had been living. But that had been in his own head, not anything she'd done.

"I will *always* come for you. Even if I have court. Even if I have deadlines."

When Aiden said, "I know," he believed it.

Mom pulled away, and said, a little gruffly, "We have a lot of cleaning to do, yes? Come. Let's get back to it."

It felt good and necessary to have something to do, and someone to tell him how to do it, and so Aiden said, "Yes."

Matt and Miles didn't play in the same division, and never had. Both of them had had the unique experience of playing with the same team throughout most of their careers, although it had taken Miles a longer time to crack a major league roster. His brother, at thirty-four, was now a veteran member of the New Jersey Scouts' blue line. He and Jess had built a nice little life in Short Hills with the kids.

It was still an event when he came to Montreal, and even better when they had a chance to actually catch up and grab dinner together the night before. It didn't always work out, with the way the travel was scheduled, and Matt was both looking forward to *and* dreading this dinner.

He'd been dodging calls from both of his parents, which meant that they were *really* worried about him, if Dad was calling. Daron Safaryan was an old-school kind of dad, the sort of guy who'd rather take you out for a silent walk in the woods or fishing on the lake than ever consider talking about a feeling. Usually that suited Matt just fine. So the fact that he'd missed a few calls from Dad's number—no voice mail—meant that the news had probably gotten back home, probably through Miles, and Mom was panicking. So Matt had absolutely no doubt that they had probably deputized Miles to try to get some news out of him.

Matt texted Miles beforehand: Hey, I can get reservations at one of my usual spots if you want to meet me?

You're the expert, Miles replied.

One of the things Matt loved most about Montreal was the variety of restaurants. Pretty much anything you wanted to eat, you could find, and not only could you find it, it would be some of the best food you'd ever eaten. For some reason there were a ton of Italian restaurants, too, which was good because both he and Miles were big pasta guys. It was possible to get a last-minute reservation, mostly because he was a regular and had gotten to know the chef a little. He sent Miles the address and got ready to go.

Miles was wearing a new peacoat when Matt caught sight of him by the door, and he grinned. "Hey, what happened to the guy who used to make fun of me for getting custom-made coats?"

"I realized how comfortable they were," Miles said, a little sheepishly. "And you know… I can afford it, so."

"Fancy." Matt extended his arms. They hugged briefly, and Miles pounded him on the back just once. It was nice to be able to have a quiet dinner without the kids, without worrying about being interrupted, but Matt thought that depending on how this went, he might want to be interrupted. He briefly wished that Aiden was here to rescue him, to send a text that would give him a ready-made excuse to escape. But of course, part of the reason he was dreading this was the fact that Aiden *wasn't* here.

"How're you doing, Matt?"

"Great," Matt said unconvincingly. "You know. Just getting through the season. You saw we had that little losing streak. Planning on snapping it tomorrow."

"Ohh, he's feeling mean," Miles teased, but followed Matt inside, out of the biting cold, without any real argument.

It was a pleasant restaurant, within walking distance of Jean-Talon, the kind of place that was always busy, but not too loud; sleek and modern, but not too trendy. The servers, who all knew him by now, didn't make a big deal about it when he came in, and people sometimes asked for autographs but usually left him alone.

They sat down at their table and perused the menus in silence. The restaurant had a pretty extensive wine list, with bottles ranging from $50 to $500. Matt picked one he'd tried before, a midrange Tuscan red that had a nice aftertaste, because Miles was usually a beer guy and couldn't tell the difference, and then they got into squabbling over the appetizers the same way they always had. It was easy and companionable, and they didn't talk about anything real, anything of import.

They made companionable small talk about Jess's work at the hospital, and Ellie's goalie practices, and Theo's latest obsession, which was paleontology. Miles asked about his knee and Matt was honest: it hadn't been great. He'd had to rely on pre- and post-game medication more often than not, and it wasn't looking like that would let up anytime soon. It wasn't until Matt had ordered them pan-fried shrimp in vermouth and a dish with breaded veal and seared tuna and a pasta to go with it while they were considering the mains that Miles looked up at him with a frown.

"Hey, Matt."

"Don't do it, Miles."

"You know I have to."

"Fuck," Matt said, and looked back down at the marble tabletop. "I mean, you don't, really."

"Come on. Mom and Dad would fucking kill me if I got dinner with you and didn't ask."

Matt heaved a long sigh, because even though he wasn't happy about it, it was true. They'd always had an easier time cowing Miles into compliance. "Okay. Fine. What do you want to ask?"

"Things with Campbell. Over for good this time?"

Matt brushed his fingers over the marble and wished the waiter had bought out the wine already. He could have gone for a drink right then. "It looks like it."

"*Fuck.* Jesus. I'm sorry. You want me to…?"

"I don't want you to anything, Miles," Matt said. He felt suddenly deflated and exhausted. "You threatening him never helped anything. You know I appreciate knowing you're in my corner. But we're not twenty-five anymore, for fuck's sake."

"It's just… I hate him *so much*, Matt. He's hurt you so much over the years. It's just…it's not fair. You didn't do anything to deserve that."

"No," Matt agreed. "But I don't think anyone does."

"Look at you, all philosophical," Miles muttered, and fell silent as the server *did* come out with the wine. They both waited while she poured. Then Matt waited while Miles gathered his thoughts together. Miles said, eventually, "What happened?"

"I don't know." It was the honest answer. "I thought everything was going pretty well. I mean, not *well*, he was clearly still fucking…depressed. Retirement has been really hard for him. But things with us were… Jesus, as good as they'd ever been. I think maybe…he thought he was saving me from something. From *him*."

"What a self-absorbed fucking asshole," Miles said, before he could stop himself.

"Please don't talk about him like that." Matt was surprised by how mild his voice sounded. "Aiden is—was—is—very important to me."

"You're really still going to fucking defend him? After he did this to you? *Again?*"

"That's the thing." Matt regretted this dinner more and more as it went on, even though the wine was good and the food would be excellent. "I don't hate *him*. It's—it's hard. I'm not going to lie, it's been really hard. And he handled it badly. But I just… I can't hate him, Miles. I've loved him for so fucking long I don't think I can feel any other way about him. And it's just… I don't think he could really help it. Whatever's going on in his head, it's pretty bad. And I was doing my best. But I'm only one guy. And my best wasn't good enough."

Miles was staring at him, wordlessly. "I don't even know what to say, man."

"You don't need to say anything," Matt said, and smiled up at the server as she brought over the first of their appetizers. He waited for her to move away again before looking at Miles. His brother had always had a bit of a baby face, despite the scar on his cheek that he'd had since they were kids. Matt had been responsible for it, by accident. They'd been roughhousing in the basement, a little too hard, and his face had hit the edge of a metal filing cabinet. "It's just… I don't know, Miles. Maybe I'm just getting older and I'm tired, but it's just, I can't control what he does. I can only control what *I* do. And I don't have any regrets about any of this. Nothing that happened over the last few months."

"*None?*"

Matt poked at the food with his fork. "Is it weird to say that even though it ended badly, I'm glad it happened? It was kind of like… I've been wondering about him for all of these years. What he's like. What he's doing. Whether he'd still fall in love with me. It's felt like an itch I can never really scratch. And this has been kind of a weird closure. In a way. He's still the same in so many ways. And whatever he did, I know he does still love me. Probably too much."

"Both of you are fucking crazy," Miles said, and swallowed a huge mouthful of wine. "You always have been. You're not even *angry*?"

Matt thought about coming back to the condo on New Year's, and sighed. He'd given in, briefly. But he would be better now. "'Pain is the opposite of strength, and so is anger. Both are things we suffer from, and yield to.'"

Miles glared at him. "Don't you fucking quote Marcus Aurelius at me, Matthew. Jesus Christ, I don't even know how the fuck I'm going to explain this to Mom and Dad."

"You don't have to explain it. All you have to do is tell them I'm okay," Matt said, and he was surprised to find, as he was saying it, that it was absolutely true.

"You're *okay*? Matty, bud, the last time this happened you had to go into player assistance."

Matt bit down his frustration. "I'm not the person I was back then. You know this. *You're* not the same person you were back then either—you're a husband and a father and a veteran. It's kind of shitty that you just assume I'd lose it like that again."

"Sorry," Miles said, looking down. "I know it's not fair, it's just… I love you, man. I worry about you all of the fucking time."

"You don't have to. Really. I don't think I even realized it before we started talking about this, but I *am* fine."

They ate without speaking for a few minutes, neither of them willing to be the one to break the silence. Matt thought about a lot of things in that time: how much Miles cared about him but how little he knew how to properly express it, the way that his whole family had frozen him in time like some kind of amber-stuck bug in the middle of an existential crisis, and Aiden, wherever he was, whether he was happy or sad or whether he was eating enough. Matt really hoped he was eating enough.

"I'm glad you're okay," Miles said, like he wasn't entirely sure if he believed it. "I'm still fucking furious at Campbell, though. Jesus, he's put you through the wringer over the years."

"Yeah, probably. But… I don't know. I'd rather have had that and dealt with the pain now than not had it at all. I hope you never find out with Jess. But he was just, well. The love of my life, probably. And maybe it'll never be the right time for it to work out. But I did the best I could do. And I'm at peace with it. Okay?"

"Okay," Miles said, slowly, staring at him. "This is fucking weird, you know. Like what the hell have you done with my brother?"

"I'm your same brother. I just went to a lot of therapy appointments and I grew up," Matt said dryly. "Okay, can we please stop talking about this? I'm okay, but there's a limit to what I can handle before I kind of want to fucking die."

"That's…fair," Miles said, a little sheepishly.

"Come on, we have a million other things to talk about. How's Coach Garcia doing, how are your rookies, et cetera, et cetera. Also, the branzino's really good, and so is the lamb, if you want suggestions."

"Yeah, yeah," Miles said, and looked down at the menu. "Give me a second, and then we can talk."

Matt sat back in his seat while Miles looked at the menu again, still turning over and over in his head the conversation they'd had. He *really* hadn't realized it until he'd said it. It felt—weird. He'd spent so much time worrying about his life falling apart after Aiden left, and now that it had happened, he was sad, but he was functional. He was playing games. He was seeing his family. He was functioning, maybe not a hundred percent, but he was...okay.

Matt rubbed at his eyes, which were stinging, suddenly. Getting older was fucking weird, all right. Maybe he'd come to an epiphany about playing hockey, too. Maybe it was just a matter of the puzzle pieces falling into place at the right time.

But right now, he wasn't going to think about any of that. He was going to enjoy his dinner and time with his brother, and then he was going to kick his ass on the ice. And all was as it should be.

At three p.m. on a Wednesday, Gabe banged on Aiden's door. Aiden sighed: the news must have gotten out, eventually. He considered waiting him out, but when Gabe was still there five minutes later, he gave in, went downstairs and opened it.

Gabe, mid-knock, almost fell forward with the force of his arm motion but caught himself before he pitched too far. "Soupy," he said, staring at Aiden with wide eyes. "Uh, wow, your hair is something else."

"What do you want, Gabe?"

"Let me in, because we're going to have a fucking *talk*, okay?"

"I don't think—"

"Nah, you *don't*," Gabe said, and pushed past him, like he always did.

Aiden sighed, and followed him back into his own house, folded his arms over his chest in the middle of the living room and watched, awkwardly, to see what Gabe was going to do.

What Gabe did was glare at him, and ask, "Soupy, what the ever-loving *fuck* are you doing?"

"What?"

"What," Gabe said, carefully, "the fuck. Are you doing. Back. In New York."

"It's complicated, Gabe."

"Is it? Really?"

"*Yes*, it is, I—"

"Because you told me you were in love with him, but this doesn't seem like—did he end it? Do I have to go to Montreal to kick his ass?"

"No! *I* came home. It was *me*. Just because you love someone doesn't mean things just work out." He swallowed hard after it came out of his mouth, louder and more frustrated than he'd intended. "There's other things that—"

Gabe seemed unfazed by his anger, narrowed his eyes. "Yeah, of course they don't work out if you don't fucking *try*."

"I *was* trying, you don't know what I—"

"Yeah, you said you were going to therapy. Talking about shit without actually doing anything to change your behavior isn't the point of going. At that rate, fucking pay *me* $200 an hour just to talk. Like, Soupy, you can't just fucking run away from everything forever, shit doesn't *change* if you do that. You're just gonna stay miserable forever."

"Gabe, you don't understand—"

"I don't know, Soup, I think I kinda do," Gabe said. He chewed on his lower lip, frowning at Aiden. "I mean, I get it. You're scared fucking shitless, I bet."

"I'm not scared!"

"Yeah, you are. If you stayed, and you actually fucking tried to change how you felt about things, if you actually *tried* to talk to Safaryan, and it didn't work? Holy shit, that would suck, right? So you just fucking run away from it because that way you fucking control how miserable you are." Gabe wasn't yelling at him, exactly, but his voice was just as high and agitated as Aiden's, his hands cut through the air decisively. Gabe had always been a hand talker, and now it seemed as though he was two steps away from trying to fight Aiden, right there in the living room. "Jesus Christ, Soupy, you are fucking choosing to be this miserable right now, do you know that? You *chose* this! You did this to *yourself*."

Aiden wondered whether he had slipped into some kind of alternate universe, whether any moment he was going to blink, and wake up, and find that he was twenty-six again and back between the posts. "I'm not choosing anything. I didn't choose anything."

"Okay, fine. If you won't do it for you, can you at least fucking do it for me?"

"What?"

"I get that you don't love me like that—and it's fine, I'm over it—but can you at least fucking give things a chance with him? So I can see that it's just possible. To play and retire and be in love with another man and have a life after hockey and shit. Can you fucking *try to*?"

"Gabe, I..."

Gabe put his hand square in the center of Aiden's chest and shoved him down on the couch. He didn't sit down himself, just kept pacing back and forth, arms hugged over his chest. "Soup, it's just...you've been my role model for so long. I've modeled my game after you, I modeled my fucking *personal life* after you. You've got everything I thought I wanted. The Cups, the awards, the franchise career. But there's always that question mark, right? Like what comes after. And it hurts me so fucking bad to look at you like this, and it scares me to think that this could be waiting for *me*, and I just want you to—I don't know. Fucking give it a chance. So I can see you do it. So I can feel like I can do it. For *fuck's sake*."

"Gabe—"

"Look, Soupy, don't say anything else to me right now. Just think about it? I don't know why you're so fucking scared of maybe being happy, but please? Please. For me. Think about it."

Aiden took a deep breath in. "Gabe, you're the oldest twenty-two-year-old I've ever met, I think."

"Yeah, well. I grew up fast. I had to. Soupy, I *love* you. Please, like, fucking forgive yourself?" When Aiden stared at his hands and couldn't answer, Gabe gave up, and sighed. "Okay. I said my part. Think about it."

He let himself out.

Aiden did think about it.

He thought about it a lot, over the next week. He thought about what his mother had said and what Gabe had said. He thought about second chances and how he ruined his, and how he probably didn't deserve a third. He thought about figuring out a way to translate his vague ideas about coaching into a reality, how much time that would actually take up if he let himself do it. He thought about the last thing Gabe had said to him. He thought about how anyone could know they were actually ready to start moving on.

He thought about Matt. He thought about how he'd hurt him, over and over, throughout the years. He thought about how his whole life had circled back around to Matt again, so many years later, a long and wobbly but ultimately inevitable orbit.

He thought about a lot of things.

The funny thing about it was that, even though Matt was holding it together pretty well, the rookies had noticed that something was wrong. He wasn't sure whether they'd discussed it among themselves, whether they had a group chat specifically for shit like this, or whether Koskinen and Cormier had cornered Jack and forced him to do the hard work of approaching Matt about whatever it was they thought was going on.

"Cap," Jack said, after morning skate. Matt was sitting on the bench by the boards, and Jack had skated up to speak to him.

They were playing Minnesota at home later that night, and it was a day where Matt had had to sit out of practice, because his knee was aching so bad. That didn't mean he wasn't present: they had video to go over with the coaches, stretching and other exercises to work on in the gym, a hundred other things he had to check in on and manage. Sometimes, he felt like he was another member of the coaching staff, with all of the suggestions he gave to his trio of rookies. There were worse things to be, he supposed.

"Yeah, Jack."

"The three of us were talking, uh, and we've been keeping an eye on you over the last couple of weeks, and we noticed that, um, Campbell hasn't been around anymore, and you've seemed pretty…pretty sad, so we just wanted to check in. You know."

Matt closed his eyes and exhaled. "I'm fine. I'm touched by your concern. But really, you, ah…don't need to worry about me."

"No?" Jack said, skeptical.

"No."

They stood in awkward silence for a few minutes. For as young and slight as Jack was, he had the steely expression that Matt had worked on adopting over the years down pat. "You know," he said, after a long moment. "Just because you're the captain and you're responsible for looking out for *us* doesn't mean you need to…like…handle all of this stuff on your own. I was thinking about what you were telling me. About the captaincy and the burden. You know? It doesn't *need* to be like that."

Matt ran a hand through his hair and smiled, a little wry. "Probably not. That's how I've always been most comfortable doing it. I don't know anything about your personal life, Jack, beyond what you've told me, but it's something that for a long time I had to keep to myself. And then I just got used to that."

"That's really kind of sad, though." Jack was still in his pads and jersey, sweat from the practice beaded on the visor of his fogged-up helmet. "Like, who can you even talk to about that shit?"

"That's what a therapist is for," Matt said dryly. "Rookies aren't therapists."

Jack rolled his eyes. He was a handsome kid, from a small town in BC called Anahim Lake, but he had adjusted very quickly to the pace and pressure of Montreal. Some people were meant to play here, Matt had always believed: he'd been one of them, and he felt Jack was another.

"I'm not saying *I'm* a therapist, I was just saying, if we can do anything for you, the way you've done shit for us over the last couple of seasons, we're all happy to do it. I don't know what that *is*, but it's on the table."

"Thank you," Matt said, weirdly touched. "I honestly don't know what that could be, either. I guess the important thing is that Aiden isn't in Montreal anymore. And I'm just…well, I'm just playing and dealing with my knee and that's all I really have to say about it."

Jack's dark eyes met Matt's, almost like he was daring him to get really crazy, be super vulnerable about it. "Okay. Well, you know we've got your back. For whatever that's worth."

"It's worth a lot."

Matt wished his knee wasn't so fucked. He wished he could just get on the ice again. He would've felt a lot better about all of this if he could've just worked it off, pushed himself with the kind of physical activity that would wipe any of the sadness from his mind and heart, at least until later. He'd have that for the game, but Jack asking him these questions felt a little like peeling a scab that hadn't healed.

"Well, I won't bother you anymore, Cap. I'll let you get ready for the game. But, I don't know. Think about it."

Matt thought about it, and about his apartment at home, the laundry piling up and the dishes he hadn't had time to wash, and nodded. "I will."

He did not think about Aiden. He didn't.

It was bitter cold outside, but Aiden rolled the window down as he took the car to Midtown. He rarely had a reason to go there, and he tended to avoid driving in the crowded New York streets especially. But that's where the framing shop was, and that was where he had to go. He certainly couldn't lug the jersey back on the subway.

The proprietor looked up in surprise when Aiden came into the store. He couldn't tell if that was because the voice mail about the pickup had been left in July and it was January now, or because Aiden was fairly unrecognizable these days if he didn't pull his hair away from his face.

"Uh, sorry this took so long," Aiden said, "I'm here to pick up my jersey."

He stopped to look at it in the car. Like always, they had done a professional, quality piece of work. Despite the fact that he spent an hour sweating his ass off in it that last game, it looked smooth and pristine beneath the glass. It sat on the passenger seat, like it was watching him accusingly.

It wasn't one of his favorite jerseys the Libs had ever worn, he had to admit. In Aiden's mind the only true shade of Liberty green was the one he had worn his first few years. The periodic attempts at redesign always left him cold.

But that was all it was: his last jersey, framed.

He had thought it would feel different picking it up. Crushing. He didn't feel any of that. Mostly he just wanted to get it home because he had a lot of other things he needed to do.

Aiden had been getting his hair cut by the same woman in Brooklyn since the year he moved to the city. He texted her in between dropping the jersey off in his memorabilia room and packing his bags to see if she could fit him in.

She texted back, for you? of course. can you be there in 20?

Aiden eyed his bags, which were already mostly packed. It hadn't taken long: he had a house full of stuff, but none of it was really necessary right now. And it was even possible that most of his clothes were still in Montreal.

He wrote back, yes, and headed out to his car immediately. His flight wasn't for another few hours, but when he wasn't flying on a team plane, Aiden was the kind of person who showed up at the airport at least an hour early, just in case. He'd almost missed enough flights and buses in his career to know better. A quick visit to Alyssa probably wouldn't kill him, though.

Her eyes widened a little when she saw him, but because she was a professional, she didn't say, *what the hell happened to you.* Instead, she asked, "What would you like me to do?"

"I just want to look like myself again," Aiden said, a weird lump in his throat. "It's…been a while."

The thing he always liked about Alyssa was that she didn't make him talk when he wasn't in the mood to, and her hands were firm and gentle. She worked in silence, and it was like he could feel the weight of the hair falling away as she did. He watched himself in the mirror, and he could see Aiden Campbell slowly emerging from beneath all of it.

"Do you want me to get rid of the beard, too?"

"If you could just trim it."

When she finally finished, Aiden looked at himself again. Alyssa cut his hair similarly to the way he used to wear it. It was just a little lighter, the kind of dark brown-and-gray that was only noticeable in the right light, or in the clumps of it on the floor, somehow more visible there. He didn't look the same as he did when he first took over as the starter from Ward, but that was to be expected.

He was thirty-seven; he wasn't a boy anymore. His face had the laugh lines and frown lines he had earned over the last sixteen years. The freckles were still the same, maybe more of them, but his eyes were so tired. Really fucking tired. And he looked sad, even at rest.

"Are you okay?" Alyssa asked.

"I'm going to do my best to be," Aiden said, surprised to find that this time, he fucking *meant* it.

The flight Aiden picked got him into Montreal while the Royal were at l'Arène, in the middle of a game against the Minnesota Northern Lights. It was cold but not as cold as Winnipeg, and so while he was technically underdressed, he could suffer through. He dropped his shit off at the hotel room he had reserved, just in case. He took a cab to Matt's condo and sat down on the steps to wait. There wasn't much to do, and it was actually cold enough that his phone was going to die if he took it out of his pocket, so he just sat on the stoop, zoned out and concentrated on his breathing.

Aiden didn't even know what time it was when Matt

approached the steps, but he did know he had lost feeling in his fingers.

Matt stopped abruptly when he noticed Aiden sitting there, and Aiden wondered whether he was just going to turn around and walk away, even though it was his own condo.

"Matt," Aiden said, getting awkwardly to his feet. The blood rushed back in, the pins and needles echoing the jumpy, nervous feeling in his chest. "Please, can we talk?"

"How long have you been out here?" Matt asked. His voice was soft and even, hard to read.

"I don't know. What time is it now?"

"One in the morning."

"I don't know. Four hours? Four and a half?"

"Jesus fucking Christ, Aiden. And you—your hair—you cut it?"

"Yes. It was time. Can we?"

Matt's teeth dug against his lower lip and Aiden could see him doing the math of all of this behind his eyes.

Aiden took a deep breath. "I understand if you don't want to, I understand I fucked it up again, I understand you don't owe me anything—I just—I'm so fucking *sorry*, Matt, and I want to explain."

Matt exhaled. "Okay. Come on up."

He followed Matt into the living room. The condo felt different than when Aiden left it last. Because he'd been home so often and Matt hadn't, Aiden had assumed the responsibility of keeping things spotless and organized. Tonight he saw how Matt had been living without him, which was piles of laundry on the couch, some dishes and pots stacked in the sink and a general air of chaos that hadn't been there when Aiden was.

And Matt himself: he looked just as exhausted as Aiden felt, and Aiden wanted more than anything to take him in his arms, wrap his arms around Matt's waist, throw himself at Matt's feet and beg for forgiveness. Anything. He stood there instead, trying to rub the feeling back into his hands, red from the cold.

"Talk," Matt said. He had his arms crossed over his chest, still standing.

"I'm sorry," Aiden said, realizing, belatedly, that he hadn't thought about what he was going to say once he actually got there. "I love you so much that it kind of makes me a little crazy. Or maybe I already was…and I'm sorry. This last year has been—I haven't handled it well. I didn't know *how* to handle it. I thought I was trying, but I was afraid to be honest with you, about how bad things were and how frightened I was, of fucking this up, of losing you again—"

Matt made a noise in his throat that Aiden couldn't decipher but didn't move toward him. Aiden kept talking.

"It just felt—like I could be happy again when you were here, when I could pretend I wasn't flailing and drowning and miserable, and then when you left it was like—all of that just came rushing back in, and I wanted you to be happy, and I thought you were happiest with the team, playing. I didn't want to force you into a situation like *me*. And then I was thinking about doing this for another season, what would happen when you realized I wasn't getting better, when I fucked things up again, and I panicked, so I—so I just—I ran away. I was scared, and I ran away, because that way I could control it. I'm sorry… I'm *so* sorry. I hope you can forgive me eventually."

He could see Matt's face, watch the corner of his mouth twitch, the way he couldn't look anywhere except Aiden. Finally, Matt said, "I didn't know how to feel when you left. I never knew how to feel when you left. I didn't expect you to come back this time, either."

"I wasn't planning to come back until Gabe slapped some sense into me and I realized if I didn't, I'd regret it for the rest of my life and—I don't know what's going to happen, what I'm going to be able to actually do, but I just want you to know that, that if I'm doing anything, I want *you* to be there. I want to do it with *you.* I want you to be in my life and I want to be in yours and, and I'll do my best to actually deserve that this time."

"Jesus, Aiden, it was never about *deserving it.* It was just about being here, staying here, letting me in your life and being in mine, and trying to… I don't know. Trying to make it work however we could." He stared at Aiden like if he did it hard enough, Aiden would finally, *finally* understand what he was trying to say, that intense dark gaze that stripped him right down to the bone. "The last few months, having you here again? Coming home from roadies to you? Having you here in our home and taking care of me…making me laugh. Being able to take care of *you*—you have no idea what that's meant to me. I love you, you know that? Always fucking have. It's *always* come back to you, no matter how I tried not to."

"I'm going to try. I promise you, Matty. I'll do whatever it takes."

Matt held out his arms and Aiden half-stepped and half-fell into them. Matt took Aiden's freezing hands in his own, his breath hot on Aiden's fingers. "Just be honest with me."

"Yes."

"Stay with me."

"Yes," Aiden said. "Yes."

"Come to bed?"

Aiden said, again, "Yes."

They were both exhausted, Matt from the game and Aiden from everything else, but side by side in the bed, staring at each other in the dark, Aiden couldn't help leaning forward to kiss the stupid smile off of Matt's face, couldn't help running his hand over Matt's cheek and jaw, couldn't help sighing with dumb, pleased satisfaction when Matt mouthed wetly at his neck.

They were too tired for anything except making out like teenagers, Matt grinding sleepily into Aiden's thigh, his breath hitching when Aiden took his cock in his spit-slicked hand, groaning when he slid it down Matt's length, laughing when he got his hands down Aiden's pants and Aiden's confident motion stuttered.

Aiden didn't want this to end, and for the first time he realized that it didn't have to. There would be tomorrow, and the day after that, and the day after that. To his surprise he realized that his eyes were stinging, and then that his cheeks were wet. His face was hot, the humiliation of his body doing something he couldn't control. But once they'd started, he couldn't seem to make them stop.

"Aidy?" Matt asked, his thumb brushing the track of moisture away.

"I'm sorry. I'm *happy*, I don't know why the fuck I'm crying."

He could still see Matt's face, in the dark, and the intensity of the emotion in his eyes did nothing to stop those stupid fucking *tears*. Looking at Matt, just now, it seemed insane to him that he'd ever wanted to leave, even if both times, he'd thought he was doing something kind and necessary for someone he loved more than anyone or anything.

"You know I always liked it when you cried," Matt said softly. So fucking fond. His other hand slowed where he'd been jerking Aiden off, thumb swiping over the head of his dick.

"These aren't sex tears," Aiden muttered. "They're just…they're just happening to me."

Matt didn't answer. Instead of his thumb, his mouth: lips pressed against the tear tracks, kissing the corner of Aiden's eyes, hand cradled gently against Aiden's cheek until he wasn't sure if he was still crying or not.

Matt said, "I can't believe you came back to me," and Aiden said, "I can't believe you let me come back."

Matt kissed him again, one of those unbearably soft kisses that had always made Aiden feel like Matt could see right through him. "You belong here. You belong with me."

"Do I?"

"You fucking do, Aidy. You always have."

That was how Aiden came, eventually, legs tangled in Matt's, smiling into Matt's mouth.

When Matt woke up in the morning, Aiden was still asleep, curled up in the bed next to him, and the sun was streaming through the blinds in the window. His alarm was going to go off in a few minutes, so he'd have time to get ready for practice in the afternoon, so he fumbled for his phone and turned it off so he wouldn't wake Aiden. As he sat up, he felt approximately fifty pounds lighter: Aiden coming back, being so honest with him, here to stay for good had done that.

He already knew what Miles was going to say. *You're like Charlie Brown and that fucking football, Matthew. What're you going to do when he yanks it away again?* And he already knew he was going to have to ignore it, because saying *it's different this time* would sound silly and hollow. Because it *was* different this time, and he didn't know how to explain it except for the deep sense of peace and satisfaction that he felt currently, his hand tracing the line of Aiden's shoulder, thumb brushing over the freckles splattered across it.

Then he sat up, and felt the aches of his body, in his knee and in his back, which had taken a particularly nasty cross-checking during the game last night. If he were a different kind of player, today would probably be a therapy day. This late in the season, he needed to conserve his energy, but they were still in a playoff spot, and he wanted to keep them there. Shifted his weight and slid out of the bed.

When he did it, Aiden's eyes opened and for a brief second, they shuttered between sleepy confusion and panic.

"Hey," Matt said, "I haven't gone anywhere."

Aiden sat up and Matt couldn't help staring at his naked body, draped in the soft nest of blankets in Matt's bed. It still shocked him, how beautiful Aiden was. His lanky, spare muscle and surprisingly broad shoulders; the soft, dark hair on his chest. His face, with those soulful eyes that had cut right through Matt's defenses the very first time he'd met them. Fifteen years later, Aiden threw him off guard just as violently as he had in that handshake line.

"Sorry," Aiden was saying, sheepishly. "It's been… a rough couple of weeks. I haven't been sleeping very well. Slept better last night than I have in…fuck, I don't even know how long."

"Me, too." Matt's mouth was smiling without his brain's input. "Look. I have to go to practice later today, but I…well, I still have all of the shit you like to eat, so let me make you breakfast."

"Thanks," Aiden said, and then hesitated. "If it's okay with you, could I…come with you to Brossard? To watch?"

There were things happening in Matt's chest that he couldn't describe, things he couldn't even begin to put into words. "Aiden," he said, finally, "I would *love* that."

It wasn't that things weren't awkward, because they were a little awkward. Aiden sat at the kitchen table while Matt made him coffee and toast with cashew butter, running his hand through his hair like he couldn't believe how much of it was missing. With it cut, he looked less like a tragic Arthurian knight and almost like the kid he'd been when Matt had first gotten to know him. There were hints of gray sweeping through it, but the style made him look years younger. It was completely disorienting.

"You keep staring at me," Aiden said. "Look, I promise, I'm not going anywhere this time."

"It's not that." Matt slid the plate across the table. "I just got used to your mountain man look, you know?"

Aiden laughed, self-conscious, and touched the back of his neck. It was bare again. His hair had been long for long enough that his skin was a shade lighter there, where it had been covered during the summer. "I wasn't doing a very good job of taking care of myself." He looked down. "Sometimes it kind of felt like I didn't deserve to."

Matt took his own coffee cup and said, carefully, "You're going to go back to the therapist?"

"Yeah." Aiden nudged at the toast with one finger. "I owe it to you. But also to myself. It's…it's kind of terrifying, trying to think of a way to be happy without hockey, but I'll never know if I don't try, right?"

"And it doesn't have to be without hockey. I know it's not the same, but if you ever, I don't know. If you ever want to skate with the team, or suit up for practices, I'm sure—I'm sure I could make it happen. I'd love to be able to get on the ice with you again regularly."

"Yeah?" The corner of Aiden's mouth tilted up in an almost shy smile.

"Yeah. Aidy, those times we were able to skate together over the summer? Those are some of the best memories of my whole life."

"Wow," Aiden deadpanned. "Pretty sad life, considering."

"Actually, it's been awesome. But when we could skate together, it was like the two best parts of it were finally together…you know?"

"Yeah. I do. And it was satisfying as hell to save all of those shots on you."

"Joke was on you," Matt replied, taking the empty plate away from him, "I was just using you as a study for shootouts."

Aiden gave him a sour look. "We were about even on those, all things considered, after that first one where you *distracted* me."

"I didn't do anything!"

"You didn't have to. You were just you. I have *eyes*,

Matthew," Aiden said, and Matt couldn't help it, he leaned down to kiss him again, his mouth that tasted of black coffee and cashew and burnt toast.

Aiden did come with him to practice, let Matt rest his hand on his knee as they drove across the bridge to the practice facility. They wouldn't be able to skate together today—Aiden still didn't have his own gear, but they could take care of that, Matt thought, already trying to figure out how to get it packed and shipped from New York—but having Aiden in the stands would be a novelty.

It felt right, having him there. Usually, the practices were open to the public, but the lower stands were blocked off and spectators had to congregate by the glass on the upper level. Because Aiden was Matt's guest, he had made it through the usual security, and was sitting on the bleacher, closer to the ice. Not in the front row, of course, but he was noticeable anyway, in his dark hoodie and leggings, scrolling through something on his phone so he didn't need to look up at the team as they came through the tunnel and the door to start warming up.

The team didn't fail to notice, either. Cormier skated up to him. "Cap? Everything cool?"

"Yeah," Matt said, and looked over at the stands, where Aiden was watching them, a little nervously. Before Aiden had left, again, he'd been around the team, he'd been part of the group chat, but Matt had never really *said* it. Saying it would've made it real; saying it might've shone a light on something that wasn't ready to be revealed. All of that was over now. "My boyfriend decided he wanted to watch us skate after all."

Boyfriend sounded pretty stupid, considering what

Aiden was to him, *had been* to him over the decades. But it was the only word he had.

Cormier tilted his head to the side, like he was processing the information. He was a big kid from a small town in rural Quebec, and he had a slow, thoughtful way of speaking in English that made him seem a lot older than his twenty-three years. He'd spent a few years in the minor leagues, but he wasn't going back anytime soon. "It's still weird to me. Not that you have a boyfriend. Just that it's *him*. You are both...probably going to the Hall of Fame."

"That's a *big* presumption," Matt said, embarrassed. He wasn't used to it when the rookies said things like that to him, even though he knew that he was kind of a legend to them, for finally bringing home another Cup to Montreal. "A really, really big presumption."

Cormier shook his head, green eyes crinkled in a smile. "I don't think so. I mean, if you guys combined your trophy room, it would probably be... I don't know. Maybe you'd need two rooms. It is difficult to wrap my head around."

"If you think it's strange for you, you can imagine how I felt when it happened to me." It was strangely—good to be able to talk about it like this, in the open, again. He'd felt the same sense of relief when they'd started telling their teams the first time around. The weight of secrecy lifted. Except this time, he didn't need to worry about it all crashing down around him. "Come on, Rémi, better get in place for the drills before Coach Roy's ready."

Aiden was still watching him, and when he saw that Matt was looking back, he smiled.

* * *

Even though he'd made the decision to stay, it wasn't any easier when Matt left for road trips. The empty condo was too quiet. It wasn't like Aiden had *nothing* to do: he was still keeping things together, cooking, seeing Dr. Gauthier. Something about leaving and then coming back had been like a light going off in his head.

It wasn't just his relationship with Matt that he'd had one foot out the door for, it was therapy, too. When he told Dr. Gauthier that he'd been avoiding really trying because he was terrified of what it would mean if he fucked things up anyway, she just smiled at him, the kind of serene smile that wouldn't have been out of place on the ice.

"It was important that you had this realization yourself," she said. "I am proud of you, Aiden."

"Yeah, so," he said, and swallowed. "Also I think… maybe I want to look into medication? I don't know if it's going to be right for me. Or a conceivable long-term solution. But until I can feel a little more…even."

"That's absolutely something we can explore together. I can refer you to a colleague of mine who can prescribe."

"Thank you." The clawing fear was still there, of the unknown, of failure. But he'd told Matt he was going to do everything he could to be better, and the fact was: he just didn't know if he could dig himself out of this hole with willpower alone.

"Of course," Dr. Gauthier said, and then looked down at her notebook. "Is there anything else you'd like to discuss today?"

"The short list, or the long list?" Aiden asked, and settled in for the session.

Later that night after the game, Matt's familiar face on video chat made something clench in his chest, but he forced it down and made himself smile. "Hey, Matty. How's the knee?"

"Holding up," Matt said, with a little grimace. He was already in the bed, shadowed in the dim hotel lights, surrounded by crumpled sheets. It was insane, how good he looked to Aiden just then, the broad expanse of his shoulders and chest, bruised and battered. "I'm probably going to need another round of steroid injections and Toradol if it keeps up like this, though."

"Don't push yourself," Aiden said, even though he knew it was useless. He'd played through so many of those nagging injuries himself, and Matt was even more stubborn about his Iron Man streak than Aiden had been. "If you need to sit, you should tell them you need to sit."

Matt laughed, the exhausted, adrenaline rush of a laugh you had sometimes after a game. He was half-sitting and half-lying in the pile of pillows, and Aiden wished more than anything that he could be there, that he could curl his body like a comma against Matt's. "Baby, it's my contract year. I'm not going to tell them I need to sit."

"About that," Aiden said. He swallowed again. His mouth felt dry, which was funny, because his palms were suddenly sweating. "I know it's not the best time to talk about this, but...are you thinking about next season? Still?"

Matt's dark eyes were just as tired as his voice, looking Aiden over with a combination of fondness and concern. "I'm thinking about a lot of options. I haven't made a decision yet, though. It's just, you know how hard it is to *stop*."

"Yes. Well. At least you probably won't be as bad at retirement as I am."

"Look—this isn't a good time to talk about it. I want to do it in person, when I do make the decision."

The gnawing fear again: would Matt be playing again next year? Would he be switching cities? Would Aiden have to uproot his life again, learn how to survive somewhere new, without even the scarce familiarity of Montreal?

And then he realized, all of a sudden, with the sudden force of a puck to the cage: it didn't matter.

Wherever they went, however long Matt was away: *it didn't matter.*

No matter where they were, Matt would always be coming home to Aiden, and Aiden was going to do what he needed to do to be there when Matt came home. To make it work. Maybe it wouldn't always be easy. Maybe he'd do a horrible job at that, too. But Matt loved him and Matt was willing to wait for him and maybe Aiden didn't deserve it at all, but he had it. All that mattered now was what he chose to do with it. That was within Aiden's power, and it always had been. He'd screwed it up in the past, but now he was looking at the future. Now he *could* finally look at the future.

Whatever happened, it was going to be *okay.*

"Aiden?" Matt said, concerned. "Are you okay?"

"Yeah, I… I just realized something. It's nothing."

"You looked like you just saw a ghost. Seriously? You're good?"

Aiden smiled and said, "Yeah. Okay, Matty. I've kept you up long enough, eh? You should sleep."

Matt's brow furrowed, like he didn't quite believe it. "Okay. Hey, Aidy."

"Yeah?"

"I love you."

"Yes." For the first time in a long time, Aiden said, and meant it: "I know. I love you, too."

After they hung up, Aiden reached for his laptop. There was a folder of pictures he still had on the hard drive that he'd never quite been able to bring himself to delete, even after things had ended. Knowing it was there had always felt a little like a barely healed scab, something that would start bleeding at the lightest touch, even years later. A Pandora's box that should never be opened.

Aiden was finally ready to open it.

The road trips through the New York and Philly area had always been bittersweet for Matt. When he and Aiden had fallen headfirst into their relationship the first time, it had been a chance to see him, one of the few times they ever had during the year. And then after Aiden had dumped him, it was an exquisite kind of torture, being so close to him but not able to touch. The reminder of the things he'd lost.

So to say it was strange playing in New York without Aiden in the crease was a little understatement. He'd been that one constant, that lodestar. Gabe Walker had done a good job of taking over even though they were big skates to fill. Matt watched him warming up, stretching on the ice, and sighed. He should say something. It was probably going to be awkward as hell, but he should say something.

He skated over.

Gabe looked up immediately, a little wary. "Safaryan," he said, as he got up out of the stretching position he'd been in so he could look Matt in the eye. This close, Matt could see so clearly how young he really was.

"Hey," Matt said. "Sorry. I didn't want to make this weird. I just… Aiden told me what you did. When he left. When he came home."

All around them, both teams were in the midst of stretches and the beginning of the warm-ups. The skaters whizzed by; at the corner of his hearing Matt could hear the steady bang of pucks against the boards.

"Home?" Gabe hunched a little forward. "He did, huh."

"Yeah. I wanted to say, I don't know. Thank you. I'm sorry about…everything, you know. But thank you. He's…it's meant a lot to me to have him back."

"Yeah." He sighed, an exhale that Matt saw rather than heard. "You're welcome. I just—promise me one thing, Safaryan."

"Yeah?"

"Take good care of him. I fucking love that guy, probably more than you know. And he needs someone to take good care of him. Even if he'd never say it. You leave him on his own and he's…well. You saw how the last year went. He's kind of a disaster. Promise me."

"I promise you," Matt said. It was almost comical, talking about Aiden that way, like he was a starving rescue dog. But in a way that's what he had been when he came to Montreal over the summer, raw and more than a bit feral, ready to snap at any hand offered in kindness. Matt thought about him in the condo, how comfortable it was coming home to Aiden's warm body in his bed, Aiden's cooking in the kitchen, Aiden's company on the couch. "I promise. I'll take really good care of him. I *do*."

Gabe cocked one eyebrow. "Okay. Hey. We probably shouldn't be talking like this, huh? I don't want to get to know the guy whose ass I'm gonna kick in like twenty minutes."

"Shit," Matt said, and laughed. "You sure have a high opinion of yourself."

"Earned," Gabe said. He smiled, and Matt could see immediately why Aiden was so fond of the kid. "Okay. Just as long as you know what you got yourself into."

The game was a tough one. No matter how hard he tried, Matt couldn't get one past Gabe, and it was clear that Gabe was taking no small amount of satisfaction in blanking him. The rest of the team stepped up, though: it was a nail-biter that went down to OT. And then one of Gabe's teammates banged in a rebound past Fourns, an angle he had no chance of reaching, while Matt watched from the bench.

He sighed, watching the Libs come out to congratulate Gabe and give him his hugs and helmet taps. Matt could give him that one: Gabe might've won the game, but Matt had the guy.

"What're you smiling about, Safy?" Jammer asked. "We *lost*."

"Oh…nothing. Just looking forward to going home, you know?"

The last game in Long Island was agony to get through, because at this point all Matt wanted was to be home with Aiden. It had been a long time since he'd been so eager to just *get home* after a roadie, and he still wasn't sure if that was having someone waiting, or whether he was just getting old and tired. Aiden had been weirdly squirrelly in text messages, kept saying that he was busy and couldn't talk. So the fact that he was getting cross-checked in front of the net by Tyler Gallant, one of the Railers' big d-men, wasn't really helping matters.

By the time the plane had landed in YUL and Matt had driven himself home, he was almost bursting with how much he wanted to see Aiden, to touch him, to hold him.

When he opened the door, Aiden was waiting, looking weirdly nervous and shy for someone who'd basically moved himself into Matt's life months ago, whatever hiccups they'd had along the way. Matt couldn't stop staring at him: it was still surreal, that he was back here. He was so fucking happy, and still part of him was terrified that Aiden was going to disappear again.

"Aidy?" Matt said. "Is everything okay?"

"Uh, yeah. It's fine. I just—well, I got you something? Made you something? I hope you aren't upset with the walls. I don't have a security deposit to pay you back or anything."

"What are you—" Matt started, and then he turned and saw the wall. "What… Jesus, Aiden. You did *all* of this?"

"I hope you like it," Aiden mumbled, unable to look him in the eye.

Matt's condo had always had a lived-in, comfortable feel, but it was a little impersonal. He had his pictures from the Cup celebration and some family photos on the fridge, but most of the art that he'd hung on the walls was the kind of stuff you could buy off of the shelf in Homesense. It wasn't as empty and soulless as Aiden's pristine brownstone, but it was reflective of the fact that throughout the years, Matt's life had been… kind of empty.

The wall was the opposite of that now.

While he'd been gone, Aiden had made prints of photos, in varying sizes, and framed and hung them. Just looking at the collection, Matt could feel his heart beating faster, his hands shaking a little. It wasn't the effort that Aiden had gone through, but the pictures he'd chosen.

They were pictures of Aiden, and Matt, and Matt and Aiden together, from the very beginning when they'd first started hanging out in the offseason through a selfie Aiden had taken of the two of them from last week. Seeing them all laid out like that was overwhelming: he almost couldn't make his feet work so he could go look at them closer. Seeing them all laid out like that just reminded him how fucking young they'd been when they first got together, how old they were now and how Aiden was still the most important person in the fucking world to him.

"Do you like it?" Aiden said again, sounding worried.

"Aidy," Matt said, and turned to him. There wasn't anything he could do except kiss him: swallow up Aiden's surprised little gasp in his mouth, stroke his thumbs along the line of Aiden's face, his soft beard and his equally soft mouth. "Aidy, I love it."

"Oh," Aiden said, flushed. "I wasn't—I wasn't sure if it was too much."

The oldest picture was one that Matt remembered well. It was after the first playoff series they had dueled each other: Aiden had kept the Libs in it, and Matt had been the only one on the Royal who seemed like he could score on him. The Libs had ultimately won the series, and they had met in the handshake line after. Aiden had said, *nice try.* He'd meant it as a compliment, of course, even if it hadn't come off that way. In retrospect it was insane that Matt hadn't immediately realized that he'd fallen in love basically at first sight, he could see how stunned he looked in the photo of the two of them clasping hands.

There were others.

A selfie in a hotel room at their first All-Star Game.

Matt assembling IKEA furniture in the apartment Aiden had gotten in their first offseason together.

The two of them in London, a daring kiss stolen in an empty side street.

The first night that Aiden had taken Matt to meet his teammates in New York, and they'd spent the whole night chirping him until Matt, in a drunken, righteous fury, had ripped them all a new one, a defense Aiden hadn't needed but had certainly shown his appreciation for later that night. In the picture, Aiden sat with Matt's arm over his shoulder in the dark, crowded bar, just enough plausible deniability so that the embrace wouldn't be noticeable. Matt still remembered how fast his heart had been beating, how sweaty his palms had been, how warm Aiden felt melting against his side. He'd felt like everyone was staring at him and it hadn't mattered at all.

Their legs tangled together in a hammock during one of those island getaways over the summer, when it felt like the whole world outside of their hotel room didn't exist.

The more recent pictures. A lot of them.

The sunset from Matt's condo roof deck.

Aiden wearing Matt's jersey at a team party.

A picture from karaoke night, one Matt hadn't seen before, Aiden tucked under his arm and leaning into his body.

Matt, asleep in bed and twisted up in the covers, Aiden's hand splayed on his shoulder.

"It's completely insane," Matt said, "and I *love it.* I love *you.*"

"I love you, too," Aiden said, and seemed like he exhaled for the first time. When Matt held out his arms, he went to them, easily, an embrace that felt like Matt could maybe crack his bones. "I've always loved you."

"Aiden, I just—what made you *do* this? What did you even…?"

"I was just thinking. About how long you've been in my life. How long I've been in yours. All of my best memories are of you. Sometimes I think my *only* good memories are of you. And I just… I know I've fucked up a lot. I know it's not always going to be easy. But I just wanted to show you. Somehow. How much you mean to me. How much you've always meant to me. And to tell you, somehow, that I'm not going anywhere this time."

Matt pulled back, just enough that he could look Aiden in the eye. Aiden's face, familiar and unfamiliar all at once, a face he'd relearned over the last year. Soon he'd know the frown and laugh lines as intimately as he'd known Aiden in his twenties. Aiden, who looked almost shy, embarrassed by the gesture he'd made.

Aiden had a legacy if *anyone* had a legacy: the Cups and the individual awards and the hushed way new players coming into New York spoke of him. He'd *been* the Liberty for so many years. He'd had a legacy; he was probably a first-ballot Hall of Famer now that he was retired. And none of it had helped him. He'd been miserable in retirement, so miserable that even Matt hadn't known how to help him, and the legacy had been a cold comfort. It had been all Aiden had, and it hadn't done one damn thing for him.

Matt thought about Marcus Aurelius again: *"But look at how soon we're all forgotten. The abyss of endless time that swallows it all."* He thought about *"everything fades so quickly, turns into legend, and soon oblivion covers it,"* and how for the last few seasons he'd been trying to reconcile those ideas with the need to leave something tangible behind in Montreal. Matt thought about Aiden, here and now, and the concrete reminders on the wall, the evidence of the memories they'd made over the years together. How he could never have forgotten Aiden even when he'd tried.

In that second, all of the doubts and questions Matt had had about his future resolved.

"Hey," he said, "come to bed?"

"Thought you'd never ask," Aiden said, and smiled.

Aiden woke up in the middle of the night, sore and disoriented and way too fucking warm. And then he remembered exactly where he was and what he had done, and realized he felt like this because Matt was plastered against his back, arm over Aiden's hip. His hot breath tickled the back of Aiden's neck. Aiden felt like he had been here before and instead of feeling panicked, he exhaled and realized that he would be here again, and again, and again. He shifted to free the arm he'd been lying on and felt Matt stir into wakefulness.

"Hi, baby," Aiden said. The word felt awkward on his tongue, even though he'd said *buddy* and meant something else so many times over the years that it was basically the same thing. The sleepy smile on Matt's face when he heard it was worth it. "Go back to sleep."

"No, in a minute," Matt mumbled into Aiden's shoulder, voice slurred with exhaustion. "Have to tell you something first."

"Oh yeah? Maybe you should wait until you actually wake up, bud."

"'M awake enough. Been thinking about it. I'm not doing free agency next season. I'm not *playing* next season. When the postseason ends, that's it for me."

"Really?"

"Yeah. I'm ready. Whatever happens next—it's gonna be you and me, baby. Together. We'll figure it out together this time."

Aiden remembered, suddenly, a question Matt had asked him once, years and years ago. *What would make you satisfied?* He'd thought he'd figured it out back then, but he'd been young and naive and thought he'd known everything, hadn't had any idea what the future held in store for him.

Maybe he wouldn't be satisfied, ever, and maybe he thought he'd figured out contentment before. And maybe he could learn to be content with what he had now.

But what came out of his mouth, with the honesty of exhaustion, was: "Matt, I'm really… I'm really happy."

"Good," Matt said, still into his shoulder. His eyes were closing; Aiden could feel the movement of Matt's eyelashes against his skin, a faint brush that tickled his skin. "Now make *me* happy and go the fuck to sleep."

We'll figure it out together this time.

Aiden trailed his hand down Matt's back as he felt his breath shift slower, deeper, and smiled.

He went the fuck to sleep.

IV.
THE FUTURE

CHAPTER ELEVEN

An Article in *The Players' Voice*
"You'll Always Be a Goalie"
Aiden Campbell
Retired Major League
August 7, 2030

The eternal question: do people who are *like that* become goalies, or does being a goalie make people *like that*?

I think a lot of people would probably say that I never even had a chance. First of all, I'm Canadian. Second of all, my dad played professional hockey for a time. Third of all…well, I guess you could say I'm *like that*.

Some of my fondest memories as a child are watching games with my dad and my younger sister. My mom, who *isn't* Canadian and is always busy, wasn't usually around for that. So that was our special time with him, and I think he loved it as much as we did. I learned the game from him, on our beat-up couch in Winnipeg.

Hannah always loved watching the defensemen, but for me? It was *always* the goalies. One of my earliest memories is watching Jeremy Brown—the Falcons' goalie at the time—diving to make a desperation save and thinking: *I want to do that when I grow up.* In fact, I loved watching the goalies so much that I broke Dad's heart when I forsook the hometown Falcons and became a Royal fan, just because of Brendan Carrier. But who could blame me? When you watched a goalie like him, it wasn't like watching sports. It was like watching a dance or an artist painting.

From the moment I saw Brendan Carrier play, I didn't just know I wanted to be a goalie. I knew I was *going* to be a goalie.

I'm not going to tell you about the years of hard work, about getting drafted and making the team, about the awards and the Cups and all of the rest of it. Everyone knows that stuff. What I'm going to tell you about is how being a goalie became *me*, my whole identity, to the exclusion of almost anything else. And I embraced it. And I welcomed it.

I've always been a little…different, I think, from other people. And being a goalie really *helped* with that. Suddenly I had something to channel my focus into. Suddenly, the fact that I was kind of a weird, awkward kid didn't matter. It was a feature, rather than a bug.

It's something they don't tell you when you start playing hockey. How easy it is to make it your personality, to focus only on the moment, to develop a kind of intense tunnel vision about your career and your role that makes the rest of your life seem secondary and almost unreal. It feels natural and right in the moment. It feels like the way things *should* be. Why worry about anything when you can play hockey, when you can stop pucks in front of twenty thousand fans every night, when you can feel that thrill? Why think about the future?

It's great until it's not. Because I only ever thought about hockey, I almost lost the most important thing, twice over.

So it went like this. I was twenty-two years old when I met the love of my life, although I didn't know that's who he was at the time. I saw, *really saw*, Matt Safaryan for the first time in the handshake line after the Libs beat the Royal in a hard-fought playoff series, and at the time I was mostly annoyed by him because he kept scoring on me.

The rest of the story is mine, but what you need to know is: I fucked everything up so, so bad, because I couldn't see how a life with Matt was compatible with hockey. And at the time, I couldn't even begin to separate myself from playing. Losing Matt destroyed me, but it was the safer option.

When I retired, it felt a little like dying. When I wasn't playing hockey, I had no idea who I even was. Without hockey I felt like…nobody. Like less than a person. And when I started to figure it out, I still didn't like the answer. It turned out that Aiden Campbell without hockey was sad, lonely, and didn't know what the hell to do with himself. It was during that time—floundering around for any kind of a lifeline—that Matt fell into my life again.

How many of us get second chances? I almost couldn't believe it. Here I was, with an opportunity I'd only ever dreamed of in my arms. But it turns out that even when you reconnect with an ex you never fell out of love with, if you don't have your own shit together, it doesn't matter. You're just going to end up sabotaging that, too. And that's exactly what I did.

This is what younger players coming up need to understand: you *need* to build a framework for your life outside of the sport. As easy as it is to construct your whole identity around being a goalie, you *can't* do that. It's safer at the time to wear those pads like armor, to refuse to look beyond the mask. But you can't do that, because one day your body is going to give up on you, or your team is going to trade your contract, and then you'll end up like I was: ruining the best thing that ever happened to you for a second time because you were too fucked up in the head to see how goddamn lucky you were.

How many of us get *multiple* second chances? I'm pretty sure I'm the luckiest man in the world, because I've fucked things up so badly, and I'm still here at the end of things, with him. Because he's loving and brave and forgiving and he understood that even though I *couldn't* be better at that time, I had desperately wanted to. Because he picked me up off of his front stoop in the middle of January and warmed my hands and my heart and asked me to stay with him.

And I said *yes*.

And since then, I've been saying yes to a lot of things. Yes to actually trying to implement what I've learned in therapy, yes to SSRIs, yes to going back to school for a business degree. Yes to refusing to view my retirement as an ending and yes to starting to reframe it as the beginning of the next phase of my life. Yes to being a better partner. Yes to staying in Montreal with Matt, and yes to opening a thriving hockey clinic with him.

I might not be a major league goalie anymore, but what I've learned since my retirement is that I'll always be a goalie. It just might look a little different now. I might not be playing in front of twenty thousand fans anymore, but I'm teaching kids how to guard the net, and I'm trying to teach them, too, healthier and better ways to look at the game. I spent a lot of years existing only in the moment to the exclusion of the past and the future, and that almost destroyed my life. It's been so damn rewarding to be able to talk to the kids who will be playing the game in the future. To hope that one day, they'll be able to avoid my pitfalls.

What's next for me? I have no idea.

I haven't told Matt yet, but I've started a feasibility study to see whether we might be able to purchase our own dedicated rink for the clinic in a few years. It's been growing by leaps and bounds, and I think maybe that's the next step. I can already hear what Matt would say: "You don't think this is a potentially terrible idea that could end in disaster?" And I already know how I'd respond: "When has that ever stopped us, Matty?"

And that's the beautiful thing. I'm not worried about the rink. I'm not worried about the possibility of actually making it happen. I'm not worried about the feasibility. If it works out, it's going to be amazing. And if it doesn't, it doesn't. I'll move on to the next thing.

Because that's the thing: I have the rest of my life to figure it out. It's taken me years to get there, but that's the truth.

The rest of my life. And I can't wait.

—*Aiden*

* * * * *

ACKNOWLEDGMENTS

This book would not have been possible without the help of so many people and I am grateful to all of you.

Thank you to Deidre Knight, my agent, for your continued belief in me.

Thank you to the entire Carina team—Stephanie Doig, Mackenzie Walton and everyone behind the scenes—for the opportunity to continue telling the stories that have rattled around in my head for years.

Thank you to Cait, without whom this series would not have been written.

Thank you to everyone behind the scenes who read early versions of the book, talked me through my anxieties about the book and went just as crazy about these characters. Thank you to Max, who came up with a sticker slogan I still cannot get out of my head; thank you to Bec and your playlists and your brainstorming: Aiden's history wouldn't have been the same without you; to Tia and your live updates and for being there for my first live hockey game in years and for adopting some of my screwed-up little guys as your own; and to Louisa for being just as feral about Matt and Aiden as I am.

As I've said before: it takes a village, and I couldn't do it without all of you. Thank you.

Turn the page to read an excerpt from *Unsportsmanlike Conduct* by Ari Baran, the next book in the Penalty Box series.

CHAPTER ONE

October

The plane had landed on time, but somehow, Leo Cohen was still late.

Devon hadn't been expecting much from Cohen and the reality was, somehow, even worse. He looked up at the arrivals board and, sure enough, the plane out of Denver with its layover in Vancouver had landed over half an hour ago. The baggage carousel whirled, but only one sad, beaten-up-looking bag remained. He tried not to look at his own face on the Skyhawks-themed decorations in the middle of the carousel, let the sign in his hands fall and went over to grab it. He checked the tag.

Sure enough, it was Cohen's. Devon yanked it up one-armed and scanned the doorway to see if there was any sign of the guy, but there was nothing. A few stragglers came through. Just a frazzled-looking set of parents and very small children.

He wondered whether it would be too much to text the Skyhawks' general manager something like, *Brad, you fucking jackass, why did you do this to me specifically? Haven't I done enough? Haven't I given enough?* But that would never have gone over well. He didn't like to curse where other people could hear him. He didn't want to rock the boat. Instead, he composed a particularly bitchy email in his head to make himself feel better.

Because that was the thing in Edmonton. It didn't matter that he'd won the Defenseman of the Year Award last season, that he had scored 92 points last season, or that he was +142 for his entire career there. It didn't matter that he wore an A and consistently mentored the younger defensemen even though he was only twenty-five himself. They hadn't won a Cup in over a decade, so *none* of it mattered. There was always more to give until they did.

It did seem particularly unfair, though, that their blue line had been so decimated in the offseason, and Jackson was behind schedule on his recovery and there were rumors he wasn't a long-term fit in Edmonton anyway, and Rantala had gotten hurt in one of the preseason games and was probably going to be out an entire four-to-six months, and they had a bunch of promising prospects but no one who was ready to take the next step. It was looking…grim. They needed bodies, and if nothing else, Leo Cohen was, for sure, a body. It did seem particularly unfair that Devon was the kind of guy a general manager would look at and say: *you. You're the one who's going to babysit this fuckup and make sure he doesn't fuck up quite so bad.*

It was his own fault, for a variety of reasons. It wasn't about fairness or luck, and that was the worst part. He had no one to blame but himself.

Well, himself and Leo Cohen, who was now on his sixth team in almost as many seasons. Cohen had a reputation as a rat for a reason. And Devon wouldn't have had to do any of this if Cohen weren't…thirty minutes late and missing somewhere in Edmonton International. Devon exhaled and considered the mindfulness exercises his therapist had suggested for when he felt the hot flush of rage rising up his throat or the cramping pain in his stomach. He closed his eyes and concentrated on the noise around him: the squeaking wheel of a baggage cart, the whir of the carousel's motor, the distant tinny echo of an announcement.

He didn't exactly feel better when he opened them, but he had himself under better control. Which was a good thing, because that was the moment that Leo Cohen burst through the doorway and Devon realized exactly how much of a Herculean trial this season was going to be.

There were a few reasons for this realization.

The first was that Cohen was fucked up on *something*, or several somethings, judging from his unsteady lope through the doorway.

The second was that Cohen's outfit was probably the most ridiculous thing Devon had ever seen a hockey player wear. Scuffed combat boots, sunglasses even though they were indoors and it was nearly midnight, ripped black jeans, a beat-up black leather jacket with metal studs lining the shoulders, and an equally beat-up white T-shirt that he could only catch a glimpse of here or there. What he could see were bold black letters: *COMMUNITY DICK*.

Instead of saying anything, Devon slowly raised the sign that said COHEN and coughed loudly.

Cohen caught sight of him, pushed the sunglasses down with one finger, smiled in a way that was halfway between a leer and a smirk, and the third reason, belatedly, hit Devon with the force of an out-of-control snowplow.

And that was, unfortunately: Cohen was fucking *hot*. It wasn't something he wanted to notice, but he couldn't help it. He had eyes, after all. And Cohen had them, too, big dark eyes fringed with thick, lush eyelashes, even if they were bloodshot. Cohen had wavy dark hair and expressive eyebrows and high cheekbones and the kind of full, pouty mouth that would look amazing wrapped around—

Okay. Jesus. Get it the fuck together, Fraser.

"Leonard!" he said, with a forced cheer he didn't feel. "Nice to meet you."

The smile immediately vanished. "My name isn't Leonard."

"No?" Devon said, smiling and smiling and smiling. He smiled until his cheeks hurt and then kept going. "My mistake. Come on. It's getting late. I'll take you home."

Cohen opened and closed his mouth like he was just itching to make some kind of smart-assed remark. In the end, he only said, "Yeah, sure," and with a flourish of his hand and an exaggerated bow, "lead the way, Mr. Defenseman of the Year."

Devon imagined shoving Leo's head in the toilet and flushing.

He exhaled.

He was present in his body, which was currently seething with fury.

He bit his tongue, and he carried Cohen's bag.

Leo wondered whether maybe it hadn't been the best idea to do a few bumps of coke in the airport bathroom before going through security and then getting drunk on the plane. Like, okay, in the moment it had seemed like a really good idea, especially because coke usually evened him out—it had since Andrea had given him a bump when he was...almost thirteen, probably.

Anyway, that didn't matter. What mattered was getting waived *again*. Most guys could say stuff like "it's not every day you get traded and/or waived," but Leo wasn't most guys. For him, it *was* pretty much every day that he got traded and/or waived, or at least every season.

It was starting to get to him. Getting fucked up helped a bit, even if he knew he was making a horrible first impression on his newly assigned babysitter. The fact that the team had very obviously assigned him a babysitter was insulting. When he'd gotten the call from his agent, he'd asked whether he would be able to pick out an apartment or whether he was going to need to stay in a hotel.

Oh no, my boy, Dan had said, *you fucked up way too bad for either one of* those *options.* You *are going to be living with Devon Fraser.*

Devon fucking Fraser, Mr. Defenseman of the Year and Media Darling, with his stupid, perfect smile and his stupid, perfect stat line. And his stupid, perfect social media, with its stupid, perfectly curated images of him volunteering at two separate shelters, one for dogs, and one for LGBTQ+ youth, and he looked equally and sincerely happy to be at both of them. And his stupid, perfect post-game interviews, which Leo hadn't spent a lot of time watching, because if you'd seen one, you'd seen them all, because Devon Fraser never said anything interesting or out of place or wrong.

Perfectly boring, perfectly perfect, perfectly *nauseating.*

And this was the guy Leo was going to have to live with this season. Leo followed him through the baggage claim, glaring at his stupid broad back and his stupid red hair and the stupid freckles that splattered across the back of his stupid neck and his big stupid feet. Almost as though he could sense the force of Leo's hatred, Fraser said, "I don't live too far from the airport, and the traffic won't be bad at this time of the night."

"I got nothing but time," Leo said, scowling over the frame of his sunglasses at his first glimpse of Edmonton. It was as ugly as he expected. And it didn't even matter if he was being fucking uncharitable to an airport. All airports were ugly, and Edmonton's could definitely be the ugliest. "I can carry my own bag."

"I'm being polite," Fraser said through gritted teeth, like the words pained him. Leo looked with interest at his jaw, which had clenched.

"I bet you grind your teeth something *awful* at night," he said before he could stop the words from slipping out.

Fraser stopped walking abruptly and set the bag down on the cement. "I'm sorry, I don't think I heard you properly." It had the kind of forced pleasantness he usually radiated when speaking to the Edmonton media about the fact that the Skyhawks had choked before the final round of the playoffs again. "Would you mind repeating yourself?"

Leo might have been kind of fucked up, but he wasn't stupid. He knew Fraser was very politely telling him to back off. Unfortunately for him, Leo had never backed off from anything in his entire life. He smiled. "I said, I bet you grind your teeth something awful at night. You seem awfully tense. Hey, you want a whiskey? I asked the flight attendant if I could buy an extra one and she gave me two for free."

Fraser continued to stare at him. His eyelashes were a gingery color, too, and his eyes were a greenish hazel. His cheeks were getting redder and redder, so all of the freckles stood out even more, and so were the tips of his ears. Leo imagined him like an old Looney Tunes episode, about to explode with a hiss of steam. Fraser said, "Do I want to drink a whiskey, at midnight, right before I have to get in the car to drive *your* drunk ass back to my house?"

"Well, when you put it that way…"

Fraser exhaled. He muttered something under his breath that might have been a curse but might also have been counting to ten. "Cohen, do us both a favor and just stop talking."

"Sure thing, boss," Leo said, and flipped him an ironic salute. He followed Fraser to the garage across from the terminal, and they went up the elevator in silence. He made a point of yanking his bag back, although it wasn't easy keeping his balance and lugging it along, either. There wasn't much inside: just a few changes of clothes, his laptop and other essentials. The rest of his belongings had already been packed up and would be shipped off to Canada from Denver within the next week or so. It had happened to him so often that he was an old pro at the process of moving his entire life from one country to another in the span of a day.

Fraser stopped next to an immaculate black Audi RS Q8, and Leo sighed. Of course it was an expensive but deeply boring car. It fit Fraser, who was also expensive and deeply boring. The only reason Leo didn't tell him that was because Fraser avoided looking at or speaking to him as he unlocked the door and threw Leo's bag in the trunk.

The Penalty Box series is available wherever books are sold, including Harlequin.com.